Jillian stopped cold, as surprised by the sudden kick of her heartbeat as she was to see Garrett standing there in the half shadow. It stunned her to realize she relished a moment like this to simply look at him. Unobserved. Unguarded.

His back was bare, his tanned skin roped with contoured muscle. But for the occasional scar—she assured herself she didn't want to know how he'd gotten them—he could have been a model advertising the stunning results of a state-of-the-art physical fitness machine. Only this was no cover boy standing with his bare feet braced wide apart in her kitchen.

This was a man.

This was a warrior with the battle scars to prove it.

Like her, he'd showered again. His hair was still wet. A trickle of water ran down the deep indentation of his spine and disappeared beneath the waistband of his jeans.

Maybe it was the way his jeans broke over the arch of his bare feet. Maybe it was the bruise on his shoulder that even now was transitioning from red to smudgy blue. Or maybe it was the weariness she sensed in him.

Against all odds, she felt an overwhelming urge to go to him again. To touch him. To tell him she was on to him. Let him know that she knew that he wasn't as hard as he looked. And that it was okay. He didn't have to be. At least not with her . . .

TO THE EDGE

THE BODYGUARD SERIES

Cindy Gerard

St. Martin's Paperbacks

TO THE EDGE

ISBN: 0-312-99091-X
EAN: 80312-99091-6

Printed in the United States of America

St. Martin's Paperbacks edition / May 2005

St. Martin's Paperbacks are published by St. Martin's Press, 175 Fifth Avenue, New York, NY 10010.

10 9 8 7 6 5 4 3

This book is dedicated to our fighting men and women who protect our freedom and our way of life while promoting peace and enduring all that is asked of them every day.

And to my mother, Vera Adams. I love you, Mom. Here's your big book.

ACKNOWLEDGMENTS

As a writer of close to thirty romance novels, I have been blessed to be associated with a number of amazing individuals who have been there for me over the years. Some of these incredible people have been around from the beginning. They've seen me through the good news, the bad news, the moments when I needed a little lift, the moments when I needed a big one. Words cannot express the debt I owe them. I'd like to acknowledge their contribution to my life and any writing success I've enjoyed.

Tom: I love you. You know all the reasons why.

Glenna McReynolds: You are my friend, my sister in spirit. For your generosity of time, your treasured talent, your honest critiques and unending faith in me, thank you, thank you, thank you.

Leanne Banks: You are one of the most incredibly generous and savvy women I know. There is no writer in this business whose opinion I rely on more. Thank you for being my friend and for always knowing what I need to know and sharing it with me.

Susan and Jim Connell: My Florida connections and good buddies. Without you, this book wouldn't be what it is. Without you, I wouldn't be what *I* am—warm and tan in the middle of February.

Maria Carvainis: Thank you for your experienced guiding hand. I am fortunate, indeed, to have such an advocate and adviser in an agent.

Monique Patterson: Thank you for buying this book and for your unflagging enthusiasm over the entire project from the beginning. It's a pleasure working with you. And to all the fine folks at St. Martin's Press, your confidence in me is inspiring.

Acknowledgments also to Dean Garner, literary agent, photographer extraordinaire, and former U.S. Army Airborne Ranger (Hooah!), for sharing information with a stranger who accosted him in cyberspace with endless questions. Dean, your generous contributions to this work have been invaluable. Thank you so very, very much.

Debbie Sheets, Patti Knoll, Anna Eberhart, and Darlene Layman: In some way, shape, or form you were all there in the beginning. You will never know what a difference it made. Thank you.

TO THE EDGE

U. S. Army Airborne Rangers Motto:

Sua Sponte—Of Their Own Accord

I

EVEN AMONG THE MASSES POPULATING West Palm Beach, Florida, Nolan Garrett found hundreds of places to be alone: in a packed corner deli, in the crush of tourists on a Sunday afternoon by the seawall, in his vintage Mustang on a deserted midnight street with the gas pedal down and the city's finest asleep at the wheel. Tonight, in this seedy bar where the Latino beat was sultry and loud, the beer flowed as free as air, and smoke hung like rotor wash in a drop zone, he made sure he stayed alone.

The sharp crack of a cue sent a dozen pool balls scattering across worn green felt. He tuned out the sound of the game along with the music and the raucous laughter, thick with undercurrents of the streets. The stench of stale spilled beer faded to background scent as well, as he wrapped his fingers around the shot of bar scotch sitting directly in front of him on the scarred table.

Slumped back in the chair, he spared a glance at the blatant invitation from a leggy blonde with hungry eyes and a black leather skirt that barely covered her crotch. Her Barbie breasts, loosely harnessed in skimpy black lace beneath a white see-through blouse, pressed provocatively against his shoulder as she squeezed slowly by him. A *do-me* smile tilted the cherry red lips she moistened with a suggestive sweep of her tongue.

He dismissed her with a long, cold look. It not only

dimmed the wattage of her smile; it startled a shocked wariness into her eyes and sent her scrambling toward the other side of the room for action. What he wouldn't let himself find in the booze he sure as hell wasn't going to find in her—no matter how clear she made it that she not only came cheap, she came often, and in ways that guaranteed him several shots at mindless, numbing oblivion.

If he'd been looking for oblivion, the table would be littered with a dozen empty shot glasses instead of one full one. He stared at the scotch, imagined the drugging taste of it on his tongue, the welcome burn as it slid to the pit of his belly.

On a slow breath, he unclenched his fingers and made himself focus on the big-screen television suspended above the congested bar. It wasn't the evening news that drew his brooding attention; it was the woman delivering it.

Jillian Kincaid.

She was publishing mogul Darin Kincaid's darling daughter; she was bona-fide Palm Beach royalty and local television's answer to Diane Sawyer. And even cloaked in the journalist persona she played to the hilt in her Worth Avenue suit that most likely cost enough to finance a small third-world coup, she also played a leading role in every straight man's X-rated fantasies.

Through the medium of television, he knew her famous face well. Knew the auburn and ginger hue of her long, lush hair, knew the multifaceted shades of her clear, bright eyes that transitioned from sea to forest green like the Atlantic shifted colors beneath a hide-and-seek sun. He knew the shape and the fullness of the lips she sometimes wrapped around a line of professionally delivered copy. Often she wrapped them around an exposé that made strong men squirm. Regularly she made a man with a weakness for dewy-eyed debutantes imagine those lips wrapped around something that didn't make for polite table conversation.

Until this morning, everything he'd known about Jillian Kincaid had been limited to the media. That had been just fine. He hadn't wanted to know any more about her. The fat dossier locked in his glove compartment along with his gun, however, had fleshed out the picture in three-dimensional color.

And now it no longer mattered what he had or hadn't wanted to know.

On a breath that was weary and weighty and resigned, he rose, dug into his hip pocket for his wallet, and tossed some bills on the table. After one last look at her incredible mouth, he headed out the door.

In less than an hour he was going to invade Jillian Kincaid's pricey City Place penthouse with his Beretta locked and loaded. And then he was going to wish he'd drained that shot of scotch.

2

"YOU KNOW, A *TRUE* FRIEND WOULD ARGUE *my* side on this, Rachael," Jillian muttered into her cell phone as she stepped out of the Town Car her father had insisted on sending to drive her home from the station. "She wouldn't be aligning herself with my father like he spoke with the voice of reason."

She bid Arthur good-bye with an *I'll be fine now, thanks* smile and a friendly wave. Her father's longtime chauffeur had dutifully delivered her to the front door of her building after her eleven o'clock newscast for the fourth night running. Jillian tolerated it more for Arthur's sake than for her father's. Arthur was a sweetheart and she didn't want to get him in trouble on her account.

"That's because your father *is* the voice of reason . . . at least on this." Rachael Hanover sounded both weary and concerned on the other end of the line as Jillian walked briskly through the front door.

"Evening, Ms. Kincaid." Eddie, the security guard, looked up from his desk in the small alcove to the left of the main doors. "You're home a little early tonight."

She'd give Arthur that. He made good time. When she drove, she generally didn't make it home before the stroke of midnight. Arthur had whipped in and out of traffic and delivered her home by 11:45.

"Hey, Eddie." Jillian stopped in the foyer and tilted the

phone away from her mouth while Rachael ran on about risk and credible threats. "Emily still holding out on you?"

Jillian had lived in one of City Place's penthouses overlooking the Intracoastal Waterway for two years now. Eddie Jefferies, with his blond good looks, perpetual Florida suntan, and American pie smile, had been the night security guard when she'd moved in. During that time, he'd gotten engaged, gotten married, and now, at the tender age of twenty-three, he was about to become a father.

Eddie tried to hide his jitters behind a dimpled grin. "If that baby doesn't pop by next week, Doc says he's going to induce."

"She'll be fine." Jillian walked over to his desk in the alcove and squeezed his arm in reassurance before she headed toward the single bank of elevators. "They'll both be fine. Your shift about over so you can go home to her?"

Eddie shot the cuff on his blue uniform shirt and checked his watch. "Another half an hour and I'm outta here."

"Tell her I'm thinking about her, OK?"

"Will do, Ms. Kincaid. And thanks."

"Good night, Eddie."

"G'night, Ms. Kincaid." Eddie's voice trailed behind her as Jillian punched the up button.

"Surfer boy's not a daddy yet?" Rachael asked, making Jillian realize she'd tuned out her friend completely.

"Not yet." Jillian stepped into the cab and hit the button for the penthouse level. "They seem so young," she added with a frown.

"And at thirty, you're what—Methuselah?" Rachael speculated, clearly amused.

"*I'm* not bringing another human being into the world."

"OK. Hold it. When, exactly, did this train derail? We were talking about *your* problem. Or was I just filling dead air with my opinion on your stalker while you chitchatted with your doorman about his personal population explosion?"

"I don't want to talk about it anymore." Jillian pressed an index finger to her temple as the elevator cab gave a gentle lurch and started rising. "And it's not *my* stalker. If there even *is* a stalker."

Rachael responded with a long silence.

Jillian closed her eyes and leaned a hip against the elevator cab's wall, recognizing that silence as concern.

"I hate this," she said on a deep sigh. "I really, really hate this."

"I know." Rachael's voice softened with sympathy. It didn't, however, stop her from pressing the issue. "So, did you knuckle under to your father and agree to the bodyguard?"

"Agree? Sweetie, it's not open for debate. There's not going to be a bodyguard. Trust me. If you'd grown up with one riding herd on you, you'd feel the same way. You remember how it was for me."

Horrible and humiliating. That's how it was. It had been a price she'd paid for being Darin Kincaid's daughter. Security gates, surveillance cameras, and personal bodyguards had been the norm from the time she had memories.

"What was his name again?"

"My old bodyguard? Hector."

"Right. It's coming back. Big as a lighthouse, stoic as a monk, and as clingy as sweat in August."

Jillian pushed out an indelicate snort. "That would be Hector."

The memories of Hector's infringement on her childhood and of being the most popular ransom bait in southern Florida riled a resentment Jillian worked hard to keep under wraps. She'd felt as violated as if she *had* been kidnapped. His hulking shadow had always been lurking in the background, running roughshod over everything she'd done. Nothing had been sacred. Birthday parties, school dances, dates . . . and Hector.

It had been years since she'd thought of those days—and

yet some things were always with her and nudged her right back into defensive mode.

"I'm not sixteen anymore, for God's sake, and here I am—still fighting to keep my father from controlling my personal freedom. It's too much, Rach. It's not going to happen. Not again."

Jillian heard the bitterness in her voice but wasn't able to curb it. She'd scrapped like a street brawler to build a credible career in TV journalism based on her own credentials and hard work—and she'd fight again to ensure that whoever was leaving messages on her answering machine and sending threatening e-mails didn't jeopardize her control over her own life. She'd worked too damn hard to get here.

"He's just concerned," Rachael reminded her, bringing her back to the moment. "Like any father would be in this situation."

"Fine. That's fine. I understand concern," she said. "But let him give me credit for knowing how to handle myself. City Place isn't exactly a tiki hut on the beach, you know. I chose this complex and this particular building because of its tight security. And I've taken other precautions. When I bought that gun several months ago, I learned how to use it. I don't need my father intervening or undermining my decisions on how I protect myself."

She felt the dull throb of a headache coming on and, what the hell, added that to her list of complaints against her father. It wasn't only her freedom at stake here. She'd had to fight her entire life to prove her worth wasn't measured in terms of the currency that came etched with Darin Kincaid's name on it. She *still* fought it, but she'd at least thought the battle with his overprotective streak was behind her.

"God. I wish I'd never told him about the threats," she muttered, then reined in her thoughts, recognizing she was coming dangerously close to whining. "It's just some sicko's idea of a bad joke anyway."

"Death plus threat don't equal joke in my book, so don't expect me to apologize for suggesting you fill your father in. I wouldn't have been a *true* friend," Rachael added, mimicking Jillian's earlier inflection on the word, "if I hadn't."

"I know," Jillian agreed, feeling very tired suddenly. "And I'm not blaming you. You *are* a friend, Rach. I don't know what I'd do without you."

"Yeah, well, it helps that I mix a mean martini," her longtime partner in crime added with a grin in her voice.

Over the years, they'd been there for each other. Friends. Confidantes. Allies. Rachael had even tried out for the U.S. gymnastics team the year Jillian had made the Olympic squad. Most recently, Jillian had seen Rachael through a nasty divorce that had rocked the Palm Beach social scene and broken Rachael's heart. That had been six months ago, and Rachael was still recovering.

The elevator cruised to a smooth stop. When the doors slid open on a nearly soundless sigh, Jillian stepped out into the subtle lighting of a wide hallway carpeted in champagne-colored plush.

"You still with me?" Jillian asked after she was met by another long silence.

"Yeah, I'm here." Rachael's voice had grown soft. "And it goes both ways. You're my friend, too. I care. And I worry, you know?"

Yeah. Jillian knew. Their long-term friendship was rare in a Palm Beach matriarchal society that had elevated the air kiss to an art form and appeared vapid and benign on the surface. The underlying jealousies, competitiveness, and egos, however, proved it was anything but and were among the reasons Jillian had distanced herself from the whole high-profile social scene. Though it puzzled her that Rachael seemed to find some sort of solace as an integral part of it, she would never question her friend's motives.

Not that TV journalism was without its own peccadilloes. If Jillian wasn't struggling with her producer's indecisions over airing one of her investigative reports or vying for studio time with Erica Gray, the weather girl, then Grant Wellington, her coanchor, made it a point to be her very own personal pain in the tush.

"Did you catch what Grant did tonight?" Jillian asked in a blatant ploy to steer away from the subject of weird voice-mail messages and e-mails.

"You mean during the closing segment when he stepped on your lines in an attempt to throw you off-balance? Oh yeah—but only because I was looking for it. You covered it like a blanket on a baby."

"What is it with that man?" Jillian keyed her code into the touch pad of her security system and, when the little green light flashed, swung open the door to her penthouse. Once inside, she reset the lock and with a groan of pleasure slipped out of her red Ferragamo pumps.

"Other than the fact that he's an aging prima donna who knows his glow is fading, a card-carrying chauvinist, and an all-around Clydesdale's ass?"

Rachael's apt, if irreverent, take on Grant Wellington finally pushed out a laugh. "Yeah, other than that. I don't want his job," she added, sobering. "Why can't he get that through his ego-inflated head?"

Flipping on the foyer light, she stripped off her suit jacket and tossed the cranberry linen over her navy blue leather sofa as she went by. The white Italian tile felt wonderfully cool beneath her bare feet.

"You don't *have* to want his job," Rachael assured her. "Apparently you just have to show up to make him feel threatened."

Jillian hit the switch for the track lighting over her kitchen counter. Light flooded the lemon yellow walls of the galley kitchen and cast shadows into the open dining and living area. "I don't threaten people. I *never* threaten people."

"True," Rachael agreed, then added with meaning, "People threaten you."

"You managed *that* segue well." Jillian reached into the fridge for the bottle of chardonnay she'd opened last week. "But we aren't going to talk about threats or notes or bodyguards anymore, *capice*?"

"That line would work so much better for you if you were Italian."

Again, Jillian laughed. "So sue me."

"You're already being sued," Rachael reminded her with a smile in her voice.

Jillian hipped the refrigerator door closed. "Yeah, but that will all go away when the indictment comes down."

She wedged the phone between her shoulder and ear and started working the cork. When she'd popped it, she reached up and slid a wineglass from the rack suspended beneath a bank of cupboards.

"When's it scheduled, anyway?"

"The indictment proceeding on Councilwoman Abramson? Next month." She filled her glass three-quarters full.

"Ought to be a real sideshow."

"Don't we both know it." Jillian sipped, savored, and then swallowed. "Look, sweetie, I'm bushed. I think I'll hit the shower, then call it a wrap. The weekend has never looked so good. You have any plans?"

"The usual."

Which meant Rachael was involved with some Angels of Charity social function.

"How's that going?"

"Fine."

Jillian heard the fatigue in Rachael's voice. "You work too hard."

"And that would be you playing the pot or the kettle?"

"OK. So we both burn a lot of midnight oil. At least I'm going to burn mine at home this weekend. I'm holing up here and compiling my notes on my Forgotten Man piece, and like Punxsutawney Phil, I ain't comin' out till I see my shadow—or until Monday, which, unfortunately, will probably come sooner. We're still on for lunch Tuesday, right?"

"Noon, The Four Seasons. I'll see you then. Now don't get ticked—you *did* lock up, right?"

Jillian smiled. "Yes, Mother."

"Get some rest."

"You, too. Bye."

"Bye."

Jillian hit the end button, set the cell phone on the black granite countertop, and tipped the wine to her lips.

"*Vino*. Nectar of the gods," she murmured on a savoring sigh.

Rolling her head to relieve the tension burning in her shoulders, she walked into the living room, then hesitated when she spotted the blinking red light on her answering machine. Determined to ignore it and the little hitch of apprehension over what kind of a message she might find there, she headed for her bedroom, sipping wine and tugging her blouse out of her skirt on the way.

It was times like these, when she was tired and—

She stopped midthought, midstride, her heart rate suddenly revving.

Standing painfully still in her bedroom doorway, she cocked an ear toward the hall, certain she'd heard something . . . in the kitchen, maybe. She waited several beats . . . heard only a ringing silence, and let out a stalled breath when she decided it was just the icemaker dropping cubes or something equally benign.

Shaking off the little frisson of unease and the sting of

anger that accompanied it—all because some jerk had decided to spook her with death threats—she made herself pull away from the edge and picked up on her train of thought again.

It was times like these when she wished she had someone to come home to. Someone who could soothe her aching shoulders, someone who would be glad to see her, greet her with a glass of wine, then tumble her into bed for a nice, frisky round of hot, sweaty sex.

"A live-in masseuse and a dog would take care of the first two," she decided. And the other two . . . she let out a gusty sigh. The other hadn't been on the table for longer than she liked to think about. Actually, hot, sweaty sex had *never* been on the table. Or the bed. Or the floor. Polite, pleasant sex, yes, and so completely unmemorable she couldn't recall if the last time had been four or five years ago. She didn't like to think about that, either.

Just like she didn't like to think about the death threats.

But she did. Again. She thought about them a lot, even though she tried to downplay it. They were getting to her. Even in her own home, she felt wary—and she didn't like it.

A shiver she couldn't stall inched down her spine when she thought of the first chilling message that had been left on her home voice mail two weeks ago:

> *"Star light, star bright,*
> *first star I see tonight.*
> *I wish I may, I wish I might,*
> *have the wish I wish tonight.*
> *I wish you were dead, Jillian.*
> *What do you wish for?"*

The voice had been chilling, genderless, almost like a child's voice. But no child could have relayed such hatred and evil intent. The second message, sent to her office e-mail and, as yet, untraceable by the police, had been identical in content.

Stone-faced, she looked in the direction of her living room. She could no longer see her answering machine, but in her mind's eye the red light blinked on and off like a taunt. She hated herself for being spooked by the thought that another message might be waiting for her there. Hated it more that she'd been too much of a coward to confront the possibility head-on as soon as she'd walked in the door.

"Well, hotshot, there's only one thing to do about it, isn't there?" she murmured, still staring down the hall toward the machine.

She made herself walk back to the living room. The answering machine sat in mocking silence on her end table. The display blinked with the number 5.

With a jerky motion, she punched the PLAY button, crossed her arms beneath her breasts, and waited in tense silence. The first two messages were hang-ups—telemarketers, no doubt. The third was her accountant reminding her to file her quarterlies.

The fourth was from Steven Fowler.

"Jillian—please call me. It's been a month. You haven't returned my calls or answered my e-mails. You haven't let me see you. Please, we can work this out if—"

She hit the DELETE button without listening to the rest of Steven's message. The bastard. He'd sucked her in, made her think they might have a future together. It had taken him two months to get around to mentioning the wife and kids back in Chicago—and that had only been after the wife in question had called Jillian and threatened to make her the object of the biggest character assassination to ever hit the *National Enquirer* and every sleaze tabloid in between.

Jillian had been horrified. She wasn't a home wrecker. But she had been a chump.

Of course, he planned to divorce her. *Of course,* he'd

meant to tell Jillian about his "complication" sooner, but *whoops,* the time had never been right.

Pretty damn big *whoops.*

Shaking off the humiliation and the pain of that experience that still cut a little too close to the quick, she skipped to the last message.

"Jillian—it's your father. We need to talk. Please give me a call."

Her relief over not finding another threat on her machine was lost in her complicated feelings for her father. She loved him, she really did . . . but she was not going to knuckle under to him on this. He had to quit bulldozing his way into her life.

And she had to quit letting the threats rule her thoughts.

Returning to her bedroom, she set her wineglass on her bedside table, shrugged out of her blouse, then reached behind her back to unfasten the zipper on her skirt. Next she lost the bra. With a blissful sigh, she rubbed her palms along the undersides of her breasts, worrying away the irritation caused by the underwire cups.

After another quick sip of wine, then an admonishment to "pace yourself, Kincaid," she left half a glass to lull her to sleep and headed for the adjoining bathroom.

She turned on the shower, eased out of her panties, then retraced her steps back into the bedroom to turn on her sound system. Slipping her Paulinho Nogueira *Late Night Guitar* CD into the changer, she upped the volume and headed back to the bathroom.

Again a noise—unfamiliar, out of place—stopped her. She stood stock-still, one hand on the door. Heart kicking like a Rockette, she cocked her head, listened, then hissed out a breath on a concise expletive.

Nothing. There wasn't a thing out of sync beneath the beat of the sultry guitar rhythms. And she had to stop allowing this nonsense to shake her. She lived in a high-security building, for God's sake. Her penthouse was virtually impenetrable. If anyone had tripped her alarm, a patrol car with siren blaring would be parked out front right now and a contingent of private security officers would be storming the building, guns drawn.

Willing her heart to settle and her backbone to stiffen up, she stepped into the shower stall and tipped her face toward the hot, pulsing spray. She lathered her hair with shampoo that smelled of rain forest and lush tropical blooms and wished she hadn't watched late-night classic movies last week. Even in black-and-white, the shower scene from *Psycho* had been chilling—possibly more so *because* of the lack of color.

The images of the blood-splattered shower wall in the bathroom of the Bates Motel drifted through her mind as she stood there, naked and completely vulnerable and honed just one more sharp edge to the knifelike tension she was beginning to despise.

Forcing herself to hum to the CD, she made concentrated work of soaping her body. It was like a test. If she could make herself stand there for a full five minutes, Norman Bates's previously unknown spawn would get tired of waiting, sheath his butcher knife, and leave her jugular be.

Snorting at the ridiculous turn of her thoughts, she rinsed and twisted off the faucets.

The plush white towel was warm from the heated rack. She wrapped it around her body and fastened it with a tuck between her breasts. Snagging another towel, she worked it over her hair, not yet used to the color change she'd let Victor talk her into last week.

"You need a new look, darling," her beautician—or, as Rachael fondly referred to him, her half man/half hairdresser—had announced with a pouting scowl when she'd gone in for her monthly trim. "I'm thinking auburn and sassy and regal. What do you say? Tell me you're game."

She'd been a brunette long enough. "Why not?" She'd grinned at Victor's spiky gilded do and challenging smile. "Go for it."

She'd been due for a change. And once her producer, Diane Kleinmeyer, had gotten past her shock—Diane did not like even the smallest corner of her world rocked—she'd been good with it, too.

"Makes you look more mature," Diane had decided. "It'll lend credibility with our older viewers."

"I wasn't aware that my credibility was an issue."

"Oh, it's not, Jillie," Diane scurried to mollify her. When she saw Jillian grin, she relaxed. "You know it's not. But a power boost can't hurt, right?"

"Riiight," she'd said with a bewildered shake of her head, and wondered, as she often did, at the workings of Diane's mind. That Diane was brilliant was without question. That she was also often certifiable—especially right before airtime and during ratings month—was also a given.

As the steam slowly dissipated from the bathroom mirror, Jillian shoved her fingers through her damp hair, moving her hips in time to the beat of the music.

With a critical eye she studied her face. She was looking at thirty-one next fall. Like Rachael said, she wasn't exactly Methuselah, but tonight every year showed. She hadn't been getting enough sleep lately. Shelly had chewed on her about it again before the newscast when she'd done her makeup. Smudges of fatigue shaded the area just below her eyes. She touched a fingertip to that soft, bruised skin as she reached for her eye cream—and froze.

A shadow of movement drifted in ghostly slow motion behind her cloudy reflection.

She whirled around, a scream of terror trapped in her throat, and prayed it had been her imagination.

Nothing.

She let out a fractured sigh.

It *was* nothing.

Then he moved into the light.

Oh God.

And she prayed he'd make it mercifully quick.

The eyes that met hers were so arctic cold and penetratingly blue, they stopped her heartbeat.

Dead.

The word blasted through her mind like a bullet. So did images of a blood-splattered Bates Motel—only it was *her* body slashed and hacked like a gutted doll, her blood flowing down the bathtub drain instead of Janet Leigh's.

Time stopped as she held his chillingly calm gaze. She saw no mercy in his eyes. Only cold-blooded intent. Dispassionate purpose.

The aching pressure in her chest expanded, threatened to burst as the horrifying truth rose like bile.

They will find me dead in the morning.

3

"BREATHE."

The stern command registered through a fog of terror.

"Breathe," he repeated, a gruff demand this time, "before you pass out."

Jillian breathed. Sucked in air on a rush, let it out on a gasp.

"Again," he said in a voice as hard as his eyes.

Her options were as limited as cognizant thought. She did what he said. Drew several ragged breaths. And finally found her voice.

"How . . . how did you get in here?"

The fact that she was capable of speech amazed her. The utter banality of her question and the weakness in her knees didn't when he merely leveled those unsettling ice blue eyes on her face, crossed his arms over his chest, and leaned a broad shoulder against the door frame.

She sagged back against the counter so she wouldn't drop like a stone, then groped for and gripped the marble edge with the hand that wasn't latched in a death grip on her towel.

Details, erratic and disjointed, registered in stabbing little jabs of surreal clarity. He was dressed in black. As black as his scowl, as unyielding as the power in his leanly muscled frame. A long, thick scar ran the length of a heavily veined forearm. A large, lethal gun was holstered in black leather beneath his left armpit. The rock-hard bulge of his bicep pressed against it. She wondered if the gun felt cold against the heat of his skin. If he would feel remorse when he killed her.

Out of place amid such terrifying images was her awareness of the tropical, floral fragrance of her shampoo. It mingled with the scent of her fear, the feel of cool damp tile beneath her feet. Hard marble pressed against her hip. The piston-fire beat of her heart—in her throat, in her ears—was out of sync and out of time with the sultry strains of Nogueira's guitar.

Mixed somewhere in the midst of it all was the realization that she wasn't dead. Yet. Despite her knee-jerk prayer for a swift and sudden death, she didn't want to die. She wanted very much to stay alive . . . and she was going to have to pull herself together if she was going to stay that way.

Her mind raced in pathetic and frantic circles, around and around the possibility of getting to her gun. That wasn't going to happen. It was in her bedside table. His was a hand span away.

The drawer handle prodded her hip. Her gun may be in the other room—but there were weapons in the drawer at her back. Hair spray. A metal nail file. A pair of cuticle scissors.

"Watch the hand," he said with a notch of his chin when she attempted to ease the drawer open. "Get it up here where I can see it."

Jillian did as he ordered, all the while searching for some way to gain an advantage—*any* advantage—and get herself out of this alive. If only she'd listened to Rachael. If only she'd let her father hire that damn bodyguard.

"What do you want?" she managed in a voice so thick with tension she hardly recognized it as her own.

"Let's back up to question number one. Getting in here was child's play. Slipping past your security guard was the first hurdle. Nice kid. Too trusting. Someone needs to have a chat with him."

His voice was as hard-edged as his mouth, completely at odds with the conversational cadence of his words. It was also as uncompromising as the muscle stretched across the breadth of a chest covered by a snug black T-shirt and the strap of a leather shoulder holster that looked as natural on him as a tie on a power broker.

"As to the security system—" His voice snapped her gaze back to his face with a start. "It's a joke, fair game for any amateur with a good set of tools and a sensitive touch."

"I'll file a complaint in the morning." Which implied that she had to be *alive* in the morning. *Plant the seed. Watch it grow.*

Oh God. She would *not* get hysterical

"And your security code?" He shook his head, snapping her out of her little side trip to panic. "Shame on you . . . and happy birthday—late, Ms. eleven twenty-four nineteen-seventy-four."

He knew her birth date? Terror melded with bafflement and a latent but burgeoning anger.

"What do you want?" she repeated. The steadiness of her voice surprised her. The fact that his mouth didn't yield the slightest fraction of an inch didn't.

"What do I want?" He pushed out a bored grunt. "Right now, to be just about anywhere but here."

Confusion was now running a close second to fear. She narrowed her eyes—then sucked in a breath as he shifted his weight to one leg.

The result of his minuscule movement was a ripple effect on his hard, honed body. It also drove home a very salient point. She kept in shape and knew some basic self-defense moves, but she was no match for him physically.

He stood almost a head taller than her five-six frame—and every inch appeared conditioned to kill or maim. His upper body was fluid muscle. His hips were lean; his legs were long. In the unlikely event she managed to get past him somehow, he could outrun her without working up a sweat.

And yet he hadn't actually made a single threatening move toward her.

Even in her waffling state of terror, it didn't compute. She'd be dead by now if that was what he wanted. Unless that was his plan. To terrify her first. Play with her like a cat swatting a mouse.

I wish you were dead, Jillian.
What do you wish for?

She looked up again, and into his face. The razor's edge of fear had dulled marginally, enough, at least, to allow her to look—really look—at him without shock masking her vision.

She'd never seen him before. Of that, she was certain. She'd have remembered that face; it was the face of a fallen angel. The dark, thick stubble of a five o'clock shadow covered carved angles and sculpted lines. The set of his jaw was unyielding. Dark brown brows were tautly drawn over the intelligent blue eyes that regarded her with distant but studied disdain. Hair the same color as his eyebrows curled softly at his nape, sable soft, shiny as silk—an incongruous anomaly in this otherwise stone-cold machine standing before her.

That such stark male beauty could disguise the soul of a killer made the thought seem even more unholy—and less and less likely—as time ticked by. He merely watched her in a dispassionate silence completely at odds with the passionate strains of the Brazilian guitar playing softly in the background.

Her gaze slid from his face back to the holstered gun—the one he hadn't yet used, she reminded herself to help deal with the fear—then flicked back to his eyes. None of the ice had left them. In spite of the chill he generated from four feet away, for the first time since his shadowy presence had materialized in her mirror, a tiny fissure of hope slogged through her blood.

"Did you come here to kill me?"

Grim-faced, he swept a look down the length of her body, lingering at her breasts before crawling back to her face. His gaze fastened on her mouth. The muscles in his throat worked as he swallowed. Then he met her eyes.

"Now, why would I want to kill you?"

The sandpaper-coarse texture of his voice and the insolent way he watched her had her clutching the towel closer as his implication registered, took root, and grew to heart-pounding comprehension.

She closed her eyes. Felt the sting of tears behind them as the steamy rhythms pulsed in the background . . . and fear shifted to another unthinkable dimension.

Oh God. Oh God. Oh God.

She steeled herself, told herself she could survive it. She'd fight like hell—and lose—but she could endure it. More important, she would live through it. She would recover. But she would never listen to Nogueira again.

"OK. I think you've had enough," he muttered, startling her eyes open. "Rein in the theatrics, Ms. Kincaid. You're body's safe with me."

He shook his head, one corner of that hard mouth tipping up in what passed for a smile, like he'd made a joke he found both amusing and ironic.

So why wasn't she laughing?

In wary silence, she watched him dig into the black sleeve looped through his belt and pull out a cell phone. Then he turned and walked away, punching in a series of numbers.

Jillian blinked. And stared at the doorway—where he no longer stood.

She clutched her arms around her ribs to keep herself from splintering into a million pieces. For several rough heartbeats she stared at the door before letting out the air that threatened to burst her lungs.

Above the intricate licks of the acoustic guitar, she heard him in the hallway, talking softly. Wetting dust-dry lips, she inched toward the door, only then realizing how hard she was trembling. When she spotted him standing with his back to her, she didn't hesitate. She raced for her bedroom and tore open her nightstand drawer.

"Please, please, please," she pleaded in a coarse whisper as she rifled frantically through magazines and lotions and tissue. "It's got to be here."

"Looking for this?"

With a painful intake of breath, she whirled around. He stood in her bedroom doorway; her little .22 automatic dangled from the index finger he'd hooked through the trigger guard.

Pathetic, his expression said as, with a shake of his head, he tucked the gun into his waistband.

"Yeah," he said, turning his attention back to his cell. "That's right."

From beneath lowered brows he cast a frowning glance her way; then with a curled finger and a notch of his chin he motioned for her to come closer. "I think you could accurately state that I've made a believer out of her."

"Yes. Yes sir. No doubt," he continued, then scowled when she stood rooted to the spot. "Here she is."

He held out the phone.

"Come on," he said with a grunt of impatience when she stood there, stalled by the bed.

She darted a glance from his face to the phone, disoriented, distrustful. *What the hell is going on?*

He firmed his lips, walked toward her, then shoved the phone into her hand. "Your father wants to talk to you."

Her fingers wrapped reflexively around the cell phone. She stared from it to those cold blue eyes. "My . . . father?"

He blinked—a study in abject boredom—then walked out of the room.

Utterly baffled, she dragged damp hair back from her forehead and lifted the phone to her ear. "D . . . daddy?"

"Don't be mad, sweetheart."

"Mad? Daddy . . . what—"

"Look, Jillie—I know how resistant you are to the idea of a bodyguard."

"Bodyguard?" she echoed numbly.

"I told him you'd be a hard sell. I asked him to convince you how vulnerable you are—and I didn't care how he did it."

Bodyguard?

Her mind raced in a hundred different directions and finally settled on the impossible conclusion. That cold-eyed killer was her bodyguard?

The terror coiled in her chest unwound like a spring, then rewrapped into a squeezing knot of pure, primal rage.

"Are you telling me you hired this . . . this . . . *person* to scare twenty years off my life just to convince me I need protection?"

"I hired him to convince you how vulnerable you are to attack."

She lifted a hand to the top of her head, fisted her fingers in her wet hair, and tugged until it burned. "I don't believe this."

"Come home, Jillian," he insisted as if it were the only logical conclusion in the face of such obvious proof. "You're not safe there. Move back to the estate—at least until this maniac is caught. No one can get past my security."

"Do you know what he *did* to me?" she demanded, ignoring her father's suggestion, enunciating each word with care, working with everything that was in her to control the fury slamming through her blood and flushing her face with heat.

"Not precisely, no. He did tell me that he got into your penthouse with minimum effort."

Little prickling sensations tingled through her fingers and toes. She was less relieved that he hadn't come here to kill or rape her than she was livid—and she was about two breaths away from hyperventilating. "And you *sanctioned* this?"

His heavy sigh said yes, he had. "I want you safe."

"I'm *not* leaving the penthouse."

A long silence punctuated the anger simmering on both ends of the line.

"I was afraid that's what you'd say," he said finally. "If you're insistent on staying there, then he stays, too."

She actually managed a laugh, although there was little humor in it. "Over my dead body."

"Which is exactly what I'm trying to avoid. It's settled, Jillian. And so is he."

Settled? He was *settled*?

Eyes blazing, Jillian marched out of her bedroom and down the hallway. A sick feeling rolled through her chest even before she swung open the door to her guest bedroom. The beat-up army surplus duffel sitting open in the middle of the bed was an abomination against the pristine white designer spread; the scuffed black lace-up boots splayed drunkenly beside the closet door were as out of place on the polished cypress floor as a velvet Elvis in a Monet exhibit.

She spun around, her fury rising. She flew into the kitchen, her bare feet slapping tile just as her *bodyguard* reached into the refrigerator. He pulled out a bottle of root beer that he'd evidently buried out of sight somewhere on the bottom shelf.

"Jillian? Are you still there?" her father asked, his voice infused with wary tension.

"Where else would I possibly be?" she ground out.

"Sweetheart. I was hoping we could talk about this rationally."

"Oh, it's waaay too late for that."

Darin Kincaid sighed heavily. "You know, sometimes

you're just too damn stubborn for your own good. Sometimes you don't see the sense of things for your pride.

"Think about it, baby. The police department's investigation into these death threats has turned up nothing. Nothing," he repeated for emphasis. "I'm sorry, but until this
lunatic is caught, I'm not taking any chances with your life."

She shook with anger as she turned to the man who had
just twisted the cap off the bottle of soda and tossed it onto
her black granite countertop.

"What's your name?" she bit out.

He leaned a hip against the lip of granite, took a long,
deep pull from the bottle, then wiped his mouth with the
back of his hand before giving her a mock salute. "Nolan
Garrett, at your service. Ma'am."

"ID." She snapped her fingers, ignoring his insolence. He
had the nerve to grin—if you could call the sneer tipping up
one corner of his mouth a grin—as he dug into his hip
pocket and fished out his wallet.

She flipped it open when he held it out to her, then
scowled at the driver's license with his photo and name. His
raised brow said, *Satisfied?*

Ignoring him, she repeated the same clipped question
into the phone. "What's his name?"

"Garrett," her father said, confirming that the reprobate
lounging in her kitchen, drinking root beer, was, in fact, the
man he claimed to be. "I asked for him specifically. His
firm's reputation is solid. So is his," her father continued. "I
wanted the best for you, baby, and these guys are the best in
the business."

"I don't care if he can shoot the dorsal off a great white at
a hundred yards; I want him out of here." Only hard-fought
control kept her from shrieking as, apparently oblivious to
her fury, Garrett shouldered around her and sauntered into
her living room.

He turned on a floor lamp, found her TV remote, and

sank down on her sofa. When he spread his arms across the length of the sofa back, propped his feet on her marble-topped rosewood table, and started flipping through the channels, Jillian gritted her teeth so hard she was afraid she'd crack a cap.

"I want him out of here," she repeated, clench jawed, and, clutching the towel that had begun to slip, stormed back to her bedroom before she acted on the growing urge to smash her Cameo Favrile vase over Garrett's head.

"Jillian—you do realize that you're acting and sounding like a spoiled, recalcitrant child."

"Yeah, well, I tend to get a little testy when someone packing a gun breaks into my home." She punched off the CD player with an angry stab of her finger, then sank down on the edge of the bed. The pounding of the blood in her ears like kettledrums was the only sound that broke the sudden quiet filling the room.

"You've always been headstrong, but I gave you more credit than this. I haven't asked much from you, Jillian. All these years when I could have helped, you wouldn't let me. I respected that. I backed away."

She lowered her face to her hand, drew in a deep breath, then let it out.

"Well, this time I'm not backing down. It's too important. *You* are too important—to me and to your mother. If she knew about these horrible threats—and God willing she'll never find out—she'd worry herself sick over this deplorable situation. This is all about keeping you safe, sweetheart," he added after a long pause. "This is about keeping you alive."

She squeezed her eyes shut as love and guilt and the lingering and unwelcome threads of fear joined forces to undercut her anger. *Justifiable anger,* she reminded herself. He'd set her up. Railroaded her into this position.

"I love you, Jillian." He paused, waiting for her to reciprocate the sentiment.

She was too angry, felt too violated, to find it in her to respond in kind.

Another long moment passed before her father ended the discussion with two concise words: "Garrett stays."

The line went dead.

Jillian stared at the cell phone for a long vacant moment before winging back and hurling it across the room. It smacked the wall above the doorjamb with a resounding crack. It wasn't until the phone hit the plush white carpet and landed directly in front of a pair of black leather running shoes that she realized she was no longer alone.

She looked up the length of long legs covered in black denim, past a flat abdomen and broad chest wrapped in black cotton knit and a shoulder holster, until she reached those laser blue eyes. Along with a roiling anger, she felt run over by the overwhelming sting of defeat and a slowly dawning truth. He'd watched her undress. He'd seen her naked. Soaping herself in the shower. Moving to the music.

A knot of humiliation joined the anger and her sense of vulnerability.

"How much money is he paying you?" she asked in a flat voice.

Legs braced wide, arms crossed, hands tucked under his armpits, he rolled a shoulder in a negligent shrug. "Enough to know that you're one hot property, princess . . . not that it matters. What matters is that I managed to breach your *high-security* building and get access to you. It could have been anyone. It could have been someone who'd have left you dead instead of alive and pissed off. You can recover from pissed off."

At the moment, she wasn't so sure she could.

Her heart leveled several hard, irregular beats. "Get out."

He considered her with a detached regard that clearly said he wasn't considering it at all. That particular look was beginning to *piss her off,* as he so delicately put it, almost as much as his presence.

"OK, look, we can do this the hard way," he said, his tone a study in bored male tolerance. "Or we can go for easy."

Jillian gathered herself. She rose, notched her chin, and with all the pent-up terror, anger, and broken pride he'd brought to life in the past ten minutes looked him straight in the eye. "By all means, let's go for hard."

He measured her response through narrowed eyes. Made a decision. "All right. You need some time. Understood. So sleep on it, princess. Things might look different in the morning."

As far as he was concerned, it was the end of the discussion. He turned to go.

"Garrett."

He stopped and slowly turned back to face her, his expression relaying reluctant forbearance. "Yeah?"

"You're a sonofabitch."

The bastard had the nerve to smile. "Yeah, well, we all have our crosses to bear. That's one of mine. Just like I'm going to be one of yours for the duration. Of course, you could always run home to Daddy," he added with a hopeful look.

She snapped then. Dived straight off the deep end.

She balled up her fist, put every ounce of her 110 pounds behind it, and launched a roundhouse punch. Her knuckles connected with his jaw in a satisfying crack.

More satisfying was the sight of his head whipping to the side as the impact backed him up a full step. He shook his head and blinked before he got his feet under him again.

Jillian was shaking with fury when his gaze connected with hers. She was past fear now. Barely felt the pain radiating all the way up to her shoulder and the burning ache in her knuckles as she braced for a blow that didn't come.

She almost wished it would. She'd never hit another living

soul in her life, and yet she relished the idea of having reason to hit him again. In fact, at that moment, she'd have liked nothing better than to draw blood.

Fire melted the ice in his narrowed eyes as he glared at her, visibly settled himself, then nodded. "OK." He lifted a hand, rubbed his jaw. "I had that coming."

Suspicious of his acceptance, she waited in wary silence for the qualifier. It came with the same chilling delivery as the promise in his eyes.

"Hit me again, though, and we might just have to have a little come-to-Jesus meeting. You won't *like* it."

"I don't *like* you."

Another one of those maddeningly amused grins had her seeing red.

"Understood. In the meantime, let's get something else straight here. Daddy didn't hire me because I'm a nice guy. He hired me because he wanted someone who would get the job done. I think I've already proven that I'll do whatever it takes to ensure Daddy gets what he wants. And trust me—I couldn't give a shit if it comes at your expense."

She flinched when he reached out, but he only chucked her under her chin—like she was some addle-brained bimbo who didn't know black from white—before he turned away.

At her bedroom door, he stopped and scooped up his cell phone. Before he left, he glanced at her over his shoulder. "Get some sleep. We've got a lot of work to do tomorrow."

Jillian was too stunned—that she'd hit him, that he hadn't hit her back, that he had the audacity to give her orders and then smile like she was his own personal source of amusement—to do anything but stare as he walked out of her bedroom.

When she snapped out of it, she reached for the door and slammed it shut. Then she leaned back against it and let loose an outraged roar.

It all caught up with her then. The fear, the humiliation,

the defeat. For long, agonizing moments, she'd thought she was going to die—and she'd held it together as long as she could. Her knees finally gave out and she slid to the floor.

She'd thought she was going to die.

She let her head drop back against the door, closed her eyes.

She wasn't dead.

She was alive.

She was alive and the man who was supposed to keep her that way was the only man who had ever awakened a rage so primal that she'd resorted to physical violence to release it.

The adrenaline rush that had been insulating her pain let go like a long sigh. She started shaking. Uncontrollably. Suddenly her hand throbbed. She cupped it to her breast and, beaten, gave up the fight. Hating herself—*really* hating herself—for giving in to them, she let the tears fall.

When she'd cried it out, she rose on rubbery legs. After filling the bathroom sink with cold water, she pressed a cold cloth to her eyes with her left hand and soaked the sore knuckles of her right. Only after she'd slipped on a sleep shirt and eased under the covers did she let herself relish the satisfying memory of Nolan Garrett's head snapping back and his eyes momentarily losing focus.

And only after she'd drained the rest of her wine with one long, deep swallow did she let down her guard enough to grudgingly admit that *maybe* she felt safer with him under her roof.

But he was still a sonofabitch.

And she still didn't like this—or him.

She turned out her light and settled in on her side to try to get some sleep.

Right.

Like that was going to happen with him in the room down the hall.

4

"*THAT* WENT WELL," NOLAN MUTTERED AS he lay on his back on Jillian Kincaid's fussy white bedspread in her frou-frou white-on-white guest bedroom. White except for the splashy artwork hung on the walls. Abstract. Vibrant. Pricey. Like the lady.

He worked his jaw, touched it gingerly before crossing his hands behind his head on a pillow that smelled of class and wealth and a luxury he'd never in his life experienced. That she was high-strung and high gloss hadn't surprised him. But who'd have figured she'd have the balls to slug him?

He frowned at the slow-moving blades of the fan hanging from a ceiling that pushed fifteen feet. Hell. Who'd have thought there was more to her than television's plastic princess persona?

And the real kicker, who'd of thought he'd end up paid to protect her—or anyone else, for that matter? It sure as hell hadn't been part of his plan.

After eight years as a Hooah, he'd left his men, left his pride, and DX'd out of his Ranger battalion. That had been three months ago. He missed it . . . missed his men like hell. But for the past ninety days he'd been telling himself he was as happy as a damn clam. Living on the boat, nursing a record string of booze-soaked days and mercifully dreamless nights, searching for a comfort zone at the bottom of the barrel.

And he'd been on one helluva roll.

Until yesterday.

Just when rock bottom had been within his reach, life had taken a turn for the worse and dumped him back into the thick of things.

He'd had the bum part down pat. He sure as hell hadn't wanted a job, but he'd found one anyway. Or rather the job had found him—compliments of the three people who should have known better than to try to resurrect the man he no longer had the stomach to be.

Lying in a room that smelled of an incongruous mix of flowers and wealth and the oil he'd used to clean his gun, he thought of his older brothers, Ethan and Dallas, and his twin sister, Eve. For whatever reasons, they still believed in him. So did his mom and dad. Evidently, so did Darin Kincaid.

Per Ethan, who called most of the shots at E.D.E.N. Security, Inc., the security firm he had taken over from their dad when he'd retired a few years ago, Kincaid had asked for Nolan's services specifically after he'd read that fricking newspaper feature and found out about his recent separation from the Rangers. Or so Ethan had said yesterday when he'd stormed onto the *EDEN* where she was moored at a slip on the Intracoastal Waterway a little north of West Palm.

He'd thought everyone would leave him alone there.

So much for what he'd thought.

He scrubbed a hand over his jaw. Christ, was it just yesterday?

He'd been waking by slow, painful degrees, nursing a hangover the size of a Black Hawk, when Ethan had barged aboard.

"Enough," Ethan barked when he'd found Nolan sitting on the edge of his rack at noon, holding his head on to his neck with the help of both hands. "I've reached my limit of seeing you this way, Bro."

"Easily solved." His big, bad self had managed to stand

and actually stay upright with the help of an unsteady hand
on the bulkhead. "Stay the hell away from me."

Ethan had shot him a look. "Yeah, that's going to happen.
Just be glad it's me and not Dallas who showed up."

Nolan grunted but knew his oldest brother was right. As
former Special Forces, Ethan still played on his negotiating
skills from his stint as a Green Beret to win the majority of
his arguments. Dallas, however, two years Nolan's senior,
had more of a tendency to go for the throat than use diplomacy. Bucking the family army tradition their father had
started when he'd become a U.S. Army Airborne Ranger
during the Vietnam conflict, Dallas had chosen the marines.
Ten years total—the last six in Force Recon. Enough said.

Nolan loved his family. He wished his brothers and Eve,
who'd opted out of the Secret Service to join the firm last
year, all the luck in the world at E.D.E.N, Inc., but he didn't
want any part of it. What he wanted was to be left alone.

"Fair warning," Ethan had cautioned, clanging around in
the galley making coffee and bringing Nolan to tears when he
dumped a fifth of Glenlivet down the drain, "If you don't get
your sorry ass straightened out by tonight, I'm sending Eve."

Pain lanced like a stiletto behind Nolan's left eye when he
thought of his twin. Eve was a pit bull packaged like a
Twinkie. Because of all those soft curves and misty blond
looks, people tended to underestimate her—to their eternal
regret. Eve never forgot . . . and she took no prisoners.

"Christ, no."

"And Mom."

Stiff-armed, he'd braced both hands on the galley table
and dropped his head between them with a groan. He
thought of his mom, happily settled in a gated community in
West Palm Beach where she played canasta and did water
aerobics with her "ladies who did lunch" and his father shot
the shit every morning on the golf course with the boys. "I
don't want them to see me like this."

"Then do something about it."

He dragged a hand over his stubbled jaw. "I plan to. In my own good time."

"You're out of time. I need you onboard. E.D.E.N. needs you. Starting tomorrow."

The hand on his shoulder undercut the anger and disgust in Ethan's voice and reduced everything to the most basic level. They were brothers. They loved each other, and Nolan knew his actions had been the cause of much pain.

In the end, that had been the deciding factor.

"OK, fine. What, exactly, can't you three overachievers do that requires my services?"

"We can't be you. And *you*, according to Darin Kincaid, are the man."

"Kincaid?" It took a moment to dig the information out of the cobwebs mucking up his brain. "The publisher? What the hell does he want with me?"

"Shower first. Then I'll explain."

So he'd hit the head—and caught a glimpse of himself in the small mirror above the sink. Death was warmer and had more color. Except for his eyes. They were as red as fire ants and burned like hot cinders.

Feeling marginally human after showering, he'd joined his brother in the galley again. Ethan had peeled a cherry lifesaver out of a roll and filled him in on the death threats against Kincaid's daughter and Kincaid's personal request to hire Nolan as her bodyguard.

"He read the newspaper article about your missions in Afghanistan and Iraq. Has always been a big fan of Special Ops. Respects the patch . . . wants you."

As they drank black coffee, Nolan realized the booze hadn't diluted his blood nearly as much as he'd hoped. He sobered up way too fast.

"You went beyond the patch," he pointed out to his brother who had gone from Rangers to Special Forces—Green Beret.

"And I'm ass deep in alligators on the Benton case. So are Eve and Dallas. Without you, I'll lose the account . . . and Kincaid is willing to pay anything to get you."

All right. Fine. So he'd help his brother out of this pinch. But he wasn't going to be anyone's damn bodyguard. Instead, he planned to pull a quick in-and-out, scare the little princess into running home to Daddy—which was what Kincaid wanted anyway—and call it a wrap. End of story.

Or so he'd thought.

He glared toward the closed bedroom door where, down the hall, Jillian Kincaid slept in her bed.

She hadn't freaked out like she was supposed to. She hadn't flown home to the nest. Which meant he was stuck doing the job he'd been hired to do: protect her.

Restless, he sat up in her fancy bed, dropped his feet to the floor. Stiff-armed, he buried his fists into the mattress at either side of his hips and fought a wave of panic as the undeniable reality of this situation sank in.

His brother was counting on him. Darin Kincaid was counting on him. And whether she liked it or not, Jillian was counting on him. On a freaking hero if you read the papers. A U.S. Army Airborne Ranger.

Ex-Ranger. Past tense. Past life.

Only the regrets had followed him into the present.

He stared at the far wall and steeled himself against the irony. Bodyguard. Him. What a fucking joke. Yeah. He'd helped out at E.D.E.N., Inc., in his misspent youth. All of them had. A little surveillance now and then, but nothing heavy. Nothing like this.

When in the hell had everything gotten so fucked up? Especially tonight.

Nolan had thought Kincaid was exaggerating when he warned him that his only daughter was stubborn. She'd been terrified, but she'd stood her ground. Grudgingly he admired her for that. And for the spirit, if not the pride, that had prompted her to try to realign his jaw. It still throbbed like a bitch.

"She's refused my offer to provide a bodyguard," Kincaid had said when they'd briefed earlier that day at E.D.E.N.'s suite of offices at the Forum on Palm Beach Lakes Boulevard. "She's not going to want you there. Make no mistake—I don't care what, she wants. What I care about is keeping her alive.

"It's up to you to figure out a way to convince her that you're a necessary evil. And I don't care how extreme your methods are. If you have to scare her half to death, do it. Just make sure she understands and accepts that either she comes home where I can protect her or you're there for the duration.

"And Garrett, if anything happens to her . . ." Kincaid's voice had broken.

Nolan had looked away, letting the man gather himself, recognizing, with an uncharacteristic kernel of empathy, that he'd just witnessed the publishing giant at his most vulnerable.

"I'm counting on you to keep her safe," he'd finished, unnecessarily.

No lie. Kincaid was paying E.D.E.N., Inc., megabucks to ensure Jillian remained in one piece. Nolan was still a little staggered by the figure Ethan had named.

The vivid image of the stark terror etched across Jillian's face when she'd seen him step out of the shadows brought a small pang of guilt. But Daddy had said extremes. If there was one word Nolan understood, that was the one.

He'd wanted her at her most vulnerable—hair wet, face void of makeup. That she'd been naked had been an unexpected bonus.

Oh yeah. The woman was a walking wet dream.

He dragged a hand over his face, stalling the thought before it got any further. He was only human. He'd had to endure her slow, unconsciously sensual strip while he'd hidden like a rat in her closet. Getting hard.

He hadn't intended to play voyeur, but it hadn't mattered where he'd looked. There were mirrors all over the damn place. Was he supposed to cover his eyes when she turned that sweet little ass his way? Blush like a choirboy at the sight of those centerfold breasts?

He got hard again just thinking about it. She'd been a gymnast once—Olympic quality according to her file. It showed in the slim lines of her hips, the flex of smooth muscle in her strong thighs and tight, high ass. Her breasts were incredible—a breast man's dream. Nice sun-kissed-sized globes, heavy on the underside, her nipples—tight little dusky pink nubs—turning slightly upward, begging to be sucked.

And that damnable pouting mouth.

He shook off the images. Playtime was over. Jillian Kincaid was an assignment. Her life depended on his ability to handle himself and the situation—*not* to handle her.

He'd do the job. He'd lay his life on the line for her, no question. But would it be enough?

A cold sweat broke across his brow.

Snagging his cell phone, he punched in Ethan's number, wishing Daddy's darling had just gone with the plan and run home. To Nolan's way of thinking, it had been a win-win situation all the way around. E.D.E.N., Inc., got the juicy Kincaid account, Daddy got his little princess back under his wing; and for his minimal but stellar performance Nolan got a fat paycheck and the opportunity to drown himself in a few more bottles of Glenlivet instead of whatever was on special for the week.

"Only she didn't scare, did she, Garrett?" he muttered, then left a terse message on Ethan's voice mail advising him that he was in.

He stared at the phone, then set it aside. He couldn't see a way out. He was stuck in her penthouse for the night at least.

Maybe longer. And he didn't like it. He didn't like the thought of exchanging hostilities with a woman who wouldn't be pushed around, wouldn't be told what to do, and didn't appear to have a single self-preservation gene in her hot little body. Very hot little body.

Don't go there.

Bottom line: While it was beyond his ability to comprehend, it appeared that despite her daddy's billions at her disposal, she was actually *serious* about her career and her independence. That meant Nolan was *seriously* stuck with her. For the foreseeable future, he'd have to stick to Jillian Kincaid like a piece of lint to her pricey suits and actually do the job he'd been hired to do.

And there was the rub and the reason he'd been burying his head in a bottle. The last person who'd relied on Nolan to keep him alive was dead.

Since he hadn't been able to sleep, Nolan hit the shower in the guest bedroom. He'd just turned off the taps when his cell phone rang in the bedroom. He dragged one of the half-dozen plush towels he'd found in the linen closet across his wet chest and glanced at the bedside clock. One ten a.m.

He punched the CONNECT button expecting to hear Ethan on the other end of the line and muttered a subdued "Yeah."

"No-man! Brethren! That you, buddy?"

Nolan closed his eyes. It was not Ethan. It was not anyone he wanted to hear from. Not tonight.

He'd recognize Jason Wilson's nasal twang anywhere. Un-fucking-believable.

"Plowboy."

"The one and only. How the hell are you, you lucky civilian bastard?"

Unprepared. That's how he was.

He was unprepared to hear the voice of a soldier he'd

never expected to see again. He was unprepared for the
punch of emotion. When he'd left Battalion, he'd left the life
behind. All the rules. All the BS. All the regrets.

A big part of those regrets had been the men who'd depended on him. It sliced every bit as deep as he'd known it
would to hear a voice that reminded him of his biggest failure.

Scenarios too numerous to sort flashed through his mind's
eye. Ranger School at Fort Benning. All-nighters mucking
through mud and swatting mosquitoes after endless hours
with no sleep. First Airborne Ranger Bat and the guys of
Hardrock Charlie Company. A bar in Atlanta they'd closed
one night with the help of the MPs and a royally pissed-off
bartender—other nights in Columbus with used women in
used cars and a six-pack that had never had a chance to live
long enough to go flat.

Afghanistan.

Iraq.

Where he'd done what he'd been trained to do: kill bad
guys and break their toys.

"What's up, Wilson?" he asked as the *whump, whump,
whump* of the helos, the sting of sand peppering his face, and
the stench of sweat and blood and death hummed in the back
of his mind like a surreal movie brought back to life at the
sound of Plowboy's voice.

"Well, here's the deal," the Ranger said, and in the background Nolan heard hard rock blaring from a jukebox and
the unmistakable sound of a head-knocking bar crowd. "I'm
here."

A curl of dread coiled in Nolan's gut. "Here where?"

"*Here,* here. West Palm. Hey!" he yelled, apparently to
anyone who would listen. "What's the name of this fine es-
tablishment?

"Nirvana," he said after a moment. "Somewhere on—"

"Yeah. I know where it is."

Nolan's chin hit his chest. His grip on the phone tightened.

Nirvana was one of his favorite watering holes of late. It had a darkness to it that often fit his mood and just enough of a dangerous edge that a man with a death wish might get that wish fulfilled.

"What are you doing in Florida?"

"It's block time, man. We're sprung for a couple weeks. No way was I sitting out my leave at Bat. So I told Uncle to shove it and decided to haul my tired ass to the Keys for a week, where the women are as bitchin' as the booze. Told you when I asked for your cell number that I'd be comin' your way, you sorry sonofabitch. Now, hump your ass down here. I've got about two hours before my connecting flight leaves and we need to talk, man. We need to talk bad."

Panic, as thick as Plowboy's midwestern accent, had Nolan reaching for excuses. "Caught me at a bad time, bud."

"Fuck that. You want to talk bad time? They've got me by the balls here, No. Seems the locals don't cotton to us suave types muscling in on their territory."

Nolan went rigid. The Iowa farm boy had an off-duty reputation for hitting the hooch too hard, shooting off his mouth, and landing with his ass in a sling.

"What did you do?"

"Well, that's the thing. It's more like what's going to be done unto me that's—"

Plowboy's words were cut off by the unmistakable sound of a fist hitting flesh and the resultant grunt of pain.

When he came back on the line, he was breathing hard and his voice was raspy. "I sort of . . . promised these needle-dick . . . no-loads that we . . . you and me . . . we'd show 'em—"

Another thud—another punch landing—then the racket of a body crashing against what was most likely a table. More groans in the background along with the ominous *thump, thump, thump* of the receiver hitting the wall as it dangled from the cord.

Adrenaline shot through Nolan's blood as he waited the interminable length of several heartbeats before he heard someone grapple with the phone.

"Nolan, that you?"

He recognized Charlene's voice and felt a small measure of relief. Char tended bar on weekends. The forty-something divorcée with the sandpaper voice and bulldog jowls could hold her own in any brawl he'd ever seen break out in Nirvana . . . and he'd seen plenty.

He pressed thumb and finger to his eyeballs. "What's happening, Char?"

"What's happening," she ground out, "is that if this stupid shit is a friend of yours, you'd better get down here fast and pull him out before they start dismantling him. He's a tough SOB but too ignorant to keep his mouth shut."

That was Plowboy. On the clock, he was all Ranger—all business, all team. Off the clock, he had always been and would always be a loudmouth, primed for a fight.

"Get down here, Nolan. I don't want no cops and I don't want no one biting it on my shift. He's not gonna last much longer," she warned, and hung up.

5

THE FIRST SURPRISE WAS THE CRACK OF the door hitting Jillian's bedroom wall. The second was that she'd been asleep—dead asleep. She shot straight up in bed, then covered her eyes with her forearm when the overhead light flicked on, blinding her.

"Get up and get dressed. We've got to move."

She squinted through the cobwebs, then blinked at the man who'd sent her heart into orbit for the second time that right as he stalked across the room and rifled through her bureau drawers.

She was too shocked to order him out. "What . . . what do you think you're doing?"

"Saving time. Put these on."

Her hands lifted reflexively to catch the white shorts and red T-shirt he tossed at her chest.

"What?" She threw her legs over the side of the bed, dragged back her hair. Scowled. Yawned. And finally got a slippery grip on the emotion she was most used to dealing with around Garrett. "Let me rephrase that. *What?*"

"I don't have time to explain. Just get dressed and make it snappy or you're going like you are. Your choice."

Jillian wasn't sure if it was his warning snarl, the fact that her sleep-drugged mind was only half-functioning, or the very real possibility that whoever was threatening her had turned up the heat, but the moment he strode out of her bedroom she scrambled out of bed and dived for her pantie drawer. She didn't bother with a bra, but she didn't go commando for anyone, and if she was going to start, it sure as the world wasn't going to be for him.

Less than a minute later, she skidded into the living area carrying her sandals and finger-combing her hair. "What's happened?"

The black scowl on the face of the man shoving ammo into the clip of a weapon that made her .22 look like a squirt gun said it all. A lot. A lot had happened.

She noticed then what she hadn't noticed in her sleep-fogged state when he barged into her bedroom. He'd evidently showered—his hair was wet and he smelled of soap and shampoo, something leathery that hinted at sage and citrus. He was dressed all in black again. His short-sleeved T-shirt clung to his chest, damp in spots, like he hadn't taken the time to dry himself off completely.

She spun toward the door, toeing on her sandals, sensing his urgency as he armed himself. "Is someone trying to get in?"

To the gun, which he expertly holstered, he added a long, lethal-looking knife that he tucked in his boot, then covered with his pant leg.

No doubt about it. He was preparing for battle.

She was stubborn, but she wasn't stupid. For the time being, she was going to take this at face value—even though she had to gnaw on her lower lip to keep from peppering him with more questions that he clearly did not want to field.

"Let's go." He snagged her elbow and led her toward the door.

Steel. The impression of steel beneath honed flesh and wrapped around bone burned through her skin and had her keeping pace at a fast trot as they streaked out of her penthouse and scrambled toward the elevator.

"Can you at least tell me what's going on?" she whispered as they waited for an elevator that was notoriously slow to rise to the penthouse floor.

"What's going on is that you need to keep your mouth shut and do exactly what I tell you."

She was wide-awake now and her initial surge of surprise, which had transitioned to fear, was quickly listing toward irritation. No. Make that anger. She'd seen no one in the hall. Had heard nothing. And on their little jaunt to the elevator, he hadn't seemed particularly intent on keeping her close and shielding her from whatever he'd perceived as a threat.

"If this is a drill," she said after assessing the situation and finding imminent danger remarkably absent, "I'd just as soon skip the rest of it, thank you very much."

What she'd *just as soon* didn't seem to matter to him. He didn't say a word. Long moments passed and silence, as thick and palpable as the tension radiating from his body, engulfed the air around them. And oddly, hovering over it all, awareness, for the first time, of him as the man who would protect her stalled her questions and her anger and held her in a grip that rivaled his hold on her arm when he dragged her down the hall.

Along with the scent of soap and shampoo that he must have brought with him, because it didn't smell anything like the rain forest products she'd stocked in the guest bathroom, she could literally smell the testosterone, could feel his coiled strength as the relatively roomy hallway shrank to roughly the size of a microchip.

Jillian was a trained observer. It came with the job. And when she wasn't run over by hysteria—standard protocol, in her opinion, when you stepped out of a shower and found a man in your bathroom packing a gun—her mind assessed, cataloged, and filed details neatly away for later recall.

There was nothing neat about Nolan Garrett's details. In fact, the devil was clearly in his details—all raw power, consummate masculinity, and a pretty good measure of mean thrown in to thicken the stew.

The elevator finally hit her floor. The doors slid soundlessly open, then shut behind them when they stepped inside.

She knew now that he hadn't come to kill her, but she'd bet her top slot during ratings week that he *had* killed. Call her crazy, but that still made him dangerous in her book.

Fallen angel. She stood by her initial assessment.

The reporter in her couldn't help but be intrigued by him. Under other circumstances, the woman in her might even have appreciated the sheer male beauty of the man. The full lips that even now were compressed in a hard, unyielding line as he stared straight ahead at the panel of lights on the elevator wall were unsettlingly sensual. His dark hair was a little on the long side. It gave him a reckless and a bit mussed-up look—like he'd just gotten out of bed or was about to tumble someone into one. Coupled with the heavy five o'clock shadow darkening his jaw, the look didn't quite fit with the clean, defined lines of his face or the honed precision of his body, which he held in a rigid, almost military posture.

Whoa. Back up. Military.

Bingo.

She could see it now. In his ramrod straight stance, in the spring-loaded give of his powerful legs. Regardless of his casual air, it was apparent he was perpetually balanced and ready for action. The man was on red alert. Trained to act and react. Kill or be killed.

If she'd suspected it before, she was sure of it now. He *had* killed. Would kill again. For her, if he had to. And while she didn't want to be—she *wanted* to be angry and incensed—she found herself hopelessly compelled to find out more about him.

"Special Ops?" she asked into the silence that had thickened to syrup.

With the slightest shift of his gaze, he met her eyes. He looked annoyed. And something else suddenly. Aware. Of her. Of the fact that they were strangers and alone in an elevator on a hot Florida night—and that he'd seen her naked stepping in and out of her shower little more than an hour ago.

Before she could stall a damnable blush, his expression closed up again, leaving her wondering if she'd been imagining things. And she still hadn't gotten an answer to her question.

"I have a right to know," she insisted.

"You have the right to remain silent, too, but I don't suppose you're going to exercise it."

What happened then amazed her. A small grin—a mix of amusement and fatalistic forbearance—cracked that granite facade. Earlier, when he'd terrorized her in the bathroom, he'd given up some semblance of a smile. But that had been staged, manufactured to show scorn, to let her know who was in charge and to scare her into wetting her pants—which she might have, if she'd had any on.

This smile was different. It was spontaneous. Unguarded. And though it had been barely there, it had been a break in his armor—although why she thought she wanted to breach it she had no idea. Just like she didn't know why that small concession to emotion had transformed all of his uncompromising and harsh beauty into something she hadn't wanted to deal with before, either: The fact that he was real. Something more than a stranger with a gun, a protector without a heart. He became a man to her in that moment . . . a man of flesh and blood and feelings.

For some unsettling reason, it made him seem even more dangerous. It had been much easier to dismiss him as a cold-blooded machine. Now she had to entertain the possibility of seeing him in a whole new light.

"Rangers," he finally volunteered, surprising her yet again and snapping her away from those troubling thoughts.

"Lead the way," she finished the credo, then waited for a reaction that never came. Unless you considered his eyes' going dead a reaction. Given that she'd just witnessed an actual display of human emotion from him, she decided it was. A big one.

The elevator finally hit the ground floor. The doors slid open and he dragged her with him across the lobby at a fast jog, assured the change-of-shift security guard that all was well, and headed out the door.

As they scrambled toward the parking garage, Jillian tried to get a better handle on the workings of this frustrating man's mind. She was not an empath nor was she clairvoyant, and truth be known, she waffled between believing in either one. She'd researched and reported on a piece a year or so ago about a self-professed empath who had done some quasi-amazing work with the police department. While Jillian still swayed toward the side of disbelief, the absolute that she'd taken away from the experience was that some people fell into the category of sensitives. Sensitives knew when there was more to someone than met the eye. Jillian was firmly convinced that she was one of those people. Not in a hocus-pocus, booga-booga way but to a degree that made her instinctively aware when someone was withholding information, feeling guilt, or experiencing pain. Many people would simply call it intuition.

Whatever they called it, she had it. And she used it. It had helped her get to the heart of the matter more than once in an interview.

Right now, whatever it was, it was telling her that Nolan Garrett of the cool blue eyes and unreadable expression guarded not only *her* with his life; he also guarded secrets. It told her that he lived with an incredible amount of guilt. That he harbored an exhausting measure of pain.

As they moved at a fast clip toward the far end of the dark garage, she glanced at the uncompromising profile of the man her father had paid to protect her and, inexplicably, felt an almost overwhelming urge to comfort him. To tell him it would be OK.

And then she got a clue.

Not more than an hour ago she'd have cheerfully knocked him into next Tuesday. And now . . . now she had absolutely no idea why she wasn't still asleep and dreaming about ways to get rid of him. She needed some answers about what was happening. If she didn't get them soon— about where he was taking her and why—she might just decide Tuesday wasn't far enough.

She was about to demand he tell her where they were going when they reached an emerald green Mustang, from the 1960s. He stopped beside the passenger door. Turned and looked at her—and her breath stalled somewhere in the vicinity of Cuba. An unexpected and immediate sexual tension, as sharp as the knife he'd slid into his boot, suddenly electrified the air she needed very badly to breathe if she had any prayer of clearing her head.

His blue eyes transitioned from ice to fire as his gaze slid down her body in a blatantly sexual assessment. He took his time about it, lingering on her bare legs, moving slowly up to the strip of skin exposed between her hip-hugger shorts and cropped T-shirt before snagging on her breasts and boldly holding.

Her pulse leaped at the shock of his less than subtle inspection. Something else reacted in shock, too. Her nipples tightened, tingled, pressed aggressively against the tight cotton knit. She would not flinch, she told herself, yet she couldn't keep from crossing her arms over her breasts to cover her body's reaction that was both knee-jerk and involuntary. And uncalled for.

His gaze shifted to her mouth, then lifted, ever so slowly,

to her eyes, and just that fast, blue flame cooled to flinty ice.

Her breath whispered out on a relieved little rush that fairly echoed in the underground garage when he averted his attention to unlock the car door. She looked away, too. And blinked and settled herse¹f and told herself she'd imagined all that . . . raw, primal heat. But her pulse said no, she hadn't imagined anything. It had been very, very real. And very, very hot.

Good God.

Shaken by it and by the fact that she'd reacted to him on any level other than anger, she eased into the passenger seat, then dared a quick glance at his profile when he settled behind the wheel. His jaw muscle clenched—and to her utter shock, a few of her internal muscles did a little clenching, too, right along with her pulse, which was pumping in places she didn't want to feel it.

This was going way beyond crazy. She wasn't sure what had just happened between them, but whatever it was, she didn't like it. Neither did he, if his dark scowl told the story, but it sure hadn't stopped him from looking his fill.

All right. It should be easy to rationalize. A truckload of adrenaline had pumped through her system during the last few hours. That could account for some momentary brain cramps and a little skewed perspective.

It called for a quick fix: Level out. Get a grip.

He shoved the key in the ignition about the time she'd convinced herself that whatever had just passed between them not only was over; it also hadn't been nearly as intense as she'd thought.

And then she didn't have to rationalize anymore, because it took every ounce of concentration she could muster just to keep from screaming.

She couldn't help it. Jillian clutched the dash and buried her feet against the floorboard as they cut down the nearly empty streets at breakneck speeds. The needle on the speedometer had made only passing acquaintance with the speed limit— and that had been several blocks ago.

"God forbid that I point this out, but in my experience, red generally means stop," she said through clenched teeth as they flew through yet another light.

She craned her head around to look behind them.

Nothing. No cars. No trucks. No police cruiser when you needed one.

"Fill me in."

She looked from the deserted street to Garrett's face. "On color-coded traffic lights?"

He looked dead ahead, the streetlights casting ominous shadows over his hooded brow. "On the death threats. When did they start? How were they delivered?"

She swallowed back a squeal as he took a corner on two wheels, then replied in the same concise verbiage that seemed to be his stock-in-trade. "Two weeks ago. The first was on my home voice mail. This week's came to the station. E-mail. My God, do we really have to drive this fast?"

"Who do you think it is?"

Her grip on the dash and the door tightened. "I have no clue."

"What are the police saying?"

"*They* have no clue."

He snorted.

And she saw red.

"So sorry," she bit out with the sweetness of alum, "but you're going to have to translate that one for me. I'm not fluent in brooding male grunting."

Another almost smile, which she chose to ignore, lifted the corner of his mouth. "Translated: that's not much to go on."

She glared out the window as street signs raced by. "And less to get worked up about. I still maintain it's someone's idea of a joke."

"And in your experience a death threat is a laughing matter?"

It was her turn to snort. "Experience? I have no *experience* in this. I just want it to go away."

"Well, princess, that makes two of us."

She whipped her gaze to his hard profile. The anger hit her first. "Do *not* call me princess." Then came curiosity as she tried to figure him out. "If you hate this so much, why are you here?"

The look he gave her when he turned his head and met her eyes made her blood run cold and hot at the same time. "Hell if I know."

Before she could recover from another bout of inexplicable sexual heat and pounce on his cryptic remark, he braked, then whipped the car into a parking space littered with newspapers, fast-food wrappers, and the remains of a battered shoe.

Jillian looked through the windshield, blinked, and gaped.

"A bar? You dragged me out of bed in the middle of the night to take me to a *bar*?"

She stared in disbelief at a cinder-block building that sat on the corner of a backstreet where either the streetlights had burned out or—and *this* was a reassuring thought—they'd been shot out.

Amazing. He'd almost made a believer of her. As he'd driven through the city like a man avoiding a death wish—or heading toward one—she'd just hung on, trying not to be aware of him as she sat beside him in the passenger seat of a vintage emerald green fastback Mustang. His hard eyes had been glued to the deserted streets, his movements economic and proficient as he downshifted through tight corners and ran more lights in ten minutes than she had in her entire life. She'd actually thought they were running *from,* not *to,* something.

Apparently, she'd thought wrong. She'd been doing that a lot tonight. She didn't like it. And she didn't like this.

The sign on the dingy gray building read: NIRVANA.

In her worst nightmare, maybe.

The one-story structure made a definitive architectural statement: early urban decay. The plate-glass windows, tinted almost black, were streaked with grime and . . . and things she *really* didn't want to think about. The thick, shatterproof glass was crisscrossed with duct tape over spidery cracks that crept from a central circular hole. A woman a little less mired in denial might recognize it as a bullet hole. To keep from whimpering like a baby, she chose not to be that woman.

Through the cloudy and cracked glass, neon signs advertised several brands of beer on tap; below the windows unoriginal but graphic graffiti extolled the virtues of someone's mother in bold red letters. The front door—which looked like it had been kicked in . . . several times . . . recently— was propped open by an empty beer crate. Shards of brown glass littered the sidewalk where scraggly weeds struggled to grow in the gap between the building's cracked and crumbling foundation and the pocked concrete. Why anything would even attempt to grow in this environment was beyond her. So was her ability to figure out what they were doing here.

Several huge motorcycles and a couple of dented pickups filled the spaces directly in front of the building. From inside, raucous laughter—low-down, dirty, and mean— rumbled beneath the head-banging rock blaring from a jukebox and seeped into the humid tropical night like toxic waste. Through the open car window Jillian could smell cigarette smoke and beer and the unmistakable undercurrent of danger.

"Put these on."

She jerked her head toward Garrett as he dragged a pair of sunglasses from the dash and handed them to her.

"Put 'em on," he repeated when she stared from the aviator glasses to him, her expression saying it all.

Are you crazy?

"I don't want anyone recognizing you."

She actually laughed, despite his stone-faced glower. "Well, that's not going to be a problem, because I'm not going in there."

He eased out of the car and walked around to the passenger side. Just as he reached for the handle, she punched the lock. Smirked.

He rolled his eyes at her ineffective and juvenile show of defiance, inserted the key, and opened her door.

When she held her ground and refused to move, he hunkered down to eye level and reached for her seat belt.

"No," she said, batting at his hands and grabbing for the buckle. "You know what? I've had it. I've been dancing to your tune all night, but I'm done now. I'm packing in my tap shoes. You want to be my bodyguard? Fine. Be my bodyguard . . . not my social director, because if this is your idea of a fun night out, you suck at it."

When he hung his head, she got the distinct impression it was to hide a smile. "This is not a social call."

"So glad we can agree on something." She stubbornly tugged the seat belt across her lap again and fumbled with the catch on the buckle. "We'll just have to reschedule this little attempt to bury the hatchet and get chummy over a bottle of Ripple and a fifty-cent draw for some other night. Now take me home."

Nolan dragged a hand over his lower face. Gezus, she was a piece of work. He'd known her silence had been too good to last. She'd been way too willing, way too docile, in the fifteen minutes since he'd woken her up, hustled her out of the penthouse, and sped across town. He'd known the elements of surprise and confusion had been the only things he'd had going for him, and she'd just maxed out on both.

Too bad. He didn't have the time or the inclination to make nice. Or to wish there'd been a way to avoid dragging her out here. Or to wonder why a woman who drank hundred-dollar bottles of imported chardonnay knew about Ripple wine and fifty-cent draws and why the fact that she did had him fighting a smile.

He didn't have time to analyze that lapse into stag rut on the elevator, either. Son of a bitch did the woman have a body. Dressed, undressed, didn't seem to matter. She played hell with his libido, which had seen a little too much downtime in the past three months if a shrew like her was flipping his switch.

He didn't even like the woman.

We don't have to like her to fuck her—this from Skippy, his one-eyed wonder snake, who in Nolan's misspent youth had done a lot of his thinking for him and still felt entitled to express an opinion from time to time.

Now was not the time.

"You owe me, Ethan," he swore under his breath. Since his brother had pumped him full of caffeine and shamed him into taking this assignment, not one thing had happened to make him think sobriety didn't suck.

"Come on." He pried her fingers off the belt buckle and latched onto her upper arm. "Watch your peach." He covered her head with his hand to protect her from bumping it and dragged her out of the car. Then he ordered himself to ignore the way she smelled and the heat of her skin beneath his hand and the way her breast felt—soft and warm and lush—snuggled up against the back of his knuckles.

"Shut . . . up," he snapped, more harshly than he'd

intended, when she started in again. He forced himself to settle down, dropped his tone a notch, and made an attempt to make her understand.

"This isn't about you, OK? I've got a little something I need to take care of. I didn't plan on it and I don't like it any more than you do, and if it'll make you move, I promise to explain later.

"In the meantime, you cannot stay out here alone and I couldn't leave you in the penthouse. So just cut me a little slack here. Keep your mouth shut, stay where I put you, and I'll have you back in the lap of luxury in no time."

So much for an attempt at diplomacy.

Her green eyes flared fire. And he picked a helluva time to notice—again—that she wasn't wearing a bra beneath that tight little red crop top T-shirt he'd had the bad luck to pull out of her drawer. Christ. Nirvana may be way off the lady's flight path, but the way she was packed into those short shorts with her midriff bare and her nipples poking against that stretchy cotton, she looked like fair game for any knuckle-dragging asshole with a notion that she came with a guarantee to put out. And he was about to haul her into a bar full of them.

Perfect.

It wasn't enough he had to save Plowboy's ass—he had to watch hers as well. And a fine ass it was, he thought, grim faced, as he guided her along ahead of him toward the door. In fact, it was a premium ass. Looked as good in those shorts as it did out of them. No time soon was he going to be able to ditch the picture burned into his brain of her stepping in and out of that shower.

"Will you quit pushing me around?"

He stopped short of going inside, turned her around to face him, and one last time put in a bid for her cooperation. "If there was any way to avoid this, believe me, I would. For the last time, put on the shades, do not open your mouth, and do exactly as I say. Now is there *anything* about that that isn't clear?"

Apparently not. Despite the venomous look she shot him, she finally slapped on the dark glasses and let him lead her into the bar toward what, he had a pretty good idea, was certain disaster.

6

IT TOOK A MOMENT FOR NOLAN TO GET THE lay of the land amid the pall of shifting smoke and the thump of pool balls bouncing off stained and torn felt bumpers. It took another to locate Plowboy. He was slumped over a table in a dark corner—alive apparently, if the heave of his shoulders told the tale. Four tattooed, pierced, and scarred biker types held somber court, flanking him with various levels of grim, combative defiance and bloodlust.

"About damn time," Char grumbled from behind the bar, where she nervously wiped a damp, dingy rag across the scarred surface. Through the smoke drifting from the ciga- rette dangling at the corner of her mouth, the blowsy blonde gave Jillian a squinty-eyed look. "And what have we here?"

"Your temporary charge." Nolan dug into his hip pocket, pulled out his wallet, and slipped out a Ben Franklin.

When Char reached for it, he held it out of her grasp. He ripped the hundred in two pieces and gave one half to her. She promptly tucked it into her very there cleavage while Nolan stuck the other in the waistband of Jillian's shorts.

"When this is over," he told Char, "it's yours . . . but only if she doesn't have a scratch on her."

Then, ignoring her squeal of surprise, he swung Jillian into his arms, lifted her up and over the bar, and deposited her on the other side by Char.

"Stay," he ordered, and dug into his waistband for the little popper he'd filched from Jillian's nightstand.

He checked the chamber of the .22, then held it out to her. "Tell me you know how to use this."

She was still catching her breath, but her mind and her mouth were in full working order. "Stand still for two seconds and I'll give you a demonstration."

She just didn't quit. He couldn't help it. He laughed. "Hold the thought while I take care of a little business. In the meantime, anyone tries to scale the bar, you aim it right at their heart and give 'em the same look you're giving me now. Yeah, that's the one. They'll run like hell."

"You aren't running."

Those green eyes flared with fire and he just couldn't ignore the challenge. "Yeah, well. I know something they don't."

"You think I won't pull this trigger?"

"Oh, you'll pull it. You just won't pull it on me."

"And you think this because?"

He leveled her a look. "Because you want to get in my pants."

That shut her up.

"Char," he said, keeping his eyes on the bloodthirsty redhead he may have just provoked into filling him full of lead, "grab your bat and stick to her like glue. I'll try to make this quick."

"As long as your mouth's hanging open, you just as well drink something."

Jillian looked from Nolan, who was walking into a sea of sweaty long-haired, earring-wearing, beer-swilling thugs, to the shot the bartender had plunked down in front of her. She didn't even consider refusing it. She picked up the glass and downed it, no questions asked.

Then she prayed for sudden death for the second time in as many hours. *Firewater* took on a whole new connotation as the liquor burned like hot razor blades all the way down to her toes.

When she could breathe again and her eyes had quit watering to the point where she could focus, she looked for Nolan. So she could shoot him for making that asinine remark, if nothing else.

Because you want to get in my pants.

Arrogant bastard.

The smoke was thick; the sunshades were dark. The first man she saw when she pulled things into fuzzy focus was not Nolan. And one look had her tightening her grip on her gun, thankful she'd saved her bullets for the real threat.

The man looked like a scripted character from every bad biker movie ever made. He was also staring at her like she was a piece of fresh meat and he hadn't gnawed on anything but motorcycle parts in days.

Black hair streaked with gray and slick with what could have been motor oil was pulled sharply back from a face that had clearly enjoyed watching and doing things she couldn't begin to imagine. That he'd lived hard, lived long, and could give a rat if he lived longer was etched deep in every crease, crag, and crevice on his face and flared in the wildness of his dilated pupils. He was bare to the waist but for a few strips of fringed leather and a loop of heavy chain linked by two nipple rings.

My God, that had to hurt.

When he caught her staring, he flexed his left pec and the tattoo on his chest of a naked woman with a witchy red mouth and humongous breasts wiggled her hips.

"Rule number one: Never make eye contact."

Jillian whipped her head toward Char, who was watching her with cynical amusement. She couldn't help it. Fascinated, she swung her gaze back to biker man. He licked his lips, grabbed his crotch with one hand, and made an equally lewd gesture with his pool cue with the other.

The air deflated from her lungs in a rush. "Oh God."

"You did it again." Char slammed her bat in plain view on top of the bar. "Do *not* look at the animals," she ordered for good measure. "Unless you want to feed 'em."

Jillian threw her a horrified look.

"Didn't think so," she said, cackling.

Carefully avoiding eye contact with anyone, Jillian searched the corners of the bar for Garrett. She'd just spotted him when all hell broke loose.

A table crashed to the floor, making her jump as another man stood—his young face bloodied and battered—and flashed Garrett a grin so wide, it almost closed the one eye that wasn't swollen shut. To the sound of breaking glass, vicious curses, and a war cry of, *"Hooah!"* he dived into a sea of bikers in a blur of flying fists.

Jillian watched in stunned horror as Garrett, with a smile—a *smile,* for God's sake—calmly picked up a pool cue and waded in toward him.

It all happened so fast that she could barely follow the action. She'd taken a self-defense class once where the instructor had demonstrated how to place a hard kick to the thigh that, in theory, shocked the femoral artery and rendered the attacker unconscious. Jillian had never seen the technique put to practical use. In fact, she'd forgotten about it. Until now.

In a lightning fast move, Garrett proved the theory on the first do-rag dull witted enough to come at him with a knife. She sucked in air on a gasp as a beefy, oily biker took a swipe at Garrett's ribs with a wicked and lethal-looking knife. He dodged, spun, and with a well-placed kick dropped his attacker like a stone.

She hadn't even digested the violent stealth of the action when, giving a little come-on motion with the cupped fingers of his left hand, Garrett invited the next comer to experience the brunt of the blunt end of the pool cue. Garrett's precision jab to his diaphragm was followed by a hard, quick strike to his jaw. The Hulk Hogan look-alike folded with a thudding moan.

After that, the not-so-bad-after-all bad boys still standing didn't have much left in them except empty threats and bruised biker egos—not that they didn't continue to make a lot of noise. But for the most part, it was pretty much all over but the obscenities that they hurled like rocks.

All business, completely in control, Garrett snagged the Hooah boy by the back of his shirt and dragged him to his feet. Using only the pool cue as a deterrent, Garrett backed toward the door holding off anyone who might be stupid enough to challenge him. Considering that the amassed IQ of all bikers present most likely topped out around 100, she was amazed when none of them did.

"Get out from behind the bar and head for the car," Garrett ordered her quietly.

Jillian was so enthralled by the skillful and expedient violence he'd used to deal with the situation, and so relieved to be getting out of there without a little up close and personal contact with her crotch-grabbing admirer, she didn't even bother to rail at Garrett for issuing orders and expecting her to hop to—like she was an army grunt or some harpy biker babe who lived to lick his boots . . . or get in his pants.

"Not so fast, chickie." Char held out her hand.

When Jillian just blinked, the bartender dug the other half of the hundred out of Jillian's shorts.

"I'll take this kind of easy money anytime, big guy." Char shot Garrett a cheeky grin as she lifted a portion of the bar that Jillian hadn't noticed was hinged. "Go," she said, and shoved Jillian out into the room.

"Go," Garrett repeated, and for once, Jillian didn't argue. She ran for the door.

"And once, in Panama, he—"

"Jase," Garrett cut the young Ranger off with a firm but exhausted patience. "Give it a rest, OK?"

Jillian had been listening to Jason's combat stories with half an ear as she studied Garrett. She wasn't sure when it had happened, but he had a small bruise high on his right cheekbone. The knuckles on the hands wrapped tight around the steering wheel were raw and bleeding. His jaw was clenched. And evidently, the authority in his tone finally shut the young Ranger up.

Sitting sideways in the front seat of Garrett's Mustang as they sped through town toward the airport, she peered around the seat where Jason "Plowboy" Wilson slumped in a splay-legged sprawl. He was bloody and battered and quite obviously drunk enough that he felt only the fuzzy edge of pain. No more than five feet nine or ten, the fair-skinned blond with the baleful brown eyes and military buzz cut personified the term *built like a bull*.

"Lugged a lot of hay bales and wrestled my share of calves back home on the farm, ma'am," he'd said, the picture of modesty when he caught her staring at his massive biceps.

He'd been talking nonstop since Garrett had dragged him out of the middle of that knot of flying fists and booted him toward the door.

She was still amazed that Garrett had never drawn his gun or his knife. Thank God. In fact, he'd never worked up a sweat. Once he'd grabbed the pool cue, it had pretty much all been over but the obscenities.

They'd been on the road for about five minutes when Garrett carefully pried the .22 from her fingers—she'd forgotten she still held it—and, leaning over her, stowed it, without a word, in his glove compartment. Not that he'd had any opportunity to speak. Jason had been on a filibuster, extolling Nolan—*No-man*—Garrett's virtues, vices, and, in his humble opinion, godlike status.

She'd managed to piece together that Jason was a part of Charlie Company, First Bat—"that's Battalion, ma'am," he'd explained—at Fort Benning and Garrett had been his sergeant and squad leader until three months ago. Jason was on leave and headed for the Keys but had planned a layover in West Palm with the express intent of connecting with Garrett. Only problem was, he'd hit the bars first and the phone second and had called Garrett as an afterthought when he failed to come up with a compelling reason why the local populace shouldn't just kill him, feed him to the gators, and put everyone out of their misery.

No-man, she'd learned after Garrett had booted Plowboy into the backseat of the Mustang with orders to not even think about bleeding on the upholstery, was—in Plowboy's words—". . . one motherfuckin', badass, genuine balls-out fightin' machine, excuse my French, ma'am."

She'd also been assured, as Plowboy babbled in obvious hero worship, that Nolan Garrett was *No-man* to those who'd trained with him and fought with him and would die for him because no man challenged him, no man bested him, and no man who knew him was dumb enough to try. No-man was the stuff, if Plowboy was to be believed, that legends were made of.

From what she'd just witnessed in Nirvana, there might be as much truth as hero worship in Plowboy's summation.

For perhaps the hundredth time in as many minutes, Jillian took a mental step back and wondered if she'd somehow stumbled through a time warp and landed a minor role in a B-rated adventure flick without so much as a casting call.

She was a professional career woman, for God's sake. She did not lead a life that invited cryptic death threats or participation in bar brawls. While surreal, the past couple of weeks of dealing with the threats had been nothing compared to the past couple of hours. Everything that had transpired—starting with seeing Garrett through the fog in her bathroom mirror—was too outrageous to even contemplate, let alone quantify. And yet here she was . . . smelling of stale beer and cigarette smoke, keeping her eyes peeled for the bikers who had hopped on their hogs and tried to follow them, not to mention there was a U.S. Army Airborne Ranger bleeding all over the backseat, no matter that he'd been ordered not to.

"Is he all right?" she asked, concerned in spite of herself. "Does he need to go to a hospital or something?"

Garrett glanced in the rearview mirror. "How you doing, Wilson?"

"Haven't felt this good since Moby Dick was a freaking minnow, man. Hooah!"

Garrett let out a deep sigh that pretty much stated it all: *We were not having fun.* "What time does your flight leave?"

Plowboy mumbled a time.

Garrett checked his watch, swore, and turned on the Mustang's afterburners.

"The woman—she really heats your pool, huh, No?"

It was o–two hundred hours. They were standing at the curb by the terminal. Nolan gave Plowboy a look that said, *None of your business,* then glanced at the *woman* in question, who was less than a yard away, waiting in the car with the windows rolled down.

He suspected Jillian was just a tad shocky. And yeah, as the young Ranger put it, she heated his pool—which royally pissed him off. So did the kernel of tenderness he felt for her as she sat there, her eyes glazed, her expression stalled somewhere between denial and disbelief.

Wilson laughed, then winced at the pain from his split lip.

"Good luck with that. And hey—thanks for hauling my ass outta there."

"Yeah. Make sure you lose my cell number."

Another broad, wincing grin. "Like old times, huh?"

Yeah, Nolan thought grimly. *It had been like old times.*

He hadn't wanted to admit it, but he'd enjoyed it. The adrenaline rush. Saving one of his boys. He'd enjoyed it a little too much. Since Iraq, he'd been edgy as hell, always on the lookout for bad guys. When he hadn't been dead drunk, the switch had been stuck in the ON position. Facing a few out-of-shape bikers with ugly attitudes was like flipping a release valve after months of deadly face-offs with Ba'ath Party resistance and fedayeen armed with AK-47s and RPG launchers who lived to take out anyone in a U.S. military uniform.

"We miss you, No," Plowboy added, breaking into Nolan's thoughts. His expression was sober now. "Bat . . . it's not the same. Nothing's the same. Except the army bullshit. That never changes."

Silence stretched like the long shadows cast by the airport parking security lights. Nolan looked at his feet, then looked beyond Jason's expectant eyes toward the terminal. It was almost empty. As empty as he suddenly felt.

He had to ask. "How's Sara and her boys?"

Plowboy looked very young suddenly, looked every bit the boy he really was instead of the man the army and Iraq had made of him.

"Kids are doin' OK, I guess. They're in counseling," he said with a shrug. "Sara's folks are there now. Will's, too. Doing what they can, ya know. She's out of the hospital. They say there's still hope that she'll walk . . . and everything." He let out a weary breath. "You couldn't have stopped it, man."

Nolan swallowed. He could have. He *should* have. He was *supposed* to have stopped it. He was supposed to take care of his men. Keep everyone safe. Including Will. But Will was dead. And Sara was a widow . . . and whether she walked or not, her life would never be the same again.

"Something just snapped in him, you know?" Plowboy continued. "Something—"

Nolan couldn't stand it anymore. "Look, you're going to miss your flight."

His voice was as rigid as his posture, and when Plowboy just stood there, looking as bleak as the night in his torn shirt and with blood smearing his face, Nolan forced a smile.

"Christ, you're a wreck. Make sure you hit the head." He shoved the duffel into the younger man's hand. "Clean up and change your shirt or they may throw your sorry ass off the plane. And so help me God, if you show up here again and pull another stunt like that, I'll feed you to the gators myself."

"Love you, too, Sarge." Plowboy grinned and stuck out his hand. "Take care, man."

Nolan clasped him on the shoulder, then shoved his hands in his pockets when the Ranger hefted his duffel. For a long moment Nolan simply stood there and watched him walk away.

Weary to her bones, Jillian keyed in her security code and opened the penthouse door. Garrett stopped her with a hand on her arm and a quiet command to stay put.

She was about to snap out a snide remark about the probability of someone breaching security twice in one night being slim to nonexistent when her better judgment popped right up and rallied against it. First, he wouldn't want to hear it. Second, given the way her life was shaping up lately, she wasn't all that confident that Norman Bates wouldn't just decide to show up yet. Third, she was too tired.

Let's face it. She wasn't programmed to handle everything that had happened tonight. In her entire life, she'd never figured on playing a lead role in the adventures of the criminally insane. The smoke stink from the bar and Plowboy's blood on her shorts were two very tangible reminders that, in Plowboy's vernacular, "shit happens" and that truth did, in fact, rival fiction.

"I'm taking a shower," she said when Garrett walked back into the foyer and gave her a grim all-clear nod. "I smell like a brewery. Oh—and Garret . . . I do *not* want to find you in my bathroom when I come out."

She didn't wait for his response. She headed straight for her bathroom and locked the door behind her.

Yeah. Like a locked door would keep him out if he wanted in.

Feeling clean and at least marginally better afterward, she dragged a pick through her hair and applied lotion, then slipped into a pair of clean panties, and back into her oversize white silk nightshirt. She was beyond exhaustion but revved on residual adrenaline. From past experience, she knew that when she felt this kind of edgy discomfort, it could keep her awake for hours. So she headed for the kitchen in search of the bottle of chardonnay . . . and found her bodyguard standing with his back to her in the dim kitchen light.

She stopped cold as surprised by the sudden kick of her heartbeat as she was to see him standing there in half shadow. He hadn't heard her approach. It stunned her further to realize she had relished a moment like this to simply look at him. Unobserved. Unguarded.

Despite the fact that the kitchen was lit only by pale light cast from the hallway and by the soft glow from the tiny lightbulb on the refrigerator's ice dispenser, he stood out against the shadows in startling clarity.

His back was bare, his tanned skin roped with contoured muscle. But for the occasional scar—she assured herself she didn't want to know how he'd gotten them—he could have been a model advertising the stunning results of a state-of-the-art physical fitness machine. Only this was no cover boy standing with his bare feet braced wide apart in her kitchen.

This was a man.

This was a warrior with the battle scars to prove it.

If she'd had any doubts about it before, he'd allayed them tonight as he fought his way out of the bar. Every move had been precision, calculated and efficient. Controlled. He could have done much more to those men than left them bruised and battered and littering the bar floor. And that said more about him than Jason "Plowboy" Wilson's worshipful commentary.

Warrior.

Garrett's shoulders were broad with it. His ribs were lean, and where his waist narrowed beneath the low-slung and well-worn jeans his incredible backside was hard and tight. Everywhere she looked, she saw strength—of body, of purpose, of mind.

Everywhere she looked, she saw a man unlike most of the men she knew. Men who were civilized and sophisticated. The men she knew didn't wear shoulder holsters and wouldn't have a clue—much less the inclination—how to rescue a friend from a mob of mean-minded men like the ones he'd encountered in Nirvana.

The men she knew didn't make her nerves sing and her pulse jump when she looked at them, either. He did. And that reaction was something she didn't like and had yet to figure out.

She'd sort it out when she wasn't so exhausted. For now, she just let herself look.

Like her, he'd showered again. His hair was still wet. A trickle of water ran down the deep indentation of his spine and disappeared beneath the waistband of his jeans. As he

tipped his head back and downed a long pull from a bottle of
root beer, he looked too raw, too masculine, and too big for
her kitchen. And yet he looked oddly vulnerable.

Maybe it was the way his jeans broke over the arch of his
bare feet. Maybe it was the bruise on his shoulder that even
now was transitioning from red to smudgy blue. Or maybe it
was the weariness she sensed in him. Not a physical weariness, though she was sure he felt that, too, but an emotional
fatigue.

It occurred to her then that she was watching a man who
may actually be weary of the fight, weary of being strong,
weary of carrying the scars on his body that undoubtedly
scarred his soul as well. It was yet another unsettling kernel
of the notion she'd been nursing that he was human. A rein-
forcement of her theory that he harbored secrets and sorrow
and pain.

Against all odds, she felt an overwhelming urge to go to
him again. To touch him. To tell him she was on to him. Let
him know what she knew—that he wasn't as hard as he
looked. And that it was OK. He didn't have to be. At least
not with her.

And where, for God's sake, was this coming from? Why
was she even going there again? He was a hired thug. She
didn't like him. She didn't want to like him. Didn't want to
know him, either. And most of all, she didn't want him here.

Still something about him compelled her to . . . to what?

She shook her head. She must be really tired. Or maybe
feeling a little vulnerable herself.

Still standing like a thief in the shadows of the hallway,
she thought back to the scene when they'd dropped the young
Ranger at the airport. She'd stayed in the car, but the windows were down as the two men stood at the curb by the terminal doors. She'd seen. As gruff as he'd been, he cared
about Plowboy. The feeling had been mutual.

There had been more than respect and responsibility between them. There may even have been love, but as with most men of his ilk, they'd buffered that emotion with grunts and name-calling, dancing around their true feelings with silences and insults.

It hadn't been all silence. She'd heard some of their conversation.

You couldn't have stopped it.

What couldn't he have stopped? she'd wondered then. She wondered now. Wondered what had made Garrett simply stand there—much as he was standing in her kitchen now—silent and alone.

Most of all alone.

That reality resounded above all others.

She must have made a sound, because his head came up suddenly. He turned and spotted her in the shadows.

What she saw in his eyes in that unguarded moment made her heart clench.

Pain.

Raw and stark.

Deep and abiding.

She might not like him, might not want him here, but she hurt for him in that moment and respected his need for solitude. She was about to turn around and leave him—and then she saw it. A thin blade of a cut, seeping blood, ran in a raw six-inch slice across the left side of his abdomen, just below his rib cage.

She gasped, then met his eyes in disbelief. "You're hurt."

He looked down at himself, looked up again, and smiled . . . and immediately pissed her off.

She knew exactly what was going to come out of his mouth. Gone was the living, breathing, vulnerable man—the man she had almost convinced herself she could like. Back was the catch-bullets-in-his-teeth fantasy warrior.

"Don't you dare," she hissed, unable to mask her anger. "Don't you *dare* say it's nothing . . . like you're some . . . some macho marauder in a low-budget blood-and-guts action movie."

He looked surprised. Then amused. "Clearly, you've been watching the wrong movies. Actually, it hurts like hell." He gave her a smoldering look. "Want to kiss my boo-boo?"

She glared at him, instant outrage making her forget every generous thought she'd been stupid enough to consider. "Do I look like I want to kiss your boo-boo?"

7

WHAT SHE LOOKED LIKE, NOLAN DECIDED, was a woman who wanted to slug him for his juvenile attempt to make light of the knife wound. And yet he saw something else flash in her eyes—something fleeting but hot that had surprised even her. She'd given a passing thought to his suggestion . . . and it had shocked the shit out of her.

Well, hell. It shocked the shit out of him, too.

That was definitely a wrinkle he didn't need. Not when just looking at her raised more than his warning flag.

Once a Ranger, always a Ranger, he thought in disgust. Life's basics were pretty much centered around war, beer, and sex—the order subject to change with the terrain. The terrain standing in front of him in nothing but thin silk and telling eyes shuffled sex to the top of the list. Which proved another Ranger axiom: The little head did most of the thinking.

"Stay," she ordered, turned on her bare feet, and marched—or ran away from him; he couldn't tell which—back toward her bedroom. He breathed his first deep breath since he'd realized he had company. Thought about the step-by-step process of breaking down an M4 and reassembling it. Then started all over again.

It almost worked. He'd almost managed to push from his mind the image of Jillian's incredible mouth kissing his boo-boo, then trailing south across his skin toward happy valley, when she returned, her arms full of rubbing alcohol, cotton balls, ointment, gauze, and tape.

He steeled himself against the frazzled, almost fragile picture she made. "What, no Power Ranger Band-Aids?"

She flipped on the track lighting. "Shut up, Garrett."

Good idea.

"Yes, ma'am."

Bracing his hands on the granite on either side of his hips, he hitched himself up onto the kitchen counter and spread his legs, making room for her to move in between them and go to work on him.

Bad idea.

Her hands were small. She was way too close. Her touch was soft and burned like fire against his skin as she gingerly dabbed an alcohol-soaked cotton ball to the cut.

He hissed against the bite of the antiseptic and smelled . . . her. It was like inhaling a tropical forest. Exotic flowers. Soft, clean scents that should have soothed. Erotic woman scents that heated his blood and had Skippy waking up by degrees.

He wrapped his fingers around the lip of the counter and held on. *Plastic princess,* he reminded himself. *Queen bitch of the rich and pampered.*

She was an assignment. In a clingy thin nightshirt that barely covered her thighs. With sweet breasts pressing against thin silk, just begging for his mouth.

He clenched his jaw, closed his eyes. When that didn't help, he swallowed and held perfectly still. He imagined himself doing push-ups. Roping out of a helo. Parachuting out of a plane and hitting the tarmac with a bone-jarring thud that rattled his teeth and— "Ouch! Christ. Easy with the sandpaper."

Her hands stilled. And then she just stood there, like she wasn't sure what to do. Her head was down; her breath fanned his ribs. As soft and sweet as a midnight breeze, it whispered across his skin and made his nipples hard as rocks.

In that moment, he knew she was as aware of him as he was of her. And that, like him, she didn't like it or have a clue what to do about it.

Her hand wasn't quite steady when she started in on the cut again. In fact, her hands were shaking.

And he wanted, more than anything he'd wanted in too long to remember, to touch her, to bury his hands in her soft, clean hair that the track lighting cast in fiery highlights where it parted at her crown.

He tightened his grip on the lip of the counter and some-how managed to stop himself. Talk about mistakes. First rule of fiefdom: The peasant doesn't touch the princess. Not the way Nolan had in mind.

Mistake or not, he remained too aware of the night, the si-lence, the cocooning isolation of her penthouse, and the residual effects of the past few hours of heightened sexual awareness.

OK. Reality check. Tomorrow she'd have this all in per-spective. Tonight she'd been pushed beyond the limit. Stress. Exhaustion. A delayed reaction to a violence he knew far too well but someone like her couldn't possibly understand. It had softened her. Made her . . . real. Made her touchable.

Made him insane.

He couldn't help himself. Heart hammering, he lifted a hand to her hair. And sank into a softness as silky and alive as anything he'd ever encountered.

She raised her head and met his eyes. And there, in her shadowed kitchen where he didn't belong and didn't want to be, awareness shifted to uncharted territory. Altered yet again when in a gesture that told how incredibly vulnerable she truly was at this moment, she turned her face into the pulse at his wrist.

Heat. Softness. Incredible vulnerability.

He almost lost it then. Almost forgot everything he knew, about right, about wrong, about who she was and who he wasn't. He almost tipped her face up to his to see if that amazing mouth tasted the way he knew it would. Of sex and hunger and a salvation a man like him had no business seeking from a woman like her.

The need of it shot through his blood like a bullet. The wrongness of it prowled in the background like a jailer. And when he saw in her eyes that she wasn't going to be the one to stop something really, truly, royally stupid from happening, he dug deep and put on the skids himself.

He abruptly dropped his hand.

"I'm sorry," he said, and heard a gruff tenderness in his voice that shocked him. "I shouldn't have dragged you to Nirvana. I should have taken you to your father."

She blinked, seemed to focus, then grasp what had almost happened. She swallowed hard and he realized she was fighting tears. "I wouldn't have gone."

"Yeah. That's what I figured."

Silence settled, heavy and thick. It was time to scramble before he dived back into big trouble.

He pried the antiseptic cream from her trembling fingers. "I can finish this up. It really is just a scratch, Jillian. Nothing to get twisted up about."

She backed away as if he'd slapped her. "Nothing to get twisted up about? In your reality, maybe. Not in mine." She lifted a hand, a gesture of abject bafflement mixed with horror. "This is your *life*?"

Her eyes were big and round; her voice had risen and he could see that exhaustion and shock had pushed her dangerously close to hysteria. She hugged her arms around her waist like she was holding herself together and leaned back against the opposite counter as if she needed it to give her balance.

"This is really what you do?" Disbelief knotted with

revulsion. "You sneak into people's homes, violate their sense of safety, get into bar fights, and put yourself at risk?"

He shot her a glance and slid off the countertop. "Yeah, well, it's a dirty job, but—"

"Stop it! Just stop with the wiseass remarks."

He watched her warily as she dragged a hand through her damp hair, glared at him, then looked away.

"I don't want to be a part of this," she said, her voice so soft he barely heard her. When she met his eyes again, hers were filled with a fiery fear that, it was apparent, she hated, really hated, to let him see. "I don't want to be someone who has to look over my shoulder or have someone watch my back."

She glanced from the angry slash on his abdomen to the bruise on his cheek. "I don't want to be responsible for someone getting hurt. I want this to be over."

He stared from her face to the antiseptic cream, then back to her face again. "With some luck, it *will* be over. Soon. The police will nail it down and put whoever's doing this away. In the meantime, I'm just here to run a little interference, OK?"

"Interference? That's what? A tactical word for dodging bullets?"

Downplaying the repugnance in her tone by ignoring it, he spread the soothing cream on a strip of gauze, then plastered the gauze against his cut. "It won't come to that."

"You're damn right it won't. Because you aren't going to be here tomorrow."

His head came up.

"When I tell my father about the little stunt you pulled, dragging me into the middle of a biker bar fight, you'll be off the payroll before you can say 'Harley hog.' "

He gave her a considering look, shrugged. "You want to tattle to Daddy? Be my guest. I'm sure you're right—but if you think I'll shed any tears over it, think again."

He tore off a piece of tape with his teeth, then secured it over the gauze. "You might also want to think about this. He'll just send someone to replace me."

For the space of several moments he let her digest that bit of reality.

"So it seems to me, you've got a choice here, princess." He felt nasty again suddenly. He didn't know why, but he did know he wanted to take it out on her. "You can stick with the devil you know or take a chance on the one you don't know. Now if you'll excuse me, it's been a bitch of a day. I'm hitting the rack."

He left her standing in the kitchen. Before he did something really stupid. Like wrap his hand around the back of her head, drag her up against him, and massage her tonsils with his tongue.

He closed the bedroom door behind him and leaned back against it. *What the hell was he doing?* Why hadn't he just dialed Daddy's number, handed her the phone, and let her tattle her regal little heart out? It would have been his ticket out of here.

It's what he wanted. To be rid of her. To go back to his boat. Back to his booze and back to a fast track to oblivion.

He stripped off his jeans and lay back on the bed. If what he really wanted was to be gone, why had he just made a half-assed attempt to convince her he should stay?

For the same reason he'd taken care about Wilson. He was a team player. He finished the job. It came with the Ranger territory.

Or maybe, for some twisted reason he might actually want to stay.

Want to kiss my boo-boo?

Christ. He watched the overhead fan spin slow shadows across the ceiling.

He was playing with fire . . . and against all odds, he wanted to feel the burn.

So she was hot. Palm Beach was full of hot women. Women who could *heat his pool* a whole hell of a lot faster than Jillian Kincaid.

So why was he letting her get to him? It didn't compute. It was like he had this constant compulsion to bait her. Earlier he'd taken the "surprise" in her bathroom much further than necessary to make his point. He could have assured her that he wasn't a threat but that the bad guys were and she wasn't safe from them. Point made.

But he hadn't.

He'd pushed. And as she'd so aptly put it, he'd been a sonofabitch about it.

He'd been pushing ever since. Wanting her to break. When she hadn't even buckled, he'd pushed a little harder. Dragged her down to Nirvana just to show her what she'd gotten hooked up with when a call would have brought Ethan running to babysit until he finished his business with Plowboy.

Yeah. He'd pushed. Because she'd surprised him.

She kept surprising him. Just like she'd impressed him. He hadn't expected or wanted to be either.

And yet he was. And the really bad news? He wanted her. Fuck.

She moved in a world of Armani suits and slick money-men. Men like he'd never been—never wanted to be. For some reason, it pissed him off, knowing he had no place in her world. For some reason, he wanted her to understand what kind of man he was—one like she'd never seen before. And he wanted her to want him in spite of it.

Talk about a suicide mission.

He dug the heels of his palms into his eyes, rubbed.

And wished to hell he had a drink.

A few miles away, vagrants huddled under packing boxes in a back alley clogged with misery and debris. The clean salt scent of the ocean and the heavenly fragrance of grapefruit blossoms didn't make it to this part of paradise. Here paradise was lost amid the fetid odor of Dumpster waste, the stench of urine, unwashed bodies, and despair.

Halogen security lamps cast a brittle glow outside the run-down low-rent motel on Blue Heron Boulevard in Riviera Beach. Those who walked the streets this time of night shied away from the light. Their business was best done in the shadows.

It was not a neighborhood that fostered dreams. Nightmares were more the norm. Nightmares and sins. Big sins. Little sins. There was market enough for both and little market for hope.

In a sparsely furnished room on the motel's fourth floor, John Smith lived his own personal nightmare. For eighteen months he'd been atoning for what must have been a sin of epic proportions. Why else would he have ended up like this? His transgressions must have been unforgivable.

If only he knew what he'd done.

John was a religious man. He did not know this for a fact. This conclusion came from something deep within him— something so deep inside, it was knotted in the muscle and blood and bone that was left of him and told him he'd been a man of faith. Why else would he look to God for answers, appeal to God for help, curse God for forsaking him?

He was a tall man and slim, his features unremarkable but for the chilling gray of his eyes. Even to him, they looked eerily empty when he confronted his image in a mirror and saw a man who did not remember his own face as a boy.

The sheets on which he lay smelled of sex and sour regrets. The air he breathed smelled of darkness and desperation—things he knew, bone deep, had not been a part of his life before he'd lost everything he had been. Everything that he was.

Beside him, Mary slept. She was new to his almost empty

bank of memories . . . but she hadn't been new in any other way for a very long time. If he had any pity left in him, he might think it was a sad thing for someone so young to harbor such an old and damaged soul. He didn't know why she had sought him out little more than a week ago, why she continued to come to him. Or why she sometimes begged, through her tears, for him to hurt her.

In his deepest moments of despair, neither did he care. He was nothing. He was no one.

Without his memories, nothing mattered. At least on his best days, it didn't matter. It was easier that way. Easier not to care that he'd had a real name once, a name lost to him along with the other pieces of his life when he'd been mugged and left for dead. Now he was called John Smith, compliments of a civil servant who felt he should not forever be known as John Doe.

This man who was John Smith had once had a birth certificate, proof to confirm or dispute his age, which the physicians estimated as between forty and forty-five. He'd claimed citizenship somewhere; his fluency in five different languages, had thus far given little back in the way of clues. Only more frustration.

Somewhere, he'd had rights. He'd been a man who could travel and work and live where he wanted. Now he could go nowhere with legal sanction. He was trapped by a lack of identification to even allow a passport should he chose to leave and go . . . where?

He sat up, swung his feet to the floor, and buried his head in his hands. The headaches were less frequent now. But the emptiness was severe.

He stood and walked naked to the window overlooking the street. And stared, even though he'd given up looking for answers a long time ago.

He had no home filled with the dusty gatherings of a life that chronicled his transition in time. He had no job to make him feel like a man, no skills he could draw from to support himself. No memory beyond eighteen months ago when he'd awakened in a Jupiter hospital.

The mugger who had struck the blow to his head had stolen so much more than his wallet. He'd stolen his identity. He'd ended his life.

And yet he breathed.

He bled.

But no longer did he cry.

In the silence of the night, with a soft, willing body curled on her side of the bed the only tangible proof that even the moment was real, he wished he could simply die.

But he was a coward. So he lived. With a mind he'd numbed to the injustice. With emotions he'd conditioned himself not to feel. He'd reduced his human contact to the animal rutting Mary allowed. He gave his body release but kept his mind disengaged.

It was a way to survive the loss of what the doctors had given up on recovering. He would probably not remember, they'd said. Not after this long. Officially, he'd been written off as a man without a future because he was a man who had no past.

A siren howled in the distance, grew closer, then faded to nothing. The window air-conditioning unit wheezed little more than tepid air into the room and rustled the faded blue curtains. On the bed, Mary stirred in her sleep, whimpered, and he knew it was because he'd used her roughly. Remorse played a distant second to his own misery. A misery that had been compounded as he'd watched the eleven o'clock news several hours ago.

The Kincaid woman, with her camera crew and tape recorder and glossy lips, had brought it all back. The kernel of hope, the painful wish to know. She'd read his story in the newspapers a few months ago, she'd said. Sought him out to help him, she said. To tell his story to the world on television. She'd said.

Someone might recognize him. Didn't he want that? Didn't he want to know if there was a chance her story could draw national attention and possibly reach someone who would recognize him? Someone who would step forward and tell him who he was?

Pain lanced through his temple. His heartbeat ratcheted, slamming inside his chest.

Didn't he want to know?

Fear, stark and cutting, infiltrated his body like tainted air.

Didn't he want to know?

With everything in him, yes, he wanted to know. And with everything in him, he was afraid to know.

This was what Jillian Kincaid had done to him. She'd brought back the hope. And for John, hope was not a cause for elation and light. Hope was a horror of resurrected cravings for all things that were denied him. Hope was cruel. Hope bred insanity.

Jillian Kincaid, with her power and ambition, was not seeking his salvation. She was seeking her own fame.

She didn't care that his suffering had begun anew the day she had approached him. She'd stirred, to a frenzy, the utter nothingness of his existence with her camera and her microphones and her pleas to let her interview him again as she filmed her documentary. About him, The Forgotten Man.

He drew a fractured breath. Settled himself and turned to the woman on the bed.

Mary offered relief from all the bleakness. Temporary. Fleeting. He didn't believe her when she told him he was someone—someone important, someone vital—and he hated Jillian Kincaid for her relentless questions, her unnerving silences that prompted him to fill them and to speak of his sense of loss and despair.

Hers was a careless cruelty.

His would not be.

Just like he was not carelessly cruel when he awakened Mary with a harsh hand, then used her again until she begged him to stop.

8

IN LIGHT OF THE FACT THAT SHE HADN'T
drunk enough wine last night to merit even a whisper of a
headache, Jillian felt particularly uncharitable toward the
hammers pounding away behind her eyelids when she
swung her feet over the side of her bed at 7:30 Saturday
morning.

To face the day with her bodyguard.

Oh, joy.

Grim and grouchy, she headed straight for the shower,
telling herself to just deal with it. Whether this loony toons
character was simply out to scare her, which she firmly believed, or he was for real, which she did *not* believe, she
couldn't afford to let Garrett disrupt her life in the interim.
Broken speed limits, biker bars, and bloody Rangers
notwithstanding.

And let's not forget the beautiful body, her libido reminded her before she could quell the memory of Nolan
Garrett damp from a shower and naked to the waist in the
pale light of her kitchen in the wee hours of the morning.

"Oh, let's," she muttered in disgust, determined to ignore
the flicker of sexual tension lingering from last night and
licking through her belly. "Let's forget it and just get through
this."

She twisted off the faucets and caught herself worrying
about his knife wound. Stone-faced, she dried her hair and

wrapped up in her robe and then went about the business of regrouping before she faced him.

When she opened her bedroom door and smelled coffee—good coffee, by the scent of it—she knew she could face anything. Even the fact that Garrett was evidently good for something other than intimidation and stoic scowls and messing with her pheromones.

"So he knows his way around a coffee grinder. Goodie for him."

With a roll of her eyes, she stepped out in the hall . . . then stopped short and braced a hand against the wall, so stunned by what she saw, she barely found the breath to scream.

"My God. Oh, my God! What are you doing! Let her go!"

Garrett didn't so much as move a muscle. And she'd have known if he had. He wore nothing but a pair of black boxer shorts, shower dew, and a scowl so caustic it could have eroded tempered steel. And at the moment, he looked about as vulnerable as a stealth bomber.

"You know this person?" he asked with quiet and lethal calm and absolutely no indication that he was about to let up on the pressure of the massive forearm he'd pressed against Lydia Grace's throat.

Pinned to the wall just inside the penthouse door, Lydia, her eyes wide with terror, glanced at Jillian; her hands clutched at Garrett's imprisoning arm, bracing for the worst. On the floor at her feet, a garment bag lay in a tangled heap. Her purse had slid across the foyer tile and landed a few feet away.

"Of course I know her! We work together. Now for God's sake, let her go!" Jillian demanded, tripping over the bag to get to Lydia.

A strong hand gripped her arm, steadying her. She shoved it away and reached for Lydia.

"Are you all right?" She touched a hand to the younger woman's arm, then almost cried herself when a tear trickled down a cheek that looked as pale as chalk against the straight jet-black hair falling around Lydia's face.

Lydia nodded valiantly. She lifted a hand to her throat.

"Oh, sweetie. I am so, so sorry." Jillian cut a venomous glare at Garrett and steeled herself against feeling sympathy over the injuries he'd received last night. The bruise on his cheek had turned a bluish purple. His knuckles had scabbed over. She didn't even want to think about the knife wound covered by white tape. "This is my assistant, you dolt. What on earth were you thinking? Never mind. Just get out of the way. And get her some water."

Stepping over the garment bag again, she led a shaky Lydia to the living area and set her carefully down on the sofa. "Did he hurt you?"

"I did *not* hurt her," Garrett volunteered from behind them; his eyes were hard, his manner bored, as he held out a glass, then raked his wet hair back from his face with his fingers.

Jillian snatched the glass and offered it to Lydia, who shook her head. "I'm OK. Really. Just . . . just a little, oh, what's the word? Terrified?" she managed on a shaky laugh.

Jillian scooped Lydia's hands into hers. She looked her hard in the eye, hesitant to accept the attempt at reassurance. "You sure you're OK?"

"I'm fine," Lydia insisted, then cut an anxious glance at Garrett. "I . . . um . . . did I . . . interrupt . . . something?"

When Lydia actually blushed, Jillian saw the tableau from her perspective. Jillian was in her robe. Garrett wore only his boxers and the stark white bandage across his ribs. Not only his hair was damp. So was his body. He seemed to be that way a lot.

"Lydia Grace, meet Nolan Garrett. My bodyguard," she added with grim tolerance as Garrett eased a hip onto the back of the sofa. His only other reaction was a deepening scowl.

Lydia's big brown eyes made a couple of sweeps between them. "Oh . . . well . . . um . . . OK."

"Not OK. He owes you an apology."

Both women looked at Garrett, who crossed his arms over his bare chest, clearly unaffected by both Jillian's condemning gaze and Lydia's apologetic trepidation.

"I need a list of everyone who knows your penthouse security code," he said without preamble, "and then we're going to change it."

Jillian blinked. "That's your idea of an apology?"

"You want me to apologize for doing my job?"

"Bullying my assistant is your job?"

"Intercepting an intruder who arrives unannounced, unexpected," he said, pushing off the sofa and walking toward the kitchen, "and sneaks into your penthouse like a thief is part of my job."

He reached for a coffee mug from a nearby cabinet. Tanned bare skin moved fluidly over ropy muscles. Tanned, scarred skin. The one on his forearm. The ones on his back. She'd noticed them last night. And now, thanks to the nice men at Nirvana, he'd have more.

They were the marks of a warrior. Scars of battle.

He was about to face another one. "Lydia is not an intruder."

"And I was supposed to know that when I saw her sneaking into the foyer, darting glances toward your bedroom?"

"He's right," Lydia said quickly, diverting Jillian's attention back to her. "I *was* sneaking in. I was trying to leave your dress without waking you. I figured you were sleeping in today."

"My dress?"

"For the dinner at Mar-A-Lago tonight? You asked me to pick it up at the cleaners?"

Jillian frowned, touched a hand to her brow, then groaned. "Oh, damn. That's tonight? I thought it was next week."

Lydia, tactful as always, looked around for her purse,

which was still on the floor by the dress. "I can double-check my day planner, but—"

"No. No," Jillian cut her off with a touch of her fingers to Lydia's arm. "I'm sure you're right. I . . . I've been a little rattled lately. I spaced it off.

"Oh, Lyd." She searched the younger woman's eyes again for signs of distress. Lydia had worked for KGLO TV almost a year now. With her quirky smile, pale blue eyes, and jet-black hair that looked exactly right with her china doll complexion, Lydia was sometimes moody, often funny, and always caring. She was a sweet kid, a hard worker, and Jillian hated, really hated, that this had happened to her. "I really am so sorry about this."

Again Lydia managed a wobbly smile as she rose on equally unsteady legs. "Yeah, well, it'll make a great story to tell my grandchildren someday."

Jillian rose, too. "Oh, wait, won't you at least have a cup of coffee, make sure you're steady before you leave?" she pressed when Lydia headed toward the door.

"I'm good. I'm *fine,*" she insisted with a reassuring smile. "Really. Quit worrying. Besides, I've got to get to work."

Ignoring Garrett, who leaned indolently against the island countertop with one bare foot propped on top of the other, silently sipping his coffee, Jillian walked with her toward the foyer. "You're working the salon today?" Lydia sometimes moonlighted at the Breakers Hotel.

"Just for a few hours." She stooped to pick up her purse and sling it over her shoulder. "Peg called. She's sick and wondered if I'd cover for her."

At the door, she snatched the garment bag off the floor before Jillian could get to it. "Here you go. Have fun tonight."

Jillian folded the dress over her arm. "Fun is not on the agenda. I'm doing this as a favor to a friend. And I owe you big-time for doing this and for putting up with—"

Though Lydia still looked a little shell-shocked, she cut

Jillian off with a shake of her head. "I'm just glad to know you've got someone looking out for you."

Behind her, she heard Garrett grunt. She didn't have to turn around to know he was also smirking.

"If this is what I can expect from now on," she said in a clipped voice, after she shut the door behind Lydia, "we're going to have to have a little discussion of the ground rules. You are not going to terrorize my friends and my coworkers, à la Captain Commando, are we clear?"

Nolan watched Jillian's face and worked hard to appear unaffected as she tossed the garment bag on the back of the sofa on her way by, then, as stiff as a raw recruit, marched to the kitchen. Unaffected, however, was the absolute antithesis of his reaction as he listened to her rummage around in her cabinets for a coffee mug. But he was damned if he was going to let her see that.

That's why he was camouflaging his semierection by leaning into the counter.

Muscle memory applied to more than combat readiness. He hadn't met the man who didn't experience an automatic, involuntary physical response to the scent of a woman fresh from a shower, the look of a woman very obviously naked beneath a thin short robe, the heat of a woman when she was revved on a healthy burst of anger.

And then there was the lingering reminder of what had almost happened in this kitchen last night.

Almost was the operative word. Nothing had happened. He'd gotten it back together sometime during the night and was determined that nothing was going to happen. Not today or any other day while this little dog and pony show played out. He wasn't ruled by muscle memory—much to Skippy's dismay.

"I said, are we clear?" she repeated in a snappish princess-to-peasant tone.

He deliberately downed another swallow of coffee before he looked up and met all that righteous outrage. And the grim, determined set of those incredible lips. And the hard points of her nipples pressing against silk that hid the contours of her first-class body with roughly the same effectiveness as oh, say . . . nothing.

"This is what we're clear about." He forced himself to meet her eyes again and hold the line. "Whatever it takes, I'll do my job. You don't like my methods? That's a big 'too bad, so sad.' What you like or don't like is a nonissue.

"The only issue," he continued when he could see her winding up to tell him what she thought of his take on the situation, "is keeping you alive until this creep is caught. Until then, I make the calls. I set the rules. That means what I say is carved in the proverbial stone. What I do is the gospel according to me. And what happens is what I deem appropriate to happen."

He watched her through narrowed eyes, letting her have a moment to digest the utter intractability of his statements.

"Now," he said, pushing his point home to make sure she felt the jab of his very sharp stick, "are we clear?"

Anger radiated off of her in steamy waves. Her cheeks flamed red. She'd shoved her hair behind her ears and even the tips of her ears looked hot. And while she tried valiantly to stem an adrenaline response that was as involuntary as it was familiar to him, her hands trembled as she wrapped them around her mug.

"Are we clear, Jillian?" he repeated, his voice as rigid as his resolve to make her understand there wasn't an inch of wiggle room in the game plan.

She drew in and let out a breath on a controlled exhalation, then stared beyond him toward the prospect of her immediate future. When her green eyes finally met his, he saw resignation but not defeat.

"All right," he said, with no inclination to gloat over his

victory, "we've got work to do. Get dressed and, while you're doing it, start thinking about who all is on that list."

"List?" The word came out weary but not combative.

"Your security code," he reminded her. "I need names. And then you're going to tell me everything you know about everyone you work with, starting with Lydia Grace."

"You can't be serious." She read the look on his face correctly and traded protest for exasperation. "Lydia isn't doing this. She's a kid, for God's sake. A good kid."

"Who has access to your penthouse," he pointed out, "and your dressing room and I'm guessing your e-mail at the station."

When her expression confirmed his assumptions, he restated his intentions. "We start with Lydia. And then we work through everyone from grips to producers. When we're finished with them, we're going over the subjects of your special reports."

"That," she said, dragging the hair back from her face with widespread fingers, "at least makes sense."

"Because you've pissed off a lot of people with your exposés?"

"Some," she agreed, "but mainly because they are not my friends and the people I work with are."

"You're saying you count Wellington among your friends?"

Another long, slow blink from eyes so jewel green he wondered if she wore tinted contacts. "Grant is pompous, small-minded, and conniving, but he's harmless."

"So is a poisonous snake until you harass it."

She pushed out a hard laugh. "I don't harass Grant."

"But he harasses you. He cuts you off—or attempts to cut you off—at the knees every chance he gets."

Her expression turned to professional concern. "It's that obvious?"

He debated for a moment, then decided he'd just as well

get it over with. He gathered the contents of the dossier he'd been preparing to reread when Lydia's surprise entrance into the penthouse interrupted him. Watching Jillian's face, he shoved it across the countertop toward her.

Her gaze flicked to his, her eyebrows furrowed. "What's this?" She reached for the folder, thick with printed paper.

"Your file."

Her hand froze midair before she snatched it back as if that snake they'd just discussed had made a strike at her. All the color had drained from her face when her gaze met his. "I have a file?"

Her extreme reaction puzzled him. "This surprises you?"

"Surprises me? It outrages me! Someone has been snooping into my life? Spying on me?"

He crossed his forearms on the counter and got comfortable. "Pardon my skepticism, but I find it a little tough to swallow that the daughter of one of the most high-profile businessmen in the United States, a woman who has been under the protection of various security agencies for the better part of her life, a former Olympic gymnast—and, let's not forget, a media personality—wouldn't realize that somewhere someone had compiled a truckload of information on her. Hell, you're a journalist. You dig up dirt on people all the time. You know how easy it is to come by."

She plopped her tidy butt down on a bar stool like the muscles holding her up had deflated. "Bits and pieces, yes. Courthouse records. Credit checks. Public documents. But this," she waved a hand over the thick folder, "this is obviously much more than bits and pieces."

"Which is why I know Grant Wellington is a backstabber who would love to see you out of that coanchor seat and replaced by someone with less talent, less sex appeal, and who represented less of a threat to his longevity."

She was still staring at the folder like it was a violation on her life and her privacy—which, of course, it was.

"Get over it," he said, more softly than he'd intended, when she dropped her head wearily and cupped it in her hand.

Poor little rich girl, he thought with an unbidden kernel of sympathy. *All that sterling didn't come with guarantees of happily ever after, did it?*

"Let's just do this, OK?" On a deep breath, he physically as well as mentally pulled away from the turmoil he sensed roiling around inside of her. He wasn't here to play woman's home companion or worry about her state of mind. He was here to keep her safe. Finding out who was doing this was the most direct route to getting the job done and getting out of here.

"Get dressed. We'll get to work. Oh . . . and that dinner. We're taking a pass."

"Excuse me?"

She recovered quick; he'd give her that.

"It's a no-go on the festivities tonight. There's no way I can check the place out on this short notice, and if I can't protect you—"

"I'm the keynote," she interrupted. "It's a benefit for the cancer society."

He scratched his nose with the back of his hand, stood up straight, then stalled a wince when the slice on his ribs gnawed with sharp teeth.

"Keynote," he repeated, feeling an impending sense of doom.

She nodded.

Well, hell. Didn't it just fucking figure?

9

"I DON'T LIKE THIS." NOLAN TUCKED HIS
cell phone between his shoulder and ear later that day and
worked the stud into the right cuff of the dress shirt that
Ethan had arranged to be delivered along with the tux about
an hour ago.

"Yeah, yeah. You're working under protest. I'll make a
note of it in your personnel file," Ethan said drolly on the
other end of the line.

Nolan told him what he could do with his personnel file.

"When you're done bitching, tell me what you've got for
us to work on."

He bit down harder on the bullet and reviewed the notes
he'd taken from the "chat" he and his charge had had earlier
in the day. Jillian hadn't exactly parted with information
willingly, but he'd gathered a fairly long, marginally detailed list of candidates who might want her dead. "It's wide-
open territory. We could take the angle that the threats could
be coming from any number of individuals holding a grudge
against Darin Kincaid."

"With Jillian's life as payment."

"Exactly," Nolan agreed. "A man doesn't land in Kincaid's position of power without crunching a few digits on
the way up. I don't want to go there just yet, though. Hunting
down that avenue would be massive and exhausting. Time
would be better spent with something a little more tangible.

I think we'd be closer to the mark looking at some of the public figures she's nailed in her special reports."

The list of candidates she'd given him was impressive. She'd exposed some of West Palm and Palm Beach's most upstanding citizens for crimes ranging from political corruption, to sexual harassment, to racial prejudice in the elite private clubs littering the area.

He rattled off the short list he'd come up with as well as some obvious speculation. "I like Marian Abramson for starters," he suggested, and hunted up the other stud.

"Abramson? A woman?"

"You know anyone meaner than a vindictive woman?"

"Good point."

"See what other dirt you can dig up on her. According to Jillian, the councilwoman warned her to back off on her investigation involving kickbacks and inappropriate spending that led to her arrest last month. She's out on bail now but due to be indicted in a couple of weeks. Definitely motive there."

"Murder may be several steps up from corruption, but a terror campaign could fit the councilwoman's profile," Ethan agreed.

"Then there's the own-backyard approach." Nolan shifted the phone to his other ear and tackled the stud at his left wrist. "Jillian's coanchor Grant Wellington's star is fizzling. Word is he resents the hell out of Jillian's flash and dazzle . . . so much that it's starting to show on the newscasts. Sort of reeks of desperation from where I stand. Check him out, too."

He gave Ethan a few other names, including Erica Gray, the weather girl, who seemed to have delusions of fame and might have an ax to grind against Jillian for outdistancing her in local media popularity. There was also Lydia Grace, Jillian's assistant, who sounded just a little too innocent to be believed, and Diane Kleinmeyer, the producer of the newscast, who according to Jillian erupted like Mount Saint Helens at least once a week.

"Hell, there's a whole laundry list of possibles at the TV station alone, including an overachieving weekend anchor. Can't come up with her name right now. I'll fax the detailed list over tomorrow.

"In the meantime, Jillian is currently working a story about a guy with amnesia. Maybe he's got some secrets he'd just as soon leave in the dark." He gave Ethan John Smith's name and address and glared at the black tie lying on the bureau. "See what you can find out about him."

"That ought to hold us for a while."

"You're going to owe me for this one."

"Just keep your head in the game. And watch your back," Ethan warned him.

Nolan disconnected, shrugged into his tux jacket, and shot the cuffs on his shirt. He hadn't mentioned Jillian's ex-lover, Steven Fowler, or Fowler's wife, the woman scorned. Each, for their own reasons, might want Jillian dead.

For whatever reason, he didn't want to travel that road with Ethan just yet, either.

For whatever reason, he didn't want to travel that road at all.

Overkill, Jillian thought when Garrett stepped out of her guest bedroom and into the living room where she was waiting for him. The man had a talent for it. From the military tenacity over his endless lists to a jawline that was so perfectly masculine and impossibly sensual, he was just too much.

And it was almost too much for her—literally—when, grim-faced, he held out his tie.

"No clue," he grumbled, then sank down on the arm of her sofa, legs splayed wide so she had better access to him.

His scent assaulted her first when she approached him with wary determination. And his heat. The two seemed irrevocably intertwined. And both were wrapped up in all that raw and dangerous male beauty.

His breath was warm and minty as it fanned her cheek. The starch in the dress shirt smelled clean and fresh and blended with a scent unique to him—a scent she'd tried not to acknowledge when she tended to his wound in the kitchen last night.

She couldn't ignore it now as she worked on his tie. He smelled of substance. Sage. Sex. The combination set all of her erogenous zones humming.

"Problem?" he asked in a gritty whisper when she swore at her fumbling fingers and had to start all over again.

"Just hold still," she grumbled.

He didn't say a word. They both knew he wasn't fidgeting. And they both felt the electric shocks zipping from her trembling fingers to the warm, fragrant skin at his throat as she wrestled with the black silk. All too aware of his thigh pressing ever so lightly against her hip. Of his heat and strength surrounding her, caging her in. Of his gaze on her face. His breath feathering the fine hair at her temple as if he were touching her there.

Her fingers stilled. She closed her eyes, then lifted her gaze . . . to find his riveted on hers like a laser.

Again, he didn't say a word. But she read his mind like a psychic when one corner of his mouth slowly slid into a knowing smirk.

You do want to get in my pants.

"We're going to be late," she sputtered, and headed for the door.

He hadn't exactly kicked or screamed, Jillian admitted to herself a few minutes later as they cruised in her convertible down South Ocean Boulevard toward Mar-A-Lago, but he looked about as happy as a paratrooper with an iffy rip cord. It was a small thing to gloat about—which probably made her small as well—but she rather enjoyed seeing him so uncomfortable.

All right, she conceded, backpedaling a bit. *Uncomfortable* probably wasn't the correct word. *Uncomfortable* was wishful thinking on her part. In truth, *formidable* was probably a better fit for the way he looked. Formidable, competent, and, unfortunately, gorgeous in the tux that had been messengered over about an hour before they had to leave for Mar-A-Lago.

Grudgingly she sneaked a glance at his profile. He drove with concentrated proficiency, his eyes hooded, his posture deceptively relaxed, when she knew he could transition to full attack mode in a heartbeat. He was professional to a fault, her bodyguard, right down to his insistence that he drive instead of her.

She made herself look away; then she stared out the passenger window toward the ocean sweeping along the horizon in endless waves of foaming white surf and blue-green water. But all she saw was him.

Garrett's transformation from Attila the Hood to *GQ* model had thrown her into yet another dimension of sexual heat she'd been determined to keep under wraps. But he'd walked into his bedroom looking for all the world like a thug in blue jeans and emerged forty minutes later as a hard-edged Prince Charming. Or Prince Charmless, she reminded herself, if you factored in his attitude and his sparkling conversation, which up until this point had been limited to curt, sharp warnings to keep a low profile, stay by his side, and plan on making it a short night.

Oh, and his sarcastic "I suppose it's too much to ask that you change into a dress that would draw a little less attention," as he'd followed her out the penthouse door.

Shimmering in a white Dior hand-stitched with seed pearls, slim lines, and little else, she'd snagged her beaded purse from the foyer table, liking it a little too much that his detached, *I'm only the hired help* composure had cracked ever so slightly when he'd looked her up and down.

"We must keep up appearances, darling." Her affected purr had been laced with enough sarcasm to set even her own teeth on edge. "It's the price we pampered princesses pay for being born royal."

And that had been the last she'd heard out of him.

That was fine, she thought wearily. She'd heard plenty earlier in the day. First he'd made arrangements with City Place security to change the code on her entrance door. Then he'd bullied her into promising not to give it to anyone. And that meant *anyone.*

She'd glanced at the slip of paper containing the new code. "Do you eat this or do I?"

He had not been amused.

Next, he'd talked to her father and they'd agreed it was necessary for Nolan to take her mother's place at the sold-out benefit dinner. Then, for the better part of the rest of the day they'd sat with their heads together, fleshing out his precious list. Fat lot of good it would do them.

He was snarling at the wrong dogs. It wasn't anyone she knew. She was convinced of that. It was some sick soul without a life, so he'd decided to make one—and make hers hell in the process. She couldn't wait until they caught him, or her. As Garrett often pointed out, it could be a woman. Whatever, she'd like to impose a little justice of her own on the creep for what he—or *she,* she added on a grumpy afterthought—had put her through, not the least of which was dealing with her bodyguard.

With every hour that passed, everything about Garrett's tactics reinforced why she'd had a bellyful of growing up as one of the hottest kidnapping prospects in Florida. It brought back all those memories of when she was younger . . . the violation of her privacy, of her rights, the theft and disregard of her need for independence. Garrett didn't care about any of that. He cared about only one thing, and that afternoon he'd proceeded with dogged determination to fill page after page with names and detailed notes about anyone with whom she had regular or irregular contact.

He was merely being thorough, he'd said, not in defense of his attention to detail but in an attempt to get her to stop bitching.

And she *had* been bitchy. She freely admitted it. She hated this. Not just his growing laundry list of possible suspects— some of whom she considered her friends—but also because it was beginning to feel more and more like she really did have reason to be concerned.

She still wanted to discount the threat as a mean-spirited joke. It was getting harder and harder to do, though, when he continued to approach the problem from the angle that someone wanted her dead. Garrett and his gloom and doom would be a real hit at a New Year's Eve party.

When Steven Fowler's name had come up in their conversation it had ended in a stalemate. She was not going to discuss that debacle with Garrett. She wasn't all that ready to examine it herself. Steven Fowler had been important to her, and both her pride and her heart were still smarting over his duplicity. She'd thought he might be the one. She'd been ready for a long-term relationship. It still hurt that he'd lied. It hurt more that she'd cared and he'd duped her. And she was ashamed—too ashamed to give Garrett the satisfaction of knowing it.

When he pulled into the drive at Mar-A-Lago, she let out a breath of relief and drew another to brace herself.

It was showtime. And despite Garrett's unsettling and unwelcome presence at her side, she had a job to do tonight.

Flanking Jillian to the left, Nolan walked close beside her as they ascended the white stone steps leading to the flamingo pink palace that Donald Trump had turned into one of the most, if not *the* most, exclusive private clubs in Palm Beach a few years ago.

Nolan picked out the in-house security people as they walked through the main doors and into a high-ceilinged anteroom overrun with pillars and pots, glitter and gold. Thanks to the blueprints Ethan had hastily procured from an associate who worked for Bolo—the firm providing Mar-A-Lago's in-house security and with whom E.D.E.N. regularly consulted on assignments—Nolan already had a mental picture of the layout.

Fortunately, Ethan had been able to spare their brother, Dallas, for a couple of hours that afternoon. Dallas had done a walk-through of the facility and the grounds surrounding the one hundred plus–room mansion and briefed Nolan in a phone call earlier.

The good news: For the most part, house security was professional and tight.

The bad news: The razzle and the dazzle of Palm Beach society had turned out in droves for the event. The size of the crowd—250 or so Mr. and Mrs. Richie Riches rubbing elbows and bussing air kisses—wasn't exactly a security nightmare, but it wasn't without its concerns.

From the anteroom to the salon, where cocktails were being served, the place was packed with sequins and satin, diamonds and silk, as the city's most affluent and philanthropic citizens mingled and laughed with gentile grace over glasses of bubbling champagne and tables heaped with frou-frou looking finger food. God only knew what was in some of that stuff.

And God only knew how much coin had been laid out for the place. Whatever realtor had made the sale to Trump must be ass deep in caviar and imported champagne. Mar-A-Lago, which, according to detail-oriented Dallas, meant "sea-by-lake," was set on eighteen of the priciest acres on earth, between the Atlantic Ocean and Lake Worth, and lived up to its billing as a playground for the moneyed few.

Nolan couldn't help it. He whistled softly through his teeth as they worked their way farther through the salon, cataloging the twenty-foot gold-leaf ceilings, pricey antique tapestries, Spanish tile floors, and chandeliers dripping with glittering crystal. It was way overdone for his taste—army surplus had done him just fine—but he had to admit the enormous plate-glass window at the far end of the room that looked out over a sprawling lawn and beyond, to the crashing waves of the Atlantic, was as impressive as hell.

"Remember, stay close," he reminded Jillian when she accepted a flute of champagne from a passing waiter.

"You're overplaying this." Her smile never cracked as she nodded a greeting to someone across the room.

"Yeah, well. Get used to it. I live for excess."

Speaking of excess . . . her dress. Holy mother of God.

She appeared to be body-painted into a long, sleek skin of tiny white pearls stitched over fabric so sheer it looked transparent. The whole thing clung like lotion to her fantasy body and appeared to be held on her shoulders by thin silver threads.

The deep, draping V in the front of the gown showcased— there was no other word for it—the creamy rounds of her breasts. Even more dangerous than the front was the rear view. The dress fell away from her pale, bare back, dipped low at her hips, and hugged her firm, high ass.

For all its high-class sophistication, it was a *fuck-me* dress—no if, ands, or buts about it—and the moment he'd seen her in it, he'd been flashing in and out of an erotic visual image of his hands gripping her hips, lifting her, shifting her until he was buried to the hilt in all that cool, haughty elegance.

It pissed him off that she'd known damn well when she'd put it on what it would do to a man's libido. And it was small

consolation that he wasn't the only one affected by her blatant, if classy, sexuality. Judging by the bug-eyed reaction of
one particularly red-faced octogenarian, he'd bet the old
geezer was sporting his first non-pharmaceutical-induced
hard-on in years.

He rolled a shoulder and sucked it up . . . but as she
turned to say hello to a matron covered in gold and black sequins and diamonds mammoth enough to choke a herd of
mastodons, his gaze arrowed back to the slim line of Jillian's
body. He followed it downward. And into more trouble.

A floor-skimming hemline separated at her ankle and ascended to midthigh, exposing a damn fine leg covered in
filmy, shimmering silk. Her slim high heels sent the same
message as the dress. Glittering silver straps crisscrossed
over her arch—and the image of those small feet arched in
passion against a mattress shot him from semierect to full
arousal right there in Donald Trump's monument to wealth
and power.

And wasn't that special?

When she turned and, as she had been doing all night,
coolly introduced him as her associate, he gave her a final,
thorough once-over—just to prove to himself he could keep
it all together. He was on the clock here and a slip on his part
could mean the difference between life and death for her.

He moved in closer, feeling the reassuring pressure of his
shoulder piece beneath his tux jacket.

"Back off," she said between clenched teeth, attempting
to mask her anger behind a brittle smile when they were
alone again—at least relatively speaking in a crowd this size.
"Protection is one thing. Invading my personal space is another. Give me some breathing room."

"You mean you can actually breathe in that thing?"

The rise and fall of her breasts above the dipping neckline
indicated that yes, she could. So could he—just barely—
when every breath he took was laced with her perfume. Like

the dress, there was nothing subtle about the scent. No tropical rain forest tonight. Tonight she smelled like midnight
and musk and mindless, marathon sex. Like the damn dress,
it had been screwing with his head from the moment he'd set
eyes on her. Hell. He'd almost dragged her to the floor back
at the penthouse and all she'd had to do to provoke it was tie
his damn tie.

And breathe.

Gezus save him.

"There are too many people here," he growled, but could
just as well have been talking to a wall. She was on the move
again, glad-handing and dazzling this huge contingent of the
lucky sperm club. And watching her, he finally got it.

"It's part of your strategy, isn't it?"

"*What* is part of my strategy?" she asked, still smiling
across the room.

"The dress. The whole package. You're working it."

She looked at him with renewed interest, then shrugged.
"It's for a good cause."

"But maybe not without a cost to you."

"I don't know what you're talking about."

With a hand on her elbow, he steered her toward the massive fireplace on the far side of the room. "Mrs. Billionaire
can't help but notice Mr. Billionaire ogling you. Take it
times a hundred or so. Doesn't take a nuclear biologist to
figure out there will be resentment among the ranks of the
rich and the richer. Enough resentment to, oh, say . . . level a
death threat?"

"That's ridiculous. I don't play with other women's . . .
portfolios," she informed him with a dry look.

"So how do you explain Steven Fowler?"

His shot hit the mark like an RPG.

Her face drained to pale. And something even stronger
than pain glazed her eyes. Humiliation.

He felt like he'd just kicked a puppy.

Great.

Good going, Garrett. Fowler was a raw nerve. He'd figured that out this afternoon. She'd closed up like a safe when he'd questioned her about him. He'd like to think his curiosity about Fowler was purely professional. That it didn't bug the hell out of him that she'd been involved with a married man, which in his estimation placed her somewhere beneath a pit viper in his game book.

"I don't have to explain anything to you."

She moved remarkably fast in her heels. So fast, he had to scramble to catch up with her.

She'd woven her way through the crowd, exited the salon and was well into an open hallway before he finally snagged her arm. With more discretion than he'd thought he had in him, he gripped her upper arm and turned her slowly around to face him.

"I was out of line," he said, watching the top of her head while she looked anywhere but at him.

"Damn right you were."

"Look. . . ." Involuntarily he rubbed his thumb along the silky skin of her upper arm. "I'm sorry."

"Go to hell."

"Right. Look, Jillian—"

"Just stick to your job, Garrett." When her gaze met his, her composure was back, but anger flashed in her green eyes like mortar fire through night vision goggles. "And save the judgmental commentary for someone who appreciates it. Now if you'll excuse me, I'm going to the ladies' room."

IO

THERE WASN'T MUCH NOLAN COULD DO BUT watch her walk away.

He dragged a hand over his face. Sonofabitch. Hitting her with a dig about Fowler had been a low blow. A sucker punch. And at the moment, he hated himself almost as much as she hated him for delivering it.

Since he wasn't exactly martyr material himself, he was in no position to judge someone else's actions. She didn't deserve this crap from him . . . and maybe that was why, at every turn, he still found himself sniping at her. He wanted to believe the worst of her, but as more time passed, he was running out of reasons. Which meant he was running out of barriers.

She impressed him and he goddamn didn't want to be impressed. She didn't want him here, yet she was enduring. She hadn't wanted to help him with his list, but she had. She was tough and she was credible when he kept wanting her to be fallible and spoiled.

And he wanted her to give him a plausible reason for Steven Fowler. Right. Like he gave a damn. And there was the rub, wasn't it? He *did* give a damn and he didn't want to.

He cupped a hand over the back of his neck. Rolled his head on his shoulders. And swore under his breath. She was nothing like he'd expected. He was actually starting to like the woman.

Worse, he wanted to nail her so bad he'd turned into a perpetual hammer. And it royally pissed him off, to the point where if he didn't get his head back in the game, he wasn't going to be able to protect her.

Just stick to your job, Garrett.

Yeah. That rankled, too. She knew better than he did what he needed to do.

Settling himself with a deep breath, he folded his hands in front of him, braced his legs wide apart, and fully engaged with the task at hand while he waited for Jillian in the corridor that led to the ladies' room.

Couldn't be more than, oh, say, a fricking boatload of trouble spots, he decided with a sour scowl. To his left, a spiral staircase ascended to what appeared to be an empty loft. To his right was an arched doorway flanked by a pair of tables. Italian maybe. Old absolutely. And undoubtedly worth more than his miserable hide.

OK—worth one hundred times his miserable hide, he conceded grimly.

Farther along the wall, an angular hallway led to what he knew from Dallas's recon was a bar, complete with a portrait of Donald Trump in his tennis shorts and white V-neck sweater. In the center of what he'd come to think of as the meet and greet room—but in fact had once been the formal living room for the Post family—was a huge table set up with highbrow floral arrangements that showcased a conch shell ice sculpture and silver platters of everything from mussels, to shrimp, to sushi and many exotic ports in between.

He nodded grimly at several guests who were filing by the table and exiting the room through the arched doorway, then milling in the general direction of the outside terraces and the lawn where a party tent was set up to the left of a huge rectangular pool.

"Where the hell is she?" he muttered just before Jillian walked out of the restroom. Finally. She dropped a lipstick tube into a glitzy beaded purse, snapped it shut, and without a word or a look his way fell into the line leading outside.

Despite the chill he felt when she shouldered past him, the night air was warm on his face. So was her scent. It shot an arrow of lust straight to his loins. The wind that had buffeted Palm Beach all day had finally laid down to a pleasant breeze that fussed with her hair and played hell with his imagination.

He forced it all out of his mind—her scent, her hair, her dress—and concentrated on the setup as they walked across a marble-tiled veranda, then hung a left and descended mosaic-tiled steps to yet another level leading to the pool area.

The place was laid out right, security wise, he noted with a quick scan of the sweeping lawn. While lushly landscaped— pots of greenery, lots of grass—the surgically manicured grounds were subtly but well lit. No bushes or dark corners for bad guys to hide in.

Jamaican palms rustled in the balmy ocean breeze as he and Jillian entered the tent set up to seat all 250 attendees. Lots of crystal. Lots of sterling. Lots of class.

A plastic-faced dowager, well preserved—in fact, close to mummified—touched frail, birdlike fingers to Jillian's shoulders and pulled her into a pseudoembrace. "Jillian, darling. How marvelous to see you."

"Hannah. You look wonderful."

"Thank you, darling. And you . . . well. You're stunning, as usual. Not to mention you're sporting some incredible accessories tonight. Please. *Do* introduce us."

Nolan held himself in check like a good dog.

Now he was a freaking accessory?

"Hannah Baylor, Nolan Garrett. Mrs. Baylor is the sponsor of tonight's event."

"It's a pleasure," he said, hiding his irritation behind a benign smile as Jillian did the honors.

Eyes as predatory as a hawk's gleamed at him from

beneath heavily made-up lids. "You are a welcome addition to our darling Jillian's arm. Do tell me you're madly in love with her."

"A man would be hard pressed not to be." From the corner of his eye he saw Jillian roll hers. "My relationship with Ms. Kincaid, however, is strictly professional."

"How interesting." The hawkish Mrs. Baylor's gaze darted between the two of them. "Professional how?"

While Jillian had made vague references to him as an associate in her previous introductions, he saw no reason to hedge. In fact, he preferred to make it known up front that anyone wanting to get to her had to get past him.

"I'm providing security for Ms. Kincaid," he explained, then felt his skin crawl beneath his dress shirt when the woman sidled closer and gave him a blatant come-hither look.

If he wasn't mistaken, Jillian was working hard at hiding a smirk.

"Security? My dear, is there a problem?" While the question was directed at Jillian, the bird eyes never left his face; the smile never cracked. "And did you have to disable some horrible person in the process of getting this colorful bruise, you poor thing?" she cooed, touching a perfectly manicured hand to his cheek.

"There's no problem," Nolan assured her while making an unsuccessful attempt to remove himself from Mrs. Baylor's clawlike grip on his arm. "Doorknob," he added, pointing to his cheek. "Surveillance can be a bitch."

"Hannah," Jillian interjected smoothly, "I believe Blanche Winston is trying to get your attention."

He was too grateful to be irritated that Jillian had had to come to his rescue.

After a long, lingering look—swear to God, the woman was trying to seduce him—the sexually charged Mrs. Baylor sighed longingly and finally followed the direction of Jillian's gaze.

"I suppose I've avoided her for as long as I can tonight. One of the newly rich. The woman is such a bore," Mrs. Baylor confided with weary forbearance. "And the company here is so . . . titillating."

She winked at him. *Winked* for God's sake.

"We'll talk later," the woman promised, and with a final squeeze to his arm walked away.

"I do believe," Jillian said, sounding way too amused, as they made their way to a table beside a podium at the front of the room, "you've got an admirer."

He snorted. "Be still, my heart." He couldn't help it; he glanced over his shoulder to make sure Mrs. Baylor was moving toward the other side of the room. "Was she for real?"

"Oh yeah." Jillian, smiling openly now, was very obviously enjoying his discomfort. "Widowed four times. Rumor has it Arthur died in bed . . . and not in his sleep."

"Oh God." He grunted out a pained laugh. "Spare me the gory details. What is she? A hundred and fifty?"

She laughed, too, as he pulled a chair out for her and sat down.

"Doorknob?" she asked with a grin, and shook her head.

He was smiling when he sat down beside her and met the amusement in her eyes.

And for a moment, one unguarded, unplanned, unexpected moment, they shared something that didn't start with resentment or end in anger. Common ground. And damn if it wasn't a comfortable place to be.

Too soon, awareness set in. Awareness of the moment. Of the circumstances that had brought them together. Of an underlying sexual tension neither of them wanted to admit to but kept creeping in to skew the picture anyway.

She was the first one to look away and left him feeling . . . what?

What the hell *did* he feel?

He leaned back in his chair, scraped a palm across his jaw. Nothing. At least nothing he wanted to admit to. Nothing he could afford to even consider.

"I don't like this cloistered tent any more than I liked the crowd inside," he said abruptly. "How long before we can get out of here?"

Her expression carefully blank, she lifted a water glass to her lips. Sipped. "I believe we're looking at five courses. My speech runs twenty minutes. You do the math."

The edge was back in her voice. No doubt in response to his grumbling. Fine. Good, in fact. They were back on familiar ground. Hostile. He'd always functioned best under enemy fire.

He kept an eye on the crowd throughout dinner, made limited small talk when absolutely pressed, and assessed any number of variables that might present a threat. The longer the night dragged on, the higher the probability of an occurrence; so said the law of averages.

So he kept his guard and his focus, alternately scoping out his surroundings, avoiding Birdlady Baylor's come-hither glances, and watching Jillian. He had to admit he was impressed by the way she wooed the cultured crowd with her presentation. She had them laughing one minute, misty-eyed the next . . . and riveted all the way through.

When she left the podium to appreciative applause, he stood and pulled her chair out for her. They had to sit for another thirty minutes as she was besieged by no small number of well-wishers who wanted to shake her hand, buss her check, and, in the case of at least two nefarious old gents, look down her dress.

Boys will be boys, he thought drily, and gave her credit for handling the old coots with good-natured forbearance.

Finally, she stood, giving him the cue to leave.

"Thank God. Baylor's locked on me like a tractor beam and heading this way. Let's make tracks."

With a hand on her elbow, he hurried her out of the tent and across the lawn. They'd made it back inside the mansion and were about to clear the common room when she put on the skids.

"I need to stop in the ladies' room again before we leave."

He slanted her an irritated look. "You have a problem, or what?"

She actually blushed. "I get a little nervous when I do public speaking, OK?"

"You are *not* serious. You make a career of appearing in public."

She gave him a withering look and turned down the corridor that led to the ladies' powder room . . . which, unfortunately, gave Hannah Baylor an opening.

Shit.

Old hawk claws had him cornered between the ice sculpture and the champagne fountain before he could make a run for it. She cut to the chase; he'd give her that. She was blatantly offering up a private charitable event involving a bed, a vivid imagination, and an amazing amount of stamina when he finally spotted Jillian returning to the room.

Thank you, Gezus.

Nolan was in the process of trying to excuse himself when he got his first good look at Jillian's face. The vivid green eyes searching for and finally connecting with his were filled with terror—stark and raw.

His adrenaline spiked. She was in trouble.

He headed across the room at a jog, his hand automatically reaching for the gun inside his tux jacket. When he reached her, she latched onto his hand with a viselike grip.

"It's . . . oh God, Garrett. It's dead."

The extent of Jillian's shock and horror resonated in the tremor of her whisper, in the grasp of her fingers as she reached for him.

Nolan dragged her against him and looked down. The hand that wasn't clamped on his arm held a box and a crumpled piece of paper. The box was open, and yeah, he had to agree. The songbird inside was dead, its delicate neck broken, its small head twisted at a gruesome angle.

He pulled Jillian protectively to his side and cut across the room toward a small alcove not ten feet away, shielding her from the crowd that was slowly tuning in to her dilemma. Once there, he pried the paper out of her hand and read the typewritten note—and that's when he really got pissed.

There was a little girl, who had a little curl,
right in the middle of her forehead.
When she was good, she was very, very good,
but when she was bad, she was horrid.
It's going to be horrid, Jillian.
Before I'm finished with you,
you'll wish you were dead.
You're going to get your wish. I promise.

Sonofabitch.
While she pressed her face against his chest, Nolan scanned the faces in the crowd for any giveaways . . . looks of guilt, elation, satisfaction. Not that he really expected to spot anything telling. Chances were, whoever had done this was long gone, but he searched just the same.

When he turned back to Jillian, her face was pale as chalk. "Who gave this to you?"

"One of the waiters. As I left the ladies' room."

"Would you recognize him?"

When she nodded, Nolan got the attention of one of the in-house security guards, filled him in, and asked him to assemble all the wait- and catering staff. Five minutes later, Brad Herman was one freaked-out waiter as Nolan hammered him with questions.

Herman was a college student. And Nolan was going to personally see to it that he was going to be more terrified than Jillian by the time they finished questioning him.

"I swear to God," the kid insisted, his voice rising, "I didn't know what was in it. Someone found the package in the kitchen."

Herman's gaze darted from Nolan to the guard. "Mrs. Baylor . . . hell, she'd been in and out of the kitchen all night, fussing over everything from the canapés to the silver. One of the chefs, Robert, spotted the box. I guess he figured she'd left it by mistake, like she'd meant to give it to Ms. Kincaid as a gift for speaking or something."

He dragged a shaking hand through his spiky hair. "He shoved it at me, told me to find Mrs. Baylor and give it to her or she'd be setting fire to his ass instead of the chafing dish. I don't ask questions. I just do what I'm told, ya know?

"So I made tracks. Couldn't find Mrs. Baylor, but I spotted Ms. Kincaid comin' out of the can, so I gave it to her. I mean, hell, it had her name on it, so why not give it to her? I didn't know what was in it. Swear to God. I just did what I was told."

The kid was a pawn. Nolan was convinced of that. He was too scared to be anything else. Just like Nolan was convinced that whoever left the package was long gone. He wanted to question the kitchen staff a little more, but he didn't expect them to know any more than the waiter.

Nolan glanced across the room to where Jillian now sat on an antique satin sofa, Hannah Baylor at her side, duly horrified and surprisingly motherly as she held Jillian's hand. The worry on Hannah's face made her look all of the hundred and fifty years old he'd suspected her to be.

Jillian looked ready to crash. He needed to get her out of here, and he would, as soon as he rattled a few more chains. Unfortunately, though, no one in the kitchen had seen anyone leave the package. Aside from the head chef, they were cater-waiters and prep cooks, part-timers working for tuition and rent and used to the habits of the rich and famous. They'd been running their legs off to make sure all the silver platters stayed filled. They were the hired help. They didn't make eye contact. They did their job and they followed orders, no questions asked.

"Might as well take her home." The guard, a Steven Seagal wannabe, complete with ponytail, nodded toward Jillian. "We'll do a final sweep, see what we come up with, but my guess is it'll be a bust."

"If you find anything, let me know."

"Do you want me to call this in to the police?"

Nolan shook his head. "I'll call the detective in charge and fill him in."

As Nolan headed toward Jillian, a sick feeling churned in his gut. Whoever had done this had just proven, bodyguard or no bodyguard, they could get to her anytime they wanted. Which meant only one thing.

From now on, he and Jillian Kincaid were going to be as tight as white on rice. She didn't breathe without him knowing it. She didn't take a leak without him close enough to hand her toilet paper. Didn't change her clothes without him on hand to work the zipper.

She thought she was pissed about him living with her now? Just wait until she realized how chummy they were going to get before this was over.

Green eyes met his across the room. Soft as an ocean swell at sunset.

His heart did that stumble thing. Skippy twitched to life. *Christ.*

Why couldn't Darin Kincaid have had a son?

Some days it wasn't just his past John couldn't remember. Today was one of those days. Tonight was one of those nights. Sometimes, when the headaches came, they brought more than pain. Stole more than his strength. They brought confusion. Like thieves, they stole hours and the most recent pieces of his life, disconnecting him from even the minuscule moments that had become his existence.

He stared at the cracked ceiling of his motel room and tried to remember . . . anything. He'd had a headache today. At least he thought it had been today. Must have been today . . . late afternoon. Maybe.

He rubbed his temples. Closed his eyes and tried to remember. He'd gotten day work . . . yeah. With that landscaping crew out of Jupiter. It was one of the few types of work available to him. No ID required. No questions asked. Payment in cash.

He'd been trimming palms. And it *had* been daylight.

But now it was dark. He was in his room. Lying on his bed, damp and sour with sweat. And he had no idea how he'd gotten here.

The door opened.

He reared up, his heart rate rocketing.

Mary.

He let out a breath. Of relief or forbearance, he wasn't sure which. It didn't matter. He didn't care.

He'd given her an extra key. Because she'd asked, he supposed. Because no one else asked him for anything. No one gave him anything. Except her.

But even Mary took.

"Baby. What's wrong?" Her eyes filled with concern as she crossed the room and tossed her purse aside. "Oh, John." Her hands shook when they touched him. Caressed his face. Smoothed her fingers through his damp hair where he sat. Alone. Drifting through a cobwebby maze of nothingness. "It's all right. It's all right. I'll make it all right."

She pressed his face to her breasts.

Warmth. Life. Real. Too real for him to deal with right now. He was shaking, too, when he shoved her away.

She clung to him. Needy. Cloying.

"Hurt me," she whispered, and pushed him to his back. Straddled him.

Her fingers quivered as she reached for his zipper, cupped him in her hands, her soft, artful hands, and begged him to punish her for not being everything he needed.

Afterward, she cried.

He rolled away from her, stared dispassionately at the bedside table and the book of designer matches lying there. He didn't remember seeing them before. Didn't remember putting them there. For a brief moment, he wondered at the name—*Mar-A-Lago*—before dismissing it and Mary and falling into a fitful sleep.

11

NOLAN TOSSED BACK THE LAST OF HIS ROOT
beer and cast a glance into the living area. Jillian sat on the
sofa in her sexy designer gown, her knees drawn up to her
chest, her bare toes hugging the edge of the leather cushion.

She looked bruised. And agonizingly vulnerable. Dazed
even, like Cinderella had just discovered Prince Charming
was an ax murderer.

Nolan let out a puff of air and resisted the urge to walk
over and give her the hug she obviously needed. He loos-
ened another stud in his shirt instead. He'd ditched the jacket
and tie the minute they walked into the penthouse. The studs
on his cuffs had gone the same way as he'd rolled up his
sleeves and headed straight for the fridge. He'd needed to
wash the taste of the evening out of his mouth.

It was close to midnight. They'd been back at her penthouse less than five minutes and she hadn't said a word. The
place echoed with the same silence that had filled the car on
the drive back.

Frustrated, Nolan thought back to the dead ends at Mar-
A-Lago and traded his soda for the glass of wine he'd just
poured for her. He considered downing it himself in one
deep swallow or hunting up a bottle of something stronger.
He'd used lamer excuses to tie one on. Sunset. Sunrise. Self-
pity. Yeah. His big sorry self had fallen back on that one
every chance he got.

But he was on the clock here. And this wasn't about him.

Face grim, he walked into the living area and stopped in front of the sofa. Jillian watched the tube with blank eyes, far too intent on the television . . . especially in light of the fact that the plasma screen wasn't on.

He'd seen that look too many times to count. The hundred-mile stare. It was a staple for young soldiers after their first taste of combat. The numbing realization had set in that war was ugly, death was real, and in the end fate and luck might be the only things keeping them alive. He didn't like seeing it on her.

She wasn't a soldier. She hadn't signed on to fight the enemy. She hadn't asked for any of this. And he'd better tread carefully or he'd lose what little perspective he had where she was concerned, because what he felt in that moment went way past professional concern. Past sympathy. He felt possessive when he had no ownership. Felt a compulsion to take her in his arms again and let her lean on him for strength if she needed it when he had no business even touching her, unless it was to shove her out of harm's way.

What the hell was he doing? He scrubbed a hand over his face. Experiencing his own delayed reaction maybe. The way she'd looked earlier, walking toward him, carrying that damn dead bird. Christ. She'd been ghost white. Eyes wide with horror. For all he'd known the bastard had already gotten to her. . . . Hell, he'd expected to see blood. Hers. And that thought shot a fresh spike of anxiety buzzing through his head.

"Here." He held out the wine, waited the space of the deep breath he needed to get it together, and fell a little deeper into the fire when a slim, glittery strap slipped off her left shoulder.

Gezus save him, the only thing he could do was look. And want, and wait for her to set it right. The problem was, she didn't seem to realize she was about to fall out of the dress.

But he did. So when he reached out and hooked his finger under the strap, he wasn't sure if he was going to tug it up or down.

Just that abbreviated point of contact—the back of his finger to her warm, silky skin—shot a punch of arousal through his blood that was so strong and pure it damn near dropped him to his knees.

To beg no doubt. *Lean on me. I'll make it better. I'll make us both forget that life sucks and sex—hot, fast, and hard—will make it all go away.*

At least for a little while.

What a dumb fuck.

When she glanced up and blinked as if momentarily surprised to see him so close, he tugged the strap back in place.

"Drink." He shoved the glass into her hand.

Then he backed the hell away. Way away.

Like an automaton, she lifted the wine and sipped.

"More."

After a deep swallow, she steadied herself, then met his eyes. "What does it mean, that this person would take such a chance?"

She'd had a couple of hours to let the scare build and breed and latch on like a leech and drain her self-control. A couple of hours to snap out of her shock, become hysterical, and lapse into victim mode.

Why me? Why is this happening to me? Why haven't you caught him? Why don't you do something?

He'd expected every one of those questions and more. Tears, Wails. Self-pity. Once again, he'd underestimated her. She was far from hysterical. Instead, she'd sucked it up and asked the hard question. The sensible question—the same one he'd been asking himself.

What did it mean? It meant the psycho was getting off on bringing the game closer to home. It meant more trouble. It meant she wasn't going to like what he had to say.

In the end, he didn't have to say anything. Her eyes were a little glassy, but she was with the program when she drew her own conclusions.

"It was a huge risk, getting that close to me with all those potential witnesses, with the possibility of getting caught."

There was a huskiness in her voice that suggested she was more pissed off now than frightened. *Atta girl,* he thought, impressed again with her ability to, if not roll with the punches, at least haul herself up by her designer shoe straps to brace for another one.

"Yeah," he agreed. "The move reeks of stupidity, confidence, or desperation—take your pick. Whichever, the game just got more dangerous."

She swallowed, gazed toward the windows that overlooked the city. "Some game."

When she met his eyes again, hers had gone soft and hunted and that sexy all-American-girl face was as white as her dress. Nothing like an up close and personal face-off with death to make a princess come to grips with her new and harsh reality that there was unrest in the peasant ranks.

She really hadn't accepted it, he realized then. Not until tonight. It wasn't just the gruesome message of the dead bird—hell, she had to have seen worse than that as a reporter covering everything from fires, to car accidents, to murder. It was that this episode had rattled her in a way the other messages hadn't. The bird's death represented a portent of hers. Until she'd seen that bird, she hadn't truly accepted that someone wanted her dead. The part of him that still felt regret felt it now for what lay ahead for her.

Sympathy and regret weren't going to keep her alive, though. He was. And right now, he needed more distance from those melting eyes that begged him to keep her that way. Trouble was, he'd already decided that distance was a luxury he couldn't afford.

White on rice. Green on grass. Sheets on a bed. Him on her.

He stood and walked to the floor-to-ceiling windows where the lights of the city glittered in a sea of black. Head-lights snaked along the eight lanes of traffic and reminded him that of the millions of people who lived in the sprawling megalopolis strung along the Florida coast, he would be the last man she'd turn to for anything but protection.

OK. So outwardly he'd reacted like a professional. In-side, though, his guts were still knotted in a fist of fear. For her. Not for his client. For *her*. Jillian. A woman who had somehow, over the course of the past twenty-four hours, started to matter when nothing had mattered in his life for a helluva long time. A woman who earlier tonight had reached for him, melted against him, clung to him like he was the one man, the only man, she trusted or wanted to trust to keep her safe.

And that path would lead nowhere.

The adrenaline rush was over and so was fantasy time. He was nothing but the hired help. That's all he ever would and ever could be.

Some game, Jillian thought again, staring into her wine. *A deadly game.*

A shiver rippled through her. She opened her mouth, shut it, then wrapped her fingers around the crystal stem of the glass. She didn't even know what to ask. What to think. What to feel.

Except the fear. She had that part down pat. It had snaked into muscle and bone and wound tight. She couldn't shake the memory of that poor dead bird from her mind—or de-lude herself any longer. The significance of the dead bird was painfully clear. Whoever had killed it intended for her to get a deadly message. He—or she—meant to kill her, too.

> *Before I'm finished with you,*
> *you'll wish you were dead.*
> *You're going to get your wish. I promise.*

She closed her eyes . . . like she'd been closing her eyes on the truth ever since she'd received that first threatening note two weeks ago.

This wasn't a joke.

It was real.

"Hit you hard, has it?"

She must have looked a little cornered, her eyes a little wild, as she lifted her head and saw Garrett watching her from the bank of windows. His gaze suddenly softened. So did his voice as he shoved his hands deep in his trouser pockets.

"It's human nature to fall back on denial," he said. "It's part of the adjustment process. The key now is that you've got the picture. But it's also critical that you don't let yourself get mired in the possibilities of the threat. You can't let the fear paralyze you."

"Too late," she said with a tight, self-effacing smile. "Already crossed that line."

"Then you're giving him exactly what he wants." Garrett's voice broke through the wall of terror. "To get you running, get you scared. We're not gonna let that happen, OK?"

The facsimile of a laugh she pushed out was laced with barely controlled hysteria. "You're optimistic to a fault. I'm waaay past scared."

In a bit of a daze, she fought the images of bogeymen hiding in her closet, madmen lurking under her bed, danger in the eyes of strangers. Dead birds wrapped in pretty ribbon and paper.

"But you're pissed, too."

Another laugh. This one actually held a trace of humor. "Oh yeah, that's somewhere in the mix."

When he grunted, she swore she heard approval.

"You're going to be OK."

She'd started to shiver.

Until she felt Garrett's strong hands grasp her shoulders, she wasn't aware that he'd joined her on the sofa. She stiffened but didn't resist when he gave her a shake, prompting her to look at him.

"You're going to be OK," he repeated, and squeezed her shoulders.

"Right." She drew a breath that was spiced with the scent of the man scowling down at her with eyes as blue as a summer sky. He still smelled of sage and sex . . . but now sea breeze was somewhere in the mix. Combined with the touch of his big hands bracketing her shoulders and his uncharacteristic show of kindness she felt an odd blend of comfort and unbalance.

No fair.

She had enough to deal with—why did he have to pick now to act like a decent human being? He was actually trying to be . . . nice to her. What was that about? It threw her, at a time when she was already standing on quaking ground. At this moment in time, she wanted nothing more than to lean into all that solid strength and masculine heat again like she had at Mar-A-Lago.

In his arms, she'd felt safe and sheltered and exactly where she'd needed to be. And the lines between what was and what she'd needed had blurred. She'd needed a man to hold her and he'd been there. But that was then. This was now. Now she had that part of the equation back in perspective. It hadn't been a man holding her but a paid protector. Doing his job. Keeping her safe. Earning his pay.

She didn't care. She needed him to earn it again. Right

now. She wanted his arms around her. And the fierceness with which she wanted to ask him to hold her again was almost as frightening as the death threat.

Oh God. This was not good.

She was losing control and she didn't like it. Control of her life. Control of her emotions. She wasn't so far gone, however, that she'd give in to a momentary weakness over the need for a pair of strong arms around her and forget she was dedicated to disliking the man.

"Jillian?"

His soft query brought her head up. The concern in his eyes tripped her heart . . . and went a long way toward eroding that dedication.

"I . . . it's OK. I'll be fine," she stammered, not knowing how to react to all this puzzling energy humming between them.

"You *are* fine. Say it. Believe it and it'll be true."

"Right. I *am* fine," she said, managing a little more conviction than she felt.

He gave her shoulders another unexpected and friendly squeeze.

"Well, *I'm* not." He shot off the sofa. "I'm starving. I think I saw a couple of eggs in the fridge. I make a mean omelet. You up for something to eat?"

She blinked up at him. *Was she up for something to eat?*

"I . . . um . . . damn." She felt the sting of tears, the anger over the circumstances that had forced them. The helplessness of feeling totally vulnerable. The confusion over how to deal with this new, improved, and utterly baffling Nolan Garrett—not to mention her reactions toward him.

"This is bad, Kincaid. These are the easy questions. What's gonna happen when we get to the tough ones? Never mind. Let's try again. Are you hungry?"

She couldn't eat if her life depended on it, but his nodding head encouraged her to nod anyway.

"Good answer. And hell, let's live dangerously and add cheese. Clog that sucker with cholesterol."

She almost laughed at that—at his mercurial shift from taciturn antagonist to affable advocate—but if she laughed she might cry, and she absolutely wasn't going to let that happen.

"How good are you?" she asked point-blank, bringing his head up from the counter where he was cracking eggs in a bowl.

The sudden silence was so huge it felt like a physical presence in the room, electrifying the air with its energy.

Before her eyes he transformed from Mr. Sensitivity to stone-cold killer.

"No one's getting past me, Jillian."

The look of him stopped her heart while relief vied for equal billing with an unexpected compassion. What had he been through, she wondered, that he'd have no qualms about doing whatever it took to protect her, including killing for her if he had to?

She looked from him to her hands, then back to him again. "You don't even want to be here."

How was that for irony? This morning she'd been figuring the angles on ousting him from her penthouse and her life. Now she was terrified he'd run as fast and as far as he could. And the real kicker—she wasn't sure which frightened her more: losing the bodyguard or losing the man.

The man who didn't even like her.

"I've been a lot of places I didn't want to be." He held her gaze. Made sure he had her undivided attention. "It's never stopped me from doing the job. This is no exception. And the fact that you don't want me here changes nothing. I'm not going away until this threat goes away," he added, driving his message home. "So, like it, hate it, like me, hate me, it doesn't matter.

"Now I'll say this one more time so there's no question.

No one is getting past me. No one is getting to you—got it?"

Yeah. She got it. More important, she believed him. He'd protect her with his life.

As she watched him—her protector who made a mean omelet—she prayed to God it wouldn't come to that.

For the first time since she'd seen those cold blue eyes staring back at her Friday night, she worried about someone other than herself.

. . . The Little Birds swarmed overhead like marauding mosquitoes laying down air cover for the Black Hawk orbiting over the drop zone. Nolan's Rangers dangled from the Hawk's belly on thick ropes. Their squad was to rendezvous with the ground convoy that was moving fast toward the target block, and it was taking too fucking long to off-load. Finally, thank you, Jesus, the helo burped out the last of his men.

Nelson roped down blind, his boots hitting the ground as rotor wash whipped up a cyclone of Iraqi sand.

"Go! Go! Go!"

He grabbed the young Ranger by the shoulder and hunched over, herded him at a zigzagging run toward the bombed-out house where the rest of his team waited for him to call the next shot.

A fierce pocket of resistance had been playing havoc with the locals and the U.S. forces stationed in the little village north of Mosul. Two marines and an Iraqi interpreter had taken hits in the last twenty-four hours. His squad was to take them out in a surprise attack under cover of darkness.

Only the surprise had been on them. They'd dropped into the middle of the biggest game in town and it looked like every tango, fedayee, and Ba'ath Party straggler within a hundred miles had crawled out of his spider hole to play.

The fire flash from an RPG had him glancing up at the Black Hawk. The grenade's smoke trail zipped through the air toward the chopper. He waited for the ear-popping explosion, but the ordnance missed its mark. The big bird roared off without a scratch while the volume of firepower on the ground went Hollywood and what seemed like a hundred shouted orders crashed through his headset from Combat Control twenty clicks away.

When they finally reached the abandoned house, he shoved Nelson through the door so hard the lance corporal went sprawling face-first onto the dirt floor.

"Ke-rist, Sarge," the Ranger sputtered, spitting sand and hauling himself to his feet. The kid grinned, his white teeth shining in the dingy dark. "A gentle nudge would have—"

Nelson never finished his sentence. He dropped his M4 and clutched both hands to his throat. Rivers of red gushed through his fingers.

His eyes widened. In confusion. In shock. Then in haunted awareness that he was as good as dead as his life pumped out through his fingers.

"Ramirez!"

The medic was at Nelson's side before his knees hit the ground, but every Ranger there knew the doc could do nothing for him. That much blood meant only one thing. A round from a sniper rifle had severed the Ranger's jugular.

"Mom." The single word gurgled out with the blood bubbling between Nelson's lips.

Minutes later, his heart quit beating.

Inside the building, his team stood or knelt in stunned silence. It could have been any one of them . . . and to a man, they knew it. Every Ranger felt the relief, felt the guilt, felt the overwhelming sense of their own mortality. And every man—some, like Nelson, little more than kids—thought of Mom and home.

Outside, the first of the Humvees barreled by, their fifty-caliber turret guns striking fire.

It was Nolan's cue to haul ass.

"Move out," he ordered snapping his men out of their flat-eyed shock. "Now! Heads down! Let's go!" ...

Nolan lay in the dark, his hands crossed behind his head.

He was wide awake. Had been for hours, watching the ceiling fan circle round and round in the shadows as that night played over and over in his mind with the same torturous slow motion. Tonight it was the night north of Mosul. Other nights Tikrit. Still others the hellholes in Afghanistan.

He wondered if this was how it was for his dad. Hell, for Ethan and Dallas. They'd all seen their share of combat. They didn't talk about it. None of them did.

So, was it there for them, too? Every night? Rain or shine? Regular as clockwork? *Just like Old fucking Faithful,* he thought caustically. The sun went down. The nightmares started. And how convenient. He didn't even have to be asleep anymore to relive them.

He turned his head, glanced through the dark at the clock. Four thirty-five a.m.

All these months later, was Nelson's mother awake? His father? Was the silence in their nights as loud as the silence in Nolan's?

Did they try to imagine the death scene that he saw as clearly as the digital read on the clock by the bed? Did they wonder exactly where their son had been when he'd breathed his last breath? If he'd felt pain? Who had been with him? Who among them had been friends? Did they understand that he'd been a well-trained stand-up soldier who'd had the bad luck to get bought by a golden BB? A lucky shot.

Would they care that the children living in that village now went to school? That their son had died so those children might grow up to be educated, to someday lead their country deeper into democracy? Or to grow into American-hating jihadists?

He sat up, weary to the bone. Weary of the wars he'd

fought. Weary of the death he'd seen. Weary of the need for it all. And for the need for boys like Nelson to die in the name of freedom.

Feet on the floor, elbows on his knees, he dragged his hands through his hair and fought a fierce impulse to call Sara. Sara . . . whose husband *had* returned from Iraq. And died anyway.

Nelson's death haunted him. As did the others'. Steubbing. Gonzalez. Brave men who had died doing what they believed in. Brave men under his command. Soldiers, who had been as well prepared as he could make them. While he mourned them, he couldn't have saved them. War, after all, was war.

Will was a different story.

Will had been a soldier, too. He'd made it home from Iraq.

Nolan should have seen it coming. He'd known Will had been wrapped tight. Even after they'd shipped home to Fort Benning, he'd had that look about him. That glazed-eyed intensity. It's what made him a good soldier, training hard over and over until he functioned on muscle memory and guts. What he hadn't done was recognize that Will hadn't pulled away from the edge once they were back stateside.

"You know what pisses me off?" Will had stated as much to himself as to Nolan the second day they were home. "Stupid people. Stupid people doing stupid things."

Yeah. Nolan had understood. All you thought of for months was coming home. Then you got there. It should have been so simple. But it wasn't. Like Will said. People were stupid. They asked stupid questions.

Did you kill anyone? What did it feel like?

Christ. What kind of a thing was that to ask?

"And crowds," Will had continued. "I hate crowds . . . and people wanting me to get in touch with my feelings. What kind of bullshit is that?"

It had been the night after they'd all sat through what the

soldiers jokingly referred to as the "don't beat your wife briefing session" all personnel were required to attend to help them deal with combat stress and readjustment when they returned home.

Will hadn't beaten his wife.

He'd shot her instead. And then he'd killed himself.

Now the boys had no daddy. Sara might never recover and Will—whom Nolan should have saved—was dead.

He walked slowly to the bathroom, flicked on the light. The tap water was cold. He cupped his hands and brought it to his face.

Finally, he straightened. Looked at his reflection in the mirror.

Down the hall, someone else counted on him to stay alive.

And the man who stared back at him—hollow eyed, combat weary—despite his earlier convictions didn't know if he had what it took to keep her that way.

12

"You seem distracted, Jillie."

Her father's voice jarred Jillian away from her little side trip to the debacle at Mar-A-Lago last night and back to the moment. They were at Golden Palms, the Kincaid Palm Beach estate. Having lunch.

From one nightmare to another.

With a bracing breath, she glanced up from her soup plate and felt immediate guilt when she saw the concern in her father's eyes. His biggest sin was caring too much. And sometimes she felt her biggest failure was in not forgiving him for it. It ranked right up there among her feelings for her mother.

She never knew which Clare Kincaid she would find—the woman who sometimes took to her bed with a sick headache, then fell into the depths of despair, or the belle of the society ball.

Today seemed to be one of her mother's good days. She was as polished as the silver, as sparkling as the crystal elaborately gracing the table in the formal dining room that had been the norm from the time Jillian had memories.

"The staff talks," Clare had tsked in annoyance when a twelve-year-old Jillian had asked if, just once, they couldn't eat off paper plates in the kitchen.

Social appearances were everything to her mother. In her late fifties, with jewel green eyes and perfectly coiffed red hair, Clare Kincaid was very beautiful in a fragile, porcelain doll sort of way.

"Jillie, sweetheart. Are you all right?" her father pressed, the crease between his eyes deepening to a furrow.

Realizing she'd drifted yet again, Jillian forced a smile for his benefit and made another stab at the soup, the second course of today's elaborate luncheon.

"I was just thinking how nice it was of Kenneth to make the asparagus soup for me. It's delicious, as always. Please tell him it's excellent. I guess I'm going to have to break down and get the recipe."

Which, of course, was ridiculous, but it was the best she could manage at the moment. Her idea of cooking was programming the microwave to reheat takeout.

"Consider it done, dear." Her mother smiled at her prodigal daughter. "Although if you came home more often, you could have it any time you want. It's such a nice surprise to have you here, Jillian. We don't see enough of you anymore."

They wouldn't be seeing her today if she and Garrett hadn't been summoned to Golden Palms via an early-morning phone call from her father. To put it in Garrett's vernacular, she had wanted to take a pass. He'd pointed out that since she didn't cut his paychecks and her father did, lunch with the folks was now on her Sunday agenda.

Home sweet home. All ten acres and eight thousand plus square feet of cold, palatial elegance, tropical gardens, and lushly landscaped pools. The ocean estate was a monument to her father's publishing success, her mother's ticket to Palm Beach society Goddess status, and the source of some of Jillian's worst memories—the past two weeks notwithstanding.

God. Her life was being threatened and here she was, bemoaning her bad luck at being born a poor little rich girl. How pathetic was that?

Someday she swore she was going to get a handle on the mix of love and guilt and resentment that always accompanied her infrequent visits home. She set one foot inside and all the years of her father's dominance smothered her; she felt plagued anew by the fluid state of her mother's mental health.

Enough. She wondered how Garrett was holding up. He didn't strike her as a man who would be overly impressed or intimidated, but Golden Palms could be daunting. So could one of her mother's overblown lunch productions. And then there was the double threat of her parents together and the dynamics of one of their dysfunctional family gatherings.

She glanced at him across the table. Talk about dysfunctional.

She wasn't sure what she'd expected when she'd met him at the coffeemaker this morning, but it hadn't been such an abrupt about-face from last night. Notably absent was the nice guy who had appeared genuinely concerned about her frame of mind. She'd been a mess over the new threat. Such a mess, evidently, that he'd stretched his limits and actually acted human toward her. He must have used up his quota, though, because whatever notion had prompted him to make nice had vanished along with the omelet he devoured while the best she managed was to push her food around her plate before quietly excusing herself.

He hadn't said anything, but he'd watched her, thoughtful and somber, as she walked away and shut herself in her bedroom.

Today she could see Garrett's act for what it had been. A smoke screen.

The real Nolan Garrett was back. Stoic, surly, and arrogant. Fine. OK. She got it. He had a job to do. She could appreciate that he was a professional and needed to maintain a professional distance to do it. As far as that went, she had a job to do, too: come out of this alive. Regain control of her life. She had a better chance of doing it if she kept her wits about her—which meant she needed to ignore as well as deny both her unwanted attraction and what she now accepted was a mandatory dependence on him. Thanks to him, it was a lot easier to manage now that he'd reverted back to full "jerk" mode. Kind, considerate, and cooking in her kitchen was more than she'd signed up for.

So was the sound she'd heard coming from his bedroom late last night when she wandered into the kitchen for something to drink. It hadn't been a shout exactly. More like a tortured groan.

She'd forgotten about it until this very moment. Forgotten that she'd walked to his closed door, placed her fingers on the knob, and almost gone to him to see if the same nightmares that had awakened her had roused him as well.

Not likely. A man like Garrett no doubt had his own set of demons that haunted him.

"What is it you do, Mr. Garrett?" Clare Kincaid asked with distant politeness, her question making Jillian aware that her thoughts had wandered yet again.

"Nolan is an associate of mine," her father interjected.

Her father exchanged looks with both Jillian and Garrett. He'd made it clear her mother knew nothing about the threats and he wanted to keep it that way. For everyone's sake, Jillian was grateful. For all of her mother's concern about decorum, she could be capable of melodrama and theatrics that would give an Italian opera a run for its money.

"And yet he's here as Jillian's guest," her mother speculated, her tone relaying the fact that she may have accepted Garrett at her table, but the jury was still out on whether he belonged there.

While Garrett wore his trademark black—sans holster and gun—Jillian had opted for yellow capris and a floral print tank top. In contrast, her mother sat at the far end of a huge polished mahogany table, pearls at her throat, stunning in gray watered silk, her hostess smile gracious but reserved. Her delicate elegance was the perfect complement to Jillian's father's commanding presence.

"And how did the two of you meet?"

"That was my doing, Clare." Jillian's father touched a napkin to the corner of his mouth, jumping in again to run interference.

At sixty-two, Darin Kincaid was still an attractive man. His hair was silver gray, his body toned and tan. But it was his eyes—seascape gray and hard as tempered steel—that held your attention. Through them shone not only his shrewd intellect but the full measure of his commanding strength and power.

As far as Jillian knew, he had only two weaknesses. Her mother was one; she was the other.

"Your doing, dear?"

"I'm trying to convince Nolan to write about his Afghanistan and Iraq experiences and publish them with us. I thought perhaps Jillian could charm him into consenting."

Jillian had wondered how he would explain Garrett.

"Oh, you're a writer then," Clare continued. "How fascinating. And what part, may I ask, did you play in those ghastly conflicts? Were you an ambassador?"

"Staff Sergeant Garrett is a soldier. Pardon me. *Was* a soldier. A decorated war hero. He once led his squad of Rangers into a heavily armed Taliban stronghold, eliminated them and the threat to an entire village with little more than courage and hand-to-hand combat."

"Oh. My." Frowning, Jillian's mother regarded Garrett with guarded interest—like one would regard a pit bull on a leash.

Garrett remained stone-faced and silent. Up until this point he'd been holding his own, but now he was clearly uncomfortable. Just as he'd been uncomfortable when Plowboy had started telling tales about his heroics Friday night.

Lord. Had it been just two days ago that he'd dragged her into a biker bar and the middle of a fight? He still owed her for that. And you know what? Now seemed like a good time to extract a little payment. After all, he'd been the one who insisted on coming here today.

"Daddy, I do believe you're embarrassing Nolan with all this talk of heroics." She smiled sweetly, then twisted the screws. "But it's so fascinating. Nolan, please, tell us more."

"I don't think your mother wants to hear any more," Garrett stated, flashing Jillian a tight facsimile of a smile. It was not a plea to change the subject but a threat that she'd better if she knew what was good for her.

She smiled right back, her own message clear: *Fat chance.*

"Well." Her mother, oblivious to the undercurrents and eye contact, considered Garrett with renewed interest. "You *do* speak. I was beginning to think Darin was going to do all your talking for you."

"When given an opportunity, yes, ma'am, I speak for myself."

"And make good sense when you do. This talk of war. It's all rather . . . disturbing, isn't it?"

"And falls far short of civilized conversation," Nolan agreed, casting a victorious smile Jillian's way. "Jillian, why don't you tell us about the current piece you're working on?"

"Oh yes, dear." Clearly relieved that she no longer had to think about messy things like third-world strife, Clare jumped on the opportunity to change the subject, even though she rarely took any interest in Jillian's work. "Do fill us in. Just the other day I was telling Elizabeth Manchester about that little award you received last fall for one of your reports. What was it . . . a Piedmont? No, that's wrong. Help me out here, darling."

"A Peabody. She won a Peabody."

Jillian snapped her gaze toward Garrett when he supplied the information and went on to clarify the award's significance.

"It recognizes achievement and meritorious service in broadcasting."

"Yes, yes. That's it. It was for something you did on children. Car seats, wasn't it?"

"Children's safety equipment in general," Garrett clarified again, and it was all Jillian could do to keep her jaw from dropping.

Interesting that this man she'd known less than forty-eight hours knew more about her work than her mother did. Her mother, of course, was in denial. She still held out hope that Jillian would quit "that horribly pedestrian job" and take her rightful place in the Palm Beach social scene.

As far as Garrett's interest went, there was really no reason to get excited. He'd just been doing his job. Like a good little bodyguard, he'd done his homework and read her file. And deflected the conversation from himself to her. Very smooth.

She lifted a brow. *Touché.*

He accepted her concession with a clipped nod.

"What *are* you working on now, Jillian?"

"Nothing that unusual, Mother. I've been following the story of an amnesiac."

Her mother looked taken aback, then dismissive. "Why, whatever for?"

Another typical Clare reaction. Indifference bred by disinterest.

"His story appealed to me. He's been wandering the East Coast for months, not knowing who he is, whether he has family . . . what he did for a living."

Clare sniffed delicately. "Well, it all sounds a bit tawdry, doesn't it? I mean, what kind of a person can't remember who he is?"

Jillian counted to ten, settled herself. Smiled. "One who sustained a devastating head injury."

Clare rolled her eyes. "And you believe him? That he can't remember anything?"

"For heaven's sake, Mother, why would anyone want to fake anything that traumatic? The man is totally lost. I can't imagine—I can't even *begin* to imagine how difficult it must be for him."

"I suppose you're right," Clare agreed with absolutely no sincerity, "but don't you think your time would be better spent on some . . . I don't know. Some notable project perhaps?"

If she bit her tongue one more time it was going to bleed. "I do news, not society balls."

Her mother scowled. "You have always been such a stubborn child."

"This is an old and familiar argument," her father interjected with a tolerant grin, "but I'm sure we're boring Mr. Garrett. Lunch was delicious, as always, Clare, but if you lovely ladies will excuse us, I want a few private words with Nolan. You must show Jillian your new orchids, Clare."

"That was beautifully choreographed, darling." Clare smiled brilliantly for her husband. "You've averted another mother-daughter quarrel at our guest's expense. I apologize, Mr. Garrett, for our boorish behavior. Come along, Jillian. Your father has dismissed us."

Once the women were out of earshot of the dining room, Kincaid laid into Nolan like a sledgehammer.

"What in the hell happened at Mar-A-Lago last night?"

So much for polish and charm. Kincaid had scraped off the upper crust and trimmed things down to bare bones.

It came as no surprise that Kincaid had a direct pipeline to the Palm Beach PD. Someone must have called him last night after Nolan had briefed Detective Laurens, the officer in charge. He wondered how many heads would roll at headquarters before they found this creep.

Kincaid was fuming by the time Nolan finished recounting the events for him.

"And you call that protecting her?"

It wasn't a question. It was an accusation.

Kincaid had a right to be pissed. Nolan had been so busy keeping his libido under control and dodging Hannah Baylor that he'd let down his guard last night.

"She wasn't in any danger," he assured Kincaid, without making any excuses. "The plan was to terrify her."

"And you know this because?"

"Because this is personal. Whoever is doing this has a very personal ax to grind. They want their little drama to drag out . . . and they want to end it one-on-one."

Kincaid took his measure with one long, hard stare. "So help me God, if so much as one hair on her head turns up with a split end, you won't be able to run far enough fast enough."

Too bad Kincaid had such trouble making his point, Nolan thought half an hour later as he cleared Golden Palms' gates, eased into traffic, and headed back toward Jillian's penthouse.

"So . . . was it good for you?"

Nolan whipped his head toward the passenger seat of his Mustang. Jillian's eyes were closed, the skin around them pinched tight with tension.

"Let's say I have a whole new appreciation for why you opted for me."

"Don't get too bowled over. The lesser of two evils is still an evil."

He'd be lying if he told himself he hadn't started to look forward to her biting sarcasm. "Black Bart, at your service, ma'am."

Christ. After meeting the parents up close and personal,

he understood why she hadn't wanted to run home to the nest to wait out her stalker. Too much exposure to toxic material would eventually cause problems. Too much exposure to those two and she'd end up as bloodless as her mother and as hard-edged as the old man.

Or maybe not. If he'd learned one thing about her, it was that there was more than met the eye. A lot more, which probably explained why she was so different from them. Except in looks. She'd inherited the best of her parents' physical traits, including good bones. She had a backbone strong enough to stand up to the crap they dished out.

He shifted lanes and made a left on Worth Avenue. Kincaid was shrewd, manipulative, and authoritative. And her mother—hell—he honestly wondered if there was a beating heart or living soul behind that plastic, self-serving facade. Even if he hadn't read it in Jillian's file, he'd have known Clare Kincaid was on something. He strongly suspected there was more than depression medication in the mix.

Jillian's heavy sigh had him glancing her way again as he waited for a light to change.

"Sometimes all I have to do is think about Golden Palms and I can barely breathe. It's been months since I sat at that table, yet it felt like yesterday."

She blinked at the traffic without seeing it. He wondered if she was aware she was talking out loud, confiding something personal, and if she'd regret it later when she realized what she'd done.

He kept his mouth shut and drove.

"You can't go home again. Whoever said that has never been to Golden Palms. You can't *leave* home. At least my home never left me." She paused. "No matter how hard I tried to break away."

He stared straight ahead, but from the corner of his eye he saw her pinch her temples between finger and thumb.

She pushed out a humorless laugh. "And yet . . . I love

them. Man. A psychiatrist would have a field day with me on a couch."

Actually, Nolan figured she was pretty sane, considering. And pretty vulnerable, which was a far cry from the way he'd originally had her pegged.

Kincaid was a different story. Aside from demanding a security update and making his expectations clear, he had accomplished something else as well. Today's little stroll down billionaire lane had put things in perspective.

He'd put Nolan in his place. In spades. The term *filthy rich* had taken on a whole new meaning once he'd experienced Kincaid's dynasty up close and personal. He would never be able to comprehend that kind of wealth. Hell, they probably spent more on floral arrangements in a month than he'd made in an entire year in the army.

By the time he and Jillian made it back to her penthouse, Nolan had himself mired in some very salient facts. He'd never be anything but a workingman—albeit a reluctant one at the moment. He was strictly blue-collar, low-rent, low-brow. Up until the day his brother had roused him out of his scotch-induced stupor, he'd been a washed-up Ranger . . . a bum drifting toward alcoholism with nothing to show for his life but a violent past and a volatile future. A future that at last look stretched only as far as his current assignment.

All of that led to a more than obvious conclusion. An assignment was all Jillian Kincaid would ever be to him. When she'd sought him out across the room last night, when she'd latched onto his hand like he was the one thing, the only thing, she needed to make her feel safe, he'd forgotten that. He'd let it become personal.

In that moment, in his twisted-up head, he'd let himself think there could actually be something more between them. What a dumb fuck. Women like her were so far above him in social and financial status, it gave him nosebleeds just thinking how high he'd have to climb to breathe the same air. And he'd actually entertained thoughts of making it with her in the sack? Not in this lifetime.

But here was the real kicker. He'd come into this job despising everything she stood for. Yet in the past forty-eight hours those very things he'd disdained—the poise, the polish, the princess aura—he now respected.

He hadn't wanted to like her, either. But there it was. After seeing where she came from, what she'd made of herself, *by* herself in spite of it, he felt guilty as hell. She could have coasted through life, but she'd chosen the hard way.

She didn't deserve his grief. And she sure as hell didn't deserve the half-baked effort he'd been putting out protecting her. He'd made her a promise last night. He'd told her that no one was getting past him to get to her. He'd meant it. He'd meant it for the same reason this psycho meant to kill her. He'd let himself become personally involved. Despite his best efforts.

Personal wouldn't keep her safe. Disconnecting would.

As of now, that's exactly what he would do. As of now, he had his head firmly extracted from his ass.

In order for him to do the best job that he knew how to do, he had to get back to basics. He wasn't her friend. He wasn't her sounding board. He wasn't her latest roll in the sack.

Jillian Kincaid was a job. Period.

And he was a eunuch.

He didn't see her. He didn't smell her. He didn't want her.

He was her protector. Her bodyguard. Nothing more. Nothing less.

Jillian scowled across her kitchen counter toward the living room where her bodyguard sat on her sofa in brood mode.

"You want to tell me what's going on with you?" she finally asked, walking into the living area with a glass of wine.

He looked up from the notes he'd spread out over the top

of her coffee table. Scowled. "What's going on is that I'm working."

"Working. Right. Do you realize you haven't said a word in two hours?"

Even when he responded, he didn't bother to look at her. "Wasn't aware I was being timed."

That did it. "Why are you acting like this?"

He finally glanced up from his precious list of suspects, his blue eyes bored and burdened by her presence. "How do you want me to act?"

"Oh, I don't know . . . maybe like a human being?"

He shot her a look. "Must have missed that memo," he said, and went back to scribbling on his yellow pad.

"You've got a rule or something that says we can't be civil to each other?"

He expelled a big put-upon sigh. "Look, if you want professional bodyguard service, you get me. You want warm fuzzies and adoration? Get a dog."

She just stood there. Livid. Shaking with fury. And confusion. And more than a little hurt.

"Was there something else?" he asked with barely a glance, his tone annoyed and dismissive.

Dismissive. In her home.

"Yeah, there's something else. Get your damn root beer off my coffee table before it leaves a mark. And do something with that gun. I'm tired of seeing it laying around."

Mature woman that she was, she stormed off to her bedroom and slammed the door behind her. After a few minutes of grumbling and grousing she booted up her laptop, plopped down in the middle of her bed, and tried to work on her Forgotten Man piece, wishing like hell she could figure out what made Garrett tick, disgusted with herself for caring. He was exactly what she'd pegged him for the first night she'd seen him. A son of a bitch.

With a growl, she shut down her computer, picked up her phone, and punched in Rachael's number.

"We're best friends, right?" she said without preamble when Rachael answered.

"OK," Rachael said, her tone leery. "The last time you opened a conversation with those words, we were sixteen and we ended up grounded for six weeks."

"Yeah, well, what I've got in mind would net us more like fifty years to life."

"Let me guess. Still having trouble with the bodyguard?"

Jillian had called Rachael Saturday afternoon, filling her in on her new bodyguard, including the way he'd scared her half to death, dragged her to a biker bar, and manhandled poor Lydia.

"I don't get this guy, Rach," she whined, aware that she was whining and not caring to do a thing to curb it.

"Get him how?"

Jillian flopped to her back on the bed, stared at the ceiling in disgust. "For starters, he's rude, intrusive, arrogant, and crude. And those are his good qualities. When he's not bossing me around, he's as stoic as a damn monk. And he drinks root beer. *Root beer.*"

"Well, for sure, he ought to be flogged for that," Rachael said with a laugh. "But what about the important stuff? You never did tell what he looks like. Are we talking Hector like in real life or Kevin Costner like in the movie?"

"Hector? No. Not Hector. He's too pretty for his own good, if you want to know the truth."

"Pretty? Did you say pretty?"

"Well . . . yeah. And OK, not pretty. He's too rough around the edges to be pretty. Look—it doesn't matter what he looks like. What matters is that he's making me crazy."

"Is he doing his job?"

"To a fault."

"So it's a matter of crowding you?"

"It's a matter of I don't like him. And he doesn't like me."

"And that's important to you? That he like you?"

"Yes. No." Jillian didn't like where this was going. She sat up. Lifted a hand. "I mean, I just don't get the man. One minute he's supportive and sympathetic; then the next he's AWOL in every way but his physical presence."

"And his physical presence is what's giving you trouble."

"Yes. No," she backpedaled again, not liking it that Rachael might be a little too close the truth. "Quit putting words in my mouth. And quit laughing. It's not funny."

"Oh, sweetie. It *is* funny. I've never seen you this flustered over a man."

"I am not flustered. I'm angry."

"At yourself."

"OK. At myself. But at him, too. I don't like it that he has this effect on me."

"Makes you hot, does he?"

"He does not make me hot."

"It's your story. You can tell it any way you want to, but if I was telling it, I'd say you like this guy much more than you want to admit and maybe he's bruised that ego you've managed to protect all these years."

"Thanks so much for that. I'm so glad I called," Jillian said, her voice oozing sarcasm.

"No, you're not. But since you did, here's my advice. Go for it."

"Go for what?"

"For the bodyguard."

"When pigs fly."

Another chuckle on the other end of the line. "OK. You don't like him. Got it."

"Great. Now you're patronizing me."

"Isn't that why you called? To have me sympathize and patronize?"

"I'm hanging up now."

Racheal was laughing again when Jillian hung up the phone.

Nelson's blood. Everywhere, painting the sand black in the night.

An RPG zinged by overhead. Nolan ducked, shrapnel raining down as the grenade hit its target.

The cry of a broken songbird resonated above the roar of the choppers, the earsplitting staccato of the machine guns, the answering fire from an AK-47.

A man screamed. Another fell. And then she was there, running through the carnage.

"Jillian! Go back! Go back!" he screamed at her over and over, but she didn't listen. She ran out into the bomb-pocked street. A hail of gunfire followed her step for step.

"For God's sake get down!"

And then he was running into darkness and shadows and flames. He had to save her. He had to save Nelson . . . had to save Will. But he couldn't get to them. Couldn't get anywhere. It felt like he was slogging through knee-deep sand. Every step he took, he lost ground against the shifting current.

Jillian cried his name, disoriented, confused, her hands reaching for him as an explosion clogged the air with plumes of black smoke that distorted her features, whitewashing them with terror.

Through it, he saw red.

God. More blood.

Jillian's blood.

Too late . . . too late he reached her, knelt by her side in the sand; rivers of blood pooled around him.

"Help me. Save me. You promised to save me."

He dragged her limp body against him; her blood ran warm and pulsing through his fingers. "I tried. Dammit. I tried."

Mortar fire lit up the sky. A shadow fell over them. He

*looked up and into Will's eyes, then Nelson's, hard with ac-
cusation, hollow with pain. "Not hard enough. Not hard
enough for any of us."*

Nolan awoke with a jolt.

Lurched up in bed with a hoarse cry.

Drenched in sweat, his heart slamming like mortar
rounds, he stared into the night and gulped for breath.

"Jesus."

Overhead the ceiling fan turned, cooling his skin, casting
shadows on the walls.

He dragged a trembling hand over his face.

"Jesus."

13

Jillian hated Mondays. Especially when the Monday followed a weekend that included dead birds, lunch with the parents, and a new roommate who had more dark scowls than Tiffany's had diamonds. Oh yeah. And another voice mail from Steven Fowler. It didn't help that Rachael's smarty-pants conclusions rang a little too true—or that Rachael had a better handle on Jillian's reaction to the man than she did.

Yeah, she thought as they pulled into the parking lot at the studio, as bad moods went, the one that had her in its clutches today was the mother of them all. The *grand*-mother. And she couldn't have been happier that Garrett was a handy outlet for her frustration.

He'd shouted in his sleep again last night. She told herself she didn't care what kind of demons haunted him. And she didn't want to know enough about him to feel sympathy or empathy or, God forbid, feel his pain. All she cared about was getting some distance. Which, based on his actions this morning, didn't look like something that was going to happen anytime soon.

She had a good pout going when she shoved through the front door of the KGLO building, her bodyguard breathing down her neck.

"Must you cling like lint?" She enunciated each word through clenched teeth.

"Lint? I was going more for something like tights on a ballerina. Until this is over, just think of me as Lycra."

There were several *L* words that came to mind when she thought of Garrett, but that wasn't one of them. *Louse. Lout. Loathsome.* Yeah. Those words all came to mind. Plus her personal favorite: *lunatic.*

She marched down the hall and jabbed the elevator button doing everything in her power to ignore him. Like that was remotely possible with him looming like a gargoyle.

OK. So she was overreacting. She knew it but couldn't work up enough enthusiasm to take it down a notch. Garrett was making her crazy because *he* was crazy. It was like he had a split personality or something and so far she hadn't seen nearly enough of Nice Nolan, who had made a brief appearance Saturday night, and had seen far too much of Grating Garrett, who, since Sunday, had taken guttural grunts and stone-faced silences interspersed with snide remarks to an intolerable level.

She was confused and at a total loss for this turnaround.

And inexplicably hurt.

Happy, Rachael?

It wasn't that he'd ever make Mr. Congeniality. It wasn't as if she cared what he thought of her, but she'd at least thought they'd found some common ground. Now he was acting like he couldn't stand the sight of her.

If she were being totally honest, that's what bothered her the most. That and the fact that there was something else missing when he looked at her now. Something she was loath to admit she missed. Heat.

Before yesterday, when she'd caught him watching her, she'd felt the air sizzle with awareness. It had made her . . . edgy. Made her a little warm herself. OK. It had made her hot. And it had made her wonder, no matter how often she told herself not to go there, what it would feel like to have all that sexual heat unleashed instead of seized in a stranglehold.

Deep down, she already knew that sex with Nolan Garrett would not be the pristine, polite sex of her limited experience. Sex with Nolan Garrett would be of the messy, hot, and sweaty variety. Sex with him would be incredibly intense.

And way too complicated. So complicated, she'd decided it would be safer to simply be angry with him.

When the elevator doors finally opened, she stepped inside and stabbed the button for the sixth floor.

"You're going to break a nail."

She stared straight ahead. "Your concern is touching."

"I aim to please."

"Then why didn't you wear a jacket like I asked you to? Or find some other way to conceal that gun. You're going to spook the crew."

"In the first place, you didn't ask. You ordered. I only take orders from your father. In the second place, if I wanted the gun out of sight, it would be. As to spooking the crew—I hope they're damn good and spooked. That way they'll keep their distance."

The doors opened and they stepped into the maze of hallways, offices, and sets that made up the TV studio.

Aware of the speculative looks following them as they walked down the hall, Jillian replied to a chorus of "good mornings" while beside her Garrett glared at anyone who came within touching distance. When they reached her office, she tossed her purse into her bottom desk drawer and sat down in her chair. Hard. She wanted to scream, shout, something, *anything* to get a real reaction from him. A reaction that wasn't based on sarcasm or indifference.

She leaned back in her chair, studied him through narrowed eyes. "This is obviously a rhetorical question, but could you possibly *be* any more of an ass?"

If he was conscious of the picture he made leaning a broad shoulder against the doorjamb, his arms crossed over his chest, he didn't show it. He was all lean muscle, bad attitude, and piercing blue eyes. They were a deeper shade of blue in daylight. She'd noticed it yesterday. Tried not to be so hyper-aware of it now.

"Possibly," he said with a considering nod. "If I put my mind to it. Yeah. I probably could."

Translated: try me and see where it gets you.

She rose and walked to her bookcase. When she found the videotape she wanted to edit for tonight's newscast, she headed toward the door, stopping long enough to look over her shoulder and lay down the law.

"Get out of my way. Stay out of my way. I've got work to do."

So much for plan B, Nolan thought as he followed Jillian down the hall at the studio. He decided that even if it pissed her off, he was determined to keep this professional. So far all he'd managed was to act like a complete and total jerk.

Well, there was typecasting and then there was typecasting. He *was* a jerk. And so far, his method of establishing professional distance had been about as effective as teats on a boar.

Except, maybe, for the pissed-off part. Success on that front. Whoa, was she hot.

And hurt, if he read the look in those green eyes right.

He clenched his jaw and steeled himself against an un-warranted punch of regret.

The mission had been accomplished. A necessary mis-sion. He'd seen a certain look in her eyes a little too often since Saturday—a look that hinted she'd had a change of heart where he was concerned . . . that maybe "friends" wasn't so far off the radar scope. That maybe even more could be on the table if he wanted it to be.

That train track led nowhere.

He took stock of the studio and the players surrounding her, any one of whom could be her stalker.

He recognized Diane Kleinmeyer from Jillian's description. Thirty-something with short dishwater blond hair and a perpetual scowl, the producer was tall and lean, all business and hustle. She was dressed in a mannish brown suit and moved like a bulldozer on a twenty-four-hour deadline to level a village. While she was a hard read, Nolan sensed she felt more harassed than hostile when Jillian made short, clipped introductions.

"Bodyguard? Hm. Well, all right then. Let's get this over with." Without taking her eyes off him—and without so much as a "plug your ears"—Kleinmeyer brought the silver whistle dangling from a leather chain around her neck to her mouth and blew.

Wincing, Nolan stuck a finger in his ear, expecting to see every dog within a hundred-mile radius come bouncing into the studio. Not a one showed up; however, every two-legged critter on the floor did. Apparently, the whistle held a lot of sway.

"Listen up, people," Kleinmeyer said when everyone from the grips, to the cameramen, to the makeup artist hustled front and center. Even Grant Wellington sauntered over, albeit looking bored and bothered.

"You all heard about the threats on Jillian's life," the producer stated to the group in general. "We've all been concerned. I'm pleased to introduce you to Nolan Garrett. Mr. Garrett is providing protection for Jillian. So, now you all know as much as I do and we can all breathe a little easier until this is resolved, knowing she has a bodyguard. In the meantime, no gawking and no speculating, OK, people? And, Erica?"

A brunette with long, flowing hair, a come-hither smile, and mocha brown eyes stepped front and center, leading with her breasts. "Yes, Diane?"

"No flirting."

A knowing swell of laughter rippled through the studio.

Erica's smile only broadened, unapologetically acknowledging that flirting was exactly what she'd had on her mind.

"Everyone," the producer continued, "you all just go on about your business. We're on a schedule here. Now let's get back to work."

She turned back to Nolan. "I'm glad to see you're looking out for our Jillie. This is ugly business . . . but do me a favor and keep it low-key, OK? I don't want my set disrupted."

And she was gone, consulting her clipboard, adjusting her headset, and scrambling over cables toward the sound room.

Everyone scattered . . . except for Wellington and Erica, who both made big productions of consoling Jillian.

"You just let me know if there's anything I can do, Jillian," Wellington said, all heartfelt concern and caring scowls.

Nolan disliked the man on sight. Wellington was a Walter Cronkite wannabe without the integrity or the class. His designer suit and one-hundred-dollar haircut couldn't disguise the slime beneath the polish or keep the hair on the back of Nolan's neck from rising. He made a mental note to push Ethan for the report on Wellington.

And then there was Erica.

"Same goes, Jillian," Erica added, her eyes flicking from Jillian to him. She smiled, the message clear: *Name the place and time, tiger, I'm there.* "This is just terrible, but I've got to say, it does have its perks, huh? I mean, had I known bodyguards came packaged like this, I'd have hired one long ago."

From an accessory to a perk. What was it with these women?

"You can have this one," Jillian offered brightly.

"Such a kidder, our Jillian." Firmly clutching Jillian's elbow, Nolan steered her toward the news set and away from Erica, who, still smiling, watched them go. There was something about the woman that, despite her soft brown looks and blatant sexpot aura, said: predator.

"Watch your back around her," he warned in a low voice.

"That's your job."

She'd meant to put him in his place. Instead, she'd unwittingly acknowledged his role. "You're finally getting the picture."

As the day wore on and Nolan took silent stock of the entire motley crew, he decided there were few in the lot who didn't look like ego-inflated potential psycho killers to him. Jillian by both necessity and design had occasion to come in contact with each one. While most were supportive and by all appearances benign, he picked up on a swell of undercurrents that indicated there was plenty of motivation lurking at the studio.

TV news, it seemed, was a highly competitive business.

Wellington, of course, was a given as a suspect. Jillian represented a threat to his fading career. He had both motive and, by proximity, opportunity. To Erica Gray, the hot-wired weather girl, who clearly disliked Jillian but fostered a kiss-ass facade, he added Jody Bentley. Fresh-faced and just out of college with her journalism degree and cosmetic dentistry–enhanced smile, Jillian's weekend fill-in was just a little too perky, just a little too Jody-on-the-spot helpful and solicitous, to be taken at face value. He figured anyone wrapped in that much sugarcoating was probably hiding a jawbreaker underneath. Plus, she most likely wanted Jillian's job. Who knew what she would resort to, to get it?

Lydia remained a puzzle. She arrived around noon after her journalism class and made herself available to Jillian as well as anyone else who needed her services. By late afternoon, she'd breezed by them for about the hundredth time, regarding him with shy smiles and giving him a wide berth. She always seemed to be hovering at Jillian's side, ready to do this or go for that, always quick with a smile when Jillian asked her opinion on a line of copy or the slant of an article.

"Ever notice the way she follows you with her eyes?" Old eyes, he thought, for someone so young.

Jillian blinked, then followed his gaze to Lydia, who was hustling to the coffeepot. "Forget it," she said. "Just leave her alone."

"What's the story with her anyway?" he asked, ignoring Jillian's dismissal and the long-suffering sigh that accompanied it.

"She's just a nice kid with a yearning to make something of herself. Not that it's any of your business, but Lydia had it a little rough growing up; her mom was ill most of the time. She died last year."

"Died how?"

"Overdose."

Ah, so that was the connection and the reason Jillian remained so protective of Lydia. Since Jillian's own mother continued a battle with depression, she could relate to Lydia's situation.

"What about her old man?"

"She adores him. Talks about him all the time. Look, I got to know her over Diet Cokes and sub sandwiches during an eleventh-hour copy edit a couple of months back. Trust me. She's no threat."

Nolan trusted no one, but he had to pretty much agree that Lydia was harmless and figured she just had a bad case of hero worship for Jillian. Still, he'd be anxious to get the background checks he'd had his brothers run on everyone who worked within a stone's throw of Jillian.

The fact was, compared to the others, Lydia appeared to be a guppy in a tank full of barracuda and hammerheads, with Grant Wellington, Erica Gray, Jody Bentley, and a few others prime candidates vying for the lead role in *Jaws*—not the least of whom was Diane Kleinmeyer. He'd seen the producer blow up on the set earlier in a pretty disarming illustration of a loose cannon.

"Spooky little thing, isn't she?" he remarked as Lydia skirted him one more time on her way to wherever it was she went in such a hurry.

Jillian, of course, bristled. "You brutalized her Saturday. How do you expect her to act?"

"I did not brutalize her."

"Well, you didn't exactly welcome her with open arms. And quit scaring her. I've seen you giving her those 'boo' looks just to see if you can make her jump."

OK. So he was guilty. And yeah, he'd been acting pretty juvenile. All in all, it was pretty boring, standing around looking intense and trying to figure an angle on these people. He'd needed an occasional diversion . . . and Lydia was predictably easy to intimidate.

Unlike Jillian.

Whatever momentary terror she'd given into at Mar-A-Lago Saturday night was long gone. She'd sucked it up. Put it behind her.

She'd been all business from the moment they'd set foot in the studio. Cool. Competent. Tuned out to his presence no matter how tight he stuck. A tough cookie was Ms. Kincaid. But cookies have a tendency to crumble. It was one of nature's more stable laws.

Not that she was showing any signs of weakness at the end of a long and grueling day. Standing just out of camera range, he watched as she ended the eleven o'clock newscast with her standard sign-off, looking as fresh as a proverbial daisy.

"Until tomorrow . . . may all your news be good. Good night; I'm Jillian Kincaid for KGLO News."

Until tomorrow, Nolan thought grimly, watching her stack pages of copy and unclip her mike. Yeah. All his news would be good . . . providing he could keep her alive until tomorrow. And providing he could keep her in that little "hands off" niche—where he didn't think about her sex goddess lips, her siren's scent, and her unconscious and earthy sexuality.

By the time they returned to City Place, however, she had him so steamed, there was a pretty good chance he just might kill her himself.

14

"So, you're the youngest."

The oncoming lights from the traffic on I-95 shaded Nolan's face in shifting shadows as they headed away from the studio toward City Place. When he glanced Jillian's way, every angle, every plane, was hard with suspicion.

"The youngest what?"

Jillian smiled. Weary of Garrett's jaundiced take on everyone from her doorman to her makeup artist and incensed over his churlish behavior and overdone intrusion—Lycra her butt—in addition to dealing with several projects she had in the works Jillian made the time to do a little research on her bodyguard throughout the day.

God bless Google and high-speed Internet connections. It led her to a glut of material on Garrett and his brothers, who, she found out, were all ex-military, as was their father. Garrett's sister, Eve, however, had been Secret Service. Interesting.

"Of the Garrett children. Your twin sister, Eve, beat you by ten minutes."

He looked straight ahead, his hands tightening on the wheel. The muscles in his jaw were clenched so tight she wondered if he'd dislocate it.

"Your father was a Vietnam War veteran—a Ranger. Decorated. Went into law enforcement here in West Palm and later retired on partial disability from a line-of-duty gunshot wound to his leg."

In fact, she'd found out that it was after he'd retired from the police department that Wes Garrett had established his private security firm fifteen years ago—E.D.E.N. Security, Inc., E.D.E.N. being, she learned through her research, an acronym for his children's initials, Ethan, Dallas, Eve, and Nolan.

"After he got on his feet again, your father started E.D.E.N—which your oldest brother, Ethan, now runs, along with Dallas and Eve. And now you're a part of it, too."

"I'm not a part of anything. I'm just doing my brother a favor."

"I'm the favor?"

"A damn big one. Where, exactly, are you going with this?"

She looked up from her notes. The man behind the wheel was not a happy man. He didn't like his life laid out like hers had been laid out to him. A wiser woman might have backed off. Instead, Jillian acted as if she hadn't heard him and continued scanning the several pages of notes she'd printed.

She couldn't help it. His background fascinated her. In one interview with the local newspaper she learned that he'd been a high school football jock. When he wasn't drafted by the pros after college, he'd enlisted.

"I love this interview," she went on, knowing she was pressing hot button after hot button but feeling reckless and relatively safe since he was occupied with traffic. Besides, turnabout was fair play. "Direct quote: 'In college I majored in beer, football, and women—not necessarily in that order. After I graduated and I didn't get even a look-see by the pros, I had absolutely no clue who I was or what I wanted out of life except a need to continually test myself. I never wanted to go the military route like my brothers and father . . . but the next thing I knew I was walking into the army recruiter's office on Gun Club Road, signing up and saying good-bye to my cushy civilian life. A few years later,

162 Cindy Gerard

I was a U.S. Army Airborne Ranger. Leaner, meaner, and a helluva lot smarter than when I went in.'"

Jillian could vouch for the meaner part. And the other things she read supported both Jason "Plowboy" Wilson's and her father's claim to Garrett's hero status in both Afghanistan and Iraq. Apparently enamored by the "local boy makes good" and the family connection, one specific newspaper reporter had spent a fair amount of time getting to know Nolan for an article he did a few years ago.

"You want to tell me why you're snooping around in my life?"

That she heard loud and clear. His words were so short and clipped and hard, there was no mistaking his anger. Tough.

"I was curious. I'm curious about something else. Tell me, other than the fact that it was a family tradition, why does a guy with a college degree sign up in the army as an enlisted man? I mean, enlisting would've been a dumb career move, right? With your degree, you could've been a commissioned officer."

Across the front seat she saw his jaw work.

"Or maybe you just thought it would be more fun," she concluded, since he'd closed up like a clam. "More of a personal challenge to be an ordinary grunt? Although, I've got to tell you, I read up on the grueling schedule the enlisted men go through and there isn't anything about it that sounds remotely like fun. Which means your idea of fun and mine are light-years apart."

"And you'd be wise to remember that. For instance, I don't find this fun."

Sometimes, going for the throat was simply the right thing to do. "The shoe doesn't feel so great on the other foot?"

"Ah. So you see this as retaliation because I have a file on you—regardless that it's part of my job to know everything I can about you."

"Just like it's part of my job to find out what makes news. You made news."

"I'm not one of your stories."

No. He wasn't one of her stories. But he'd become someone of great interest to her. Everything she'd learned about him today wasn't pretty. Sure, there was the good stuff, the American hero Army Ranger stuff. And yes, what he'd done—his bravery, his valor—it had all impressed her. But he'd partied hard in college and so she figured he must have a flaw or two in that otherwise perfect military record.

By all accounts, he was going to make the Rangers his career. And then he'd come home from Iraq. He hadn't been back a full week when he put in for separation.

And disappeared . . . until he showed up in her penthouse four days ago.

"You didn't stay a grunt long, though, did you? You became a Ranger a couple of years later."

"If you're going to research, then get it right. I got my Ranger patch a couple of years later. You graduate from Ranger School, you get the tab, but you aren't a Ranger until you serve in a Ranger battalion."

"OK, you served in a Ranger battalion. Then what?"

He let out a breath between puffed cheeks. "You're the reporter. Why don't you tell me?"

"All right," she said agreeably, and referred to her notes again. He'd shipped off to PLDC—Professional Leadership Development Course—where he learned how to be a junior NCO. "You made sergeant, became a team leader, then . . . wait. It's here somewhere." She paged through the papers and finally found what she was looking for. BNCOC—Basic Non-Commissioned Officers Course. He'd aced it. "Eventually you were promoted to staff sergeant. Squad leader, right?"

He said nothing.

"You stayed at that rank for a long time. Stuck with the

Rangers for a long time for that matter. With your record, why didn't you go on to Special Forces? Green Beret or Delta?"

"Maybe I wasn't asked—just like you weren't asked to dig up all this crap."

"Oh, you were asked. You turned them down. Do you ever regret it?"

"I regret a lot of things. Like this conversation."

"Do you regret leaving the army?"

Nothing.

"So why did you leave?"

"You're like a damn dog with a bone, you know that?" He glared at her, then rolled his eyes and swore. "Spending ten years as a Ranger kicks anyone's butt, OK? My knees are for shit, and I was tired of the crap that goes on at Bat and in the regiment."

She waited a second, then went with her instincts, trusting that "sensitivity" factor she relied on. "But that's not why you left."

Whoa. That hit a nerve. His blue eyes glazed over with something that very much resembled pain before they hardened to ice.

"Is there a point to this interrogation?"

She wasn't sure anymore. She'd started out wanting to needle him. Now she just wanted to know . . . more to the point, she wanted him to want to tell her. "Just trying to figure you out."

Another surly silence followed while he took the Okeechobee exit. A few miles later, he pulled into a twenty-four-hour grocery store.

"What are you doing?"

"I'm hungry. That finger food they served for lunch at the station wasn't enough to keep a two-year-old alive, and you don't have any food in your refrigerator."

"I have food."

"One egg and some rusty lettuce. And I'm figuring there's a reason I haven't seen you cook anything yet."

"I can cook."

"Programming your speed dial with the phone numbers of your favorite restaurants does not constitute cooking." He jerked the car into PARK and cut the engine. "Come on. I need some red meat. And you need something to occupy your mouth."

His grip on her arm as he ushered her out of the car and toward the supermarket suddenly felt like more than a guiding hand. Just like his remark about finding something to occupy her mouth felt like a suggestion that made her cheeks hot.

"I take it," she said, hurrying to keep up with him and trying to get a highly improper and highly erotic image out of her mind, "we're not talking about you anymore?"

Nolan cast a covert glance at Jillian as he took two rare rib eyes off the countertop grill and set them on a platter. She sat placidly on a stool at the counter, one elbow on the black granite, her jaw in her palm while she alternately sipped from and played lazily with her wineglass.

Hell. He should have given her wine a long time ago. Since he'd poured her a glass half an hour ago, she'd stopped firing questions at him like bullets. Who knew that when she wasn't scared out of her mind a little alcohol would quiet her down? And who knew she'd have the balls to dig into his past . . . or the savvy to uncover what she had?

Her little fishing expedition—or witch hunt if you're splitting hairs—had caught him off-guard. He didn't like having his life story rolled out like a length of newsprint— even though he had to admit, his opinion of her had grudgingly ratcheted up yet another notch. Obviously, she'd made it as far as she had in the business on her own merit. Anyone who could dig up that much dirt in that short order couldn't be half-bad as an investigative reporter.

"Soup's on," he announced, carrying the platter and a salad bowl to the table.

She roused herself with a slow blink, as if she'd forgotten he was even there. Finally, she sort of spilled off the bar stool and with her wine in hand walked barefoot to the table. "Why root beer?"

He watched her settle herself in her chair. One of many mistakes he'd made so far. She'd ditched her white jacket and heels the minute they cleared her penthouse door. Just his luck, the only thing she was wearing besides a short white skirt that showed way too much pale, bare leg was a skimpy little coral pink top with straps as thin as spaghetti. Hell, he didn't know what it was called—a camisole, maybe. The only thing he knew for sure was that it was as sheer as silk and as sexy as bare skin. And the woman who had designed it had a deep and abiding insight about what brought a man to his knees.

Besides all the subtle shifting going on beneath it when she moved, her breasts pressed against the watery fabric; her nipples were as prominent as pencil erasers.

"Hel-looo?"

He dragged his gaze away from her chest to her face when he realized she was talking to him. "What?"

"Why root beer?" she asked, and he realized she was repeating a question.

He sat down, settled himself, and grabbed a steak knife. "Because I'm on-the-job."

"And?"

He angled her a look. "And because I like the real stuff too much."

"Hm." She considered him, sipped more wine. "I figured you more for a hard-liquor kind of guy."

"That, too," he said, slicing into his steak.

"Meaning you drink it or you like it too much?"

"Yeah to both. Eat. No more questions."

Absolutely no more questions. If she kept hammering away like she had in the car on the way back from the studio, he'd end up spilling his guts just to shut her up. And that was the last thing he wanted to do. So far, since she hadn't brought up the incident at Fort Benning, she must have missed his connection to Will. She didn't know about how he died. More specifically, she didn't know why he'd died. And she didn't know that when he'd DX'd out three months ago he'd launched a full-scale romance with the bottle.

"Did you know that you sometimes shout in your sleep?"

Her question hit him like a gut punch. He froze, somehow managed to keep his gaze from cutting to hers, then very methodically made himself resume chewing. After he swallowed, he snagged his root beer and cast a benign glance at her over the top of the bottle.

"I've heard you. In the night," she continued softly.

When he said nothing, her green eyes, like her voice, softened with something that could have been compassion.

"Nightmares?" she added with a gentleness completely at odds with the feelings burning in his gut.

He drew a steadying breath, let it out. "You just don't know when to quit, do you?"

She sipped more wine, then leaned forward, elbows on the table. Holy mother of God. The pose deepened her cleavage and all he could think about was how soft and warm and wonderful it would feel to bury his face there in the middle of the night when he woke up to the sound of men screaming and evidently did a little screaming himself.

"Occupational hazard," she said, oblivious to the heat in his eyes. "It's what makes me a good reporter."

There was nowhere to go here. Jillian Kincaid and her unending questions pissed him off to the point where he could cheerfully throttle her, and yet he couldn't stop thinking about her breasts. And that incredible mouth. God. She was chewing on her lower lip, looking at him like he was a puzzle she was trying to figure out. He wanted to do a little chewing, too. Start with her mouth, work his way to her nipples, then delve between her thighs and just feast until his tongue was so saturated with her taste and texture—

"Snooping into other people's lives makes you a good reporter? In my book," he said, countering with as much anger at himself as with her over the way he always teetered on the brink of self-control around her, "it just makes you stupid."

She blinked, amused. "Stupid?"

"You're tiptoeing into territory where you don't want to tread, and yeah, you're too stupid to realize it. Just like you're too stupid to have figured out by now that you're making yourself way too accessible and way too vulnerable to attack."

"Whoa. You're movin' too fast for me, cowboy. From nightmares, to my questionable intellect, to accessibility. You wouldn't be trying to change the subject again now, would you?"

"What I'm trying to do is rattle your cage hard enough to open you up to seeing the light. I've bided my time, thinking you'd come to your senses, but all you want to do is play games. So let me lay it out for you. You need to take some time off. Go home to Golden Palms. Let the police find your stalker while you lay low."

And get the hell out of his sight.

"Lay low? What happened to 'Don't let them get you running'? 'Don't let them get you scared'?"

"There's a difference between running and protecting yourself. There's a monumental difference between fear and common sense." And there was a difference between a death threat and the threat he represented. One could leave her dead. The other could leave *him* dead. If her father didn't kill him, he'd do himself in for being such a dumb fuck.

"Why don't you just make it easy on everyone involved and hole up until this all blows over? For once, use your head."

She tilted the head in question, shot him a pinched frown, and with that one look made it apparent she had no intention of taking his advice.

He shook his head. Stubborn damn woman. "Oh wait, listen to me. Suggesting you use your head. I forgot. You have a tendency to not always use the best judgment anyway, right? Take Steven Fowler, for example."

Crap. He hadn't meant to hit her with that one again. But she ticked him off, dammit. Evidently, so did the idea of her and Fowler together, because the thought lay like a slug in the back of his mind—until he burped it out again.

"What I meant to say was, maybe some of your past mistakes should clue you in that you don't always make the best decisions and you ought to be listening to well-intended advice."

Her frown worked its way into a glare. "Well-intended? There isn't a well-intended bone in your entire body, and that crack just proved it."

She studied his face for a long time, then, instead of blasting him, asked what he was soon to discover was a very calculated question.

"Why do you keep bringing up Steven Fowler?"

Because he was jealous of the bastard, that's why. And because it bugged the hell out of him that she'd slept with a married man. "He's a suspect. So is his wife."

"Really? I think you bring his name up a little too often and then back away."

Straws. He had nothing left but straws to grasp. Which was what he'd been doing when he brought Fowler into the conversation. "Bothers you, does it, to think your ex-lover could be responsible?"

"What bothers me," she said, looking like she'd just had a blindfold lifted from her eyes, "is that you can't admit the truth."

All-knowing and infinitely pleased with herself, she sat back in her chair, considering him.

With a smug smile, she picked up her glass and wiggled it at him. "Why didn't I see this before? You've been so certain that I—oh, how did you put it?—*want to get in your pants* that I totally underestimated how badly *you* want to get in *mine*. It bugs you to think Fowler's been somewhere you haven't."

When she laughed—evidently in response to the look on his face—he wondered if he was really that transparent.

Evidently, he was.

"Oh, this is too rich. Mr. Big-bad-nobody-messes-with-me Garrett has his tail in a knot because his hormones are giving him fits."

He sneered. "Hate to break this to you, princess, but you've got an inflated opinion of your sex appeal."

She looked him up and down. Her eyes told him that she knew she was flirting with fire. Just like her smile told him she was feeling reckless enough to strike the match anyway. "Is that a fact?"

His heart double-pumped when she rose and, never taking her eyes off his face, skirted the table and walked up beside him. Close. So close, he could see the pulse quicken at her throat, feel the heat radiating off her body. Smell the erotic scent of rain forest and wine and woman.

"So I don't do anything for you, is that what you're saying?"

He swallowed, fought to appear unaffected by her nearness, as her warm breath whispered against his ear. "You piss me off. Does that count?"

He sat ramrod straight, told himself to think about the weather, the fact that his steak was getting cold, anything but the way Skippy was happily swelling with hope and primed for action. But she generated a little too much heat, moved a little too close, and shot his concentration all to hell and back.

When she ran an index finger in a slow, sensual glide along the side of his clenched jaw, then skimmed it lingeringly down his throat he swallowed back a groan.

When she spread her fingers wide across the skin exposed just above the round collar of his shirt his mouth went dry and he stopped breathing.

And when she flattened her palm against his chest and eased it slowly downward he felt himself slip-slide down the rocky slope toward a bottomless pit of disaster.

When Garrett's hand shot up and manacled her wrist just as she reached his belt, Jillian didn't know if she was relieved or disappointed. She was stunned by the speed of his action. The feel of his hand capturing her wrist made her tremble with anticipation. And fear. And a little too much longing to keep this at the level where the stakes in her game had been all about his control.

She'd been teasing, tempting, letting the wine do a little too much talking, and banking a little too heavily on the notion that she could also use it as an excuse for playing fast and loose with her hands. But he'd just turned the tables on her. The game was no longer just about his control . . . suddenly it was also about hers.

No way was she going to let him in on that little revelation. And no way was he going to best her at a game she'd initiated.

"What's the matter, Garrett? Am I getting a little too close to the truth?"

"What you're getting a little too close to is a spanking."

She blinked at him, wasn't aware that she'd wet her lips until his gaze tracked her tongue there and he groaned.

"Well, my, my, doesn't that sound kinky."

Blue eyes glared up at her. All heat and fury and pure animal lust.

She'd just crossed a dangerous line. And she liked it. How could she be so annoyed by this man and so excited by him? And how could she have let herself believe she could hold her own in any physical contest with him?

Maybe, just maybe, she'd better back a step away from the fire before she got good and truly burned. And she would back away . . . in just a moment. There was something she wanted him to understand first.

"For your information, Steven Fowler is a liar and a cheat, but he's not violent. And to ease your troubled mind, he was never my lover. He never will be.

"And, Garrett," she added silkily, meeting his angry gaze and holding it, "neither will you."

She wasn't sure what she saw on his face—satisfaction, relief, anger, or all three—before the hard line of his mouth turned up in a smirk. "Well, that takes a load off."

Before she could wind up to get royally ticked, he tugged and she tumbled, and the next thing she knew, she was on his lap. His arms banded around her, pinning her arms between them.

She glared into the blue eyes looking down from mere inches away, told herself she was more surprised and angry than she was excited.

She lied.

He smiled. A study in male arrogance and insight. "For the record . . . you're not even a little bit curious?"

She tried to form the word, to say, *No,* but she was too occupied cataloging the scent, the heat, the hardness of him to manage even that one necessary denial.

She must have shaken her head, though, because he laughed. "Me, neither."

Then he lowered his head to nip lightly at her bottom lip. And got down to the business of making liars out of both of them.

Instant arousal. Electric heat. That such a hard, maddening man could have such soft lips and employ such gentle skill that elevated what for all practical purposes was a fairly chaste kiss to a level that went beyond erotic was beyond her comprehension. But he did and more when he covered her mouth with his.

Innocence was not a word she would ever associate with Nolan Garrett, yet the way his mouth touched hers brimmed with it. She'd expected relentless aggression. Ravenous dominance. Instead, he gave her time, gave her a chance to get accustomed to the taste and the feel of him, to experience the tightening of his body beneath hers and prepare for what came next.

With each dip of his head, each buss of his nose to her cheek, each exquisitely tender caress of his lips, he drew out the anticipation, built the urgency until she was squirming on his lap, wishing her hands were free so she could pull him hard against her and take this gentle introduction to a full-blown exploration of lips and teeth and tongues.

It wasn't that she didn't like what he was doing. She *loved* what he was doing. The slow and silky touches belied his rugged strength. The skillful give-and-take was at odds with his aggressive nature. Such gentleness clashed with the image of the hard man she'd come to know. Such tenderness opened him up to emotions he'd tried to convince her he could never feel . . . and yet she was the one who felt raw around the edges.

So raw that when he lifted his head and drew slowly away she followed, silently asking for more, begging for more, needing so much more than this gentle mating of their mouths.

Stone-silent, he watched her face, closed his eyes, then lifted her off his lap.

"Go to bed," he ordered. "Go to bed . . . and stay there."

15

JAW SET WITH STEELY RESOLVE, NOLAN ignored the confusion and hurt flicking across Jillian's face. He made himself dig back into his steak.

Like the world hadn't just rocked.

Like the sky hadn't just fallen.

Only when he heard the last of her hesitant footsteps and the sound of her bedroom door closing behind her did he let out the breath that had backed up in his lungs.

Keep it up, shit for brains. You might just dig a hole so deep, you'll never find your way out.

What the hell had he been thinking? How had he let things get so out of control?

Because she'd made it into a contest, that's how, and stupid fuck that he was, he'd decided he was going to win it. She'd issued a challenge. She'd told him flat out he wasn't getting in her bed. Well, hell. No real *Hooah* backed away from that kind of a dare. What could he do but make her understand that he made that call, not her?

So, he'd set out to teach her a lesson. To make her aware that if he wanted her between the sheets, he could damn well have her begging him to take her there. But the minute his lips touched hers . . . ah, God . . . he forgot about lessons and contests and lost himself in the wonder of her mouth.

Kissing Jillian Kincaid was everything he'd ever imagined and many things he hadn't. He'd expected the heat, but not such sweetness. He'd expected the burn, but not his own meltdown. He'd expected a fight, but she'd responded with guileless invitation.

Defenseless. She'd been absolutely defenseless. This woman who wouldn't run from death threats and tackled corporate corruption had been 100 percent defenseless against him. And it had stunned him into backing off, taking it slow, giving her the time to remember they were at war here. That this kiss wasn't about anything but power and positioning and proving who had the upper hand.

He'd wanted to make her understand that he wasn't anyone she wanted to be messing with. That kissing him had nothing to do with feelings and everything to do with sex. Just sex, because that's what he was about when it came to women. And that's what he'd thought she was about when it came to men.

Fowler was never her lover.

It was the last thing he'd needed to hear and the one thing he'd hoped for. It had been a helluva lot easier to steer clear of personal when he thought the worst of her on that count. In fact, it had been the final barrier and he'd used it to foster animosity and keep his distance.

Now that last bastion of disapproval was gone.

And it was more than enough reason to send her to bed.

Alone.

Jillian scowled at Rachael, who sat directly to her left at their table at the Four Seasons where the two of them met every Tuesday for lunch. Only today a few more players had joined the party.

To Jillian's right Lydia busily consulted her day planner and looked a bit frazzled. Beside Lydia, Nolan sat in all his bodyguard glory, and to his right, Jillian's father, face dark, quizzed Nolan about his beefed-up security measures.

"Wipe your lip, sweetie," Jillian suggested behind her napkin to Rachael, the low drone of the men's conversation covering her comment. "You're about to drool in your pâté."

Rachael grinned, her gaze never leaving Nolan's face. "I'm sorry. It's just . . . well, no wonder you're all a-dither."

"Dither? Where do you get these words?" she hissed under her breath. "And I'm not all a-*dither*."

"Right. And he's certainly not Hector."

No, Jillian agreed, and actually felt a little twinge of regret. Garrett wasn't Hector. If he was, she wouldn't be wondering what had gotten into her last night—besides the fact that she'd drunk too much wine and now had the headache to prove it. The alcohol had also short-circuited her internal wiring and killed a few brain cells. What else could explain what had happened at her dining room table? What else could account for the fact that she couldn't look at the man now and not wonder how hot things would have gotten if he hadn't called a halt to it.

Well, he was cool as a damn cucumber today. You'd never know to look at him that she'd had the equivalent of a nuclear meltdown in his lap. A lap that, by all indications, had been totally onboard with the course they'd set with a kiss the likes of which she'd never experienced in her entire life.

She lifted her water glass, sipped, watching him covertly over the lip.

It was nice to know she wasn't the only one caught off-balance by Garrett's physical appeal. Rachael's response validated Jillian's. Pheromones seemed to ooze from his every pore and no female was immune to them. Even Lydia was rattled around him, although Jillian suspected that had more to do with a substantiated wariness than sex appeal.

It was also nice to see a little life flicker in Rachael's eyes when she watched Garrett. Jillian couldn't help but worry about her friend. Rachael had pretty much checked out last year after the divorce. Brian's infidelities and the callous way he'd flaunted them had taken a toll on her confidence. Jillian would like to personally deck Brian for that. Rachael had fallen into an abyss for a long time. While her work with the Palm Beach society scene and the charities they supported had nudged her back toward recovery, she'd lost her spark.

Garrett seemed to have ignited it. Another sign of recovery. Rachael might be getting some of her confidence back. She was a beautiful woman with her pixie brown eyes, glossy black hair, and a body still as slim and sleek as a model's.

The clatter of crystal and Lydia's dismayed "Oh, damn. I'm sorry" wrenched Jillian's head to her right to see Lydia dabbing frantically at the tablecloth, desperate to sop up the spill.

"It's only water," Rachael said gently when she saw how upset Lydia was. "It's not a big deal."

The younger woman stood, working desperately over the soggy tablecloth. "I can't believe I did that. It was so clumsy."

"Water," Jillian reminded her, stilling Lydia's trembling hands by covering them with her own. "Relax, sweetie."

On a shaky breath, Lydia settled herself. Cut a nervous gaze toward Garrett, then forced a smile for Jillian. "Right. OK then. Did I get you wet?"

"Dry as a desert. Now sit and we'll get someone to replace your napkin."

Across the table, Nolan scowled between Lydia and Rachael while her father resumed their one-on-one conversation.

"Are you OK?" Jillian asked quietly, concerned about

Lydia, whom she'd asked to accompany them to lunch so they could discuss tonight's feature story in the car on the way over. "You seem a little on-edge."

Lydia flushed red and shook her head. "This business with you . . . and whoever is threatening you. I don't know. I guess it's just got me a little rattled."

She watched Lydia's face as she shifted her gaze from her hands to the men and back to her hands again.

"Well, it's got us all rattled," Jillian admitted.

While she tried to ignore the potential danger, while she was *determined* to ignore it, there was no chance of completely pushing it from her mind. It was always there, lurking in the background like a thief prowling the night, disrupting her sleep, stealing her peace of mind. And, evidently, the peace of mind of her young assistant.

"Would you mind terribly if I took off?" Lydia asked.

Nolan's head came up at that, Mr. Suspicious-of-everything-in-the world. Jillian shook her head and turned back to Lydia. "But you didn't finish your lunch."

"I know. But I've got a final in a little less than an hour and I need to do a quick review. Frankly, I don't feel much like eating anyway," she finally confessed with another darting glance Garrett's way.

Poor kid, Jillian thought. Working, studying, worrying— bearing up to Garrett's bullying. No wonder she was so fidgety.

"Here. Take a cab." Jillian dug into her purse for a twenty. "No, I want you to take it," she persisted when Lydia shook her head. "If I hadn't insisted you come along with us today, you wouldn't need the cab fare. You don't have time to argue. Just go. And ace it, OK?"

Lydia grinned shyly and pocketed the twenty. "Not much hope of that, but with a little luck I'll do OK."

With a little luck they'd all do OK, Jillian thought. When

she caught Nolan's gaze, inexplicably soft on her face, however, she wasn't so sure she'd be OK after all.

After days of brooding disdain—both jaundiced and judgmental—she could have sworn she saw approval on his face. It shouldn't have affected her. So why did it feel as if an entire squadron of butterflies lifted off in her stomach?

"So, Mr. Garrett, are you native to the area?" Rachael Hanover asked with one of the many smiles Nolan had been trying to interpret since Jillian had introduced them roughly an hour ago.

"If the area you're referring to is Florida, yes."

It was the first time the socialite had addressed him directly since Jillian had introduced them. Not that there hadn't been a lot of silent communication on Rachael's part. Christ. He'd felt like a piece of prime beef laid out on a butcher block every time she'd flashed her sly smile and flirty brown eyes his way. It wasn't that she was overtly sexual. In fact, he wasn't sure it was sexual at all.

She *was* sizing him up, though. For what, he hadn't yet decided. Rich women. Game playing. The two went hand in hand. At least, his first impression of Rachael Hanover was that she was all about playing games.

Was he a native? she'd asked. They both knew that while the populations of Palm Beach and West Palm were separated by a thin spit of water, an ocean separated them in social and financial status.

Maybe that was her point—to remind him he was rubbing elbows with the hierarchy. To put him in his place? Or to illustrate that he fit in just fine?

Who the hell knew? What he did know was that for a woman who was supposed to be such a good friend of Jillian's she'd seemed a lot more concerned about getting his attention than she was about expressing concern over Jillian's situation.

"Jillian tells me that the two of you go way back," he said, deciding to do a little fishing of his own when Kincaid excused himself to use the restroom.

"Mutt and Jeff," Rachael said with a quick smile. "What she did I did—well, at least I tried to do. Our Jillie was quite the star when we were kids."

"Like you weren't?" Jillian said with a laugh.

Rachael waved that notion away. "Drive doesn't make up for talent, and I fell short in that department."

"Rachael, that's ridiculous," Jillian insisted. "You were good at everything you set your mind to."

"Not good enough. I didn't make the cut, but Jillian made the Olympic team when we were fifteen; did she tell you that?" Rachael asked, lifting her water goblet to her mouth and sipping.

"You'd have made it, too, if you hadn't sprained your ankle the week before try-outs."

"She's too kind," Rachael confided with a smile. "I didn't have a prayer. Just like I could never top her grades or beat her out for the lead when our Thespian Club put on a play."

"Now you're being just plain silly," Jillian sputtered.

"Did she tell you that we even competed for boyfriends?" Rachael laughed at Jillian's horrified look. "Jillian and my ex—may he someday burn in hell—were an item the better part of our third year at college."

"But Brian married *you*," Jillian pointed out.

Rachael rolled her eyes. "Don't remind me. I was going to be the next F. Scott Fitzgerald," she said with a self-deprecating smile, "but I gave it up for Brian. Gotta look out for those rebound romances."

There it was, Nolan thought as he listened to Rachael self-denigrate and Jillian build her back up. The "thing" he hadn't been able to put his finger on. The "something" about Rachael that just didn't ring true. For all her posturing otherwise, he'd lay odds she harbored a shitload of resentment toward Jillian.

Kincaid returned to the table then and ended their conversation. But after lunch, as Nolan and Jillian rode across town in the KGLO news van to meet with Jillian's amnesiac, Nolan told himself that if lunch with the old man hadn't gotten him back on-track, then his gut reaction to Jillian's friend Rachael Hanover should have.

He watched Jillian across the seat from him, 100 percent concentration on her notes and the questions she would ask during the upcoming interview. Swiping a hand across his jaw, he decided not to bother mentioning his unease about Rachael. He already knew what Jillian's reaction would be anyway. She'd lay into him about unfounded suspicions, clock his IQ in the low double digits for even thinking something so asinine, and no doubt order him to leave poor, fragile Rachael alone.

He watched the traffic roll by out the window, drumming his fingers on his knee. Between their luncheon conversation and a little creative reading between the lines, he now saw the two women's relationship from Rachael's perspective, and it didn't seem quite as hunky-dory as Jillian's.

For instance, at what point does an also-ran turn bitter? At what point does second banana decide on a little retribution? Especially one who was emotionally unstable.

To Nolan, from Rachael's perspective, when Jillian dumped Brian Hanover and he turned to Rachael it stacked up something like: *Finally, I got something she wants. I'm number one . . . at least in Hanover's eyes.*

And now Brian Hanover had "done her wrong" in a very public and very humiliating way. Maybe Rachael blamed Jillian for the breakup. Maybe she blamed Jillian for a lot of things that had gone wrong in her life. And maybe he'd better bump Ethan and Dallas about the report he'd requested on Rachael Hanover to see if there might be some merit to his suspicions.

Hell, at this point, anyone looked good for their bad

guy—including Lydia of the limpid eyes and flutter fingers. And he was checking all possibilities.

"Here we are," Jillian said as the van pulled up in front of a seedy-looking motel on Blue Heron.

Nolan stepped out onto the street and got a good look at the disrepair and general decay of the area. "Nice digs."

Jillian marched ahead of him toward the motel's front door. "Word to the wise: if you need to sit down once we get in his room, make sure it's on a hard chair, no upholstery. I don't want you bringing any tag-alongs back to my place."

He held the door open for Jake and Ramón, the cameraman and the soundman, who lugged their equipment like good soldiers. A roach dropped to the floor at his feet when the door slammed behind them.

"From the Four Seasons to the Roach Motel in under an hour. Dear me. I'm liable to get culture shock."

If Garrett expected her to laugh, he was going to be disappointed. Jillian had other things on her mind.

As they walked the corridor on threadbare carpet to room 414, which John Smith rented by the week, she remembered the first time she'd met with him. Never in her life had she encountered such despair.

"The Forgotten Man."

The title she'd chosen for her piece on him didn't begin to tell the story. This would be their third meeting . . . and she wasn't sure if she could ever accurately relate what she felt when she confronted this man.

Rachael had accused her of letting him become something of an obsession. In a way, she supposed he was. To her way of thinking, however, it was more of an obsessive commitment to tell John's story. In the beginning, she was reluctant to admit, even to herself, that the man's horrible circumstances had touched something inside her. As a journalist, she was supposed to remain removed and objective.

When she'd first approached him, it had been all about the story. All about the news.

On many levels, that now shamed her. She'd always known who she was and what she wanted, and she'd gone after it with unflagging tenacity. She'd been aggressive, competitive, and focused on the brass ring. Her news stories had been a means to an end, platforms to elevate her to the next level in her career.

With John—well, somewhere along the line things had changed. It was no longer about her career. It was about— and God help her if anyone heard her put voice to her Pollyanna thoughts—helping him. It was about making a difference in a life other than her own, for a reason other than her own advancement. It was about a level of integrity she'd never realized was part and parcel of what made a good person as well as a good TV reporter.

But when he opened the door to her knock and his ghost gray eyes met hers with unrelenting nothingness, she honestly wondered if she was fooling herself into believing she was helping him more than she was hurting him.

"How does that make you feel, John? When someone turns you down for a job because you don't have a Social Security number and because you have no ID you can't acquire one?"

Nolan stood quietly in the background, watching the interplay between Jillian and her Forgotten Man, John Smith. He'd been trying for the better part of an hour to get a solid read on Smith's reaction to Jillian's questions. The poor SOB was spooky as hell. Not so much in appearance. There was nothing remarkable about him; he was paper-bag plain as a matter of fact, except for those eyes. Whoever said that the eyes were the windows to a man's soul had never met this man. His eyes gave little away in that department. His lack of emotion was chilling.

So far, Nolan had learned more about Jillian than he had

about Smith. And his respect for her professionalism had hiked up another notch.

She was very careful with Smith. Careful of his feelings and gentle with her questions. Her concern for his comfort was real even as she probed. She cared about him, Nolan had realized early on. Not just as an interesting subject but as a person who had suffered and endured. She approached him not only as a journalist but also as a fellow human being who was concerned for his well-being. She wanted to help him.

"John?" Jillian prodded gently when several moments had passed and he hadn't reacted to her question. "How does it make you feel?"

Smith seemed to come out of his semitrance. "How do you want me to feel?" he asked, staring not at Jillian but at the wall behind her head. "Angry? Defeated?" He lifted a shoulder, more apathy than reaction. "What's the point? It is the law. I can't fight it. I no longer wish to try."

They were the most words Smith had strung together since they'd arrived for the interview. Nolan could see the excitement warring with patience in Jillian's eyes. She was hoping it might be the beginning of a breakthrough.

Her gaze steady on Smith, she inched forward on the wooden chair, leaning closer to him where he sat on the edge of an unmade bed, feet flat on the floor, hands gripping his knees.

"I understand your frustration—"

"No," Smith interrupted with a sharp shift of his gaze to Jillian. In that instant his mask of indifference melted away in an inferno of rage—a rage he attempted and failed to extinguish with a long, deep breath. "No one can understand, Ms. Kincaid. Do not presume to think anyone—even you— can understand."

Bitterness. Anger. Resentment.

Nolan felt them full bore—directed at his circumstances? Or at Jillian for reminding him of them?

"Then help me understand, John," she said after a long silence. "Share with me what it does to you."

"Share what it does to hear someone call me John and know it's not my name?" His voice rose. "Share what it does to see my reflection in a window when I walk by and see only the face of a stranger?" The hands resting on his knees clenched into fists. "Tell me what you want me to say? I'll say it. Then you can leave."

Adrenaline shot through Nolan's blood like a bullet. He moved to Jillian's side as a silence, heavy with acid rage, hung in the aftermath of Smith's words.

From apathy to activist in one easy step. Smith was pissed. His ghost gray eyes fairly burned with anger.

"This is over," Smith announced abruptly.

"I've upset you."

Nothing.

"John—you do realize I'm trying to help you?"

Christ. Why didn't she just give up on him? Everyone in the room, including Smith, knew the man was a lost cause. Except her.

"You need to go now."

Jillian's shoulders sagged in defeat. "All right," she said. "When can we schedule another time?"

The venom welling up in Smith's eyes when he connected with hers had Nolan moving between them. Fast.

"We're done." Smith glanced at Nolan, then Jillian. "Don't come back."

Smith rose and walked to the door. Where he stood after swinging it wide open and waited for them to leave.

"I'll let you think about it for a while, OK?" Jillian asked in one final attempt to change his mind. "Just think about it. I'll be back in touch."

Garrett sat on the sofa in her penthouse, rolling a bottle of root beer between his palms while she stared out the windows overlooking Lake Worth. They'd returned to the station hours ago and Jillian had done her evening newscast. And all she could think about was John Smith.

"He hates me, doesn't he?"

Garrett was quiet for a while before responding.

"Smith? Probably," he said, and for some reason she was grateful he was there, understanding instinctively that she was talking about John Smith, not Wellington, who had been an ass again before and during tonight's live newscast. "Most of all, he hates his life. Hates his circumstances. The void."

"I remind him of everything he's lost."

"Yes," Garrett agreed. "Which places you firmly in the kill-the-messenger category."

She crossed her arms, cupped her elbows in her palms, and shuddered. "I hate what I do, sometimes."

"Because he's started to matter to you more than the piece?"

She looked over her shoulder, regarded him with renewed interest. He didn't miss much, this man who didn't want to engage with her on any level but professional.

"I think it's possible he's harboring some underlying hostility where you're concerned."

He was right, but he was wrong where he was going with this. "John isn't the one threatening me," she said wearily.

He considered her, his face expressionless. "I want to see every note, every piece of tape that's been shot, since you started this."

Of course he did. "Is there any point in fighting you?"

He didn't bother to reply.

She turned back to the window. It had felt so good in the beginning, when she'd first contacted John. It had felt like she'd been helping. And now . . . now she just felt tired.

"You know, you have messages," Garrett said, his voice soft.

She glanced at him and then at her phone. Yeah. She knew. Just like she somehow knew even before she listened to them what she would find.

"Go ahead," she said, then waited in tense silence as he rose, walked to the answering machine, and pressed the PLAY button.

"Delete it," she said dispassionately when Steven Fowler identified himself on the first voice mail.

The second wasn't as easy to dismiss.

It was the same childlike, genderless voice that had delivered the first threat. And the chill it sent through her blood felt like arctic ice.

> *"Humpty Dumpty sat on a wall.*
> *Humpty Dumpty thought he would fall.*
> *He pushed Jillian instead.*
> *Now Jillian is dead.*
> *And the king's men gave her father a call.*
> *Soon, Jillian. He'll be crying over you."*

Jillian closed her eyes, pressed her forehead against the plate glass, and listened through a numbing mist as Garrett dialed the police department, then asked for Detective Laurens.

John watched Mary ease carefully out of bed and limp toward the bathroom. He rubbed his eyes. His head hurt. Jillian Kincaid's interviews cut worse than rusty knives. Abraided like coarse sandpaper rubbing against third-degree burns.

"Do you need an aspirin?"

He didn't bother to look at her. Look at her standing there with blood on her lip and in pain that he'd caused and ask if he needed an aspirin.

He rolled to his side away from her—not knowing if she was savior or Satan. Not caring.

"How did the job go today?" Her voice reached him from the bathroom over the sound of running tap water.

His job. The one she'd gotten for him. Washing dishes on the night shift in a hotel restaurant was demeaning, but it was a job, the first steady job anyone had given him in three months. Thanks to Mary.

He heard her walk back to the bed. Felt her slight weight as she eased down on the mattress beside him and held out two tablets.

"Why do you do this? Why do you come here?"

"Because you need me," she said, stroking her hand over his hair. "Because I need you."

What he needed was to be left alone. To fade back into the void he'd created to escape the pain of reality. The reality— he didn't know who he was and he was beginning to care. The void had protected him from facing it.

"It's OK, baby," she whispered with a tenderness that made his eyes sting.

He rolled to his back again, crossed his arms behind his head, and closed his eyes. Lonely men had hope.

Had he ever felt this lonely?

Mary made him face the despair when she came to him. She made him feel—she and Jillian Kincaid, whose endless questions reminded him how many answers he lacked.

He truly didn't know who he hated more. Himself, for being so weak, Mary, for making him feel both guilty and cruel for using her, or Jillian Kincaid for poking at his wounds with a machette.

Mary said she wanted to share his life. Yet because of her he felt more disconnected and conflicted than ever. How could he share a life that had evolved less than two years ago, when he awoke in a hospital bed with no memory? And how, after the physical intimacies he and Mary had shared, could he feel more emotion toward Jillian Kincaid?

He hated Jillian Kincaid for her endless questions.

And he had to do something to stop her.

Mary turned off the tap, ran cold water on the washcloth, then pressed it to her face. In the other room, John slept. Tormented but spent. She understood torment. Had lived it, begged to be released from it as only a child, helpless and confused, could beg.

She was no longer a child. But she wore the child's scars, inside and out.

Harsh light from the bare fluorescent bulb over the bathroom sink cast garish shadows over eyes red and swollen from crying. She was ashamed. Ashamed of the weakness that had made her give in to the tears. Pain had been a staple in her life for as long as she had memories. So now she asked for it. Expected it. How else could she know she existed?

With John, it wasn't all pain. He could be gentle at times. Giving. It was the gentleness she didn't trust.

But that wasn't why she had come to him. And that wasn't why she stayed.

She dabbed the cloth to a small cut at the corner of her mouth and thought of exactly why she'd sought him out. Why she'd arranged for their first meeting last week to appear to be by chance.

She smiled. *Clever girl.* Then she sobered. It saddened her to use him. She knew his pain just as she knew her own. She, too, had been nothing. She, too, had been no one but not because she'd lost her memory as John had.

Staring at her pale reflection in the cracked mirror, she remembered all too well the loneliness of the little girl who had grown up with nothing.

"Both Jillian and Darin Kincaid will pay for what was done to me," she whispered.

Soon. She sensed the time must be soon. The bodyguard had become an issue. And John, instead of becoming more malleable, was growing more remote. A few more days. She just needed a few more days and Daddy's little darling would be Daddy's little dead darling.

16

headed east on Okeechobee and away from the station.

"I need to check in at E.D.E.N," he'd said.

Despite his machinelike demeanor and Jillian's conflicted emotions, they'd finally reached an unspoken and tentative cease-fire of some sort. Oh yeah, and they'd played a little kissie face in one of her major moments of weakness. Let's not forget that.

As a matter of fact, if it weren't for the elevated concern of the Palm Beach PD over the latest threatening message, Jillian would have spent the bulk of her time thinking about Garrett and the unsettling effect he had on her.

Maybe she was scared stupid.

She pressed her fingers to her temples, thought of the voice message on her machine last night. *Soon, Jillian. He'll be crying over you.*

Yeah. Maybe she was scared stupid. For sure, she was scared.

"Headache?"

Great. Concern.

She shook her head.

Whenever he expressed it—which, granted, wasn't often—it surprised her. It surprised him, too, if she read his scowl right. He didn't want to feel anything for her other than that perfect bodyguard stoicism.

It all served to further convolute things because she still thought he was a sonofabitch. But he was a great-looking sonofabitch, and at times he showed amazing intuitive powers, compassion, and, like now, concern. Even though he didn't want to. Which, for some reason, only endeared him to her a little more.

Endeared? God. That soaked it. She *was* scared stupid.

Beside her, Garret had fallen into silence, too, and she wondered if he was messing with the same thoughts she was. At Palm Beach Lakes Boulevard, he made a left, then pulled into a large high-rise office complex known as the Forum, where E.D.E.N. Security, Inc., kept a suite of offices.

While she'd groused about taking time out of her day to come here, secretly she'd been looking forward to meeting the other Garretts. She'd done her research. The whole lot were overachievers, it seemed.

"Well, if it isn't the prodigal." A pretty, diminutive blonde with a huge smile and big blue eyes met them when they walked in the door.

"Hello, little brother," she went on before turning eyes the same color blue as Nolan's on Jillian. "And you're Ms. Kincaid. I'm Eve, Nolan's sister. I've seen your newscasts. You're fabulous. Great suit," she added, admiring Jillian's slim-fitting two-piece mauve silk pantsuit.

Jillian returned her warm smile and firm handshake. "It's Jillian, please. And thanks."

According to the article, Eve was the doer of the group. Her background was in the Secret Service, and prior to protection duty she specialized in money-laundering and computer-programming issues and lent the firm the ability to offer corporate crime investigations. Again, according to the article, she was very career oriented.

"So, how's the bully treating you?" Eve asked even as she threw her arms around the bully's neck and planted a big wet one on his cheek.

Jillian was as charmed by Eve's uninhibited show of affection as she was by the show Nolan made of tolerating it. He rolled his eyes and glowered, although she noticed his arms had folded around his sister and squeezed her tight.

"Get away from me, brat," he sputtered, peeling her away from him, but there was a smile in his voice even if his mouth remained hard and firm. "You'll get makeup on my shirt."

"You could use a little brightening up," Eve tossed back, and winked at Jillian. "Don't you agree?"

Actually, Jillian thought black suited him just fine, but she nodded just to get a rise out of him.

"I did not come here for a fashion consult or to be abused by you," he grumbled. "You have some info for me?"

"Gave it to Ethan. Come on. We were about to have a quick conference. Jillian can meet the rest of the E.D.E.N. brain trust." Eve headed down the hall and they fell in step behind her.

"Did I mention that my sister has a smart mouth?"

"I heard that," Eve said over her shoulder.

"You were supposed to."

As they entered the conference room Jillian was met by another pair of blue eyes set in a dark masculine face that so resembled Nolan's she had to smile and take a guess as to which brother she was facing. "Ethan?"

"Dallas," he corrected, and extended his hand. "And you would be Jillian Kincaid."

Dallas, at thirty-three, was considered the negotiator, according to the article. A former Force Recon team leader—he'd bucked the family's army tradition and opted for the marines—Dallas had been described as open, friendly, and preppie and was primed in his usual uniform of trendy chinos and a knit shirt. His sister was quoted as saying Dallas liked his life neat and orderly.

"*I* would be Ethan." Nolan's oldest brother—he was

thirty-five if she remembered right—rose from a chair at the head of a meeting table.

Ethan was a former Green Beret. His siblings affectionately regarded him as the brooder of the group. All work, no sense of humor, he was rarely seen without his trademark suit and tie or roll of cherry lifesavers. Today was no exception. He was also very private about his personal life and his marriage that had ended five years ago.

The photograph accompanying the article certainly hadn't lied. And the family genes ran strong and true, Jillian noted as this other devastatingly handsome Garrett walked around the table and extended his hand. "It's nice to meet you, Ms. Kincaid."

"All right, all right, enough with the glad-handing," Nolan broke in. "We're not here on a social call."

"Or a fashion consult," Eve added with an ornery grin.

The three brothers, evidently used to Eve's sense of humor, exchanged knowing looks.

"The files you asked for are in my office," Ethan said with a nod toward Nolan. "Blue folder, right corner, top of the desk. Go ahead. We'll entertain Ms. Kincaid until you get back."

Nolan seemed to consider the wisdom of leaving her with them, but in the end he shot his sister a warning glare, then left the conference room. Jillian couldn't swear to it, but she sensed a collective concern on the faces of all three Garrett siblings as they watched their brother walk away.

"Does that Terminator look he's got going on work on you?" Eve asked, breaking the tension. "Because if it does, we definitely need to talk."

"How are you holding up?" Ethan asked soberly as he eased a hip onto a corner of the conference table and popped a Lifesaver out of the roll.

"I'm doing fine," Jillian said automatically. And if you didn't count the sporadic moments when the reality of her situation caught up with her and her heart clogged her throat, she *was* doing fine.

"We're all over this," Dallas added, his blue eyes seeking and holding hers as he sat down in a chair. Propping his elbows on the arms, he folded his hands, prayerlike, in front of him. "We've been working with the West Palm PD, feeding them every piece of intel we uncover that might be pertinent."

"And we'll get a handle on whoever is doing this to you soon," Eve assured her. "In the meantime, he may be hell to live with, but Nolan won't let anything happen to you."

"I know," Jillian said, and realized for the first time just how deeply she believed it.

They were en route back to the TV studio when Jillian's cell phone rang.

"You're kidding," Nolan heard her say as she wedged the phone between her shoulder and ear, then scrambled to open her purse.

She pulled out a pen and a notebook and started scribbling. "Yeah. Yeah, I've got it. We can be there in," she checked her wristwatch, "ten minutes. Fifteen if traffic holds us up. . . . Yes, tell Jake and Ramón to hoist a red flag or something. I'll find them. . . . Right. Did he say what it's about?"

Nolan cast a glance her way. Her eyes were bright with excitement, her mouth tight with concentration, as she disconnected, looked up, and got a fix on where they were. "OK—we need to get downtown *wiki wiki.*"

He snorted. "*Wiki wiki?* Is that like a technical term?"

"Just take the first exit. I know a shortcut to the West Palm police station."

"What's up?"

"Diane got a call from the police chief's office. They've

announced that he's holding a press conference at four-thirty—that's fifteen minutes from now. And to answer your next question, no, I don't know what it's about."

"But you have an idea."

"My money's on the Colburn murder. Could be they've got a lead."

Oh yeah. He'd heard about that case. If he remembered right, the story had broken a few weeks ago. The papers and even national television had given a lot of coverage to the unsolved murder of the prominent hotelier. Arthur Colburn had been found beaten to death in his suite of rooms. It was a juicy story that hinted heavily of a love triangle involving a rising male supermodel, a local female ingenue, and whispers of bisexuality. In short, it was a journalist's wet dream.

"I don't think it's a good idea for you to cover this," he growled.

She whipped her head around to glare at him. "It's my job."

"You're the only reporter at the studio who can handle it?"

"I'm the closest reporter. It's all about proximity. Besides, I want this story."

Yeah, he was sure she did.

"All right. But stay close."

"Like Lycra," she said with a smart-ass grin.

Nolan swore when, twelve minutes later, he pulled into a parking spot at 600 Banyan where space had been roped off for media vehicles. The grounds around the police station were crawling with people. Everywhere he looked there were reporters, cops, cameras, microphones, and about a million miles of cable.

"I take it you didn't get an exclusive," he grumbled as he hustled out of his car and sprinted to catch up with her. "I said stay close."

"Then keep up."

She never broke stride, and once he snagged her elbow he never let go while she dodged bodies and gave an occasional hello wave to a colleague as she plowed a course toward, believe it or not, a red flag waving high above the throng outside the station.

"Hey, guys," she said a little breathlessly when she reached her crew, who had set up shop on the sidewalk to the left of the front door, where a podium loaded with microphones had been hastily erected. "Anything yet?"

"Not yet." Ramón was all business, messing with his gear, setting up a tripod. He was, according to Nolan's notes, of Cuban descent, twenty-six years old, and a three-year employee of KGLO. Nolan didn't need any notes to tell him that Ramón with his pumped-up pecs, long black hair, and *hey, baby* eyes was also a ladies' man. His smile was quick and warm. A little too warm for Nolan's liking when Ramón flashed it Jillian's way, but he'd been professional to a fault at John Smith's interview yesterday.

Jake was a fifty-something Caucasian with a potbelly, receding hairline, and long salt-and-pepper ponytail. He constantly talked about his kids and a new grandchild on the way, all the while tending to business. Nolan figured he could count on either one of them if push came to shove and something went down here.

Speaking of pushes, someone bumped him from behind, mumbled an apology, and shoved on through the crowd. It was to become a common occurrence before the day was over.

An hour after they'd arrived, there was still no sign of Albert Fielding, the chief of police.

"And we rushed over here because . . . ?" Nolan angled Jillian a dark look.

She looked up at him and grinned. "You'd never make a good reporter," she said, and went back to checking her hair and lipstick in a slim black compact. "Nine times out of ten, it's a hurry-up-and-wait game."

He glanced over her head, scanned the crowd. "I don't like it that you're so exposed here."

"Noted. Now relax. We may be here a while yet."

A *while* turned out to be an understatement. Another hour passed and there was still no sign of Fielding.

"Can't you call in sick or something?"

She threw him a droll look. He took it as a no.

The scene had turned into a sideshow. Besides reporters from the Palm Beach and Miami papers milling around and all the TV crews set up practically on top of one another, the delayed press conference had attracted far too many curiosity seekers to make Nolan comfortable. Hell. Some guy had even shown up with a vending cart, hawking tacos and fajitas.

"I could use something to eat." Jake dug into his hip pocket for his wallet. "Anyone else?"

"Taco. Soft-shell," Jillian said, and started fishing around in her purse for cash. "And an iced tea, please. No sugar."

"It's on me." Jake waved away her money. "I'll expense it out."

"In that case, get me a chicken fajita," Ramón added with a grin. "Lots of onions."

Jake cocked a brow. "Garrett?"

Gezus. They were turning it into a damn picnic. "Yeah, sure, why not? Whatever they've got."

"And get him a root beer."

Surprised, Nolan glanced at Jillian. She ducked her head back into her purse, like something at the bottom had captured her full attention.

Well hell. Next thing he knew she'd be wiping refried beans off his chin. How domestic.

He'd been doing his damnedest to forget about that little

scene at her dining room table. Now this latest gesture had managed to remind him that there could be a lot more than a client relationship between them, and he wasn't talking just friends.

He'd also been trying his damnedest to ignore the easy camaraderie she enjoyed with her crew as well as her rivals and colleagues. She was professional, tenacious, respectful, and empathetic to the media and police. And it was apparent they regarded her as one of them. When one of the uniformed officers made his way over and started shooting the breeze with her, Nolan saw yet another side of the woman he'd once thought of as a prima donna.

She joked with the young officer who was obviously smitten with her and somehow managed to pump him up without letting him down when his friendliness turned to flirting.

She didn't hold herself above them but was one of the people as she juggled her purse and her taco, laughing as Ramón teased her about bean breath and giving back as good as she got.

But to him, she was a client, Nolan reminded himself for about the hundredth time as a flare of jealousy crept in over the familiar way Ramón touched a finger to the corner of her mouth to wipe away a smear of sour cream.

Nolan's scowl wasn't the only thing that was dark by the time the police chief finally made an appearance. The sun had long set when someone shouted, "There he is!"

Albert Fielding, a slim, fit man with a marine haircut, a no-nonsense glower, and dark eyes creased at the corners from nights of burning the midnight oil, finally appeared. Fielding was flanked by two of his senior officers and two men sporting lawyerlike suits and official airs as he made his way somberly to the podium.

It became pure pandemonium as reporters, Jillian included,

jockeyed for closer position, thrusting mikes toward the chief and lobbing questions like artillery rounds.

"Good afternoon," the chief started, quieting the crowd. "Or should I say, good evening. I'm sorry about this delay. We had intended to speak with you much earlier, but some last-minute legal issues cropped up and set us back a bit.

"That said, the purpose of this press conference is to announce that we've made an arrest in the Colburn murder case."

The reporters migrated toward the podium like a swarm of angry bees to a field of flowers. Jillian got bumped and hassled in the process and Nolan had to muscle his way in between her and an overzealous reporter from a competing station.

Nolan didn't hear another word of Fielding's statement or any of the questions the reporters machine-gunned at the chief. He had his hands full sticking to Jillian's side and keeping her on her feet, for that matter.

"Back the hell off!" he shouted when one particularly zealous newshound shoved an elbow in his ribs.

There were people everywhere. The crowd seemed to shift and swell like a rising tide in hurricane season. He didn't like it. He didn't like it a bit that Jillian was exposed to so many bodies in such tight proximity. And when one of the network vans with a satellite dish sprouting from the roof blew a major fuse, the crowd reacted to the sizzle and pop and mini–fireworks display with screams and a stampeding crush. Jillian's arm was wrenched out of his grasp.

The mob sucked her in . . . and Nolan went ballistic.

"Get the fuck out of my way!" He parted the sea of bodies like they were curtains and he was desperate for daylight.

When he finally got to her, Jillian was on her knees on the grass.

He swept her to her feet, held her steady against him. "You all right?"

"Yeah. Yeah . . . I think so."

He didn't wait to find out. Tucking her under his arm and leading with his shoulder, he wedged his way through the mass of bodies, stopping only when they'd cleared the knot of shouting reporters by a good ten yards.

"Goddamn it!" he swore, looking down on her with a mixture of rage and concern. His voice and his hands shook with it. "I never should have—"

His heart stopped when he saw the blood. "Christ. You're bleeding."

Panicked, he turned her toward the glow of a streetlight. All the blood drained from his head. A crimson stain the size of a golf ball spread like a huge, ragged ink spot from under the jacket pocket covering her left breast.

His gaze flew to hers. She blinked down at the blood, shock etched on her face.

"I . . . I don't feel anything." She lifted a hand to the bloody jacket. Blood spurted between her fingers and ran down her wrist when she applied pressure.

Swearing under his breath, wondering how she was even able to stay on her feet, Nolan wrenched her jacket open so he could get to the wound, then blinked in confusion and relief when her pale, perfect flesh was exactly that—pale and perfect beneath a lacy flesh-colored bra.

"What the hell?"

He folded the jacket back over her breasts, reached carefully inside the breast pocket . . . and pulled out a plastic bag, soggy and almost empty of blood. Inside the bag was a note that had been laminated to protect it.

> *Three blind mice,*
> *see how they run.*
> *The blood isn't yours,*
> *but wasn't it fun?*
> *Soon, Jillian . . .*

"OK," Jillian said, her eyes wild, her hands shaking as she clutched his arm. "That's it. Get me out of here."

The green eyes that met his begged. "Please. Get me out of here."

17

"Did I not tell you I *only* wear stripes?"
Wellington roared at the shell-shocked intern who'd been
unfortunate enough to draw wardrobe duty for tonight's
newscast and the bad luck to pick out a paisley tie.

"I'm sorry, Mr. Wellington. I'll replace it right away."

"Damn right you will. And make it blue. Do you think
you can handle that?"

The young woman was close to tears as she nodded and
scurried off in search of the perfect tie.

Wellington was the biggest ass known to man, Nolan decided as he listened with half an ear to the coanchor's tirade.

For the man whose star was fading it all came down to
ego, and Wellington's ego, had taken a major hit in the past
twenty-four hours. Not only did it stick in his craw that Jillian delivered the news with more style than he did, but now
she *was* the news after the incident at the police press conference last night.

The story had aired on all the major stations in the area
and it had made front page of the *Palm Beach Post* and several Miami papers. The phones had been ringing off the
hook with viewers expressing concern for Jillian. The station's e-mail was clogged with questions about her. Even
Diane Kleinmeyer had dropped her drill sergeant reserve
and pulled Jillian aside for an awkward but supportive pat on
the back.

Wellington had been in a snit all day.

Nolan wanted to grab him by his pricey lapels and shake him until his porcelain veneers popped loose. Jillian's life was in danger and it was high time Wellington got off his high horse and got a clue. She did not need his crap or the snide remarks Erica Gray was making behind her back.

"Pity about what Jillian's going through," Erica had offered, sidling up to Nolan a few minutes ago and making a point to touch his hand. Lingeringly. "Must be such a trial," she added, leaning in close and "accidentally" brushing her generous breasts against his chest, "for both of you."

"For both of us?"

"Well, it's no secret Jillian isn't exactly . . . how do I say this? The friendly sort?"

"Like you?"

"Yeah. Like me." She'd tucked a slip of paper in his hand, folded her fingers over his, and lifted a very friendly brow. "Hang on to that. You're going to want it when this is over."

Nolan had known without looking that her phone number was written on the paper. He'd tossed it in the nearest trash can the minute she sauntered away.

Talk about a head case. The more he was around both Erica and Wellington, however, the less likely they seemed as suspects. While they both had motive—at least in their minds—and opportunity, in Nolan's opinion, neither had the backbone necessary to get their hands messy by actually carrying out a murder plot.

Then there was Jody. "If you're not up to it, Jillie, you know I'll fill in for you tonight."

As usual, Jody's on-the-spot offer just didn't ring true. Ms. Cute and Perky grated on his nerves in a way that instinctively warned him to beware of her. And yet, again, like Wellington and Erica, Jody didn't feel right as the star contender. Which, in his experience, meant all three bore watching.

Last night after the fiasco at the police station and Jillian's going to bed, he'd stayed up and read the reports he'd retrieved from his brother earlier in the afternoon. Lydia's had been interesting, but the woman was spooked by her own shadow; he couldn't really figure her for the bad guy, either. Then again, it was always the one you least expected.

Then there was the report on Jillian's friend Rachael Hanover. Nothing much pointed any fingers her way, either, but buried deep in the material had been a mention of an ER visit when she'd been twelve. He'd dug deeper, but that was it. No more info. He'd called Ethan first thing this morning and told him he wanted him to locate that ER report. So far, Nolan hadn't heard anything back.

It could be he was fishing for sharks with a dip net, but something about Rachael bugged the hell out of him. So did Marian Abramson and John Smith. They were his most viable suspects. The potential for violence and the need for retribution on those fronts had red flags waving all over the place.

Nolan also had Darin Kincaid to deal with. He was livid over the latest incident, had cracked a few heads down at the West Palm PD for letting the story get out—as if they could have stopped it with the department crawling with media. And because of the news Jillian's stalker had made, Clare was now aware of Jillian's danger. Apparently, she wasn't handling it too well.

Nolan dragged a hand through his hair as he stood in the makeup room doorway. He tuned out Wellington's ranting behind him and the dressing-down Kincaid had given him on the phone and watched the makeup artist work on the dark circles beneath Jillian's eyes. She couldn't take much more of this. The wondering when, wondering if, wondering who . . . wondering how.

She looked bruised. Battle weary. And that wall of restraint he butted up against daily when it came to her buckled a little more because of the strain she was under. As she eased out of the makeup chair and walked to the set in preparation for the late newscast he realized that if ever a woman needed a man to shore her up, she was that woman.

And he sure as the world couldn't be that man even though last night she'd allowed herself one brief moment and turned to him. *Get me out of here. Please get me out of here.*

After that, she'd sucked it up like a soldier facing combat, because of course he hadn't been able to take her anywhere, at least not for a while. Ramón and Jake had come looking for them, spotted the blood, and closed ranks around her in a protective ring even as she assured them she was fine.

Only she hadn't been fine. But she'd held up. Through the police questioning. Through the ride back to the studio. Through the newscast she'd insisted on doing last night.

She hadn't even broken down on the ride home. She'd sat quietly in the car beside him, then walked straight to her bedroom and shut the door. Now here they were. Over twenty-four hours had passed since the attack and she was still rock steady. At least that's what she wanted everyone to think.

Not one tear had yet leaked down that porcelain cheek. Not once had her full lower lip quivered. As he stood out of camera range while she completed the news, he thought of all her strength. But as she finished the Thursday evening newscast with her trademark, "Until tomorrow . . . may all your news be good . . . ," he detected the slightest bit of corrosion in the wall of steel she'd erected around herself.

He didn't think anyone else noticed that her hands were shaking as she unclipped her mike. Didn't think anyone noticed that her gaze sought his and locked on him like a laser beam in a silent plea for help that she wasn't even aware she'd issued.

But he saw it anyway, all the while trying to ignore the clutch of compassion and pride and concern that tightened in his chest and drew him toward her. He needed to get her the hell out of here before her steel will rusted through. She was about to crash, and he knew her well enough by now to know she wouldn't want anyone to see it happen. She, no doubt, would perceive a justified case of the screaming "ohmy-gods" as a weakness when most mere mortals would have collapsed under the pressure long ago.

He'd just reached her side when she stiffened to stone. He searched her face. What color she'd maintained during the newscast drained to pale as her gaze locked and held on something over Nolan's shoulder.

He turned to see a man whose photo he'd studied in a file and whom he'd detested on sight. Until that moment, Nolan hadn't realized how much he'd been relishing a confrontation with the creep.

"Jillian." His brows beetled in concern, Steven Fowler walked toward her, his arms extended. "I just heard. I flew in from Chicago immediately. I've been so worried about you."

Snake oil and scams came to mind. Fowler was slick to the point of being oily in his custom-tailored beige suit and with his hundred-dollar manicure, the picture of support and concern.

Nolan stepped in front of Jillian. "Back off."

Behind him, she pressed her forehead between his shoulder blades, as if she simply could not take one more hit and needed him to keep her upright.

"Who the hell are you?" Incensed, Fowler looked Nolan up and down.

"I'm the man who's just itching for a reason to rip off your head and shove it up your ass," Nolan assured him with a deceptively congenial smile. "So back off, jack. The lady does not want to speak with you."

Fowler's face turned the color of a stop sign. Nolan could see he was thinking about challenging him—for all of two seconds—before he backed away.

He made sure that Nolan, with Jillian tucked under his arm, had cleared him by a couple of yards before he worked up the courage to insult her. "So this is the kind of man you go for now? A pretty-boy muscle-head with a pin-sized brain?"

Around them, the already quiet set stilled to a vacuum of silence.

Nolan stopped, drew a weary breath. As he turned slowly toward Fowler, he caught a glimpse of Wellington and Erica hanging on every word. Might as well give 'em a good show.

"Well, hell. Now you've hurt my feelings." He shook his head, somber and sad. "What do you think, Jillian? Can I hit him? Just once?"

In spite of the tension, she caught on quick. He saw her first real smile in twenty-four hours.

"No, Thor." She patted his arm like he was a pet in need of persuasion and steered him toward the elevator. "You'll just get your hands dirty. Besides, he's not worth your energy."

"So you're saying that I can't hit him." A disappointed Rocky.

"No, darling. I'm sorry, but you can't hit him." She punched the elevator button, both of them aware of Fowler's and everyone else within earshot's stupefied gazes following them. "Come along. I'll buy you a present to make up for it."

He grinned—Forrest Gump on a chocolate high. "Something shiny, OK?"

They stepped into the elevator and the doors swished shut behind them. For a moment, they just stood and grinned at each other.

Then a stilted laugh burst out of her. " 'Rip off your head and shove it up your ass'?"

Still smiling, he shrugged. "I thought it was pretty inventive."

"Not to mention graphic."

"Yeah. That, too. I figured he needed a real clear picture."

"God." She laughed again, shook her head. "The look on his face was priceless."

So was the look on hers. For the first time in many, many hours she didn't look haunted or hunted. For the first time in longer than that, she'd forgotten about the faceless lunatic who hated her so much they wanted her dead.

Their eyes held for another long moment.

"What?" Other than amusement, he couldn't read what it was he saw in her eyes.

"Would you really have hit him?"

It was his turn to laugh. "In a heartbeat."

She nodded. "Good."

They became quiet then as the elevator hit the main floor and the doors opened. He stepped out ahead of her, checked the hall, and motioned that it was clear for her to follow. Yet she stood there, just looking at him.

"At the risk of repeating myself . . . what?"

She seemed to consider, then put her head down and stepped into the hall. "I was just thinking that I figured you would be the last person in the world capable of making me laugh."

Yeah. Him, too. "Comes with the service," he tossed out because he *did* get a read on what she was thinking this time.

She was thinking he wasn't such a bad guy after all. She was thinking that maybe, just maybe, he might be someone worth knowing.

She was wrong.

Her next statement confirmed it.

"You should smile more often," she said, her look contemplative. "It looks good on you."

"Plays hell with my tough guy image, though."

Lame. That was so lame. But so were the thoughts rumbling through his head. Thoughts that didn't just tiptoe over the line he'd drawn between them, they leaped over.

He was in trouble again. Those soft eyes and that lush mouth were doing a number on him.

"Speaking of tough guys, how's the cut on your ribs?"

"Fine. I'm a fast healer."

Too bad he wasn't as fast on his feet. If he were, he'd have figured a way out of this by now.

They walked in silence to his car. When he opened the door and helped her inside and all he could think about was how wonderful she smelled, he knew he was going down for the count.

Big trouble.

The kind of trouble it was going to be hard as hell to stay ahead of.

When he slipped behind the wheel and her hand covered his on the gearshift, sending electric shocks zinging up the length of his arm, he didn't see a lot of hope of outrunning it.

"Take me somewhere."

He stilled. Tried not to turn and look in her eyes—and failed miserably.

They were so green. So softly pleading.

"I don't want to go home. I don't want to face another blinking red light on my answering machine. I don't want to face another night in my bedroom wondering when and if this will all be over."

She looked away, looked at her hands, and a single teardrop spilled onto that delicate crease where her thumb joined her palm. "I need something . . . some reminder that somewhere life is normal, that people laugh and dance and don't think past the moment."

OK, this was the time when he needed to be tough. He needed to remind her the streets weren't safe, that she was vulnerable and, short of her father's estate, her locked penthouse was the best place for her to be. That's what he needed to do.

But she turned that beautiful brave face up to his again. A glittering sea of unshed tears pooled in her eyes and clung to her upper lashes.

And he was a goner.

"I know a place," he said, accepting that he was making a huge mistake but defenseless against her tears.

She smiled, let out a ragged breath. "Thank you."

"Yeah. For sure, this is going to cost you. Thor still want shiny present."

The smile she gave him in that moment was worth any price . . . even if he paid it in blood.

He shifted into gear and they roared off into the tropical night and, most likely, into more trouble than either one of them was prepared to handle.

Nolan didn't dare take Jillian to a public place in Palm Beach. It was too risky. After cruising on and off I-95 to make sure they didn't have a tail, he drove south of the city to a backwater restaurant and bar where the beer was cold and the only silver the place had ever seen was the cap in the cook's tooth.

La Casa de la Mamá was nestled in the middle of the block in a quiet and not quite tidy neighborhood. The blue-collar working folk living there were bilingual and raised their kids with kisses and swats and mowed their lawns when they felt like it. When they wanted groceries, they walked to local green markets and the corner store. When they wanted a cold beer, authentic Latin cooking, or the best cold stone crab in Florida or maybe just the chance to un-wind to a little salsa music, they went to Mama's House. Everyone was welcome there.

Nolan decided it might be the perfect place to take Jillian.

She needed a break, but he needed to be careful. He was straddling a very thin wire here. It was more than the fact that she was vulnerable and he had an unfortunate case of the hots for her. There was that subtle difference in the way she'd been looking at him lately to deal with. It wasn't just that she was at the end of her rope. It wasn't just that she was scared. She saw him as a buffer. And she saw him as someone she could depend on, someone she wanted to get to know better.

That was where the trouble had begun. Here, however, he decided, getting it together on the drive, was where it was going to end. Let her see how he lived was how he figured it. Let her see him in his element . . . in surroundings that were as far from what she was used to as hot dogs were from caviar. Where silk was a luxury instead of a staple and then most likely it wasn't silk at all but something that did a bad job pretending to be.

Yeah. Let her see how the poor folk—his folk—lived. Let her party in a bar where the Latino beat was sultry and loud and people danced on worn and cracked linoleum instead of imported Italian tile. Let her realize he was most comfortable in a world where the biggest financial deal made within a ten-block radius was likely over the price of a very used car.

In short, let her see who he was.

That'd scare her off. And he hoped in the process it would also make her forget about her situation for a little while.

He parked along a street where pineapple palms and wooden planters filled with blooming flowers vied for space with bits of litter. Jillian said nothing as he pocketed his keys and opened her car door, but her eyes were busy taking in every detail. Mama's House sat on the corner of a long lot. But for a flashing neon sign of vivid blue, yellow, red, and green letters blinking "La Casa de la Mamá" over the door, the cracked lavender stucco building was unremarkable in a neighborhood of colorful buildings.

He placed a hand at the small of her back and guided her ahead of him through a door painted electric pink. Music, laughter, and the richest scents known to man—Cuban food, wine, tap beer, and cigar smoke—greeted them. Mama's was always jumping, and tonight was no exception.

"No-lon!"

The shout, full of pleasant surprise and welcome, pounced on him the moment his head cleared the front door.

"Esteban," Nolan called across the room, and lifted a hand in greeting to a short barrel of a man with a snow-white mustache and a headful of Einstein hair. *"¿Cómo usted es?"*

"Bueno. Muy bueno, mi amigo."

Esteban scurried out from behind the bar, wiping his hands on a damp towel and affecting an affronted scowl as he wove his way through tables and patrons to get to them. "Where you been for so long now? Mama worries." He paused, a broad smile splitting his face when he saw Jillian. "Ah. Look here. Usted se ha encontrado un gato verde, pequeño y bonito de eyed, se?" *You've found yourself a pretty little green-eyed cat, yes?*

Nolan cringed and hoped Jillian didn't speak Spanish. "Sí, ella es muy bonita. Pero ella no es la mina." *Yes, she's very pretty. But she's not mine.*

Eyes twinkling, Esteban looked from Nolan to Jillian and grunted. "Quizá usted tuvo mejores cosas para hacer que vienen y nos ven." *Still, maybe you had better things to do than come and see us.*

Nolan laughed, shrugged. "Si usted lo dice." *If you say so.*

"Welcome, pretty cat, to Mama's House." With an elaborate old-world gesture, Esteban brought Jillian's hand to his lips and kissed it. "No-lon . . . he's taking as good care of you as I take care of Mama, yes?"

"All right," Nolan cut in before Jillian could do any more than smile. It was obvious by the look on her face that despite the coarseness of the surroundings, Esteban had charmed her. "We're here to listen to the music, maybe get something to drink, not play twenty questions."

"Then sit, No-lon. You and your pretty cat." With a wink at Jillian, Esteban led them to a table in the corner of the crowded bar. "I'll tell Mama you're here and send Maria over with something to drink. Corona for you, yes? And for the lady?"

"Root beer for me," Nolan corrected, ignoring Esteban's curious look. "Jillian? Chardonnay?"

She nodded, then shook her head. "No. Let's do this right. Make it a margarita. Rocks."

"Smart girl. I make the best margarita east of the Gulf. You will lap it up like a cat eating cream."

With a chuckle, Esteban wove his way back through the tables. He poked his head over the top of the swinging doors that led to the kitchen first, said something in rapid-fire Spanish, then tucked back in behind the bar.

"Word to the wise," Nolan said once they'd gotten settled. "No lapping. Sipping only. I don't want you wrecked on tequila to the point I have to carry you out of here."

The minute he said it, he wished he could take it back. It was exactly the image—Jillian plastered, loose limbed, and snuggled in his arms—he did not want stuck in his mind the rest of the night.

So much for what he'd wanted.

When Maria brought their drinks Jillian gaped at what looked like a liter of Jose with just enough salt and lime for color.

"Christ," Nolan said with a groan.

Jillian laughed. "I'd say lapping and sipping are both off the table. I'm going to have to attack this like I mean it if I plan on finishing it off. Somebody, get me a straw."

18

ALL RIGHT. SO IT WASN'T NICE TO MAKE FUN
of someone else's discomfort, but Jillian couldn't help it.
Nolan looked so sour and concerned and he'd gone to great
extents to take her someplace where she could unwind. The
best part was, it was working.

Mama's was so full of delicious sights and scents and
sounds, it was a full-time job just taking it all in.

"Where did you learn to speak Spanish?" she asked, sipping her margarita like a good girl.

Beside her, he grunted, Mr. Malcontent. "Here and there."

"Well, that cleared it up for me."

He merely blinked.

And that word came up again as she looked at him. *En-
dearing.*

Would wonders never cease?

There he sat, stern to the bone, doing his damnedest to
give her a little relief from the stalker stress, yet worried she
might have *too* good of a time—or, God forbid, worried that
he might have too good of a time—which could lead to them
having a good time together.

Heavens. Wouldn't that just be too awful for words?

"What?" he growled when he realized she was looking
at him.

She had to lean in close to be heard above the music and
the talking and the laughter. "I like Esteban."

"Everyone likes Esteban."

"And I like this place."

He considered her, then shrugged.

"You didn't think I would?"

Another shrug. A long swallow of his root beer. "Didn't know. Just figured it would take your mind off things."

"Like Steven Fowler?"

He stared at his bottle of root beer, wiped his thumb along the damp label. "Not that it's any of my business, but what did you ever see in that guy?"

She thought about it, shook her head. "I'm not sure. I think . . . I don't know. Maybe it was more circumstantial than anything else."

"Circumstantial how?"

She took another sip, licked salt off her lips. "It's a woman thing. You wouldn't understand."

He groaned. "I'm going to regret this, but try me."

Since he was as reluctant as he was curious and since she felt a need to explain, she decided to give it a go.

"OK. Let's say you're a twenty-nine-year-old woman. It's been a very long time since you've been in a serious relationship . . . mostly because everyone in your circle knows you as Darin Kincaid's daughter and you figure any interest from the opposite sex is generated by an avid interest in Daddy's money first and you a distant second.

"Along comes a man who is wealthy in his own right, who seems to be impressed by you, not your bloodlines. Maybe you're a little . . . unsettled at the time. Maybe you've been thinking you've been too focused on your career and you're missing out on something . . . I don't know. Something more. Something important. And maybe you think Steven is what you've been missing in your life, especially when he convinces you that you're what's missing in his."

She shrugged, looked out at the dance floor where a

lovely Latino couple was putting some spice in the salsa as they moved in beautiful harmony to the music.

When Nolan didn't say anything, she cast a glance his way. "Or . . . suppose *your* take on the situation was painfully accurate and I was stupid."

"Yeah. Well. We've all done things we regret."

Something in his eyes said he had many regrets. And something in his posture said his regrets were staunchly guarded and strictly off-limits.

"I liked your brothers," she said, deciding to exercise the better part of wisdom and not push for information. "And Eve. She seems very sweet."

He snorted, but there was affection in his almost smile. "Sweet as a hand grenade. People often make the mistake of misjudging those blond bombshell looks. Believe me, there is no marshmallow inside. She's smart, shrewd, and has no compunctions about going for the jugular if there's a need."

"I take it she's gone for yours a time or two?"

This time, he couldn't hide the smile or the pride. "Oh yeah."

Before she could decide if she wanted to press him to elaborate, a Latino woman with striking good looks, glossy black hair, and a body made for lingerie ads glided toward the table.

"No-lon," she purred, flipping her long hair over her bare shoulder and reaching for his hand. "You are so bad to stay away for so long."

Nolan rose at her slightest tug and returned her long, familiar hug . . . while Jillian tried to decide if the knot of tension fisting in her chest was what she thought it was.

Yeah, she decided when the woman pulled away, then planted a lingering kiss on each of Nolan's cheeks. It was. She was jealous. Well, well. Just one new wrinkle after another.

"You look good, *mi amor*." The woman looked deep into Nolan's eyes as she clasped his cheeks in her hands, then ran fingers tipped with siren red nails down the side of his face. "And Esteban tells me you have brought a friend."

The dark eyes that had adored Nolan turned to Jillian. Measuring, assessing.

Measuring and assessing what? Jillian wondered. *The competition?*

She was ready to dislike the woman on sight, if for no other reason than she was so excessively beautiful, stunningly sultry, and wore the flowing floral skirt and off-the-shoulder blouse like a heroine in a south-of-the-border movie. Beside her, wearing a black camisole beneath a buttercup yellow jacket, and a short yellow skirt, Jillian felt like a kindergarten teacher. A dowdy old maid kindergarten teacher.

"Who have we here, No-lon?"

"My . . . friend," he said hesitantly. "Jillian. Jillian, meet Mama."

This was Mama? This sultry Salma Hayek look-alike was the Mama that Esteban took care of?

"Did I not tell you she was a pretty cat, darling?" Esteban joined them at the table.

"Complete with claws," Mama said, smiling with satisfaction at Jillian. "Keep them sharp, *chica;* you will have use of them if you want to keep this one. But you have no worry with me. Unless, of course, you hurt our No-lon."

Esteban reared back his head and laughed as Mama snuggled up to his side, her gaze lingering on Jillian's for a moment longer in a clear warning that if she did hurt their *No-lon,* the consequences could be dire.

Jillian was still thinking about Mama's incorrect assumption that she had any kind of hold on Nolan when Maria arrived with a basket of chips and salsa.

"I must dance with my woman," Esteban announced with a lusty smile, and steered Mama to the dance floor.

"Amazing," Jillian said when she could find the words. "Look at them. My God. They're incredible together."

What they were was pure sensuality. At first glance, Esteban was an aging, white-haired, grandfather type of man. Couple him with Mama and the chemistry sizzling between them as they moved to the hot Latin rhythms, however, and Esteban transformed to a virile and dangerously attractive man.

She'd never seen anything like it. By the time they'd finished the dance, their eyes locked on each other, their arms entwined, bodies sliding sensuously close, Jillian felt as if she'd witnessed an intimacy generally reserved for the bedroom.

Unsettlingly aroused, she worked her way out of her jacket and hooked it over the back of her chair. "Is it getting warm in here?"

When she looked up and into Garrett's eyes—and found them locked on her breasts like steel to magnet—she understood at least one of the sources of heat.

She felt herself melt into the chair as he swallowed and looked away.

"Maybe we should go," he said in a dark voice.

He may have dragged his gaze away, but she still felt the heat . . . and the hunger. Clear to her bones, she felt it. The residual effect of his blatant appreciation spread warmth from the tips of her breasts to pool low in her belly. Never in her life had she seen such desperate desire in a man's eyes. Desperate and raw . . . so raw it frightened and excited her.

Hot. Cold. Harsh. Soft. He was a study in contrasts and intensity all right. She'd never encountered anyone like him. One minute, she trembled in anticipation of the thought of what it would be like to make love with him . . . in the next, she wondered if she could survive a physical encounter with the man.

He would not be gentle. And he would not be meek.

A shiver cooled her flushed skin.

Yeah, she thought, branding herself as a coward, maybe he was right. Maybe they should go.

But *should* wasn't her favorite word at the moment, and if it had been she would have attached it to something other than *go*. Like life is short. For all she knew, she could be dead tomorrow. Maybe she *should* live dangerously for once and find out exactly what Mr. Garrett could teach her about sex and sensuality and all parts in between.

When he rose, however, and, stone-faced again, dug into his hip pocket to pull out his wallet, she knew the moment had passed.

Sanity ruled.

How typical.

Disappointed, she cupped her fishbowl of a margarita glass in both hands and allowed herself a final, deep swallow. But when she stood to reluctantly head for the door, all she saw of Nolan was the back of his head as Mama dragged him toward the dance floor. The next thing she knew, Esteban had clasped her hand in his, kissed it, and with a laugh guided her out there as well.

She was laughing, too—as much from surprise as uncertainty—when he pulled her into his arms.

"I'm afraid I'm not much of a dancer."

"Oh no, no. Everyone dances at Mama's. Just feel the music. Yes. Yes. Like that. Very good."

And to her surprise, she did feel it. And it felt good. Following Esteban's expert lead, she moved to the music, felt the rhythm and the beat.

And more heat. Lord, it was hot. A bead of sweat trickled between her breasts. More dampened the fine hair at her nape. The dance floor was packed with warm bodies and spicy scents. The air reverberated with licks from the sensual Latin guitar. Everyone was having a good time. Moving to the music. Drifting on the tempo. Even Nolan, whom she caught a glimpse of with Mama, was smiling. And oh, did the man have some wicked moves.

It was hard to keep track of him and concentrate on

keeping step with Esteban, but by the same token, it was impossible not to. Nolan was a dark, graceful animal, lean hips swaying, sensual mouth smiling, as he gave in to the music and let himself go.

If the change in Esteban had been amazing when he'd danced with Mama, the transformation in Nolan was indescribable. All the hard edges seemed to have melted to smooth, fluid lines. Lines Jillian wanted to stroke. Even his face, usually hard as stone, had softened to a languid, slumberous beauty that stole her breath and deregulated her heartbeat to the point where she felt light-headed.

The crowd swallowed them and she lost track. Probably a good thing. Her heart couldn't take much more of this. Still, she couldn't help but search for him. She was so busy searching, in fact, she didn't realize that he and Mama had danced up beside her and Esteban. In a move as fluid and effortless as breathing, Esteban twirled her into Nolan's arms, wrapped Mama in his, and left the two of them together.

For a moment, all Jillian could do was stand there, her hands braced on Nolan's hard forearms. She stared up into the face of a man who had terrified, bullied, protected, and disarmed her as no other man ever had. Terror was far from her mind, though, as he seemed to snap out of his own momentary shock and start moving to the music with that slow, loose-limbed grace that had fascinated her so.

The first sensation she became aware of was more heat. It radiated from his body in undulating waves. With it came his scent as she gingerly slid her hands up his arms to his shoulders and started moving with him. The sagey, sexy, intoxicating scent of male she associated with him surrounded her. She breathed it in. Deep and slow. And felt the tips of her breasts, now pressing against his chest, harden to tight, painful peaks.

She struggled for equilibrium . . . and lost. All she felt was awareness. Of his nearness, his hardness, of a sound welling up from deep in his throat that could have been pain or appreciation or defeat.

Whatever it was, it sent her tummy tumbling. So did his hands as he wrapped her tightly against him, lowered his head so his stubbled cheek brushed her temple and he drew her tighter still.

Oh God. Lately it seemed that all she had to do was look at him and a tension coiled so tight inside it made her chest ache, her muscles clench. Now she was touching him. And he was touching her. And the ache intensified to a need.

The dance transitioned to something more. Something intimate and suggestive and deeply arousing as his hips brushed her stomach, and the length of a very apparent erection nestled against her belly.

She supposed she should be shocked. But what she was, was entranced. She loved how he felt moving against her. She loved the feel of his hands on her waist. As restless as his ragged breath, they slid to the small of her back, then to her hips, his fingers splayed wide as he gripped, kneaded, caressed, and glided lower.

"This," he whispered against her ear, "was a really, really bad idea."

At least, that's what she thought he said. Her senses were so consumed by the music and the man, she tuned out everything around her and just let herself experience one of the most sexually charged moments of her life. The sway of his hips was pure invitation; the subtle brush of his thighs against hers, a caress; the feather of his warm breath against her face, a promise.

And his mouth. She'd always known it couldn't be that hard and unyielding all the time. He'd proved it late one night at her table. There was gentleness there, and passion. As his lips whispered across the shell of her ear, his message was very clear. His mouth was made for other things than scowling. Lovely things. She flashed on a sensual image of his lips tracking across her bare skin, enveloping a nipple, tugging.

They were dancing. Merely dancing. But it felt like so much more. A lingering caress of his hand on her bottom told her where he really wanted it. A moment when his thigh wedged between hers clarified what else he'd like to press there. The heel of his palm sliding slowly upward along her ribs pressed inward when it reached her breast, plumping her against him until she was so hypersensitized her legs could barely support her. The man left no doubt what he would do to her if they were alone.

But they weren't alone, no matter how badly she wanted them to be.

She was still drifting on intoxicating, erotic images of them together when the song ended on a lingering note.

His feet stilled long before his body stopped moving against hers. The sudden silence around them made her achingly aware that it was over.

So did his face when he pulled away.

Mistake, he said without speaking as his expression once again turned to stone and his eyes hid his thoughts like twin curtains.

Well, she thought, disappointed. There was reality for you. It forced you to deal with the here and now. The reality was, if they'd met under different circumstances and she hadn't been forced into getting to know him, she would never have given him a second look. The reality was that while he was sexually attracted to her, he could barely abide her on any other level.

Those absolutes cooled her head as they walked in silence back to their table. Yes, they cooled her head, but not her blood. Her hands trembled as she slipped back into her suit jacket. Her legs felt roughly the consistency of thick latte as they walked out of Mama's, little sparks of sexual heat sizzling along her nerve endings like live wires, little yearnings to know what it would be like to be made love to by him still fluttering inside her chest.

Nolan was past making excuses. He was past self-recriminations and ready to face the truth. He wanted this woman.

As he drove north away from Mama's back toward West Palm, he admitted to himself that he wanted Jillian like nothing he'd ever wanted in his life. He wanted to breathe in the scent of her, lose his hands in the silk of her hair, lose his mind pumping deep inside that gorgeous body.

He wanted his mouth on her. Everywhere. He wanted to feel his tongue glide across her nipple, listen to her moan, listen to her breathless sighs as he slid between her thighs and stroked and sucked until she was mindless with wanting him. He wanted to make love to her until she was screaming his name. Until he was screaming hers.

He wanted her hard and fast.

He wanted her often and in ways that would probably make her blush.

And he wanted her with a blistering intensity he'd never felt for another woman.

He sucked in a deep breath of warm night air as it rushed in through his open window. Flexed his fingers on the steering wheel. He'd never felt this out of control. He loved it. And he hated it.

That was as honest as he could get. And it was the honesty that made him face the reality he'd never wanted to admit.

Jillian . . . hell, she did things to him, brought out things in him he'd not only buried, but he'd never known existed. He'd never deluded himself about women. In high school it had all been about testosterone. In college it had all been about partying. And in the Rangers—he'd seen what the life did to relationships—it had been all about avoiding that kind of trouble.

When some sweet doe-eyed girl started making noises about forever, he was gone before he got sucked in too deep. And he made sure the women in his life knew the score. Sex. That's all it had ever been for him. A little bump and grind between the sheets . . . everybody was happy, and everybody walked out before morning.

In a different life, in a different time, he'd be all over that scenario with Jillian. But if ever there was a life, if ever there was a time, where he could be with her in that way, it wasn't now.

Let's get real. It would *never* be now for someone like him with someone like her. And yet, for a while there, on the dance floor, with her slumberous cat green eyes gazing up at him, with her body soft and pliant against his, he'd actually considered taking her to bed just to get her out of his system.

As if tonight was the first time he'd thought of it. Late at night, in stark moments of insanity, with her sleeping down the hall, he'd thought about it then, too. A lot.

But he knew about her kind of woman and sex. A woman like Jillian indulged in sex for more than physical gratification. She'd expect all that touchy-feely stuff afterward about feeling closer and more connected. He didn't do touchy-feely. And he didn't connect on any level but the in-and-out kind where it made him feel good and her feel good and they agreed to disconnect before morning.

With another kind of woman, yeah. A woman who understood he was a bad bet on the best day. It was the best- and the worst-case scenario. He liked sex, but the catch-22 was he'd never really liked the women who accepted his terms. They were shallow and unfeeling . . . and didn't that just say a whole helluva lot about him?

Jillian wasn't that kind of woman. She was smart and funny and—hell. She was a regular Girl Scout. A Girl Scout who truly didn't know the score. And the real kicker: He liked her. He respected her. And he couldn't use her like that.

That was what really sucked in all of this. Of all the good-time girls he'd had and all the good girls he'd walked away from because they thought they loved him, how was it possible that at *this* time in *this* situation he was thinking about wanting more? More than sex. More than . . . what?

His palms began to sweat. He felt that swift, sinking spiral of anxiety that always preceded him into combat. A warning that he was about to go someplace he'd never been before, someplace he'd be better off steering clear the hell away from.

He was not falling in love with her. No way. Hell, he didn't even know what love was. He did know it was something he was incapable of feeling.

So no. Not love.

Not here. Not now.

And not with her.

He signaled for the off-ramp and cruised onto Okeechobee.

And felt like he was letting go of something . . . vital.

In spite of it, in spite of all the things he wanted to do with her, *because* of all the things he wanted to do to her, it wasn't going to happen.

He was going to stick with the plan. Do his job. Forget about the kiss they'd shared. Forget about the dance that still shot an arrow of lust to his groin. The only thing he was going to do for Jillian Kincaid was keep her alive.

The scene that met them when they arrived at City Place redefined his mission with a stark clarity that had him digging deep for control and filled Jillian's eyes with terror.

Jillian saw it before he did as Nolan turned off Okeechobee onto Sapodilla Avenue.

Her hand flew to his arm, latched on. "Oh, my God."

Nolan followed her gaze, saw what had her so upset, and swore. A half-dozen squad cars and an ambulance lined the street that ran directly in front of City Place. Instead of driving around to the parking garage, Nolan pulled up behind a squad car.

"Sorry, folks." One of the uniformed officers stopped them at the front door. "If you don't have business here, I'm afraid I'm going to have to ask you to leave."

"Ms. Kincaid lives here," Nolan said. "What's going on?"

"Kincaid?" The officer consulted his clipboard, slanted Jillian a look, then flipped out his communicator. "You can go up," he said after a brief conversation with someone on the other end.

In the background the muffled chatter of police radios competed with the rush of traffic and the strobe lights from the patrol cars and ambulance flashing eerily into the night.

"Who was hurt?" Jillian's fingers dug into his arm. "God, please . . . please tell me it's not Eddie."

"Eddie?"

"The security guard. I don't see him anywhere."

"Ah. I'm not supposed to release any information."

"Just tell us if he's all right," Nolan cut in, knowing Jillian would move heaven and earth to find out.

The officer considered with a scowl, then finally caved. "He's got a bump on the head. Slight concussion. Paramedics say he'll be fine. He's awake now and alert."

Beside him, Nolan felt Jillian's body shudder with a breath of relief.

"Look. Detective Laurens can fill you in. He'll meet you upstairs."

Jillian's grip on Nolan's arm tightened. "Detective Laurens is upstairs? At my penthouse?"

The officer cut Nolan a look. He read it for what it was. Whatever was up there was bad. Real bad.

"Come on." Nolan nudged Jillian toward the elevator.

When they reached the penthouse floor, Detective Laurens met them in the hall.

Laurens was a Charles Bronson look-alike whose eyes

showed his years on the beat and the integrity inherent in a man of his reputation and experience. "Wait. Wait just a second, Ms. Kincaid."

Nolan cupped Jillian's shoulders in his hands and kept her from rushing to the penthouse. "What's going on, Detective?"

"There's been a break-in."

"Oh God." Jillian tried to pull away. Nolan held her fast.

"I'm afraid they pretty much trashed your place."

"Trashed?"

"Look . . . maybe you ought to just wait a bit until we can—"

"I want to see it," she insisted.

After a considering look at Nolan, Laurens nodded. "OK. But don't touch anything. And I need to warn you. It's . . . well, it's pretty obvious that whoever did this is the same person who's been harassing you."

Nolan walked with her to the open door where crime scene tape blocked their way. Together they ducked under the tape and stepped inside.

"Jesus," Nolan swore as he took in the scene.

Beside him, Jillian stood statue still.

Trashed didn't even come close to what had been done. *Destroyed. Desecrated.* Many similar words came to mind. But the one that pounded at him stood out above all others: *hate.*

Whoever had done this hated Jillian with a passion that bordered on insanity.

In a parked car, at the corner of Okeechobee and Sapodilla, Mary gulped deep breaths of the balmy night air and tried to settle her hammering heart.

What a rush . . . destroying what was Jillian's. Defying her to guess who had done it.

Was she crying now?

Was she dying a little even now in her fear, in her terror?

Did she feel horribly alone?

Mary knew all about being alone. The weight of it suddenly pressed down like lead.

She lowered her head to the steering wheel.

And then she sobbed.

For the baby sister she'd lost.

For the comfort she'd never known.

For the pain her mother had caused when Mary had been the only outlet for her wrath.

She lifted her head. Dried her eyes. Then she drove away into the night.

Soon she wouldn't have to cry anymore.

19

SHE WAS QUIET. *TOO QUIET*, NOLAN thought as he guided Jillian along the maze of docks toward the slip where the *EDEN* was berthed. On the drive over, she hadn't even asked him where he was taking her or why he was bringing her there.

But then, how quiet was too quiet when a part of your life—your home, which was supposed to be your sanctuary—had just been violently violated?

The moon was full, the sheltered mooring along the Intracoastal waterway silent but for the gentle lap of salt water to the *EDEN*'s fiberglass hull where she rode, along with a hundred or so other vessels with barely a notion of movement. Brine and sea scented the air. A soft breeze felt warm against his skin, barely ruffling the silk of Jillian's hair. And yet he felt her shiver when he cupped her elbow in his hand to steady her.

"Watch your step," he said, negotiating the ramp to the *EDEN* and helping her aboard.

The original plan, after the police had said they could leave, had been to take her to her father at Golden Palms. When he'd said as much, she'd spoken the only word she'd uttered since she'd taken in the carnage of her penthouse.

"No."

He could have argued, but he'd understood. After Sunday lunch with the parents, he'd understood in spades why she

couldn't find any refuge there. He hadn't known where else
to take her where she'd be safe but here—and he'd had to get
her away from the penthouse and the visceral reminder of
how badly someone wanted her dead.

He'd called Kincaid on the drive over, broken the news
about the break-in. Before Kincaid could start issuing de-
mands, Nolan informed him that for the night Jillian was safe
but incommunicado. Then he'd disconnected and shut off his
cell phone. He figured he'd be out of a job in the morning,
but until then at least she'd have some peace of mind.

He walked her along the side deck, ducked under the
cover of the aft deck, and with his key unlocked the sliding
door that led to the main cabin.

"Five steps down." He guided her down the companionway steps. "The last one's a little taller than the others. All
right. Just stand tight for a second and I'll get us some light."

Not that he wanted to shed any light on the place. If
memory served him right, he'd left it in a helluva mess.
Nonstop bingeing was messy business. When he flipped the
switch on the table lamp near the L-shaped sofa and light
flooded the cabin, he couldn't hide his surprise. "Holy crap."

The place was spotless. No newspapers spread around.
No empty liquor bottles or boxes of half-eaten takeout or the
stench of either one. The white curtains at the sparkling salon windows were neatly tied back. The blue toss pillows on
the white upholstery of the sofa were neatly fluffed. No dust
gathered on the teak wall paneling or galley table. The carpet had been vacuumed.

Come to think of it, the aft deck had been shipshape, too,
the all-weather furniture neatly arranged instead of scattered
about helter-skelter as he'd sworn he'd left it.

"Something wrong?"

He laughed, dragged a hand over his face as he stood in
the middle of the salon, taking it all in. "No. Just a surprise

is all. Looks like the cabin fairies were here with their magic fairy dust. This place was a pit when I left it."

"Is she yours?"

"*Ours.* The family's. Dad bought her new back in '88." All fifty-six foot of her, with her twin Caterpillar 275-horsepower diesel engines and all the comforts of home. "God, he was proud," he said aloud before he realized he'd taken a quick stroll down memory lane, where life had been simple and sweet. They'd had a blast onboard over the years.

"Do you . . . live here?"

He turned, saw that she was listing a little toward starboard. She was exhausted. Running on fumes. And still a little shocky. He motioned for her to sit, waited until she did before answering. "Temporarily. No one's taken her out for a while, so I claimed squatter's rights for the time being."

He crossed the few feet to the open galley and snagged a note stuck to the refrigerator door by a magnet shaped like a seagull.

> *Cookies and chicken casserole in the freezer. You're such a slob, sweetie. You owe me.*
>
> Love, Mom

He grinned. "My mother," he said by way of explanation when he felt her gaze on his face.

"Aka the cabin fairy?"

He nodded and stuck the note back where he'd found it.

"So . . . how long have you been staying here?"

"About three months." He wandered back to the master cabin and found it as spotless as the rest of the boat.

"Since you separated from the Rangers," she calculated as he ducked back through the doorway.

He met her eyes, girded himself for another game of twenty questions. Only the funny thing was, he didn't feel nearly as resistant to answering them as he had in the past. He wasn't sure what that meant, but he figured it wasn't good. So he made sure his answer was short and to the point in the hope of warning her off.

"Yeah. Since then."

She got the message. And for the better part of a very long minute she just sat there, perched on the edge of the sofa, her hands folded on her lap, glancing around the cabin in a way that said part of her was here, cataloging and familiarizing, but that another part—the scared-out-of-her-wits part—was still back at her penthouse, reliving the shock.

"Do you want to talk about it?" he asked, leaning back against the galley counter and crossing his arms over his chest.

Her gaze darted to his, then back to her hands. She shook her head. He couldn't see her face, but he could see the way she'd clutched her fingers together until they were white. Could see the catch of each breath, the valiant way she held her shoulders stiff and her legs together, like a soldier working to prove with everything in him that he wasn't afraid to die. Hell no, she didn't want to talk about it. Yet he knew that it was probably all she could think about.

All of her leather furniture had been cut to pieces, wooden tables hacked and marred, paintings viciously slashed, pricey antique vases smashed.

Her bedroom . . . God. Down feathers were everywhere; her white sheets and comforter had been ripped to shreds— her clothes, too. And every mirror in the house was shattered.

But the worst part . . . the very worst was the huge pool of blood congealing in the middle of what was left of her bed.

So no, she didn't want to talk about it or about Eddie the doorman, who had taken a rap to the head hard enough to knock him out. He was awake now, but he'd never seen what—or, more important, who—had hit him. The intruder had known what they were about. The security station's desk had been jimmied open. Inside the desk had been all the security codes for the building, which explained why the alarms had never sounded.

Nolan watched her for a moment, making some denials of his own. Like the need to go to her, pull her onto his lap, and let her lean and latch onto him for as long as she wanted, as long as she needed. But he knew where it would lead. He wasn't that self-sacrificing. And he didn't have that much self-control.

"How about the fifty-cent tour?" he asked, and told himself it was an attempt to distract her instead of an act of desperation.

She looked up. Forced a smile. "Sure. That way I won't stumble over something in the night if I get restless."

OK. Fine. Whatever. He didn't want to think about her wandering around in the night. Restless. Just like he'd be restless in his own bed.

So, he showed her the *EDEN* from stem to stern, then took her back topside to the foredeck, where they stood in silence, listening to the water, the occasional wisp of a conversation, and watched the small scattering of lights that indicated other boats were occupied as well and that they weren't as isolated as it seemed.

She removed her shoes, then sat with her bare feet dangling over the bow. Hands on the bow rail, she looked over the side where the *EDEN* rode several feet above the water's surface.

"So, you had some good times here."

Well behind her, leaning a shoulder against the flybridge, he watched the moonlight cast creamy shades and shadows over her hair. "Yeah. I don't know how the folks stood it. There wasn't a one of us who wasn't hell on wheels when we were kids. Eve included."

"They named the boat after all of you. Something tells me they stood it very well.

"She's a nice piece of craftsmanship," Jillian added, running her hand across the polished deck. "I envy you the times you spent on her with your family."

Nolan had seen pictures of the Kincaid yacht. While the *EDEN* was shipshape and seaworthy, in contrast the yacht made her look like a dinghy. An old, weatherworn dinghy.

"Daddy uses his yacht for entertaining. I don't know if it's ever been out of port. Crazy, huh? It's fully staffed twenty-four-seven and I don't think he's been aboard more than once or twice this past year."

"Are you a sailor?" He could picture her in open water, her face turned into the wind, her eyes bright with excitement.

"Me? No. I love the water, but when I was a kid I was pretty much involved with gymnastics all the time. It didn't leave much room for sailing."

"How about other things?" he asked, moving forward to help her when she stood.

"Other things?"

He shrugged, then leaned down to pick up her shoes. In the process, he noticed that her toenails were painted bright red. "Didn't you ever get into trouble?"

She laughed, but there wasn't much humor in it. "I was a good girl. Good girls don't get into trouble. They get good grades, toe the line, and set goals."

"Sounds boring."

She started walking aft along the side deck until she reached the ladder that ascended to the top of the flybridge. Instead of climbing it like he thought she might, she leaned back against it and stared up at the stars. "I was too busy to be bored."

He grunted, dragged a cushioned patio chair out of the aft deck, and sat down. Because he was tired, he told himself, not so he could see her face better in the moonlight. "And I was too busy raising hell."

"I'll bet you were one of those guys all the girls drooled

over." A speculative smile tilted one corner of her mouth. "Football hero. Good-looking. All attitude and ego."

He slouched back in the chair, laced his fingers together over his abdomen. "Because you smiled when you said that, I'm not going to let myself feel too wounded."

"Tell me about your family," she said abruptly. "Not the newspaper, magazine article stuff. The real stuff. The things that tie you together."

Her hands were above her head now, clutching the handrails on the ladder at her back, her pose unconsciously seductive, unequivocally sexy. Her yellow jacket fell open, the black camisole pulled snug against her breasts. Her short skirt showed enough leg to make his throat feel thick. He noticed her red toenails again.

Details. He'd always had a knack for details.

He looked away. The alternative was to stand up and press her deeper into that ladder with his body, then figure out the fastest way to get her horizontal and naked. He didn't care which order.

But he'd already had this conversation with himself and he already knew that couldn't happen. So he thought about what she'd asked him. And then he started talking and smiling as he remembered.

Once he started, she wouldn't let him stop. She coaxed him with smiles, charmed him with her laughter, delighting in the simplest tales that he'd always taken for granted as his due. But in the small hours of the morning, with the water and the sky and the woman listening in, he slowly realized they were very special and very cherished memories.

Some of which he'd completely forgotten.

"We had a banyan tree in our backyard. My mom was so proud of it. One year a storm came through and cracked one of the trunks. We'd heard Dad talking about how he needed to saw it off before it broke off. He was still on the force then. I must have been . . . I don't know . . . maybe five.

Anyway, one day Ethan and Dallas decided they'd take care of that limb for him.

"So there they were, both of them straddling it. The sucker must have been ten feet off the ground. Anyway, they were sawing like crazy and I was whining on the ground because they wouldn't let me help."

He paused, remembering with a smile. "Finally they sawed through. Only problem was, Dallas was sitting on the hanging side of the cut. When that limb cracked and fell, so did he. Knocked the wind out of him and scared Ethan to death. Me, being the baby and the brat, went running to the house screaming to Mom that Dallas had fallen out of the tree.

"Mom went into a panic. She grabbed me by the shoulders. 'Oh, my God, Nolan. How far did he fall?'" he said, imitating his mother. "Meaning, how many feet did he fall? Because she was scared, I got scared and started bawling. 'All the way to the ground, Mom! He fell all the way to the ground!'"

He paused. Shook his head while she chuckled. "My dad loves telling that story."

"And you like hearing him tell it."

He sat up, leaned forward, and, legs splayed, propped his elbows on his thighs. "Yeah. I guess I do."

And he did, he realized. He liked talking about his family. Got a little melancholy thinking about it. Let down his guard. Because the next thing he knew, he found himself thinking out loud about things he'd never confided to anyone. About things he'd rarely let himself dwell on.

"He's a quiet man, my dad. Normally doesn't have a lot to say. I've never heard him talk about his experience in Nam. And I'd always wanted him to. Wanted to understand his military experience. How he'd felt about coming home to protesters when he'd only been fighting for what he thought was right."

"I imagine he felt much the same way about it as you did."

His gaze cut to hers. "Not the same. Sure, we've had our share of peace protests, but it wasn't the same as what they experienced coming home from Nam."

"Have you ever talked about it? About your experience with anyone?"

Quiet. It had grown so quiet.

And then before his inner hall monitor could step in and take control, he started talking. Just started talking. About Afghanistan. About Iraq. Little bits and pieces just sort of burped out. Then bigger slices. The poverty. The fear in the children's eyes. The soldiers who had died. The bomb-cratered countryside and the sand that seeped into his pores and stung his eyes and he still woke up tasting in his mouth.

"I loved it," he heard himself say. "And I hated it."

And when he looked up and saw by the position of the moon in the sky that he'd been talking for damn near an hour, he shook his head and swore softly.

"Why didn't you shut me off?"

She had slid to the deck long ago and sat with her legs folded under her hips. "Because I wanted to listen. And because you needed to talk."

Yeah, he realized. Yeah, he had.

And yet he hadn't told her the whole story. He hadn't told her about Will. The man he'd let down. And the reason he was going to move heaven and earth to keep from letting her down, too.

He stood, stiff from sitting for so long, and reached a hand down to her. "Come on. You've got to be beat. You shower first. I'll find a T-shirt for you to sleep in."

She took the hand he offered. Like him, she'd been sitting in one spot too long. She lost her balance and fell against him.

He caught her, cupping his hands on her shoulders to steady her. For the longest moment they stood together that way. Her face tipped up to his. Her eyes glittering in the moonlight. He wanted to pull her flush against him, feel her evening-cooled skin against his, experience the woman softness of her body, and simply sink into everything she was.

But because he was everything she didn't need he made himself set her away.

The only light may have been the wash of moonlight and the slant of lamplight shining on the deck from the cabin, but he read the look in her eyes for what it was.

Disappointment.

Christ. Did every fricking moment have to be a test? Hadn't he served? Hadn't he defended? Did he have to keep the vigil and protect her . . . even from himself when she didn't have the good sense to protect herself from him?

Yeah. He did, because she sure as the world didn't have it in her tonight. She'd been through too much. Her defenses were at rock bottom if she was looking to him for those kinds of answers.

"Come on," he said in a weary voice. "What you need is sleep."

And a lock on her stateroom door.

It was sometime after three in the morning. The *EDEN,* snug in her quiet water mooring, rocked just enough to lull Jillian into a suspended sort of relaxation. The distant creak and groan of the pilings blended with the water sounds and the silence to encourage sleep.

If only she could.

The bed was soft and roomy and the sheets smelled of fresh air and sea breeze. The port stateroom was smaller than the starboard one, and while Nolan had insisted she take the bigger berth, *she'd* insisted he needed the bigger bed. She could be stubborn, too.

After a quick shower and a change into an extra-large

white T-shirt that fell all the way to her knees and smelled like the sheets and like him, she'd shut herself into the smaller bedroom and honestly tried to sleep.

But she could hear him moving quietly about in the cabin. She heard the pump kick on when he took his shower, and imagined him standing under the spray. All wet, naked male. All dark, muscled perfection but for the scars he carried on his body . . . and the scars inside his soul.

He'd revealed some of those to her tonight. So instead of sleeping, she lay there and thought about what it had taken for him to open up to her that way. She thought about how it had felt to be kissed by him, how wonderful he'd felt pressed against her on the dance floor, how he'd looked in the moonlight with his guard down and his expression wistful as he talked about his family. How that same face had hardened with both misery and pain when he'd told her of war and death and all the things that made up the life of a soldier.

When the boat became midnight quiet and she knew he was finally settled in his own berth, she wondered if he was lying in the dark thinking about all of those things he'd told her, too. Of all the things he hadn't.

He had told her that he wondered at the mind-set of a nation that had taken a horrible event like 9/11 to inspire a renewed sense of patriotism when patriotism had almost been lost in complacency. He hadn't told her that at thirty-two he was world-weary, that he'd left the Rangers in the midst of some sort of crisis of conviction. That he was a man now searching for his niche. That he was as vulnerable as she'd thought he was that first night when he stood in her kitchen bleeding.

No, he hadn't told her those things in the words he'd said, but he'd told her in the ones he hadn't. She'd seen it in his eyes. Heard it all in his voice. In the tension in his throat when he'd swallowed, caught himself, and changed tack.

Who were you protecting, Nolan? Who did you think would have difficulty with the truth? You? Or me? Just as she wondered when, exactly, she'd fallen in love with him.

She stared into the night, wanting to believe it was the tension, the danger, the uncertainty, that had led her down that path. That when this was over, if it was ever over, she'd come back to her senses, see him for what he was, and wonder at the workings of the human mind that had caused this momentary lapse in sanity.

She wanted to believe that. But the truth was, there was only one absolute in this entire muddled mess. She *had* fallen in love with him. Completely. Irrevocably. Scars and all. Scars most of all.

So where was the sense of euphoria she'd always thought would accompany that life-altering four-letter word? Where were the fireworks? Where was the elation?

Like some of his secrets, it was all buried. It was all buried beneath the reality that he most likely didn't feel the same way and, even if he did, he'd be self-sacrificing and stubborn and insist he wasn't the man she needed. And it was buried under the very real possibility that she would not live to see tomorrow. A quick mental trip back to her penthouse was all it took to remind her of that.

It was also all the impetus she needed to toss back the covers and sit up. She looked through the darkness toward the stateroom door with a sense of urgency. Heart pounding. Breath short.

All her life, she'd done things the right way. She wasn't going to change her methods now. It was right to go to him . . . no matter that she already knew he was going to fight to the end to convince her it was wrong.

20

IT WAS DEAD OF NIGHT NOW. NOLAN WAS alone in his bed. Remembering something he'd read several years ago—probably in a book about war and the men who waged it.

As a man grows older, he sometimes goes dead inside.

He'd known some of those men, had sworn then that he would never become one. Yet somewhere along the line, he had. Somewhere along the line, he'd even started wanting to be one. In the dead of night, with the sky lit by mortar rounds and the bodies of Iraqi soldiers scattered like broken dolls in the bloodied desert sand, shutting down had been the only way to keep his sanity.

Not more than an hour ago he'd told Jillian some of the events in his life that had led him to this point. This point where he'd become one of those men he'd once sworn he would never become.

Restless, he shoved the sheet down to his waist. A soft breeze drifted through the open porthole and cooled his bare skin. He crossed his arms behind his head on the pillow and stared into the night. It had taken Afghanistan and Iraq and Will to get him to this emotional shutdown. It had taken seeing Sara in ICU struggling for her life and knowing there was nothing he could do to help her. It had taken the looks on her boys' faces—lost, confused—and feeling helpless and responsible. It had taken years of conditioning, gallons of booze, to successfully shut the systems down.

Dead inside. Yeah. He'd thought he finally made it.

Only it seemed he wasn't quite dead after all. Jillian Kincaid wasn't going to allow it.

Christ. How did it happen that in less than a week one small, stubborn redhead had managed to scrape away his insulating calluses, set his lifeblood flowing again, and force him to feel something other than numb?

He'd come into this job feeling indifferent, immune. The most he'd ever thought he'd feel for Jillian Kincaid was contempt. For who she was, for what she represented, for the queen bitch he'd expected her to be. But contempt had given way to respect. Respect to grudging admiration until she'd gotten him to the point where he actually liked her.

Then along came this schoolboy infatuation—and he'd be damned if he'd cop to anything more than that. Infatuation and a hard-core case of lust. Lust, not love. He wasn't going anywhere near that word again. It was too damn scary.

And she was too damn . . . vital.

He let out a resigned breath.

Hell, even when she was pissing him off, she made him feel alive. And he goddamn didn't like it. She'd dragged him right back among the living . . . right back to wanting, needing, wishing for something he couldn't have.

He stared toward his closed stateroom door. Jillian wasn't more than ten feet away.

And he wanted her.

Like some snot-nosed kid, staring through a candy store window, he wanted everything in sight, but he knew he couldn't have it. She was every piece of candy in the freaking store. She was the dream—his life was the reality. And there was no place for her and these feelings she'd resurrected in it.

When he heard her stateroom door open, then close,

heard her footsteps fall, then stop just outside his door, his heart kicked the hell out of him.

Anticipation.

Need.

That's what she made him feel. Feel it with a force that made him weary. Of the wanting. Of the fight to keep from taking it.

Yeah. He was weary. And when he was weary, he got angry—and then he felt nothing but mean.

Why not take it all out on her? It would be so easy to use her. Hell, she was making it easy. So why not?

Because buried somewhere in the depths of his worthless soul a kernel of integrity was determined to make her understand he wasn't anything she needed in her life.

When his stateroom door opened, he leaned up on an elbow and glared at her—at least he tried to. The moonlight reflected off the water and danced in through the window. It made more than a dent in the darkness. He could see her face where she watched him from the doorway, see that his T-shirt had slipped off her shoulder, make out the softness of her breasts beneath it.

She wouldn't make much of a poker player. The look in her eyes was as easy to read as a comic book, but nothing about it made him feel like laughing. She'd come to him for one reason; it could garner only one result. They'd both end up bleeding. They'd both end up with more scars. He had just about all the scars he could handle. And he wasn't going to be responsible for putting any more on her.

He dragged a hand through his hair, made a production out of a yawn, and hoped to hell she didn't see through his act. "What are you doing here, princess?"

Silence. A hesitant step toward his bed. And panic more than honor had him groping for ways to stop her.

"Oh . . . I get it," he said, shooting for bored amusement that he hoped would tick her off enough to send her hiking.

"Still a little keyed up, are you? Figure a roll in the sack with a big bad bodyguard type might take the edge off?"

Her eyes narrowed.

He pushed out a snort. "Sorry, babe. That particular duty isn't in my contract. So you just tippy-toe on back to your own bed, OK? I'm too tired to work up the energy for that kind of action. And for the record, I'm really not all that interested."

It wasn't exactly surprise he saw on her face. He wasn't even sure it was shock. If he were a betting man, he'd wager that she'd been expecting him to try to brush her off and wasn't buying a single line of his bullshit. Her next words confirmed it.

"You're a lousy liar, *babe*," she said, and stepped farther into his stateroom. "Contract clause or not, I think maybe you need me as much as I need you right now."

She did need someone. That much he could see. She'd been through hell the past few days and he wanted nothing more than to invite her to his bed, be that someone for her, and make everything all right. But he had nothing to give her but grief.

Resolve made his voice hard. "If you haven't figured it out by now, I don't need anyone. And if you're thinking this is going to play out something like 'you use, me, I use you, and everybody walks away with happy hormones,' you're dead wrong."

She smiled. She *actually* smiled, and damn her, it was not an *I'm laughing with you, not at you* smile. "That's not exactly the way I see it, but if it helps you to think of it that way—"

"I don't want to think of it at all," he lied, cutting her off. "Since you're not getting the message, let me make it a little clearer. I want you out of here."

She took another step toward the bed. Her beautiful face was limned in moonlight. The scent of his shampoo in her hair was as intoxicating as any scotch. He felt his blood go south.

"So, you're trying to scare me away, is that it?"

Yeah. Hell yeah, that's what he was trying to do. But she didn't look scared. She looked amused, damn her. And he felt hot. And cornered.

"One of us needs to be scared, and it sure as hell isn't me," his big bad self lied, then compounded it with another. "Go away. I told you, I'm not interested."

Her knee hit the bed, dug into the mattress, and tugged the sheet tight over his hips, making them both achingly aware of the tenting action going on beneath it.

She looked from his lap to his face. "Your nose is growing, too."

He could only take so much. And he'd just reached his limit. He reared up, grabbed her by the shoulders. Shook her. Shook her again. "Goddamn it! You think this is funny? You think this is just another game? Well, it's not."

Nose to nose with her, he gave her his best bad dog snarl. "You've forgotten who and what you're dealing with here, princess. So let me jar your memory. I'm not on your father's short list of men you can bring home to dinner. I'm not a nice man. So if all you're looking for is sex . . . just keep this up and you're liable to get it. And don't expect some polite little in-and-out and 'oh, darling, that was lovely.' You come to my bed, I'm going to fuck you, and there won't be anything polite about it."

He shoved her away, breathing hard with the effort to keep from tumbling her beneath him right there, right then. Ignoring the stunned look on her face, he grabbed a handful of sheet and rolled onto his side, away from her. "Now get the hell out of here before we both do something *you're* gonna regret in the morning."

A long moment passed when the only sounds in the room were the blood pounding in his ears and his own harsh breathing. He waited for the door to slam. And waited until her voice finally broke the tension.

"Did you get that all out of your system?"

He groaned, swore. "I told you to leave."

"Um . . . OK, well, no. Your turn."

He rolled to his back, propped himself up on his elbows, and prepared to glare at her. But all he could do was stare, his mouth dust dry as she lifted his T-shirt over her head and let it drop to the floor by the bed.

He swallowed hard, his heartbeat rocketing as she crawled across the sheets on her hands and knees and straddled him . . . all golden limbs, berry pink nipples, and sweet naked ass.

Gezus God, she was beautiful . . . everything he remembered . . . everything he'd dreamed. Everything he wanted.

"I'm a big girl, Nolan," she whispered, her mouth a mere breath away from his. "I don't need you protecting me from myself. I just need you."

He was only so strong. And she was so much of everything essentially missing from his life.

"Damn you," he murmured, reaching for her. "Damn you."

His hands were hard, his mouth on hers rough and greedy, as he kissed her, gripped her hips, and flipped her to her back.

She wasn't smiling anymore. Her eyes were big with anticipation and maybe with a little fear. But mostly what he saw when he searched her beautiful face was trust.

Trust.

It stunned him.

She trusted him. Despite his warning, despite his big bad speech, despite the way he'd handled her.

Trust.

He'd lost all trust in himself when he'd lost Will . . . and with one look, one soft caress of her eyes, she was giving it back.

The feelings welling up inside of him were too much to catalog, too complex to name. But the result was pig simple.

He surrendered. Gave up the fight.

So much for his threat. So much for sex, just sex. There was only one thing he could do now. Only one thing he wanted to do. He gentled his hold, eased the pressure of his mouth over hers, and gave in to the need to make love to her.

It had been so long, so, so long, since he'd had anything this soft in his life. So long since he'd been responsible for anything this fragile. And she was fragile, no matter how tough she pretended to be.

She was cool, smooth silk stretched out beneath him. Her skin. Her sighs. Her hands where she touched him. Nothing had ever aroused him more than the gentle exploration of her fingers as they sifted through his hair. Nothing had ever made him feel this needed, as the flats of her palms drifted down his back, then lower to cup his buttocks and squeeze while she pressed her heels into the mattress and lifted her hips into him.

No woman had ever had this effect on him. Made him feel this indescribable rush of tenderness and lust. This tug-of-war between wanting to take her hard and fast and a gnawing craving to slow it down and take the time to explore what made her tremble, what made her yearn. What made her come apart in his arms.

She was so small. So incredibly giving. And he was so fricking hard he hurt. Yet he gentled his kiss, catering to the burgeoning need to simply lose himself for a while in the taste of her.

Her mouth. *My God.* Her mouth was lush and wet, mobile and giving. She opened wide, let a velvet moan ride on her breath as he delved deep with his tongue and matched the rhythm of his hips as they rocked against hers. He lifted up on his elbows, caged her head in his hands, and changed the angle of his mouth over hers. He could have kissed her like that forever, just played with her lips, swallowed her lusty sighs, and experimented with methods of extracting more, if she hadn't reminded him with her restlessness that there was more, so much more, she could make him feel. And so much more he could give her in the process.

He wanted skin on skin, but the sheet had gotten tangled between them. He made himself pull away, rolled to his side, and ripped it free. As hard as he was, as bad as he hurt, as much as he wanted to bury himself inside her, he stayed where he was beside her. Fed the need to look at her. Just look at this soft, strong woman who had managed to drag him out of a pit of nothingness and make him glad he was alive.

He was a hard man. He'd never in a million years seen himself as a poet, but at that moment he wished he could be one. Moonlight and Jillian. It was a potent combination. He wished he had the ability to tell her what the sight of her body did to him. How her touch inflamed him.

But he was a man of action, so he showed her with his hands instead. He splayed his fingers wide over the flatness of her belly, mesmerized by the contrasts: his dark skin to her light, his scars and calluses to her silky perfection.

Each touch sparked some new sensation. Tenderness, impatience, lust, as he trailed his fingers up her rib cage, then cupped one supple breast in his hand.

Her breath caught, her nipple pearled. Desire dived deep, then surfaced as hunger. He lowered his head, tugged on her nipple when she arched toward him, cupped his head in her hand, and pressed his mouth to her flesh. He opened wide over her, sucking her in, sipping at the sweetest feast, the most incredible softness.

One sensation fed the need for another. With his mouth still playing at her breast, he skimmed the back of his knuckles down the centerline of her body. A delicious tremor of anticipation eddied through her when he cupped her and he did a little groaning of his own when she parted her thighs in a wanton invitation for him to touch her there.

She was so wet and so hot and so sweetly swollen when

he slipped a finger inside. She was incredibly responsive when he stroked her, bucking against his hand, moaning her impatience and her pleasure. And when he lifted his head and saw the honesty of her response on her face, he slid down her body and let himself finally taste that part of her he'd been wanting to taste since the first night he'd seen her step naked out of her shower.

He loved that she wasn't so sure about what he was doing. Loved that she tensed, rose up on one elbow, and knotted her fingers in his hair.

"Too much," she gasped. "Too . . . fast."

He kissed her stomach, lifted his head, and looked up the length of her body. Unbelievable. The desperate longing in her eyes actually settled him. He, however, had no intention of settling her. He wanted her wild. He wanted her writhing. And by the time he trailed kisses and nips across her abdomen, tracked a warm, wet path across her hip point with a lingering glide of his tongue, she was equal measures of both.

The curls covering her sex were silky soft. The fold of her lips lush and pink, slick and swollen. He nestled deep, made a long pass along her clitoris with his tongue . . . and felt her sudden intake of air.

Then he set about stealing her breath altogether.

She screamed when she came. Sobbed when he drew out her pleasure. And when he brought her down from her high with slow licks and gentle suction, his name was on her lips, just as her taste would be forever embedded in his.

Light-headed, saturated in the most consummate pleasure she'd ever imagined, Jillian drifted on the aftermath of sensations too devastating and intense to sort or name. She drew in a shallow breath, let it out on a ragged sigh. Boneless. She felt boneless and spent and deliriously happy, content to float forever on the backside of the most incredible sexual experience of her life.

Nothing had ever felt this good. Nothing could ever feel this good again. There wasn't even a point in trying. Yet thinking about it, remembering the unbelievable rush, she had high hopes of duplicating it. But not anytime soon. The mind was willing, but the body . . . oh, the body was exhausted and spent and still tingling in the afterglow.

When Nolan crawled back up her body, taking his time to linger and nuzzle and nip, it took every ounce of strength to wrap her arms around his neck and pull his mouth to hers for a long, lazy kiss. A kiss that tasted of sex and of him and of her. A kiss that rekindled by languid degrees the low pulsing ache deep in her belly.

When he parted her legs with his knee and in one long, slow thrust entered her, the upward spiral into sensation began anew . . . and he took her even higher than before.

All she could think of was him. Inside her. A part of her. Filling her so full she could barely absorb the pressure. She felt like she was flying; she felt like she was falling as he drove into her over and over again. Deep. Hard. So absolutely male. So dangerously needy. She wanted it to go on forever . . . yet if something didn't happen soon, she knew she was going to die in her attempt to reach it.

"Please . . . please . . . please . . ."

It could have been her begging. It could have been him. She no longer knew where her breath ended and his began. No longer knew if she was earthbound or soaring. And when he thrust one final time, lifting her with him, taking her along, she no longer cared. All that mattered was sensation. All that mattered was the moment.

And the man.

Oh, the man.

When he collapsed on top of her, she welcomed his weight. When he tried to roll away to ease the stress, she wrapped herself around him like a monkey and held on so tight he couldn't have left if he wanted to.

He didn't want to. That knowledge brought a sleepy, content smile.

No matter that he'd snarled and growled and pulled every threat out of his bag of tricks to scare her away, he hadn't really wanted her to go. He didn't want her going anywhere now.

She could feel it in the whipcord strength of his arms locked around her. Sense it in the way he buried his face in her hair and breathed her in like she was life and without her he didn't want to live it.

She held him tightly against her in the hours while he slept, loving the heat and the weight of him, satisfied with the steady, exhausted cadence of his breathing, not caring that her arm had gone to sleep, that her neck had grown stiff. She knew he didn't always sleep well. Was happy beyond reason that she was able to give him this respite.

It was a small but necessary act for her to protect him from the demons that haunted him in the dark. Small but necessary given the fact that he protected her with his life.

Nolan lay on his back in the bed, arms crossed behind his head, staring at the water's reflection flashing on the paneled ceiling. Beside him, curled up like a kitten, her head on his shoulder, her arm draped across his chest, Jillian slept, a wonder of woman softness and giving heat.

She was lush and warm and everything a woman should be. He allowed himself the moment to relish the feel of her nestled against him. To remember the way she'd shattered in his arms, that sweet place between her thighs. The taste he would never forget.

When he'd made love to her, he felt things he hadn't felt since he was a boy—like the experience of that first exhilarating ride on a roller coaster. The first dive off the high board. The first time solo behind the wheel.

The first time he'd thought he was in love.

The first time he'd *known* he was in love. Which, by his best estimation, was the first time he'd set eyes on her.

He swiped a hand over his face. He was so fucked.

For a man who'd given up on living, he'd picked a helluva time to find a spark of life. For a man who was paid to protect, he'd committed the cardinal sin. He'd let things become personal. He'd let their relationship transition from adversarial to allied. He'd let her get too close. Told her things. Personal things. God . . . he'd spilled his guts last night.

Because of it, she'd decided *she* needed to save *him*. How was that for, fricking irony?

"You're thinking too hard, Garrett."

He looked down to see her green eyes smiling up at him. The sun was just breaking over the *EDEN*'s bow, slanting gentle morning light through the starboard window of the stateroom.

"If I was thinking—"

"No." She rose up on an elbow, pressed two fingers to his lips. "Don't say it. Don't say that if you were thinking, this wouldn't have happened. And for God's sake, don't apologize. Don't tell me how wrong this was or what a bad, bad man you are or how stupid I was to let it happen."

He clenched his jaw, averted his gaze to the ceiling again to avoid looking at her pretty breasts pressed against his chest, her incredible mouth, swollen and pink from his kisses.

"You're the boss," he said with just enough meanness to regret it.

She slid a knee over his stomach, brushing his penis in the process. True to form, he involuntarily rose to the occasion.

Oh no. He wasn't going to compound things by making love to her again, no matter how badly he wanted to.

He started to sit up. "We'd better get dressed and check in with your father."

She pushed him back down. At least he convinced himself she did.

Her fingers traced the tattoo on the inside of his bicep. "What's this?"

He didn't have to look down to see what had drawn her attention. "My Social Security number and blood type."

"Do I want to know why they're there?"

He watched her brows draw together into a frown. "Probably not."

She ran her fingers slowly back and forth over the numbers and he had to grit his teeth to keep from tumbling her beneath him. When she lifted her gaze to his, it was filled with a determined but wary curiosity. "Tell me."

He debated for a moment, then decided it was something she needed to hear. "When you go to war, you never know if you'll come back, and if you do, you never know *how* you'll come back. Sometimes the only way to identify a body is by parts. I was just hedging my bets."

Tears shimmered in her eyes.

He steeled himself against the urge to kiss them away.

Using his chest for leverage, she pushed herself up and over him, settling all her warm, damp heat over his groin.

"Make love to me," she whispered, all dewy soft skin and shimmering eyes and a body so damn hot he thought he'd combust.

"Please," she said, bending down and brushing her breasts across his chest, her lips across his mouth.

Defenseless against her as he'd never been defenseless in his life, he gave up, gave in. He let her take him deep into her body. Let her infiltrate a little deeper into his blood. Let himself believe, if only in this moment, that everything was right with his world as long as she was in it.

21

NOLAN WOKE UP FROM A DEAD SLEEP. HIS eyes flew open. His heart pounded like marching feet; his breath soughed out, harsh and choppy.

Even after he realized where he was—not Iraq, not watching Nelson bleed out—the adrenaline still ripped through his blood. He stared at the ceiling, slowly became aware of the slap of the water against the *EDEN*'s hull, of the warm body sleeping beside him, and the nightmare skulked back into the dark.

He breathed deep. And smelled her.

Outside, gulls screeched like rusty gears. In the distance he could hear the muted purr of motor craft negotiating the network of slips and heading out to open water. He closed his eyes, fell back on the relaxation technique he'd used countless times after countless enemy engagements, and finally felt himself level out.

Beside him, Jillian slept, oblivious to his nightmare.

She was exhausted. And why the hell wouldn't she be? If the tension from her stalker hadn't done it, what they'd done in this berth during the night had.

And he was getting the hell away from her before he lost his mind again and pushed her past exhaustion and into a coma.

He eased carefully out of bed so he wouldn't wake her. Then he stood there, unable to make himself move away.

Christ. Look at her. He dragged a hand through his hair. Even sound asleep and wrecked on sex, she looked regal, like the princess she was.

It was time for a reality check. Only it felt more like a gut check, because for the first time in his life taking a woman to bed hadn't been all about sex. Yeah, it had been great sex. OK, unbelievable sex. But it had also been more.

At least for him it had. It had been about caring and sharing and . . . love.

How was that for a kick in the ass?

If it weren't so pathetic, it'd be laughable.

He could fight it, deny it, lie to himself until Iraq became the fifty-first state, but he couldn't outrun it any longer. The truth dogged him like a shadow, relentless and demanding that he face it.

In the dark of night he finally had. When she'd come to him, small and strong, fragile and determined, he could have stuck to his guns and sent her away. He *should* have sent her away. For her sake.

He hadn't. For his sake.

He'd needed her. More than breath. More than water. In that moment and every moment since he'd needed her to take away the emptiness. Needed her to fill the void. Needed her so bad he'd ached with it.

And so he'd taken. And she'd given. Now he had to fix the mess he'd made with his selfishness.

She thought she had feelings for him, too. She might even think she loved him. He knew better. Because he knew who he was. She didn't. Once she did, once she saw past the image of him as a protector, she'd realize she was simply caught up in the terror of her situation and that he'd become her "savior." When the threat went away, so, eventually, would she.

Better to just end it now. Cut and run before he sank in any deeper, because it was a bona-fide lost cause from where he was standing.

He grabbed his jeans from the floor and headed for the galley. After making coffee and snagging a couple of cookies from the freezer, he hit the head and the shower. He was standing on-deck, soaking up his hit of caffeine and squaring away his arguments, when he heard her walk up behind him.

"Hi," she whispered, wrapping her arms around his waist and snuggling up against his back. "Great morning."

Gently prying her hands away, he put distance between them and turned to face her. "Barely that. It's almost eleven."

She squinted against the sun, then smiled up at him. "Then it's almost time for a nap. Care to join me?"

She'd dressed in his T-shirt again and it was obvious by the way the wind plastered it against her slight body that she wasn't wearing anything else.

"I called the hospital, checked on Eddie Jefferies." He tried to drag his gaze to the harbor and out of trouble. No such luck. Even ruined from his hands and his mouth, she was the most beautiful thing he'd ever seen. "He's doing fine. Most likely, they'll release him today."

Relief washed over her face. "Thank you for checking on him. I'm so glad he wasn't hurt any worse than he was.

"Now . . . about that nap." With a playful smile, she reached for him.

It killed him, but he shook his head, backed away. "Look, Jillian. About last night."

Her hand paused midair. She looked at him. Hard. "Wait. You're not really going to give me an *about last night* speech, are you?"

He downed a swallow of lukewarm coffee, tossed the rest over the side of the boat. "You don't want a speech? Fine. I'll cut to the chase. The sex was great. Are you on the pill?"

She looked stunned but nodded.

"Then we're good. I'm healthy. I figure you are, too. So, now it's back to business."

Some of the shock had left her eyes. In its place was

incredulity. "Gosh and gee-whiz. I'm just bowled over by your morning-after love talk, Romeo."

"Look. You came to *my* bed, remember? I gave you what you wanted. Now I need you to give me what I want."

Her eyes, hard as emeralds now, searched his. "What *do* you want, Nolan?"

He steeled himself against her wounded look. "What I've wanted from the beginning. Distance."

Reeling with shock and pain, Jillian watched him walk away. For all of a second. Then outrage kicked in. "Distance? You want *distance*?"

As she'd hoped, her question stopped him cold when he reached the aft deck. He turned and looked at her through bored eyes. Strike that. He looked past her, over her shoulder, because he couldn't look her in the eye and lie to her again.

And he was lying. Badly. It all fell into place then. Relief spilled over the frustration. "You are so full of it, Garrett. You don't want distance. You want me . . . and it's driving you crazy."

Everything inside her that she'd ever trusted to lead the way screamed at her now to believe her gut instincts. "You want *us*. You couldn't have made love to me the way you did last night if you didn't."

His jaw worked. His blue eyes iced over. "Why can't you just leave this alone? Why do you make me hurt you? Make me say things I don't want to say?"

He swore. Dragged a hand through his hair and pinned her with a hard look. "It was just sex, Jillian. Don't confuse it with anything else."

She didn't bat an eye. "I don't believe you. I don't think you believe it, either. You just don't want to deal with the truth because you don't have control now. What you feel for me does."

She'd fight to make sure he understood that. Then she

was going to fight to make him stay. But right now he was running scared and she had to figure out a way to stop him.

"For God's sake, Nolan, do I frighten you that much?"

He studied her face, then gave her one of those *I don't give a damn* shrugs. "If that's what you want to think—"

"Oh, I do," she fired back, Joan of Arc on a mission. She was mad now, fighting mad. "I think you're scared to death. Scared to take a chance on me. Scared to take a chance on you."

Bingo.

In the fraction of a second before he hid his surprise with another one of his patented brooding glares, his eyes gave him away.

He wasn't just scared. He was terrified. And suddenly she knew where to look for the source of that fear. If she'd been reading between the lines when she dug up all that information about him on the Web, she'd have figured it out long ago. If she'd thought a little harder about what Plowboy had said—*You couldn't have stopped it*—she'd have known where to start long before this.

"Who do you think you let down, Nolan?"

Silence—as taut with tension as a lifeline. His eyes cut into hers like lasers. *Back off.*

"Who was it?" she pressed, risking his wrath. "Who didn't you save that made you decide you weren't man enough to be a Ranger anymore? Who died and made you so sure you're not man enough for me?"

"You don't know what you're talking about," he said in a flat voice, though she could see his pulse pounding double-time at his throat.

"I know that you have nightmares."

He closed his eyes, then visibly tried to settle himself. "Show me a combat veteran who doesn't."

"And you show me one who can handle everything on his own and still keep his sanity. Talk to me."

He snorted. "What? Are you my shrink now?"

She shook her head, ignored his glower. "No. I'm the woman who loves you."

He pushed out a harsh laugh. "We spent one night in the sack, for God's sake. You can't love me."

"Why? Because you're not worth it?"

"Now you've got the picture."

He turned and headed for the cabin door.

She raced after him, all but ran to catch up as he descended the companionway steps. "Why aren't you worth it? Because men in your squad died in combat? Because you have nightmares telling you that *you* were responsible?"

"Hell yes, men died!" He spun around to face her. Agony, rage. It was all there on his face. "Good soldiers. Good men."

One foot on the step, the other on the floor, she gripped the railing. "Men you think you should have saved."

He hung his hands on his hips, let out a weary breath. "I couldn't have saved them. But I should have—"

He cut himself off. Wiped a hand over his jaw.

"You should have what?" she asked softly.

He whipped his head her way, pinned her with a defiant stare. And then he just sort of crumpled. His shoulders sagged. His face grew slack. In that moment she could see the weight of the entire world pressing down on his shoulders.

"I should have saved Will, all right?"

"Will?"

He blinked slowly. "Will Sloan. He was one of mine. Came through the war zone like Superman. And then he came home . . . and I lost him."

The cords in his neck worked as he swallowed.

"What happened?"

Weary. He looked so weary. She could see it in the tight lines rimming his mouth, hear it in every breath.

"What happened," he began, turning his back to her, "is

that I should have seen it coming. What happened is that I should have stopped him."

Stiff-armed, he gripped the galley counter with both hands, hung his head. "Sara had come to me. She'd told me that even before we'd redeployed to Iraq she couldn't take it anymore. The time Will spent away from her and the boys. The worry. The way he'd changed into someone she no longer knew. She wanted him to go to counseling with her or she wanted out."

"And what part of this is your fault?"

He turned back around to face her. He leaned his hips against the counter, crossed his arms heavily over his chest. "I was his squad leader. I shouldn't have let him convince me they could work it out on their own. I shouldn't have listened. But he was scared. If they'd gone to counseling, his mental health would be questioned. Even a whisper of a problem isn't career safe in the army and Will was career track to NCO. He lived and breathed army. He didn't want to lose it.

"Sara gave him an ultimatum," he continued when Jillian waited for him to let it all out. "And he . . . snapped. He shot Sara and then he killed himself."

Tears stung her eyes at the raw pain in his voice. "I'm sorry. I'm sorry about your friend."

"Yeah. Tell that to Sara. Tell it to her boys."

"And how would she feel if you told her you felt responsible for his death? Would she agree? Would she blame you?"

He had nothing to say to that.

"She wouldn't, would she? She wouldn't because it wasn't your fault.

"It wasn't your fault," Jillian repeated, going to him. "The only one who thinks so is you."

He stood like a tree. Rigid. Unyielding.

OK. Fine. He wasn't ready to consider it. And he wasn't going to talk about it anymore. She knew him well enough by now to understand his moods. The one he was showing her now was stubborn defiance.

She hadn't reached him. She wasn't going to.

They were in the Mustang, on the way to Golden Palms, when Nolan's cell phone rang. Probably Kincaid again. When he'd finally turned on his phone to call KGLO and tell a very concerned Diane Kleinmeyer that Jillian wasn't going to be in today, there had been at least ten messages from Kincaid. Most of them had something to do with wanting his head on a platter.

"Yeah," he said, and braced for the barrage.

"Got the old ER report on Rachael Hanover." It was Ethan.

Nolan checked his rearview and changed lanes. "OK, shoot."

"Sexual abuse."

He almost rear-ended the Mercedes in front of him. "Say again?"

Ethan repeated the stunning news. "Seems the family managed to bury it. Not deep enough, though."

"Did it name the perpetrator?"

"Negative. Supposedly, someone broke into her bedroom, did the deed there. She never saw his face."

"And the investigation just got dropped?"

"At the family's request. Apparently they didn't want to put her through any more trauma."

Interesting, he thought after Ethan rang off, *that it never made the papers.*

"How long have you known Rachael?" he asked his silent, brooding passenger.

Jillian whipped her head toward him, tugged a flyaway strand of hair away from the corner of her mouth. "Rachael? Rachael Hanover?"

He nodded, averting his gaze back to the road. He couldn't

look at her without remembering last night. Couldn't think about last night without wanting her.

"Why do you want to know?"

"Just passing time, OK?"

"No," she said. "It's not OK. You don't engage in idle conversation. Wait . . . don't tell me you think Rachael's a suspect?"

He ignored her question and fired his back at her. "How long have you known her?"

"Since we were in diapers, and so help me God, if you involve her in this—"

"She ever say anything to you about being assaulted?"

That gave her pause. "Rachael was assaulted? Oh, my God. When?"

"She was twelve."

She stared into the passing traffic, brows furrowed in disbelief. "I would have known."

"Not if she'd been traumatized. Or if she was told not to tell."

"Not to tell? What are you getting at? What kind of assault? Oh no. No," she repeated, incredulous when she read the look on his face. "Not sexual. Oh God."

"What kind of relationship did she have with her father?"

Shock. Denial. It brimmed in her expression. "You can't be implying that Mr. Goddard . . . I can't even say it."

"What kind of relationship?"

"Fine. As far as I know, it was fine. He was an involved parent. I liked him. But I don't like this. Even if it happened, what does it have to do with what's happening to me?"

"Just covering my bases."

He still wasn't sure what this new revelation about Rachael Hanover meant, didn't know if it had any bearing at all on Jillian. But it started him thinking about the messages the stalker had sent. Most of them had used children's nursery rhymes. One had alluded to the king's men calling Jillian's father.

Nursery rhymes plus child plus childhood trauma plus the father reference.

If there was a connection, it was a stretch, but at this point nothing seemed like too much of a reach. Still spinning it around in his head, he dialed Kincaid's number. It was time to face the music. They'd been incommunicado since he'd brought Jillian aboard the *EDEN* last night.

"God*damn* it, Garrett!" Kincaid roared. "Don't you *ever* cut off communication with me again! Where's Jillian? How is she?"

"She's with me. She's fine. And we're about two miles from Golden Palms. We'll be there in under five minutes."

Nolan hung up—but not before Kincaid hit him with a few choice words and ripped a strip off his back. He'd gone from golden boy to vermin in ten easy steps. It also seemed that the moment he delivered Jillian he was out of a job.

That was fine, too. Nolan didn't want to play this game anymore. Or think about why he'd spilled his guts to her. Or how she'd looked at him with love in her eyes and hope in her heart and made him feel like he might just deserve both.

He didn't. And she didn't love him. She just thought she did. And he wasn't going to turn into one of her lost causes.

He dragged a hand through his hair. Damn the woman. She pushed and pushed until she backed a man up against a brick wall, and then she took a wrecking ball to the damn wall.

Well, she could push all she wanted, but he was taking her to Golden Palms and dumping her there. Putting her under lock and key if he had to. She may have forgotten what her penthouse had looked like, but he hadn't. This lunatic was running on a small reserve of sanity. It wouldn't be long now before the final scene played out, and he wasn't taking any chances with her life.

"I'm not staying with my parents," she said, defiance ooz-ing from every pore.

"You can't stay at your penthouse. Even if it wasn't trashed, you aren't safe there."

"What's wrong with staying on the boat?"

Everything, he thought. Everything was wrong. Every-thing would be wrong until he could get the scent of her out of his sheets and the taste of her out of his system.

And he wasn't going to have this argument with her about it.

Driving through the security gate at Golden Palms again, Nolan knew he'd been right to bring her here. And he would be right to walk away.

"Jillian!" Clare, stylish as ever but looking a bit frazzled and haunted around the eyes, greeted them at Darin's side. "Darling, we've been so worried." She drew her daughter into her arms, the first honest show of affection Nolan had seen.

"I'm fine, Mother. Daddy, you can quit glaring at Nolan. I asked him to take me somewhere quiet last night. I'm sorry. I just wasn't up to dealing with anyone."

"Laurens wants you to call him," Kincaid said, none of the steel leaving his eyes. His look defied Nolan to butt heads with him again.

The Kincaids hustled Jillian toward the east wing of the house while Nolan stayed in the foyer and dialed Laurens's number.

It didn't take long to figure out they hadn't found any-thing more to go on. Whoever had destroyed Jillian's pent-house had known what they were doing. No prints. No fiber. Nothing to connect the dots and lead them to the stalker.

"What about the blood?"

"Same as the blood planted on Jillian at the press confer-ence. It's animal. Lab's on it, but they haven't come up with anything yet."

Nolan relayed the information on Rachael Hanover. Laurens was of the same mind: it was interesting, but it was a stretch. Still, the detective said he'd follow up on it.

Nolan disconnected and followed raised voices to the library. The Kincaids—all three of them—were deep in a debate about where Jillian would be staying until this thing played out.

"Make it three to one," he said, siding with Darin and Clare against Jillian as he walked into the room. "You're staying here. And you're not leaving until this is over."

"Over? Don't be ridiculous. It could go on for months."

"Then you stay here for months."

"I have a job. And at the risk of sounding like a broken record, I'm not going to let this maniac run my life. You're hired to protect me, Garrett. So protect me."

"Sorry, princess. I'm officially off the case."

"What?" She looked from Garrett to her father.

"I fired him," Kincaid said.

That was the least of what Kincaid had done or said in the voice mail messages he'd left. The word *lawsuit* had come up several times.

Nolan flashed Jillian a hard smile. "Problem solved. You're staying here." Where she was safe, not only from the killer but also from him.

"Your mother needs you, Jillie," Kincaid put in.

"Mom has you," Jillian insisted. "And I have a life."

"You do if you stay put." Nolan took one long last look. "Take care, princess."

He turned to go.

"OK. OK."

Her adamant tone stopped him.

"I give up. I'll stay here tonight, all right?"

The library rang with silence in the aftermath of her reluctant concession. Then she dropped the bomb.

"On the condition I get my bodyguard back."

Her mind was set. He'd never seen such stubborn determination in her eyes.

"Come again? Thought you'd be jumping for joy."

She ignored him and addressed Kincaid. "Garrett stays, or I go, too," she said, daring her father to test her. "The Palm Beach County Civic Awards banquet is tomorrow night. I'm going—with him, without him. It's your choice. But I *am* going. This person has stolen my sense of security, stolen my peace. I'm not going to let him steal everything I've worked for. I want this award. I deserve it. And I'm going to be there when it's presented."

22

THE DULL RAZOR ABRADED HIS SKIN AS John drew it across his jaw. The cheap motel soap provided little in the way of reducing the friction. A sharp, quick jab of pain stilled his hand. With disconnected fascination, he watched as a thin trickle of blood oozed from the fresh nick on his flesh.

How ... odd that he bled, that his heart still beat, when for all practical purposes he was little more than a ghost. An apparition.

If not for Jillian Kincaid and her endless questions, that ghost would have been laid to rest long ago and he would have finally found some semblance of peace.

Her questions had finally pushed him to the point where he now had but one of his own: Had he ever hated anyone as much as the woman who insisted he mattered when nothing in his life confirmed that he did?

He wanted relief. He craved it.

As he wiped the last of the shaving cream from his jaw and prepared for what must be done tonight, he had never felt less like a human.

After tonight, he would have relief. Mary assured him it would be so.

"Ready?" Mary asked gently from behind him.

He stared past his reflection to see her face behind him in the mirror.

She smiled, and he nodded. And set his mind to what must be done.

The place might be spectacular, but the setup at the Breakers was a security nightmare.

Nolan sat beside Jillian at one of the tables reserved for tonight's Civic Award recipients. He tuned out the industry chatter around him, routinely checking every one of several sets of double doors leading in and out of the room.

The Venetian Ballroom was located at the back of the hotel, on the ground floor, overlooking the Atlantic. It was the largest of many such banquet rooms where these types of functions were routinely held. And similar to the shindig at Mar-A-Lago a week ago tonight, it was packed with a who's who list of Palm Beach notables. They'd turned out in droves wearing their glittering finest to see and be seen and to pay homage to the carefully chosen recipients of awards presented by the richest county, per capita, in the good old capitalistic USA.

Black-and-white-dressed hotel waitstaff scuttled about during a lengthy seven-course dinner, faultlessly profes-sional, catering to every need. Pricey sterling clinked deli-cately against patterned china. Ice tinkled in fragile crystal. In the background a string quartet played some highbrow music that could have been Mozart or one of those other dead composers. Jillian, no doubt, knew who it was and the name of every piece.

Nolan would rather have heard a little Aerosmith. A little hard-driving rock to match his mood and the crash of the breakers slamming against the beach no more than twenty yards from the east windows. Not that he could hear them to-night. The noise made by three hundred plus people bounced down from ceilings over twenty feet high; the windows with their spectacular view of the Atlantic wearing away at the pristine sand beach were at least half that. Even a blue-collar like him could appreciate the elegance and history of the hotel. Another night, another time, he might even have enjoyed some snooping around.

But not tonight. Tonight was all about one thing: keeping Jillian alive.

He had a bad feeling that tonight was the night he was going to earn his money.

He tugged at the collar of his dress shirt, wished to hell he could lose the black tie. The back of his neck itched—another sign to support his instinct that things could get dicey before the night was over.

He'd taken every precaution possible on short notice. Ethan had provided security for other events at the hotel, so the blueprints were on-file at E.D.E.N. Nolan had spent a good part of the day at the office studying them and knew the location of every exit. There were too fricking many of them in the rambling landmark hotel. Hell, there were five banks of public elevators and the damn things were spread all over the place. Even with hotel security on alert, it was impossible to seal them all off, let alone screen in excess of one thousand overnight guests and only God knew how many others attending one function or another on a balmy Saturday night.

With that many guests, you also had to figure there were any number of employees. Ethan and Dallas were in the process of running the names the hotel personnel office had grudgingly handed over less than an hour ago. If anything of interest popped, they'd call him.

Beside him, Jillian conversed with forced animation with some Civic Center mucky-muck who'd been given the honor of presenting her award tonight.

"It's a night for celebration," Jillian had informed Nolan when he picked her up at Golden Palms an hour ago. "Smile, darling." Her sarcasm had been honed to a razor-sharp edge. "There may be little children there. You'll scare them."

He couldn't have smiled if he'd been told he'd won the

lottery. Hell, he could barely breathe when he caught sight of her.

He hadn't seen her in more than twenty-four hours. When he left her at Golden Palms yesterday, he made tracks. And he hadn't been running, dammit, no matter that she was convinced he was. He was just being smart.

He'd needed to regroup. The bomb she'd dropped about attending the Civic Awards had hit him as hard as it had the Kincaids. She wasn't backing down. There wasn't going to be any stopping her from attending. She'd already made her concession. She'd agreed to spend the night at Golden Palms . . . providing Nolan was rehired as her bodyguard. End of negotiations.

He'd been caught between the proverbial boulder and rock wall. If he refused to come back onboard, she'd go to the banquet without him. Yeah, Kincaid could have hired an army of guards to protect her. But would she have let them? And could they have done the job?

He wasn't willing to take the chance.

And wasn't that a 180-degree turnaround?

He'd come into this scared spitless that he didn't have it in him to protect anyone, let alone Jillian. Now he wasn't willing to trust anyone else with the task. He knew what lengths he'd go to. He'd die before he let anything happen to her. He couldn't guarantee the same from anyone else.

So, he'd ended up holing up at E.D.E.N., Inc., the rest of the day and half the night, poring over every piece of information his brothers and sister had gathered on Jillian and the dozens of potential suspects who might be gearing up to make their final move.

He'd been determined not to think about the night he and Jillian had spent in his bed. Determined not to think about the things she'd said.

I'm the woman who loves you.

She just thought she did.

Do I frighten you that much?

Hell yes, he was afraid.

Who do you think you let down?

Will. Sara. And everyone who cared about them. He didn't care what Jillian said or what she believed. He was responsible. He'd let them down. He wasn't going to take a chance of letting Jillian down, too.

But he was going to keep her alive. And when this was over and whoever was trying to hurt her was dead or behind bars, he was walking away. End of story.

She laughed, a clear, ringing sound, and he had to—he just had to—look her way.

She'd been a knockout in shimmering white and seed pearls a week ago. She was unbelievable in emerald silk and rhinestones tonight.

While the dress she'd worn to Mar-A-Lago had exposed lots of creamy skin and incredible cleavage, this one covered her from head to toe—yet it left nothing to the imagination.

The high neckline ended just below her chin; the sleeves were long and narrow, just like the dress. The rich green silk hugged her body like a thin film of lotion overlaid with shimmering trails of tiny white rhinestones that crisscrossed in horizontal lines to the floor. Beneath the slightly flaring hem, her bare toes peeked out of silver sandals that were all straps and four-inch heels.

"You're doing it again."

Slowly, he lifted his gaze from her breasts to her eyes. "Doing what?"

"Scaring the children." She smiled, but there was a brittleness in her eyes that he'd put there.

She'd told him she loved him and he'd laughed it off. She'd shown him how much she cared and he'd thrown it back in her face.

She'd given him the most amazing night of his life . . . and he'd discounted it as just sex.

Fat chance.

"The children are on their own. In case you hadn't noticed, I have a few other things on my mind."

She drew in a serrated breath, glanced around the room. "You really think something's going to happen tonight?"

"I'm paid to think something's going to happen."

"Oh, right. I forgot. It's all about the job for you."

He held her gaze. Told himself it didn't faze him when a mist of tears gathered. "Yeah," he said, understanding that she'd given him one last chance to convince her otherwise. For her sake, he held the line. "It's all about the job."

Soft to hard. Hope to grim acceptance. He saw it all in those hopeful eyes that had wanted so much to believe in him.

She'd given up. He knew right then and there that he'd finally managed to kill whatever feelings she thought she had for him.

And he felt a loss as consuming as cancer.

Jillian felt like a stranger among strangers as she sat in the banquet room, a fabricated smile firmly in place. She even felt like a stranger to herself tonight. It was possible that someone in this crowd loathed her, rejoiced in terrifying her, relished the thought of killing her. Nolan was certain the vendetta was personal. The proof had been in the destruction of her penthouse. Every room had been trashed. Every room but one. The kitchen. Whoever had done this knew she was no cook, didn't care about cooking, could care less about learning how. So they'd left her the one thing they'd known would be no loss. Just so she'd know how very personal it was.

She looked around the room, wishing Rachael could have been here. A friend would have been good tonight. No matter what Nolan thought, Rachael could never be responsible.

Rachael. She hadn't been far from Jillian's mind since Friday, when Nolan had suggested she might have been sexually abused. By her own father. The thought made Jillian nauseous.

Laughter broke out around her. She laughed, too . . . because everyone at the table was laughing. Because she had to get it together. She had a part to play tonight. Somehow, she had to maintain the status quo . . . while the one person she wanted to count on and believe in and turn to and confess how truly frightened and desolate she felt had shut off his feelings like they were a light.

She might consider despising him for that if she didn't love him so much. For all the good either emotion would do her. She couldn't reach him. Obviously, she didn't know how.

"Jillian?"

She jumped when Nolan said her name.

She glanced his way. His eyes were dark with concern. "They just announced your name. Are you OK?"

She heard the anticipatory applause from around the packed ballroom, and shifted into autopilot mode.

Manufacturing a huge smile, she stood, then, very aware of the unsteadiness of her legs and of Nolan's hand at her back supporting her, wound her way carefully through the maze of tables toward the front of the room.

Calling on all her reserves, she climbed the three steps to the dais. Then, doing her best to ignore Nolan's lurking presence a few feet behind her, she stepped up to the podium and began her speech.

Nolan stood on the platform behind Jillian, scanning the darkened room for anything out of order. The problem was, he couldn't see anything. They had dimmed the lights; the entire ballroom was dark but for the single tapered candle on every table and a set of spotlights mounted high above the dais that swept the crowd in crisscrossing arcs like this was some freaking Hollywood movie premiere.

He didn't like the way they'd set up the dais, either. An

elevated platform held a podium equipped with a mike. The platform was positioned at the south wall of the ballroom. Behind it, three sets of huge double doors led out to a wide corridor. He'd been assured the doors were locked, had checked them himself before he and Jillian settled in.

This was the part of the evening when Jillian was at her most vulnerable. Nolan hadn't been more than a foot from her side all night. Now he was forced to stand a little over a yard away, out of the spotlight, in the fricking dark.

When the cell phone clipped to his belt vibrated, his pulse jumped several beats. The display lit with Ethan's number.

"What?" he said quietly so as not to disrupt her speech.

"John Smith, Jillian's Forgotten Man? Seems he recently started working at the Breakers as a dishwasher. He's on the schedule for tonight."

Warning bells clanged like fire alarms as Nolan disconnected. And when a door approximately fifteen yards to the left of the dais cracked open—a door that was supposed to be locked—his adrenaline spiked off the charts.

A thin shaft of light spilled into the room, backlighting the figure standing in the open doorway. Even at this distance, there was no mistaking it was John Smith—just like there was no mistaking the flash of light glinting off something metal Smith clutched in his hand.

Nolan shoved Jillian behind him. "Get down!"

A collective gasp ripped through the room like a wind gust.

"Down!" he repeated, shoving her lower as he reached inside his jacket for his gun.

"What . . . what's happening?" she whispered, breathless.

"Smith's out there."

"John? John's here? Why would he . . . oh. Oh God."

When Smith spotted Nolan, he ducked back into the hall and slammed the door behind him.

"Stay down. And *do not* leave this room." Another gasp and a scattering of screams echoed through the ballroom as Nolan jumped off the dais and sprinted toward the door.

Leading with his gun, he wrenched the door open and inched carefully into the hall. All he saw of Smith was the back of his head as he rounded a corner at a dead run.

Nolan debated for all of a nanosecond before he took off after Smith. He didn't want to leave Jillian, but he couldn't let Smith get away.

"You!" Nolan collared a hotel security person who had come running when he'd heard the commotion. "Get to the Venetian Ballroom. See to it that Ms. Kincaid is all right. Then stay with her and call the Palm Beach PD. Detective Laurens. Tell him I think we've got the stalker. Move!" he yelled as he skidded around another corner and into a full-out run.

"Are you all right?"

Still on her knees, her heart in her throat, Jillian dusted herself off and looked up and into the eyes of one of the few people who could have made her smile in the face of terror, "Oh, thank God. Where did you come from? Never mind," she said, pushing shakily to her feet. "I'm so glad to see a friendly face."

And someone she could count on. She hadn't realized until then just how shaken she was, how desperately vulnerable she felt without Nolan at her side.

She felt her heartbeat quicken even more. Felt her hands begin to shake and tingle, her head begin to spin, as her breath became more and more erratic.

She was about to hyperventilate.

"Get . . . me out of here. Please. Before the whole mob descends."

"Come on. I'll sneak you out the back door."

On rubbery legs, she rushed down the dais steps, tried to force away the panic. "I don't suppose you've got a paper bag on you? I'm going to either barf or pass out on you."

"Fresh air's a few steps away. Hang in there . . . and then tell me what's going on."

He'd lost him.

Sonofabitch!

Hands braced on his knees, sucking air, Nolan cursed his physical conditioning. Three months ago, Smith never would have outrun him. Three months ago, he'd still been in shape.

Straightening, he dragged his hand through his damp hair, jerked the tie from around his neck, and shoved it in his jacket pocket. Heading back toward the ballroom at a jog, he pulled out his cell phone and dialed Laurens's number.

The detective, already en route, answered on the first ring.

Nolan told him what had happened, where he'd lost Smith, and that he was headed back to Jillian. His heart was slamming from much more than physical exertion when he burst into the ballroom—and didn't see her.

"Where is she?" he roared at a frazzled-looking security guard.

"I got waylaid," the guard said, trying not to look cowed. "I just got here. I'm sorry. She's gone."

"Gone? Where?"

"How the hell should I know?" the kid bristled. And he wasn't much more than a kid, inexperienced and out of his element, something Nolan hadn't seen with his adrenaline soaring and his mind set on nailing Smith.

"Quiet. Quiet!" Nolan yelled at the crowd milling around the ballroom in agitated excitement. "Did anyone see Ms. Kincaid leave?"

An elderly gentleman with a red face and rapidly blinking eyes pointed toward the double doors behind the dais.

Nolan set out at a run. He burst through the doors into the middle of a wide hallway. Twenty yards to his right and he'd end up back in the interior maze of the hotel. Twenty yards to the left, exterior doors led to the seawall. His gut instinct had him running for those doors.

Outside, low-moving clouds obscured the moon. Less than twenty yards from the seawall, the wind whipped the Atlantic into rolling, foamy breakers that crashed against eroding sand. Tall palms swayed against the stout tropical wind, fronds clicking like fingernails on glass.

He ran to the edge of the seawall and looked to his right where green grass and lighted walkways led to an outdoor pool running parallel to the ocean and farther west to a maze of hotel shops. To his left about forty feet, the seawall ended, as did the northernmost part of the hotel. If he remembered the blueprints right, there was a narrow paving to the north of the hotel where delivery trucks unloaded.

Again, instinct and a gnawing feeling in his gut had him releasing the safety on his Beretta and sprinting in that direction. He cut across the grass back toward the northeast corner of the hotel. When he reached it he pressed his back up tight against the outer wall, his gun grasped with both hands, and collected himself.

That's when he heard it. A soft, terrified cry.

He lunged around the corner . . . and felt his heart drop to the ground. "Jesus."

Jillian lay on the ground as lifeless-looking as a rag doll.

His breath stalled. In the surreal and murky glow of a security light he could see blood. Everywhere. And bending over her, sobbing hysterically, was Lydia Grace.

"Get away from her! Get the fuck away from her!"

He ran to Jillian's side, fingers jumpy on the trigger as he trained the gun on Lydia.

Lydia turned a tear-streaked face to his, her hands covered in blood. "He . . . he . . . oh God, he stabbed her. You've got to catch him. You've . . . oh God, oh God . . . you've got to do something. Get an ambulance! Hurry. Please . . . please," her sobs grew louder. "For God's sake, hurry!"

The wind buffeted his face. Nolan was peripherally aware of the wail of sirens screeching in the background, the scream of tires on asphalt, the burst of floodlights dancing through the dark. Layered over it all was the distant sound of hovering Black Hawks, mortar fire lighting the night, screams of downed soldiers.

He shut it out, disconnected from everything but the gruesome sight of bloodstained grass, bloodstained silk, as around him he heard a muffled shout: "Police officer! Stop or I'll shoot!" and Lydia's heartbroken sobs. She knelt with her bloodied hands clutched in her lap beside him.

He heard it all, all that was real, all that wasn't, with the clarity of a vivid dream, but what he lived was his worst nightmare.

Jillian must have hit her head when she fell. Concussion? Worse? Hell. There was too much blood. He had to stop it. He had to save her. He searched for the source of the blood with his eyes, with his hands, with everything in him, and finally found it.

Her upper arm. Christ. His heart wrenched as he thought of her lifting her arms to protect herself. Instinct. Reflex. Whatever, the knife had missed any vital organs but still managed to nick an artery and threaten her life anyway.

He dug his necktie out of his pocket, made a tourniquet with it, and used his cell phone to adjust the pressure. He pressed his ear to her chest and damn near wept when he heard a heartbeat and the shallow evidence of her breath. She was going into shock. Blood loss. God, there was so much blood.

"Hang in there, princess," he whispered, and blinked

back moisture from his eyes. "Don't you dare, don't you dare, don't you dare check out on me."

"We'll take it, man."

"Back the hell off!" he snarled as hands gripped his shoulders and urged him away.

"Garrett. Come on, man. It's OK."

A familiar authoritative voice broke through. He looked up to see Detective Laurens squatted down, balancing on the balls of his feet in front of him. "Let the paramedics take over. Let them do their job."

He blinked once, looked around, and realized an ambulance had pulled up on the lawn. A team of paramedics hovered nearby, somber, wary.

"Do not let her die," he said, and reluctantly turned her over to their care.

He stood just as John Smith, in handcuffs, head down, was escorted to a waiting patrol car.

23

". . . AND NOW THAT WE'VE BRIEFED YOU ON this breaking story, we here at KGLO TV are happy to report that everyone's favorite anchor is now resting comfortably. Our sources tell us that Jillian should be released from the hospital soon."

Looking convincingly sober and concerned, Grant Wellington stacked his copy in front of him on the news desk. "Quite a story, Jody."

"Incredible, Grant," Jody agreed, sympathy and incredulity painted on her perky face.

"And, Jillian," Grant turned concerned eyes to the camera, "if you're watching, get well soon, OK? We're all thinking about you.

"That's our news for tonight. Until tomorrow, this is Grant Wellington—"

"And Jody Bentley," Jody piped in with a toothpaste ad smile, "signing off for KGLO News. Good night, everyone."

Leaning back against the pillows in her hospital bed, Jillian stabbed the remote toward the television and clicked it off. "So glad I could provide a little boost in the ratings."

"Not to mention give Grant something to posture about," Rachael added with a grin. "Such concern. I could gag."

Jillian turned her head on her pillow and smiled at her friend. She couldn't look at Rachael now and not think about what she might have gone through.

"Oh, sweetie, you're feeling pretty rough, aren't you?" Rachael asked, mistaking Jillian's concern for pain.

Jillian forced a smile and wondered if Rachael would ever open up to her about it. "I'm doing OK."

"Do I have to preach at you to ask for pain medication when you need it?"

"No, Mother."

"Speaking of which . . . how's she handling this?"

"Pretty well, actually. She and Daddy were here most of the day and she didn't once ask me to give up my job."

"Well, there's always tomorrow," Rachael said brightly.

"Yeah, there's always tomorrow," Jillian echoed. "Thank God."

They both grew quiet for a moment, reflecting on the very real possibility that *tomorrow* might have been off the table for Jillian.

"I still can't believe it," Jillian said wearily.

"Don't think about it now, OK? Concentrate on getting better. Right now the best thing you can do is rest, which is why I'm going to scoot." Rachael leaned over the bed, kissed Jillian on the cheek. "Call if you need anything, OK?"

Jillian squeezed Rachael's hand . . . then went utterly still when she saw a shadow fill the doorway.

Nolan. In all his beautiful, dysfunctional glory.

Nolan, who'd been very obviously AWOL. Jillian hadn't seen or heard from him—unless you counted the flowers and get-well note from E.D.E.N., Inc., as hearing from him— since she woke up in the ER last night. Even then, she'd only caught sight of him lurking in the background before she'd been pronounced stable, and then he'd just disappeared.

For the longest moment, she simply looked at him.

He was so unreasonably beautiful. His eyes were so blue and completely void of emotion as he stood there, his body as rigid as the hard planes of his face.

He was in warrior mode. And since he'd already slain her dragon, that pretty much left only one other thing for him to fight: his feelings for her.

"Hi," she said, like her heart wasn't flipping around in her chest. *Keep it light. Give him room.* "Thought maybe you'd left the country."

"Considered it." He nodded to Rachael. "Figured your old man would find me anyway. It was just a matter of time."

"Well," Rachael said after another protracted silence. She cleared her throat as her gaze darted between the two of them. "Guess I'll just be going now." She sent Jillian a concerned look, skirted around Nolan, and moved on out the door.

"How are you?" Nolan finally asked.

Cautious of his mood, still hurting that this was the first she'd seen of him, she tried to get a read on his emotions. "I'm doing OK."

"You're lying."

She quirked a brow. "Busted. OK, it hurts some. But they've got good drugs here.

"So," she added when the silence thickened again, "how are *you* doing?"

"Me?" He shrugged. "Nothing wrong with me."

Face grim, he walked farther into the room, then basically ignored her. He shoved his fingers into the back pockets of his black jeans, glanced at the ridiculously large number of get-well bouquets, at the cheery balloons dancing on the whim of the climate control system, and finally out the window into the night.

"I *am* fine, Nolan," she assured him again softly, knowing instinctively that he blamed himself for her injury.

He didn't say anything. He just stood there, his legs spread wide, his knees locked, his shoulders heavy with the weight of his perceived transgressions. "The sonofabitch hurt you."

She couldn't see his face, but she could see the muscles of his throat working. He was darn good at laying the sins of the world on his own shoulders. "You did everything you could."

"Yeah. Everything but stop him."

"Hellooo? I'm here. I'm alive because of you."

His chin dropped to his chest. "Because Lydia scared him off."

"Because you were on top of it. Because you stopped the blood loss before the paramedics came. They said I probably would have bled out if it wasn't for you."

"Goody for me."

As hammers went, he was beating himself over the head with a whopper. She considered, then decided they both needed to hear the entire story. She needed to hear it because there were a lot of blank spaces. He needed to hear it to realize he'd done everything he could to save her.

"Tell me what happened. Tell me everything you know. No one else has been willing to answer my questions. Daddy must have decided I couldn't handle it and issued an edict or something. Do that for me, Nolan. I need to know."

He turned to her. "Tell me something first. What in the hell were you thinking when you left the ballroom?"

Ah. Finally. Emotion. The anger in his eyes was a live thing. She understood it. He'd told her to stay put. She hadn't listened.

"What was I thinking? I don't know that I was thinking. I saw Lydia and, well, she's a kid, but she's a sweet kid and she's taken care of things for me for almost a year now. I needed to get out of that room. I panicked."

"You knew I suspected her. You didn't think it was odd that she just showed up?"

Not only was he going to dress her down for disobeying his orders; he was also going to belabor the issue, no matter that it was a moot point.

"No, it didn't seem odd. She works there part-time, re-member? She also knew about the award presentation and had told me she might stop by to check things out before she went home. Nolan, why are we talking about her?" she asked, suspecting this was just another one of his tactics to avoid talking about them. Him and her. "She didn't *do* anything."

He dragged his hand through his hair. "That doesn't let you off the hook."

"OK. I did a bad thing." Weary to the bone, wanting an-swers and some sign that he'd missed her as much as she'd missed him, she let her head drop back on the pillow.

He flew to the side of the bed when she winced. "What? Do you have pain? I'll call a nurse."

She turned her hand in his when he gripped it. "I don't need a nurse. I just bumped the spot where he hit me, OK?"

Clearly, it wasn't OK, but he backed off. "They say you have a concussion."

"*Slight* concussion, which is probably why I can't re-member anything past when Lydia and I ducked around the corner of the hotel. After that, everything's pretty much a blank."

She couldn't stall a shiver that ran through her. Knowing what had happened and actually talking about it . . . well. It was difficult.

"This was a bad idea. I don't think you're up for it."

"No." She clutched his hand. "Please. I need to hear the rest of it. Give me credit for being adult, OK? No one else will."

He looked from their clasped hands to her face, then slowly moved away from the bed. She bit back the hurt she felt at his physical withdrawal. She liked the feel of his big, rough hand holding hers. She needed the physical connection.

He, however, felt he needed something else.

What do you want, Nolan?

What I've wanted from the beginning. Distance.

Couldn't say he hadn't laid it out for her. Yet somehow she'd hoped that what happened might have made him re-think things.

But he was a man of conviction, her bodyguard. A man still mired in denial. She resigned herself to the fact that she'd just have to accept it. For now. When she was stronger, she'd butt heads with him. Now, she just had to know the rest of the story.

"Smith doesn't have much to say," Nolan finally told her. "He says he's sorry. That he's glad he was caught. That he deserves to die."

"Does he say why he tried to kill me?" Even now that it was behind her, it was hard to believe.

"He just says he was already dead, but you wouldn't let him stay that way."

"I should have left him alone," she said quietly. "I could tell it was hurting him when I questioned him. He . . . said to me once that I'd given him hope. And then he said he'd been better off without it. Hope caused him pain. Hope reminded him of all he'd lost."

"If it hadn't been you, he'd have focused his anger and frustration on someone else. He was a bomb waiting to deto-nate. Sad, but there it is. There was no malice in what you did."

"But there was thoughtlessness. That's a form of malice."

"Lose the hair shirt, Jillian. You didn't do anything wrong. Smith was a lost cause."

She heard anger in his voice. And she hurt enough and was just tired enough to feel anger of her own. Suddenly she needed answers to a different set of questions. "What about you? What about us? Are we a lost cause, too?"

For a moment, he looked wearier than she felt. What that moment didn't say he did with his next words.

"I've got to go."

And just like that, he was gone.

Nolan slouched in a chair on the aft deck of the *EDEN*, his ankles propped on the rail, his hand wrapped around the neck of a half-full bottle of scotch.

The moon hung like a damn china egg as it worked its way slowly from east to west across the Southern Hemisphere. He lifted his bottle in salute. *Bad egg. Rotten egg. Yoke's on you.*

God, he was funny. And the scotch tasted great. Goddamn great. Even if it wasn't as smooth as he remembered. Even if it didn't numb nearly as fast as he needed it to.

Even if it couldn't make him forget how Jillian had looked lying in the grass after Smith had attacked her. She'd been broken and bleeding and so close to gone that his hands still shook at the memory.

But he'd still managed to get good and piss-faced drunk. *Hoo-fuckin'-aah!*

The booze was all he wanted now.

It was all he needed.

Yup. Him and Glen. Together again. A fricking family reunion. Making the rest of the world go away. A world where there was a woman who looked at him through clear green eyes that told him she believed he was more than he was. More than he was capable of being.

Will had known better. Will had known his worth. He wasn't worth shit. Not at crunch time.

Tears streamed down his face. Just like Nelson, Will was dead. Dammit, why hadn't he come to him? Why hadn't he let him help?

And Jillian . . . he'd almost let her die, too.

He lifted the bottle, swallowed deep, wiped the tears away from his cheeks with the back of his hand. Gone. The one woman who had ever mattered was gone—and he'd made damn sure to see to it she stayed that way.

But at least she was safe.

She was safe.

Please, God, let her always be safe.

And please, let him stay drunk forever so he could forget that look on her face. The one that said, *I love you.* The one that said, *I need you.*

The one that brought these fucking wimpy-ass tears to his eyes and proved what a poor excuse for a man he really was.

24

NOLAN CAME TO THIRTY-ODD HOURS LATER. The sun burned through his closed eyelids like lasers. Vultures circled overhead. He cautiously cracked open an eye. OK. Not vultures. Gulls. With a little luck they'd have been vultures. A sure sign he was dead. He'd be out of his misery then.

But dead didn't hurt this much. He was pretty sure of that.

He shifted in the deck chair, groaned at the stiffness in his limbs, and struggled to a stand.

And promptly puked his guts out over the side of the boat.

Where he'd gone wrong, he told his sorry self as he stumbled down the companionway steps into the cabin, was that sometime during the past two days he'd stopped drinking. He eyed the remaining full bottles of scotch sitting on the counter in the galley and gave a thought to repeating the drill. Just for the hell of it.

But heart and mind didn't come to terms with the idea any more than his stomach did. So he hit the head, showered the stench off his body, shaved two days' worth of beard, then brushed the sour taste from his mouth.

And all the while thought about Jillian.

Would he ever stop thinking about Jillian?

Moving like an automaton, he reached into the freezer for the chicken casserole his mother had made and left for him.

While it defrosted in the microwave, he made coffee and dressed.

By noon, he'd kept food and coffee down and, nursing a bitch of a hangover, thought about Smith, tucked away in jail where he couldn't hurt her ever again.

Smith. It had been so obvious. And yet he'd missed it.

So obvious.

Standing at the aft deck rail, fortifying himself with more coffee, he realized that notion had started working on him somewhere between his "poor little drunk ole me" routine and his morning gut spill.

Something wasn't right. Something about Smith. He couldn't get a bead on it, but something was off-kilter.

His gut—what was left of it—kept telling him there was more to the story. He should have questioned Smith that night at the Breakers after he'd attacked Jillian. But he hadn't been firing on all cylinders then, any more than he was now, for that matter. All he'd been able to think about was Jillian. The blood. God, the blood.

He shook himself away from the memory. Got it back together. And did a rewind of the series of events leading up to the attack. He couldn't pinpoint why, but something besides the residual effects of the booze he'd practically mainlined into his system was eating at him.

Personal. From the beginning, he'd seen the threats to Jillian as personal. Messages on her home phone—an unlisted number. Messages on her e-mail—again, someone close to her who knew her address. And the nursery rhymes. How in the hell did those fit in? And how did they tie in to Smith?

The more he thought about it, the more questions he had. Smith lived in a dump of a motel. No computer. Little money. Fewer resources. From what he'd gathered reading Jillian's interview transcripts, watching the videos, the guy couldn't even get a library card. His accessibility to a computer and a printer was slim and none.

And how did he always know where she was going to be—like at the police chief's press conference and at Mar-A-Lago?

Nolan felt his pulse kick up a couple of beats. *Personal.* He kept coming back to that. From the beginning, he'd thought—hell, he'd *known* these attacks were personal. Her penthouse that she'd since pulled in markers to have refurbished had been destroyed. Her clothes. Her bed. Everything but the kitchen. The one room in the place Jillian could have cared less about.

Personal.

Smith might have seen her as a threat to his personal space, might not have liked it that Jillian had invaded it, but he could have simply disappeared rather than endure her probing questions if he really wanted to avoid her. Why kill her?

Nolan felt a jolt of memory that damn near sent him to the floor. A date—one he'd seen on Jillian's interview transcripts as the date she'd contacted Smith to set up their first interview.

Christ. Jesus H. Christ.

The date was several days after she'd received her first threat. Which meant that Smith couldn't have sent it.

Heart pounding like a sledgehammer, he snagged the Mustang's keys from the counter and headed for the docks at a run.

"Smith says he'll see you," Detective Laurens said as he led Nolan down a maze of hallways, then nodded for the guard to unlock the door to the bank of cells. "Don't know why. He hasn't said a word since we booked him. Keep it short, OK? I don't want his PD screaming foul."

Nolan waited in an interview room, agonizingly sober, wondering what he was going to say, what he was going to do, when he finally saw Smith. Murder and mayhem came to mind, but that wouldn't solve anything. He wanted some answers. If only he knew what the questions were.

He looked up when the door opened. Smith, dressed in an oversize jailhouse jumpsuit, walked in looking lost and defeated. And Nolan knew he'd been right to come here.

This was not a man. This was a lost shell of a man.

And that, Nolan realized in that instant, was part of what had bothered him all along.

He recognized lost when he saw it. He understood it; at least he thought he had, until he looked deep in John Smith's eyes.

This was a man who was beyond lost. This was a man who was absent of strength, of purpose, of any emotion strong enough to prompt anything as violent and feeling as a death wish—let alone carry one out.

There wasn't enough left in him to sustain the kind of hatred required to kill.

"You weren't in this by yourself, were you?" Nolan asked, his pulse spiking because he knew, he just knew, there was more to the story.

Smith's eyes lifted slowly. Nolan saw recognition before Smith shifted his gaze to a spot at the middle of Nolan's chest. And said nothing.

"Who told you to hurt her?"

Smith swallowed, blinked, then met Nolan's eyes. "She should have left me alone. She shouldn't have asked so many questions."

Nolan fought the urge to jump across the table and wrap his hands around the man's throat and choke an answer out of him. Which would net him exactly nothing.

"You've been through a bad time," he said, settling himself, settling Smith. "Jillian wanted to help you. See if she could find someone who knew you. Family . . . friends. Someone who could give you back your identity."

"She . . . she made me—" Smith stopped, exhaled a

breath that came from the depths of his empty soul. "She made me want that. To want . . . you don't understand. You can't understand. Wanting is too painful."

But Nolan did understand. He wanted. He wanted Jillian. Wanted her so much it hurt like hell. "So, you decided to kill her."

"I did not decide. It just made sense."

"Who said it made sense?"

Smith glanced up again, then away, then seemed to reach a decision. "Mary."

Nolan's breath caught. *Mary.* The name had spilled off Smith's lips, part prayer, part hatred.

"Mary?" Nolan repeated, amazed at the calm in his voice when he felt as revved as a rocket inside. "She's someone special to you?"

"She is just . . . Mary. She knows things."

"Things?"

A long hesitation. "She knew that Jillian Kincaid was a bad person. That she had to be stopped."

Nolan needed to be careful here. He needed to be precise. "Mary told you to kill her?"

Smith's shoulders sagged a little more. He tipped his head toward the ceiling, world-weary, worn, and beaten. "Mary has been hurt, too. She understands. So . . . I tried. I felt I owed her. She said she cared for me. She spoke to me when no one else would. She got me the job at the hotel."

Nolan had to physically restrain himself from jumping out of the chair. "She sounds like a good person," he said, practically choking on the words.

Smith shook his head. "No. Not good. Just like me."

"Yet you tried to kill Miss Kincaid. Because Mary told you to."

"Yes. She said Jillian Kincaid deserved to die."

Nolan fisted his hands together on the top of the table. "Was she there? That night? Was Mary there?" He had to ask . . . even though he had a sick feeling he already knew.

Smith nodded.

Nolan closed his eyes, steadied himself. "Tell me about Mary. Tell me what she looks like."

With stilted words, Smith described Mary to him.

Gezus God.

Nolan shot out of the chair. Pounded on the door. Yelled for the guard. When he burst through the door, Laurens came running.

"Christ," Laurens said when Nolan told him who really wanted Jillian dead.

Nolan's hands were surprisingly steady as he dug his cell phone out of his pocket and dialed the hospital while he ran for his Mustang.

"Shit!" He swore when he found out Jillian had been released at ten that morning.

He hit Jillian's penthouse number on his speed dial. She answered on the second ring.

"Tell me your parents are with you."

"Nolan? Is that you?"

"Jillian, are your parents with you?"

"No," she said, sounding confused. "They left a few minutes ago."

Shit.

"Call security. Tell them not to let anyone up to see you."

"Nolan? For God's sake! You're scaring me. What's this about?"

"Just call security. No one is to get up to see you, understand? I'm on my way over."

"Then we'll have a party."

"What are you talking about? Who's there?"

"No one. Yet."

Then she told him who was on the way over.

His throat constricted to the size of a very thin straw.

Calm. Stay the hell calm.

"Jillian, listen to me and listen carefully. I want you to get your gun. I put it—"

The line went dead.

"Nolan?" Propped up against her new pillows in her new bed, Jillian frowned at the phone and foolishly repeated his name even though she realized they'd been disconnected.

Willing herself not to panic, she clicked the receiver a couple of times for a dial tone. Nothing.

OK. Regroup. The line was dead. It happened. Construction workers sometimes hit cables. Power outages were caused by many things.

Like cut wires.

Where the silence of her penthouse had been a welcome change from the constant disruptive noises of the hospital, it suddenly felt sinister.

Gun.

He'd mentioned her gun.

Wincing as pain bit into her arm when she moved, she sat up and checked the top drawer in her bedside table. Everything was in there *but* her gun.

First things first. Call security. Her cell phone was in her purse. That was the good news. The bad news was that her purse was on the kitchen counter.

Light-headed, a little off-balance, she stood, then gave herself a minute to get steady legs under her.

"Hey, what are you doing out of bed?"

Startled, Jillian's good hand flew to her throat. She let out a breath of relief when she looked up and saw who was standing in her bedroom doorway.

"OK. Heart attack's over. You scared the bejesus out of me. God, Lydia, I'm glad you're here." And glad she'd given Lydia her new security code.

"What about me? Glad to see me, too?"

Diane poked her head in the door and held up a huge bouquet.

"Absolutely." She managed a smile and eased back down on her bed.

"Hey, what's up?" Lydia walked to her side. "You look rattled."

"Good call." Jillian steadied herself with a hand on the mattress. "Nolan just phoned. He told me to tell security not to let anyone in."

Diane stepped up by the bed. "Why?"

"I don't know. Just like I don't know why he told me to get my gun just before the line went dead."

Lydia went pale. "Holy cow! What do you think's happening?"

Jillian shook her head. "Again no clue. Maybe John Smith escaped? Is that possible?"

Diane frowned. "Doesn't seem likely."

"That reminds me. Could one of you get my purse from the kitchen? My cell phone's in there and I'd better make that call to security."

"I'll do it," Diane volunteered. She turned to Lydia. "Don't you have to get going?"

"Yeah," Lydia said, her voice filled with regret. "I have a class. I wish I could stay, but I had to see for myself that you were back in your own bed." Lydia crossed the room and hugged her carefully.

"Better scoot, kiddo." Diane walked toward the door urging Lydia to follow.

After a final hug, Lydia followed Diane out of the room.

"Be right back with that phone."

Restless, on-edge, Jillian sank back against the pillows, angered by her physical weakness, more than a little spooked by Nolan's call.

She heard the front door open and close, then the sound

of Diane's footsteps tracking back toward her bedroom. "Find it?"

"Actually, no. But I found this."

Jillian looked up to see Diane standing in the bedroom door, a strange, serene smile on her face, the butcher knife from Jillian's chopping block clutched loosely in her hand.

25

IT WAS TAKING TOO FRICKING LONG TO GET there. Three blocks from the police station, Nolan cranked the steering wheel hard to the right. The Mustang skidded around the corner on two tires as he buried the gas pedal. Behind him, Laurens followed, siren screaming. A half-dozen other units joined the parade a block or two behind them.

"Sonofabitch," Nolan swore, and stood on the brakes, his back end fishtailing. He barely managed to avoid rear-ending the BMW directly in front of him. In front of the Beemer, a dozen other cars clogged lanes as a freight train creaked slowly across the intersection. A long fucking train.

He shoved the Mustang into park, hit the button on the glove box, and pulled out his Beretta. Then he shouldered open the door and ran toward the moving train. City Place was less than three blocks away on the other side of the tracks. Three blocks and several hundred tons of rolling steel and rusted iron were not going to stop him.

The freight train slowed, clanked to a shrieking, skidding stop, then reversed direction with a lurching grind of metal to metal. Gut check time. Nolan watched, counted out the rhythm, and timed his jump.

He was airborne before Laurens, skidding to a stop behind him, could scream for him not to do it. He landed on, then jumped from the coupling linking two boxcars in one well-timed and miraculously lucky leap. When he hit the pavement on the other side of the tracks, he rolled as he'd been taught to roll on a parachute landing, taking the brunt of the fall on his shoulder.

Grunting through the pain, he shoved himself to his feet and flat-out ran toward City Place. He burst through the door before his shadow caught up with him. Eddie's substitute, a retired police officer who filled in on an as-needed basis, looked up from his magazine as Nolan sprinted across the foyer to the bank of elevators.

"Who's visiting Jillian Kincaid?" Nolan demanded, punching the button.

"Ms. Kincaid? Why . . . a young woman. What—"

Nolan didn't wait to hear more. He had to get up there. He had to get to her before it was too late.

"I never should have counted on John to take care of you."

Jillian sat perfectly still. Her mind, however, ran sprints. Her stomach turned somersaults. "What . . . what are you talking about?"

"He was supposed to kill you," her producer said casually as she walked to Jillian's dresser, examined a bottle of perfume, then opened it. "Your father buy this for you?"

Jillian blinked, beyond confused.

In a mercurial fit of rage, Diane hauled back and threw the perfume at the wall above Jillian's head.

Jillian ducked, eyes wide as the bottle shattered. She felt the prick of a glass shard nick her forehead, smelled the sweet musky fragrance of French perfume spilling down the wall and seeping into the newly installed carpet.

"Scared, Jillian? Oh yeah. You're good and scared. The thing is, you should be good and dead. I should have known Smith didn't have the guts to get the job done. And leave it to that simpering little lapdog of yours to muck things up.

What, do you pay Lydia to step and fetch for you? Must be a trip to inspire such loyalty and devotion."

Hatred and sarcasm seeped like toxic waste from every word.

Jillian stared at her producer. She shook her head, her brows furrowed in abject bafflement, her pulse thrumming with the cadence of fear. "John Smith was supposed to kill me? You . . . you wanted him to kill me?"

She had to be dreaming. Or delirious.

Diane? All along it had been Diane Kleinmeyer? Quirky, all-business, fly-off-the-handle Diane? Whose wild eyes were now filled with hate?

This couldn't be real. This couldn't be happening. None of it made any sense.

"Diane? I don't understand. Any of this. Why?" She lifted a hand, swallowed back a wave of nausea, as Diane absently prodded her own palm with the tip of the knife. Blood trickled down her wrist, dripped in slow, steady drops to the floor. She seemed as oblivious to the pain as she was to the overwhelming scent of the perfume that consumed the air.

Insane.

"Why?" Jillian asked again, a plea this time. "I don't understand?"

"You don't have to understand. You just have to die. But hey, I'm a team player. And in the end it's only fair—more pleasurable for me, too—that you know what you're going to die for."

Jillian said nothing. Couldn't put together a thought that wasn't shrink-wrapped in terror to make any sense of Diane's hatred.

"I like that. I like that look," Diane said, nodding in approval. "Scared shitless, aren't you? Good. Now you know just a fraction of the fear I felt growing up. You'll know a lot more before I finish this. I think I'll take my time with you."

Jillian dug deep, pulled herself together. "Diane . . . whatever you think I've done to you—"

"Shut up," she snapped, then smiled, her eyes brimming with maniacal rage. "And don't call me Diane. My name is Mary. Mary Gates. Ring any bells?"

Jillian searched her mind, came up blank. "Did we go to school together?" she tried, attempting to make any kind of connection.

"No, we didn't go to school together. Interesting. But not a surprise that Daddy dear didn't tell you about the Gates family."

"Did . . . someone in your family work for my father? Is that what this is about?" Had her father fired Diane's father or something? Was she taking it out on her?

"God, without a full complement of written copy you can't come up with a single original thought, can you? No. No one in my family worked for your father. But your father did work over my mother. Fucked her good. Literally," she said, venom spewing from her eyes as well as her mouth. "And then he walked away. God damn him, he got her pregnant and then he walked the hell away!"

The words registered through a fog. No. None of what Diane was saying could be true.

"And now you're going to pay for what he did. And in the process, he'll pay, too."

Her voice rose with her words. So did the knife. She sliced it through the air in front of Jillian's face. Laughed gleefully when Jillian flinched.

"Diane . . . Mary. I still don't understand. But whatever needs fixing . . . whatever's wrong, I can help you sort it out."

Diane shook her head, contempt and sarcasm coloring her smile. "Of course you can. As a matter of fact you've already helped me by being so gullible. Did you really think you were hired because you were the outstanding applicant for the anchor job?" She laughed, an ugly self-satisfied sound. "You're good, Jillian, but you got that job because I made sure you did. I had it planned for years. I followed your career, made sure our paths crossed. Made sure I ended up at KGLO when you hired on, then made sure you ended up on my team.

"Oh, I know what you're thinking. Why go to so much bother? Why not just kill you one night when you walked to your car? Or run you off the road?

"There's no skill in that, Jillian. No finesse. No way to show your father that there was someone more clever than you. Someone smarter than you. Just like my baby sister would have been."

Jillian had to steel herself to keep from going numb—with shock, with disbelief.

"And now you want to help me," Diane restated with a twisted smile. "Sweetie, you can. You can help me by dying. The time is finally right. Then your darling daddy will know what it's like to lose something he loves." Her voice rose again, fluctuating between little girl lost and hate-filled demon.

"Diane, please. Let's talk about this."

"It's way too late to talk. It's time to show your darling daddy," Diane screamed, "how life can be a living hell. Just like he made mine!

"She's dead now, you know." Spittle flew from the corner of her mouth as she moved closer still. "My mother. He killed her! Oh, not with a gun—but just as effectively. He knocked her up, walked out on her, and left her with a new baby. My little sister. My beautiful baby sister! He should have loved her. He should have loved my mother! Lived with us! Tucked *us* into bed at night. Told us nursery rhymes! Not you! Never you!"

Jillian's eyes widened as she tried to make sense, any sense at all, of what Diane was saying. But there was no sense to be made here. There was only madness.

If she was going to live through it, she had to find a way to calm Diane. At least until Nolan got here. He was on his way. She was sure of it. More sure than she'd been of anything else in her life.

"You think I'm crazy?" Diane asked, her eyes narrowed and mean. "Yeah. You do."

Jillian shook her head. "I don't think that at all."

Diane smiled. Then laughed and moved closer to the bed, the scent of Jillian's perfume drenching the air. "When your darling daddy finds you, and he smells this perfume he bought for you, he'll see you dead every time he smells it. And he'll grieve. He'll feel my pain when my mother died and took my little sister with her. And the best part? He'll never know why."

She sank down on the bed, poking the tip of the knife deeper into her palm, over and over and over until blood ran in a thick river onto Jillian's thigh. "Do you understand now? This is about redemption. This is about paybacks."

Jillian understood only one thing. She had to dilute the hatred. Had to get Diane thinking about something else.

"You . . . you hurt yourself," Jillian said. "You're bleeding. There are supplies in the bathroom. Maybe you should get them."

If she could get Diane out of the bedroom, maybe she could get out, too. Maybe. If she didn't pass out first. She'd lost a lot of blood from her stab wound. Her head still pounded from her concussion.

In the end, it didn't matter. Diane was as oblivious to her suggestion as she was to her own blood.

"It's OK, Jillie. I'm used to shedding blood. And I'm going to enjoy shedding yours. Maybe I'll make it quick after all," Diane said, reconsidering, suddenly turning generous, caring. "Because, after all, you worked hard for me. You got me great ratings."

Oh God. This was it. If she didn't do something, it would be her blood mixing with Diane's to stain the pillow.

Jillian flinched as with her bloodied hand Diane brushed Jillian's hair away from her forehead. And raised the knife.

Jillian screamed, in outrage as much as denial and fear. It caught Diane by surprise. She hesitated for a split second, her knife hand poised above her head in strike position.

Diane's hesitation was long enough for Jillian to grab the phone and swing it with all her might.

"Fuck!" Nolan roared when he realized the elevator was stalled on the penthouse floor. He sprinted for the stairs, cursed his hangover as he raced up the steps, taking them two at a time. His thighs burned. His lungs were on fire by the time he made the fourteenth floor.

The gun in his hand, however, was rock steady.

He inched the stairwell door open. The hall was clear.

He eased inside. Hugging the wall, he moved carefully toward Jillian's door. The doorknob felt cool beneath his hand. He punched in the security code and quietly opened the door.

He entered the penthouse low, in firing stance, arms extended directly ahead of him, the Berretta gripped in both hands. His labored breath and the pumping like pistons of his blood through his ears were the only sounds he heard. The strong, cloying scent of perfume was almost gagging. He was trying to gauge the significance of that detail when he heard the voice. Childlike. Almost giddy. Undoubtedly insane. And barely recognizable as Diane Kleinmeyer's.

It came from Jillian's bedroom. Other than the scent of perfume that grew stronger as he crept down the hall, only one thing registered in his brain: he didn't hear Jillian.

Breath stalled in his chest, he prayed he wasn't too late as he paused, his back pressed against the wall just outside

Jillian's bedroom door. Despite the sweat trickling down his
back, when he heard the voice again, then, thank you, God,
Jillian's cautious reply, relief combined with fear to feed the
icy chill shivering down his spine.

*"Maybe I'll make it quick after all. Because, after all, you
worked hard for me. You got me great ratings."*

The silence that followed stopped his heart. The scream
that rent the air in its wake curdled his blood.

Fuck caution.

He shot into the room like an RPG. Sized up the situation
on the run and dived for the bed.

He caught Diane around the waist and jerked her away
from Jillian just as she slashed the knife downward.

Grabbing a handful of comforter, he rolled, taking Diane
with him. She fought like a wild animal as they thrashed
across the bed, then spilled together in a tangled heap on the
floor.

"It's over!" he said, rising to his knees above her. Straddling her hips, he pinned her wrists above her head on the
floor. "It's over," he repeated while she kicked and sobbed
and wrenched her head around.

"Nolan. Ease up, man. We've got her."

Breathing hard, Nolan glanced over his shoulder to see
Laurens. The detective and two of his officers had moved in
to restrain the crazed woman.

Nolan rose slowly, only then aware that the butcher knife
Diane wielded had nicked him in the forearm. And even then
barely aware of anything but Jillian.

Her gaze darted from him to Diane, who, even now,
handcuffed and flanked by two burly officers, screamed at
Jillian.

"No. She needs to die!" Diane screamed, fighting to
break free. "She needs to die. Don't you see? I have to kill
her. To pay him back for what he did to me. To my mother.

To my baby sister. I promised. I promised." She broke down with heavy sobs.

"Get her out of here." Nolan cut his gaze from the pain washing across Jillian's face to Laurens. "Just . . . get her out of here."

Even after the officers had bodily removed Diane and shut the penthouse door behind them, her maniacal screams echoed, then finally faded away.

Nolan dragged a shaking hand through his hair. Looked toward the bed.

Jillian. He was damn tired of seeing her bathed in blood. Damn tired of feeling his heart ripped to shreds at the thought of losing her.

He wanted to ram his fist through the closest wall and just keep hammering until he felt more pain than she did. He walked to her side instead. Sat down. Gently wiped the blood from her face with the corner of the sheet. "Tell me none of this is yours."

She met his eyes. Lost. So lost.

She shook her head. Steady to the end.

Except she couldn't quite pull it off this time.

She fought it, but her face finally crumbled; hot tears leaked down her cheeks. And hard as she tried to swallow back the haunting, keening cry, it pushed its way out from the very depths of her soul and rose to a heartbreaking moan.

Something very nearly like tears filled his own eyes as he carefully wrapped his arms around her and let her grieve.

Something very nearly like life filled his chest to bursting as her fragile, trembling warmth melted into him.

Then he simply held her . . . to keep himself from falling apart.

He smoothed the hair from her eyes, murmured assurances. Promised her it was going to be OK. Whispered that

she should cry it out. Rocked her until the sobs subsided.
Held her until she finally slept.

And as he leaned back against the headboard with this
strong woman spent but not broken in his arms, he tried not
to think about tomorrow and where they went from here,
even though he knew what had to be done.

26

JILLIAN SEARCHED THE FACES OF HER
mother and father as sunlight slanted in through her penthouse windows. They sat beside her on the sofa while she
clutched a toss pillow on her lap. The penthouse was eerily
quiet, the gurgle of yet another pot of coffee brewing in the
background the only ordinary sound in an otherwise extraordinary situation.

After she'd awakened from her meltdown late yesterday
afternoon, Nolan had fed her, then helped her clean up. Then
he'd put her to bed again. In the guest bedroom. Away from
the blood. Away from the memory of what had almost happened to her.

Unlikely as the possibility had seemed at the time, she'd
fallen into a dead sleep. And there she'd stayed until almost
ten o'clock this morning.

Nolan was gone.

Her mother and father were there, had been, it seemed,
since late yesterday.

Concern dulled their eyes. Weight pressed down on their
shoulders in the aftermath of her near-death experience.

It was over. She was alive.

She was alive, but lives, it seemed, had changed. Her father's. Her mother's. Diane's. And her own.

Now more than ever, she needed Nolan by her side. The

problem was, she didn't even know where he was. She shut out the pain that knowledge fostered, traded it for another kind of sorrow. Her father was suffering.

"It appears that Diane Kleinmeyer's real name really is Mary Gates," he said, and for the first time in Jillian's memory he looked toward her mother for support.

Clare covered his hand with hers, squeezed.

"And a long time ago I did have an affair with her mother."

Even more painful than his admission was the impact of seeing her father this way. Jillian had never seen him like this . . . off-balance, subdued. He was always a powerhouse of purpose and energy. Today, however, her mother appeared to be shoring him up. The role reversal was a little much to absorb.

It was even more of a stretch when it was Jillian's mother who picked up the threads of the conversation when her father seemed incapable of going on.

"We never discussed this, darling, but you were never intended to be an only child." Clare smiled sadly. "But you were our gift. Our one to a customer, it seems. I . . . I miscarried several times over the years after you were born. It . . . well, I'm afraid I struggled with the whys and the anger and the pain of it all for a long time. So much that I went into a very deep depression for several years. I still struggle with it." Again she stopped, smiled. "But then I don't have to tell you that, do I?"

"Mom, you don't—"

Clare shook her head. "It's all right. Let me finish." She glanced between Jillian and Darin, apology in her eyes. "I wasn't much of a mother to you during that period of time. Wasn't much of a wife to your father, either, I'm afraid."

"It still doesn't excuse what I did." Jillian's father's words came out slow and heavy. Like his breath. He averted his gaze from his wife to his daughter.

"I regretted the affair immediately," he said abruptly, and then, in something more typical of her father, he summed it up in abbreviated, concise words. "I never meant for it to happen. God. One night I had to get out of the house. I just drove. Finally stopped for coffee at this . . . hell. I don't even remember where it was."

He paused, shook his head. "Anyway. Mary's mother was there."

"And you were lonely," Clare supplied, tears welling in her eyes.

Darin swallowed, looked at his hands. "Her name was Ruth Gates. I remember her telling me about her daughter. Mary was her name. She was just a little girl then."

He rose, shoved his hands deep into his pockets, and stared out the bank of windows. "I never saw her again. But it seems there was a child conceived as a result of my indiscretion."

"The baby sister." Jillian remembered Diane's words out loud, her mind struggling to wrap itself around these revelations. "You didn't know about the baby?"

Her father shook his head. "If I had I'd like to think I would have done right by the child."

Weary. He looked so weary. She was aware of the fact that her father was not a young man. Another first.

The silence seemed to stretch out to an unbearable length by the time her father spoke again. "The police have managed to put a sketch of a story together on Diane—Mary," he corrected, then, with a nod of encouragement from Jillian's mother, continued.

"Diane—I'm sorry—Mary, well, it goes without saying that she's a very troubled young woman. It appears that her mother—" He stopped. Tears filled his voice.

"It's all right, dear." Clare picked up the thread of thought when Darin choked on the words. "Her mother was apparently prone to psychotic episodes. The police have tracked Mary to a suburb in Miami where she and her mother and sister lived. Records indicate that Family Services had been called in many times due to various reports from Mary's school, from concerned neighbors."

"She was abused?"

Her father nodded. "It was never proved, but yes, every indication is that she was. Mary's been very vocal since she's been transferred to a psychiatric facility. She . . . well, she's related in graphic detail some of the terror her mother inflicted on her and the other child."

And again Clare came to his aid. "Mary tells stories of being burned with cigarettes, cut with knives, being shut in dark closets for days. And all the while, it seems her mother told her stories about Darin and how he had fathered Mary's sister and how much pain that child had caused her. Eventually, she killed the child and herself. With a knife," Clare added after a sickening moment. "Mary found them."

Jillian felt physically ill. "Oh God."

"Apparently, it was years ago when Mary was still a child herself. She ended up in foster home after foster home, a very disturbed child. The system lost track of her after she turned eighteen and the rest is conjecture at this point, but the psychiatric staff is proceeding with her treatment on the assumption that Mary suffered her own psychotic episodes. No matter how unstable her mother was, she still represented Mary's only constant. Her only anchor. When she died, Mary took it upon herself to avenge her mother's and her baby sister's deaths."

"By killing my daughter to get to me," Darin added numbly.

Heartsick over her father's torment, Jillian added her hand to her mother's where it covered Darin's. "It's not your fault. You didn't know about the child. You couldn't have. And I don't have to think about it. I *know* you would have done the right thing by her."

"I don't know if the two of you can understand this," he

said, conviction returning to his voice as a bid for understanding filled his eyes, "but since I couldn't help that little girl, I feel compelled to help Mary now. She'll need psychiatric treatment, legal assistance. And she's alone."

"Of course we'll help her," Clare said gently, astounding Jillian yet again with her generosity of spirit and support. When the full story hit the news, the scandal would rock the Palm Beach social scene to its well-heeled roots. It would not go well for Clare.

Jillian had never felt more love or more pride for her. And never had Jillian felt more empathy for her father. His suffering made her realize there was even more than she'd thought to this strong man who could anger her to the point of seeing red, frustrate her into speechlessness, and yet love her unconditionally.

"I love you, Daddy. I love you both," she whispered as tears misted her eyes. "We'll all help her."

"Nothing?" Jillian met Ethan Garrett's somber gaze across his desk at E.D.E.N., Inc., two weeks later. "You've heard nothing from him?"

Looking like a *GQ* ad in his dark suit and tie, Nolan's older brother glanced between Dallas and Eve, who had joined them in his office. "Sorry," Ethan said, avoiding Jillian's eyes. "Haven't heard a word. I wouldn't worry about it, though. He'll turn up . . . in time."

He'd had plenty of time, to Jillian's way of thinking. Two weeks was enough time for anyone to outrun the truth. Two weeks was enough time to outrun it, figure it out, *and* come to terms with it.

It had only taken her one. And in that one week, she'd gone through all the stages. Played "poor me," then "vindictive me," then "doubtful me," and finally "determined me." She loved him. He loved her. And she wasn't going to let him mess this up for them.

That's why she'd spent the second week trying to find him. And that's why she'd ended up here.

"How are you doing?" Eve asked, crossing her arms and easing a hip on the corner of Ethan's desk. No power suit for Nolan's twin today. She looked feminine and curvy in a watered silk pantsuit in rosy mauve.

"I'm good." Jillian smiled at the genuine concern in Eve's expression. And she *was* fine. She was rested and for the most part she was physically healed.

The rest would come eventually. Eventually, she'd come to terms with the lengths Diane had gone to in order to try to kill her. God, she'd even been instrumental in getting Jillian her position at KGLO. In retrospect, it all fit now. Diane had had complete access to her schedule, had always known the best time to get to her. She'd had the pull to get John Smith a job at the Breakers and the savvy to manipulate him into helping her. Poor John. He was so lost and had been used so badly.

"Jillian?"

She looked up to see Eve watching her with concerned eyes.

"I'm sorry. Little lapse there. I'm really fine. And if I haven't already thanked you for the flowers, they were beautiful. It was very thoughtful of you to send them. All of you."

"We're just glad it's over for you." This came from Dallas, looking all-American delicious in his button-down shirt and khakis.

Dallas, however, was wrong. Very wrong. It was not over. At least not where she and Nolan were concerned. Despite his siblings' concern and their united front, she didn't doubt for a minute that they knew exactly where Nolan was. Blood, after all, was thicker than anything she and Nolan had managed to forge together. At least, the Garretts thought it was.

They, however, didn't know what she did: She loved their

brother. And he loved her. If she had to hit Nolan over the head with that information, so be it. But she had to find him first.

"You don't have to look so guilty," she told them with a resigned smile. "It's good that you all care about him. But I care, too. And with or without your help, I will find him."

Although she'd just given them absolution, the siblings exchanged guilt-filled glances. She shook her head, couldn't help but smile. Lord, they were a gorgeous lot. It made her ache inside to watch the brothers; their looks, their voices, even their actions, were so reflective of Nolan's. Even Eve, with her petite blond-bombshell look, was unmistakably a Garrett.

Knowing she was wasting her time here, Jillian bid them good-bye. Didn't bother to ask them to give her a call if they heard anything. It would be another waste of time and breath. And who could blame them for aiding and abetting him? Were she in their shoes, she'd be helping him hide out, too. After all, who in their right mind would want to get involved with the media circus her life had become since the "rest of the story" had broken?

Not that she thought Nolan was in his right mind, but it was no wonder he'd run away. Now, however, it was time for him to come back. To her.

She'd just reached the elevator when Eve called her name. "Jillian."

Nolan's twin smiled as she approached. "Men," she said, and if her inflection on that single word hadn't summed up her opinion of the species, her next words did. "They're idiots. It's like they all take a vow of stupidity or something."

Jillian returned Eve's smile. "That's a given, but what does it make us when we continue to fall in love with them?"

"Idiot squared, I guess." Eve sobered and studied Jillian's face. "You do love him, don't you?"

"Yeah," Jillian confessed. "I do."

"Give him another week. Then check the marina. He'll be there. On the *EDEN*."

Jillian couldn't help it. She reached for Eve, hugged her hard.

"Well, damn. Don't cry." Eve laughed, but she was a little teary eyed herself when she pulled away. "And don't thank me. I'm not so sure I'm doing you any favors. He's a knot-head and probably more trouble than he's worth."

"Knot-head, yes. Trouble? Absolutely. *My* kind."

"Good luck," Eve said with another warm smile. "And, Jillian . . . for what it's worth, I think you're exactly the kind of trouble *he* needs."

27

JILLIAN PULLED INTO A PARKING SPACE AT the marina and cut the motor. She'd given Nolan his week. Then for good measure, she'd given him another, telling herself it was to afford him a little more time to deal with his insecurities. It was possible though, she thought, staring toward the *EDEN*'s slip, that her own uncertainty may have made that call.

What if she was wrong? What if her radar had completely gone off the scope on this one and she was wrong about Nolan's feelings for her?

She hesitated as she checked her hair in the rearview mirror, damned the nervous tremor in her hand as she freshened her lip gloss. Maybe she should just leave well enough alone. Forget about the fact that for the first time in her life she'd fallen head over heart in love. Forget that she missed him so much she physically hurt with it.

She let out a deflated breath. Maybe she should simply figure out a way to factor Nolan out of her life and just . . . just get on with it.

Coward.

"Yeah, yeah, yeah," she muttered, and reached for the cooler she'd stowed on the front seat beside her. She'd be a coward if she didn't at least confront him and make him tell her to her face that he didn't want to be a part of her life.

But he *did* want to be. He *had* to want it. And she was just the woman to make him admit it.

Buoyed up by that conviction, she headed for the docks. She'd never played the shrinking violet in her life. Never used tears or threats or a quivering lower lip to get what she wanted. As she approached the *EDEN*, she was determined she wasn't going to start now. The stakes were too high. She was going to face this like she faced everything else in her life. Head-on.

"This is it, Kincaid," she told herself as she stepped onboard.

She reached for the companionway door, then hesitated when she heard a muffled sound from the bow.

Bracing her shoulders, she stepped around the back of the flybridge . . . and felt all the air sough out of her lungs at the sight that met her.

Whether nerves or battle mode caused it, her heart pounded so hard it competed with the growl of a sailboat motoring by toward open water.

Nolan was doing push-ups on the deck, looking tough and buff and . . . incredible. His hair was wet with perspiration; his skin was oiled with it, too, as he pressed his body to the limit, muscles straining, sinews stretching. She'd forgotten how truly beautiful he was. How could that be? And how could it be that all she had to do was look at him and she could feel the kiss of his breath on her skin?

Powerful. It was so powerful, this love she felt, that a physical ache tugged way down deep in her center. So powerful that she needed these few moments before he spotted her to reacclimatize herself to the reactions zinging along her bloodstream like pinballs.

When he finally rose and, unaware of her presence, wiped the sweat from his forehead with his upper arm, she told herself she was ready. She could do this, she thought as he crossed the deck and lifted a fishing rod from a holder fastened to the bow rail and slowly reeled in the line.

Ducking behind the cover of the flybridge, she opened the cooler and drew out two ice-cold bottles. Then she stepped out of the aft deck and walked toward him.

There was no backing out now.

Nolan had been back in West Palm and aboard the *EDEN* for two weeks. He'd done a lot of thinking in the past month. A *lot* of thinking.

He'd also done a lot of fishing. He hadn't caught a damn thing. It hadn't kept him from trying. Over and over again, he'd baited up, cast in, waited patiently, and reeled in an empty hook.

As he reeled in yet again, it seemed his luck was holding true—or was it? he thought when he heard footsteps on the deck behind him.

He turned around.

And there she was.

The catch of the century.

God, she looked amazing. Healthy. Vibrant. Hot.

He'd known she was well again. He'd kept tabs, but damn, seeing her like this, long bare legs, short white shorts, tight red top, it damn near stopped his heart.

In each hand she gripped an ice-cold bottle of root beer. So cold the bottles were fogged over, dripping wet with sweat. Or maybe his eyes had fogged over. For sure, his brain was a muzzy mess.

"Hot today," she said, like it hadn't been thirty fricking days since he'd seen her, like his heart wasn't clogging "Lord of the Dance" against his rib cage.

She extended a bottle. "Thought you might be thirsty."

Oh yeah. His mouth was as dry as a desert-bleached bone.

Gaze locked on hers, he took it. Still watching her, he twisted off the cap and sucked down a long, deep swallow, all the while trying to pretend she hadn't rocked his world like a daisy cutter blasting through an Afghanistan mountain.

He should say something. He needed to say something, but he couldn't get his fill of looking. Didn't ever want to stop looking at her. Pale, creamy skin. Red-gold hair. Dark glasses covered her eyes, but the vivid sea green of her irises was burned into his mind like a brand. He'd seen those eyes in his dreams—the welcome ones that had replaced some of his nightmares.

"So," she said, the picture of a woman in control. "Catch anything?"

His breath. Maybe. If he was lucky.

He snagged the towel he'd looped over the railing, then dragged it across his face, wiping the sweat from his eyes. So he could get an even better look.

Sweet Gezus, she was a sight. He remembered those shorts. They were the ones she'd worn the night he'd dragged her to Nirvana. He remembered that little strip of pale skin between them and her skimpy red top, too. Remembered most of all how that skin tasted, how silky soft it felt against his tongue.

And suddenly he realized she'd known exactly what seeing her in them would do to him.

Well, I'll be damned. His princess was here on a mission, all decked out in her battle gear. And wonder of wonders, she'd come to fight for her man, not tell him to take a long walk off a short pier.

Yeah, she was tooled for battle and she wasn't planning on being gentle about it.

A relief so huge it damn near buckled his knees swept through him. Elation so overwhelming it hurt swelled in his chest like a wet sponge. He'd been dying to go to her, crawl over broken glass on his hands and knees to beg for another shot, and here she was, bringing the action to him. It took everything in him not to break into a big, gooney grin.

Oh man. He was the luckiest SOB in the world. He didn't

deserve her—wouldn't in a million years—and he damn well should have stayed the hell away. But she was the best thing that had ever happened to him and if it took the rest of his life, he was going to figure out a way to become the best thing that ever happened to her.

Right now would be a helluva fine time to start, to confess that if she hadn't shown up today, he was coming after her. So while he'd like nothing better than to run up the white flag and let her have her way with him, she deserved the chance to hit him with her best shot. So he stood there and prepared to take his licks like a man . . . a man in love.

"You come all this way to talk about fishing?" he asked when what he wanted to do was drag her into his arms and plaster her against him like glue.

She looked past him toward the bow . . . the first sign that she wasn't as sure of herself as she wanted him to think. "No. But I did come to talk."

When he didn't say anything, she lifted the bottle to her lips, swallowed. The face she made set the corner of his mouth twitching. *Definitely not champagne, huh, princess?*

"What's on your mind, Jillian?"

"You," she said with unabashed frankness.

He searched her face and, for the first time since he'd discovered her on the *EDEN*'s deck, realized what he'd done to her. She'd suffered because he'd skipped. And yeah, one hundred times yeah, he'd suffered, too. That's why he was back. He'd missed her. Missed her like hell. Missed her until his insides felt as empty as a retired tank. Rusted. Hollow. Gutted of purpose.

"You want to tell me why you ran, Garrett?"

Ouch. OK. Where did he start? Maybe with what was going through his head at the time.

"The job was over. It made sense that I leave." Not one of his brighter moments.

"Ah. So that's how you justified it."

He tilted his head, took his lumps. "Yep. That's how I justified it."

"That doesn't play for me."

Oh yeah. She was revving up for the mother of all battles all right.

"The way I figure it, you were running scared. As a matter of fact, I think you're *still* running scared."

She stepped closer, waggled her bottle at him. "You know, sometimes it's beyond me why I think so, but you're not a stupid man. So why, I ask myself, can't a man who not only faced the Taliban and the fedayeen but outsmarted them figure there is nothing to be afraid of where we're concerned? Why can't he face the fact that love is something you run to, not away from?"

Music. Even with all the static she was dishing out, it was music to his ears.

"I told myself it was OK when days went by and I didn't hear from you," she pressed on, shaking her head in disgust. "Let him think. Let him sort it out. This is a huge adjustment in his life.

"*I* was a huge adjustment," she continued. "I mean, after all, you didn't even want the job. And you sure as the world didn't want to *like* me, let alone fall in love with me."

"Jillian—"

"No." She poked her index finger into his sternum. "All you have to do right now is listen."

He winced, rubbed at the spot on his chest. His true love didn't seem to care that she might have punctured a lung. What she cared about was setting him straight.

"You did your job. You protected me. You saved me. Well, I don't need saving anymore, OK? Especially not from you. I love you." She glared at him. "Without illusions. I love you because you are fallible and because your poor misguided testosterone-corrupted brain has you doing cartwheels trying not to be. I love you because of all you are and because of all you're not. And because, no matter what, you are all the man I'll ever need."

He wanted to smile. She'd go for his throat if he did. So he screwed his face into a scowl and tried to stop her again. "Jillian—"

"No! There is only one thing I want to hear from you. Now suck it up, Garrett. Admit it! You love me."

It was so huge, this capacity he'd developed for needing her. Her fire. Her sass. Her smart-ass bossy mouth.

He set down his empty bottle. Gripped her shoulders in his hands and looked deep into her eyes. "I love you."

She opened her mouth. Shut it. Then seemed to deflate like a hot air balloon with a ripped seam.

She searched his face.

Searched it again.

And then he saw it. Hope. *Guarded* hope—sullied by suspicion.

"Why was that so easy?"

On a deep breath, he pulled her against him. Pressed his lips to the top of her head and simply wallowed in the scent and the softness and finally in the nearness of her. "Trust me, there was nothing easy about it."

She tipped her face to his. All the anger and desperation had left her eyes. In their place was the trust she gave him so freely. "Tell me."

"Everything," he promised, and drew her to her toes for a long, deep kiss. "Later. There's something I've just got to do first." Then he led her toward the companionway door.

Her damp hair felt like silk against his shoulder. Nolan sifted it through his fingers, playing with its cool weight, loving the feel of her naked and spent beside him.

They'd made love like wild monkeys. Then they'd showered and fallen back into bed and made love again. Sweet and slow this time, with all the pain of their separation and all the joy of their reunion threaded through each stoke of his body into hers, each tug of her welcoming warmth.

"When I left," he said, knowing she was drifting on the edge of sleep beside him but needing to finally get this out, "I had no plans to come back here. As far as I was concerned, I was gone. End of story. Out of your life. Out of your hair."

She snuggled closer, all sleepy warmth and woman softness. "I'm so, so glad you came back."

He squeezed her arm. "Yeah."

"Where did you go?"

"Couple of places." He told her about Nelson, how he'd lost him in Tikrit.

"I went to see his folks. To tell them. You know. That he was a stand-up soldier. That he loved what he did. That he died a hero."

They'd cried. He'd cried with them. And then they'd asked him to keep in touch.

He let out a deep breath, felt the warmth of her love surround him.

"I went back to Georgia." He'd had unfinished business there. "I had to see Sara. Had to sort things through with her."

Jillian rose up on an elbow. Concern shone in her eyes as she searched his face. "How is she?"

"She's . . ." He paused. "She's getting there. Physically, she still has some healing to do, but she's walking again. Her prognosis is good. And she looked good," he added. It still surprised him that she actually had. "She's coping."

"She sounds like an incredibly strong woman."

"Yeah. And you were right." He rubbed his hand up and down her arm. "She doesn't blame me. Never has."

"And what about you?" She touched her fingers to his lower lip. "Do you still blame yourself?"

He caught her hand loosely in his. Kissed the tips of her fingers. "Still working on that."

"That's good," she whispered. "You just keep on working."

Yeah. He would. He would keep on working. Because now he had something worth working for. "I went back to Benning, too."

"So . . . what was it like? Back at base. Seeing your buddies."

"Good. It was good to see them. Wilson sends his lust, by the way."

She grinned. "How *is* Plowboy?"

"Spending a lot of time with Sara and the boys." That had been another surprise, that other side of Jason Wilson. "He's great with them. I think he's good for Sara, too."

"A new romance brewing?"

He rolled a shoulder. "I don't know. Maybe. Time will tell."

And time, he'd finally come to realize, was something he wanted a lot more of. With Jillian in his life, he was no longer just killing time. He was living it. And he was going to live it to the hilt.

"Tell me again," she whispered.

He knew exactly what she wanted to hear. And for the first time in his life, he wanted to say it. Felt the words deep, so deep down in his soul. "I love you."

"I love you, too. But, so you know, I hate, really, really hate, that horrible root beer you drink."

He rolled her beneath him. "Then we'll just have to find something else for you to swallow."

Laughter bubbled in her eyes. "You are a bad, bad man."

"That," he said, pressing his hips into hers, "is what I've been trying to tell you."

But he'd never been a better man, would never *be* a better man, than when he held her in his arms.

. . .

The next day, the *EDEN* cut smoothly through a light chop as she cruised south from Palm Beach through open water toward a sunset rivaling any Jillian had ever seen, even in Key West.

"She handles well," she said, standing beside Nolan on the flybridge, loving the rush of the wind through her hair, the scent of salt water, the sun glinting from the prow of a gleaming white catamaran out for a sunset sail. Dozens of vessels dotted the horizon—from freighters, to sand suckers, to pricey yachts and sleek clippers.

"It feels good to have her out again. Been a while." Nolan checked his heading, then throttled down to an idle so they could drift in relative silence and enjoy the view.

"Why is it," she said, brushing the hair from her eyes, "that something this huge and restless has such a restful effect on people?"

He thought, shrugged. "Sheer size and volume, maybe? Maybe even a little intimidation? In the face of all this power, what point is there to feeling anything but small? Humbled. Restful."

Jillian watched the face of this complex man, wondering, now that he was slowly opening up to her, just how many new facets of himself he would reveal. "I knew there was a poet in you somewhere."

He glanced at her, his face no longer a curtain over his emotions but a window to them. "Yeah, well. I'm a constant source of surprises."

He was happy. She was making him that way. She was going to keep him that way. "Yeah," she said, deliriously in love. "You are.

"Drop anchor, would you," she said on impulse. "Then come below. I want to show you something."

Before he could ask her what was up, she planted a kiss

on his mouth, then scuttled down the ladder steps to the aft deck. It seemed impossible that they'd been back together for less than twenty-four hours, she thought as she let herself into the cabin. Twenty-four hours of amazing, incredible revelations. And love.

And sex. Oh, my God, the sex.

Jillian shivered as she stole into the captain's stateroom, stripped, and arranged herself in the middle of the bed.

Together. What a wonderful word. Of course, Jillian wasn't taking anything for granted. She loved him, he loved her, but he hadn't said anything about their long-term future and she wasn't about to press her luck. For now, it was enough that he was here, he was happy, and he was hers.

When the stateroom door swung open and he saw her, the look on his face was all she needed to make her very, very happy, too.

His gaze raked her body before settling on her face. She would never tire of seeing fire flare in his eyes. And she would never get tired of teasing him.

"If you come in here, *babe,*" she said, rising up on an elbow and affecting a warning glare, "you're going to get exactly what you're looking for. Maybe you've forgotten, but I'm not a nice woman. So if you're looking for sex . . . you're just liable to get it. And don't expect some polite little in-and-out and 'oh, darling, that was—' "

He dived for the bed, flattened her beneath him, and ended her mocking monologue with a searing kiss.

She was giggling when he lifted his head and glared at her, all the while struggling to get out of his shirt. "You're going to remind me of my noble little speech for the rest of my life, aren't you?"

"I think so. Yeah. Wait." She stilled, sobered, then gripped handfuls of his hair and dragged his head away from her breast so she could look into his eyes.

"You said: the rest of your life." Her heart pounded so hard she could hardly get the words out.

"Yeah," he said, his words a soft whisper. "You want to make something of it?"

Her breath caught. "Like . . . what?"

"Like something permanent?"

Oh God.

Tears filled her eyes as she looked at his beautiful, serious face.

"Marry me, princess. I'll give you my kingdom—small potatoes that it is."

She couldn't talk. She couldn't think. She couldn't—

"Jillian?" Absolute and undeniable love shone in his eyes.

"Hm?"

"Breathe."

EPILOGUE

IF THERE HAD EVER BEEN ASSEMBLED A more beautiful collection of beefcake than the Garrett men at a family get-together, Jillian would pay very big coin to attend.

"Your brothers are so hot," she said as she placed her foot over her red ball, which was nestled up against Nolan's blue ball, and gave it a hard whack with her mallet.

Nolan watched his ball fly into the rough in his dad's tidily manicured backyard as his brothers and sister hooted in appreciation of Jillian's shot.

"You will pay for that."

"All's fair in croquet, big guy. Suck it up and take it like a man."

He hooked his elbow around her neck, dragged her against him, and planted a kiss on the top of her head. "I was talking about the way you're ogling my brothers."

"Add your dad to the mix. He's gorgeous."

"She thinks you're gorgeous!" Nolan yelled, earning him an elbow in the ribs and a hissing and embarrassed "Big-mouth," just as Wes Garrett stepped up to his green ball and eyed the hoop in the middle of the course.

"It's OK, Jillian." Susan Garrett joined the group, carrying a huge tray laden with lemonade, root beer, and tumblers. "I happen to agree wholeheartedly."

"It just goes to show that your lady has an excellent eye."

Wes grinned up at Jillian, winked. "Can't fault her for missing the mark with you though, Son."

"Do you see the grief I have to put up with?" Nolan sputtered as he walked over to relieve his mother of the heavy load and set the tray on the patio table.

Jillian felt the warmth of a hundred suns as she watched him. It had been a month since she'd sought Nolan out on the *EDEN*. A month of getting to know him better and falling deeper in love with him and his entire family.

A lot had happened in that month. Eddie was back on the job and doing fine, as was his wife and their new baby boy. CNN had given the story of Jillian's attempted murder a lot of airplay. It was still painful to see her parents go through their very public exposure over Mary Gates and the changes her situation had brought to all of their lives. John Smith, at least, was on the road to a new life. More accurately, he was on the road to his old one.

The wide media coverage had netted incredible results for him. A woman had stepped forward after hearing John's story and seeing his photograph, which had been aired almost nonstop during the first week after the story had broken. While all the details hadn't yet been woven back together, the woman—who claimed to be John's sister—appeared to be credible. John Smith might actually be Maynard Schroeder, a Nova Scotia–born factory worker, who had moved to the United States fifteen years ago and who had lived alone and kept to himself most of that time. All of his family had been in Canada and hadn't known of his disappearance until his story had been picked up on the international wire. Many other details of his life, however, were still a mystery.

Jillian was on it, though, just as she was on the legal staff she'd hired to help him through his trial.

In the meantime, her career was red-hot. She'd even received a call from CNN offering her a position. Time would tell what she decided to do about that. Her contract at KGLO was up for negotiation, so who knew? Much of what she decided would depend on Nolan. Right now, it appeared he was leaning toward joining E.D.E.N, Inc., as a partner. They would weigh the pros and cons together.

At the far corner of the croquet course, Eve swore roundly, then threatened some serious damage to Dallas's reproductive equipment if he even thought about bumping her into the rough.

Her ball went sailing. Eve swore again and Susan rolled her eyes and shook her head. "That girl."

Now Jillian knew where Eve got her soft curves and blond hair. She was a younger version of her mother, who, despite her feigned disgust with her daughter's language, was clearly proud that Eve could hold her own with the boys.

Dallas and Ethan were as different from each other and Nolan in temperament as they were similar in looks. Dallas was what Rachael would refer to as a Neaty Petey. He always looked perfect. Always said the perfect thing. Always had the perfect smile.

It made her wonder why the perfect woman hadn't snapped him up. She'd said as much to Eve once.

"Because there hasn't been one born who can measure up to what that boy is looking for. Can't wait until some not-so-perfect woman comes along and knocks the pins out from under him. It's going to be a real ride watching her take him down."

The story with Ethan was a little different. He'd found the woman of his dreams—and lost her. Jillian had asked, but Nolan didn't know exactly what had driven them to divorce. While Ethan was pleasant, engaging, and sometimes even showed he was capable of Nolan's irreverent sense of humor, he kept his feelings very close to the vest. Nolan knew only that Ethan had loved his wife, and had been pretty certain she'd loved him, too.

Jillian had decided that Ethan wasn't over his ex. She wasn't sure what made her think that—possibly the emptiness she saw in his eyes when he didn't think anyone was watching him. Or possibly she was just so blissfully happy, she was a little too sensitive to someone else's pain.

"Take that, you reprobate," Eve said on a laugh, and Jillian looked up to see a yellow ball—Dallas's—go sailing into the flower bed.

She'd decided early on that she would bleed for Eve, if for no other reason than the tip she'd given her the day she'd tried to pry Nolan's location out of his brothers. Eve had understood. And Jillian pitied the man who tried to take her on. He'd have to be quite the man, Jillian thought with a smile, because Eve was going to put him through the wringer.

"I love your family," Jillian said when Nolan returned to her side with a glass of lemonade for her and a root beer for him.

"So you've said. Several times."

"They're just so extraordinary and normal," she finally decided.

He blinked at her. "I'll need a minute to process that."

She laughed and wrapped her arms around his neck. "Extraordinary because they're so special. Normal because they're so grounded."

"Doesn't take much to make you happy, does it?"

"Just you."

"So," Dallas said, walking by with his mallet propped on his shoulder, "how much longer do we have to endure all this sloppy kissy-face stuff?"

"You only wish you had someone to slop over," Nolan said, looping his arms low at Jillian's back, and played a little kissy-face that started out for his brother's benefit but ended with a heated whisper: "Let's go find someplace with a little less traffic."

She grinned up at him. "I like it here."

He narrowed his eyes. "Just once, could you pretend to agree with me on something? Or are you always going to be this obstinate?"

"Try me."

"Black," he said.

"White."

"Yes."

"No."

"Stay."

"Go."

"Great. Knew I could get you to see it my way."

Oh yeah, she thought, as they said hasty good-byes to several pairs of knowing blue eyes. She planned on seeing it his way for the rest of her life.

Read on for an excerpt from
Cindy Gerard's next book

TO THE LIMIT

NOW AVAILABLE FROM ST. MARTIN'S PAPERBACKS

WEST PALM BEACH, FLORIDA

Dark she could do, Eve Garrett thought as she sat by the curb, her motor running. The rain was another story. She didn't do rain.

"Or wind," she grumbled as a strong gust rocked her little Mazda, and the downpour pelted the windshield like BBs.

Why couldn't she be curled up in her apartment, comfy and dry and reading a good "It was a dark and stormy night" mystery novel, instead of muttering to herself out here in one?

She was a long way from her apartment. A long way from comfy. Instead, she was wiping steam off her driver's side window on a night that was also damp and muggy. And she wasn't even a little bit at ease about parking on this smarmy back street just off Blue Heron Boulevard in a seedy neighborhood that stank of garbage and rot while she waited for Tiffany Clayborne to show.

She squinted into the rain. *Where was that girl?*

Eve cared about the little brat—God bless her—but Tiffany had better have a damn good reason for dragging her out in this crap or when she finally did show up, there might be serious hair-pulling involved.

And why the theatrics? Eve wondered uneasily, losing the battle to clear a spot on her window. Why the tears and the almost incoherent begging that Eve meet her here, no explanation provided?

"Just come, Eve. Please. Please hurry."

With Tiff, lately, there often wasn't an explanation. Starting with her eighteenth birthday six months ago, Tiffany had turned into the quintessential spoiled little rich girl, monetarily gorged, and emotionally starved for attention.

She'd really fired up the afterburners in the spoiled-rich department lately—like anyone could really compete with Paris Hilton. But it still gave the paparazzi plenty of fodder for sensational stories about her exploits. Eve had figured it was a case of Tiffany's age proclaiming she was capable of making adult decisions, but her brain not yet come to terms with the new reality of maturity.

Come to terms, little girl. Soon.

The steam finally got the best of her. Eve rolled down her window, thinking back to Tiffany's eighteenth birthday party. You had your basic cake and balloons and candles. And then, in Tiffany's case, you had your instant access to a multi-billion-dollar trust fund.

Eve was thinking that all that money had screwed with her head. Well, so had Tiffany's father, but that was a whole other story.

"Come on, Tiff. It's getting wet out here."

Eve checked her watch and told herself that to an eighteen-year-old, fifteen minutes did not constitute late. To a thirty-two-year-old who had to be on the job at seven the next morning, however, fifteen minutes constituted the beginnings of a very bad mood.

Disgusted, she flipped her cell phone open and punched in Tiffany's number. Straight to voice mail.

"What the heck is going on?" she wondered, then sharpened her focus outside her window when she saw a flash of movement by one of the buildings directly across the street.

She leaned over in the seat so she could get a better look through the rain and saw movement again.

"Tiff? Is that you?"

Whoever it was stopped when Eve yelled, hesitated for a moment, then ducked between two buildings.

It didn't much matter that Eve had spent seven years as a Secret Service agent. Didn't much matter that she'd logged her share of stakeouts during that time. At least it didn't matter to her heart rate because it ratcheted up several beats per minute as a healthy, intuitive wariness and a spike of adrenaline had her popping open her glovebox and digging for her flashlight.

She hesitated over the .38 S & W she pretty much went nowhere without, then tucked it in her waistband at the small of her back. With a muttered oath, she stepped out into the rain.

"You'd better have a good reason for playing this game, little girl," she sputtered under her breath.

But even as she said it, Eve sensed, gut deep, that this wasn't a game. Something was wrong. She just hadn't wanted it to be. Tiffany was vulnerable. Prime predator bait. And what Eve had just seen duck between the buildings had looked like a predator.

She was completely drenched by the time she ran across the lot and ducked in next to a dingy gray cinderblock building. The adjacent building was an ugly, mustard-brown brick. The walkway between the two was narrow and dark; the weeds growing in dirt that had softened to mud were the primary landscape materials.

And Tiffany was the primary reason Eve was about to put her life on the line. She reached behind her back for her gun, flicked off the safety, and gripping the weapon in both hands, swung into the gap.

Water gushed from the roofs, bypassing debris-clogged

eaves. Nothing. She could see nothing through the deluge. And then she felt nothing. Nothing but pain as an arm hooked around her neck and dragged her back against a body as hard and unyielding as the building she was suddenly slammed into.

She could barely breathe, wouldn't be on her feet if her attacker hadn't pinned her between him and the rough cinderblock wall. Somewhere at her feet was her gun. And somewhere in the dark, she heard the wail of a far-away police siren.

"You're dead," he said, his hot breath fanning her ear as the rain poured like a waterfall around them.

"Who—"

The forearm crushing her throat jerked viciously. Pain knifed through her windpipe. She gasped, sucking for a breath that wasn't gorged with rain and pain and willed herself not to pass out.

"You're dead," he repeated, his voice as void of emotion as the night was void of light. "You just don't know it yet."

Exquisite, mind-searing pain ripped through her system. She felt a scream boil up just as another jolt tore into her and her muscles started to spasm. By the third jolt, her eyes had rolled back in her head.

And by the time he let her fall in a boneless lump to the muddy ground, the prospect of death was a welcome relief.

Texas Cattleman's Club:
The Secret Diary Series

BOOK I

Black~Tie Seduction

by Cindy Gerard

NOW AVAILABLE FROM
Silhouette Desire